CHASING TYRANNY

ONE SMALL STEP ^{OUT OF} GARDEN OF EDEN ™

Series

Part One: Call of Destiny

Part Two: Chasing Tyranny

CHASING TYRANNY

Being the second part of

ONE SMALL STEP OUT OF THE GARDEN OF EDEN

Robert Wagoner

Beechstreet Publishing
Vermont

CHASING TYRANNY

A Beechstreet Publishing Publication

ISBN: 978-0-9826285-1-5

Printed in the United States of America

First edition, printed April, 2010

To my wife and children.

i. A Young Man

David's polished mahogany casket lay tellingly closed in front of the Gillens. David's pastor stood facing them on the opposite side of the casket.

... Michael couldn't listen anymore. The words were too painful to bear. He couldn't listen to how much the disadvantaged Weightless *had benefited from David's sacrifice. The* Weightless *had killed him! He hated the* Weightless *now! He hated all of them bitterly! He hated Mos Thieren, their enigmatic leader, that much more!*

*　　　 * 　 * 　 * 　 * 　 * 　 * 　 * 　 **

That was when Michael heard the sounds of the newscast in the background. The words, Outer Rim: Elara *displayed in small print as the reporter continued his address:*

> *"So we only know this: Clifford Gillen, the grandson of the late Jonathan Gillen, the infamous inventor of the gravitational field generator, has been assassinated along with his wife, Marjorie ... the victims of a grizzly transport bombing."*

The report continued to spout its insanity—that was how Michael regarded it. "I can't believe this is happening again." ... He was alone in the universe—the last Gillen alive. The fault once more clearly lay with Mos Thieren and those despicable Weightless.

ii. A Great Mission

"... I am pleased to announce that on Friday, October eighteenth, 2505, the National Space Exploration Administration will launch the first-ever deep space exploration mission. ... The ship will spend the next twenty-four years traveling to the Alpha Centauri sun, a triple star system and the closest stars to Terrae Solaris, just over four light-years away."

iii. A Terrible War

The pictures were from Ceres Fleet Base, an Earth States military base located on the borders between the Inner Rim and Outer Rim. But now, that base lay in ruins!

... Tashjian stood there in shock—just like the rest of them—watching the terrible pictures. "Do they know who did it?"

"No," Cyril Davidson replied. "Not officially. But we all know who it is: the Europans."

Michael was at a loss for words. He didn't think about the personal impact the attack would have on him; he didn't remorse over the fact that NSEA canceling the Alpha Centauri mission was a foregone conclusion.

No, Earth States would soon be at war.

*　　　 * 　 * 　 * 　 * 　 * 　 * 　 * 　 **

*　*　*　*　*　*　*

Tom came in all the way (into Michael's office on board the ESS Comanche*), shutting the door while Michael turned off the music. Tom kind of gulped, "Well, it's been twenty-three months since I came on board with you...."*

"And you want me to finally make good on my promise to let you go to Intelligence?" Michael asked, finishing the sentence. ... "I guess our mission to drop off those Coverts on Europa was too much for you," Michael lamented, remembering the dangerous mission the previous week. The crew had barely made it back to Allied territory alive.

*　*　*　*　*　*　*

... Argall saw their inquisitive gazes and pointed to the small transport traveling in the middle of the Allied convoy. "That ship is the Executive One*. The President is in desperate trouble—and he needs your help."*

Michael realized what a dire cup fate had handed him.

*　*　*　*　*　*　*

Michael Gillen sat in his command chair, suffering through the onslaught and at a loss. With all the other Allied vessels gone, Comanche *found itself all alone defending the President's transport.*

... Comanche *was dying ... Michael had only seconds to react ... he could only think of one other hand to play. "Morelli, prepare to ram."*

... Comanche, *now less than a half of a kilometer off the nose of the beast, came to a dead stop. The destroyer was moving fast ... inertia carried the behemoth directly into the mid-section of the* Comanche.

... Comanche *split in two. Its fore section tumbled away into space. Not going very far, the aft section bounced several times off the destroyer's hull ... until the power plants inside gave way, erupting into a blinding explosion.*

The mighty Jupiter-Class destroyer quickly became engulfed in the violent explosion. Bulkheads melted under the intense heat, while section after section shattered away. Fuel and ammunition reserves erupted violently. The chain reaction continued until the whole destroyer's fore section ... became nothing but charred remains.

The beast was dead.

... but Executive One *sped on undeterred toward Allied territory. The President was safe.*

*　*　*　*　*　*　*

Twenty-six-year-old Michael Gillen found himself lying in a pile of rubble that was once his bridge.

... Then the truth hit him: He was hurt. The blood covering him was his—not another crewman!

So this is what it's like to be forsaken, *Michael Gillen thought, mourning the feeling.*

... All the strangeness of the last moments coalesced into a cold, grim reality. Grief overwhelmed him, and his reaction caught him off guard. During the entire battle,

the young captain had prepared himself for the end. But now that death was upon him, Michael became filled with the sensation of incredible loss.

None of these thoughts really mattered to him—yet they consumed him too. He still labored to breathe. A cold darkness was quickly enveloping him; death was beckoning. Death comes to everyone, no matter what they believe, *he thought.* Of course, young Gillen found no consolation in that thought.

… Finally, darkness enveloped him.

iv. A Loyal Friend

Tom Andrews knelt in the rubble that used to be the bridge of the ESS Comanche, *pointing the small searchlight down at where Michael Gillen lay.*

… It didn't matter to the young man that he needed medical attention, or that some of the crew were still alive under the rubble and needed help too. It didn't matter to him that the fore section of the Comanche—*or what was left of it—was on the verge of collapse. It didn't matter to him that the ship remnant, tumbling through space since the collision, had been righted. He didn't even care that Europan soldiers had boarded the ship and were rushing the bridge.*

No, even as two Europan soldiers came over him, pointing their rifles squarely at his head and telling him not to move, Tom Andrews paid them no mind, at least not right then.

No, all he could do is look down at the lifeless body of his best friend.

v. A Skilled Surgeon

Kara took in with great fondness the sight of Michael reciting his vows to Kate. She hung on every word, as if Michael were speaking to her. She remembered her days back at the academy: how she had pined over Michael for so long, how she had thrown caution to the wind to win his affection—how she had failed miserably.

… Watching Kate slip the gold band over Michael's finger … Kara let the tears and the lump in her throat have their moment.

* * * * * * * *

Kara Ricci stood over her operating table in the surgical bay of the ESS Windsor, *overwhelmed by an incredible sense of despair.*

The bay looked like something out of a horror movie. … She could still see herself swimming in wounded soldiers, men—sometimes women—with such ghastly injuries. They had looked at her desperately. Their haunting gazes had transfixed her as they were dying. Many of them did die—she had seen so many die that day. Their faces, twisted from the agony, still haunted her mind.

And she knew the images would never leave her—ever.

* * * * * * * *

Finally alone with her tortured thoughts, Kara stared at herself in the mirror for a long moment. The terrible images from that day began unloading on her. The faces of those she had let die—mostly by her own decision—began haunting her.

… Becoming increasingly inconsolable as her body slithered down the dull surface in surrender, Kara began to weep loudly and bitterly.

As the young woman fell to pieces, in a place where no one could see her cry, in a place where no one could hear her desperation—and foreseeing many similar missions to the front—Kara realized just how familiar the tiny room would become.

vi. A Faithful Wife

Twenty-four-year-old Kate Gillen walked through the entrance to the main floor, following the office manager assigned to settle her in to her new position at Earth States Intelligence.

… The young woman sighed and began setting up her workstation, not sure how she had ever come to this place. Yet there she sat: in some obscure Intelligence office on Earth, doing some sort of clerk job. The assignment didn't make sense.

… Before long, Kate spotted the woman at the nearest workstation coming over to her. … The woman held up her left hand, proudly displaying her own wedding ring. "Welcome to the Kept Wives Club."

*   *   *   *   *   *   *   *

After sinking into the plush couch and nestling her bare feet up underneath her, Kate took a sip of coffee, laid her head back, and closed her eyes. She was finally home.

But she really wasn't home.

… The young newlywed wondered why she had looked forward to arriving or why the long weekend had seemed so appealing. Now that she was home, Kate realized that a long weekend was nothing more than another opportunity to spend even more time worrying about Michael, another opportunity to become even more furious over him leaving her behind too.

*   *   *   *   *   *   *   *

The more Kate listened to the admiral, the more her expression changed. Simple concern changed to disbelief; disbelief deteriorated into Kate defiantly shaking her head in denial.

Kate resisted imbibing the bitter truth. The admiral's words continued as if piercing her mercilessly. Overwhelmed, Kate's defiance melted. She shook her head back and forth once again, and her face twisted painfully. Then Kate fell into the admiral's arms and wept.

A LOOK BACK

CHAPTER ONE

Long Ago on Europa

The beautiful Europan woman stood at the window of the modest apartment, watching the turmoil engulfing Tyre, Europa's capitol city. The eternally black sky—home to the foreboding sight of Jupiter—pushed down against the dim lights of the city, and the small dwelling remained intentionally dark. She preferred it that way; she could watch the uprising from the shadows without any chance of being caught doing so.

From her vantage point, she could see the faint traces of heavy rioting among the crowded buildings in the distance. Firelight, streaming through the transparent ceilings of the pressurized habitats near ground level, danced against the walls of those towering structures. Most certainly, thousands of protesters filled the streets and open areas there—though she couldn't see them directly. The conflict centered around the majestic Parliament building far on the horizon. Military craft descended on the location from all directions, though other military vehicles scoured the city on an outward trajectory too.

The young woman would have laughed at the suggestion that Europa would someday rise to international prominence—as it would; that a lunatic would wield the incredible power of the coming Europan Empire to terrorize the whole solar system. No, Europa existed in the ashes of its former glory, a place of danger and incredible misery. The unrest overtaking the city had become commonplace in the post-Ceres Skirmishes era on Europa.

However, the danger had recently become much more personal to her.

Her striking beauty and pleasing form fell out of place among the shadows. The vixen had grown accustomed to being adored, to being the center of attention in the most affluent of venues, to luring only the most worthy suitors to her side. She had used her natural charm and grace to overcome the curse of her common blood, to secure what she wanted from life. She had even won the hand of a young, aspiring junior senator. The modest wedding ring she wore was a trophy of sorts.

Of course, the dark times had descended once again, and so she trembled among the shadows.

"*Livia*," her husband unexpectedly called from behind her. She spun around, as he and his closest confidant hurried into the darkened apartment. Both men were dressed in nobles' clothing, with her husband boasting his junior senators' regalia. However, neither young man inhabited anything else suggesting true Europan nobility. No, living as commoners for so many years had permanently marked them, thus betraying their fledgling status.

Letting out an incredible sigh with her ice-blue eyes aflame, Livia rushed over to her husband, wrapped him in a tight embrace, and kissed him.

"I was so worried about you," she cried, clutching him with abandon.

"I came as soon as I could," he tried to assure her. However, his face betrayed his anxiousness. "It's not safe to stay here anymore. We need to hurry."

"*To where?*"

The other young man leaned in toward her. "It's best that neither of you know."

Livia recoiled and nervously searched her husband's face in the sparse light. "What's he talking about?"

"I'm going to take you to safety," the confidant said.

"But what about *you*?" she looked back at her husband.

"I have to go into hiding," the man lamented, causing her countenance to fall that much more. "Though I doubt I'll last the night." Unable to bear the dread washing over her face, the young senator hurried to the bedroom. When both she and the confidant followed, he added, "My name appeared on an *enemies list*. The new Prime Minister is insane! I don't know what the Mars Federation was thinking by appointing him to head up the new government."

"They thought he'd be a puppet ruler," the confidant grimaced, helping his friend lay out two empty suitcases on the bed.

"We don't have much time," her husband warned, stepping over to the dresser and opening one of the drawers. He threw a handful of her clothes from the drawer into one of the suitcases. "They'll be here soon to arrest you and execute me."

Livia, watching the two men hastily packing the separate suitcases, shook her head. "I'm going wherever *you* go."

"That would be unwise," the confidant barely looked up as the two men continued packing. "We need to get you to safety."

"No, I'm *staying* with my husband!"

However, the two men only worked faster. The closer they came to completing the task, the more anxious her face grew.

"*You can't leave me now*," she pleaded to her husband. However, he remained more than preoccupied with his packing. So she grasped at him, forcing him to stop and look at her. "*I'm pregnant.*"

Even his best friend fell idle at the surprising news. The stunned junior senator gazed at her for a long moment. Finally, he cracked a pleasing smile and took her by the thick of her arms. "*Really?*"

"*Yes.* I just found out today. *You're going to have a son.*"

With tremendous joy overcoming him, the young man embraced her, even picking her up and spinning her around a few turns. "This is wonderful!"

However, his friend, watching from the side, never cracked a smile. Instead, his sober expression only intensified. "This changes everything."

The comment brought the unexpected celebration to a sudden end. Never letting go of his wife, the young man returned the serious gaze and reluctantly nodded in agreement. "What do you suggest?"

"Hiding Livia on Europa is no longer good enough. According to Europan law, a son inherits his father's succession rights. That makes him a threat to the ruling party. If word leaks back to the Prime Minister and his thugs that she's pregnant, he'll hunt her down and execute her. And if she escapes and carries your son to term, the Prime Minister will never stop looking for the child."

Livia's face filled with dread. "*No.*"

Still holding his wife, the junior senator traded sober looks with his friend. When the confidant offered a sympathetic nod, the young man waxed endearingly at his wife, who began turning her head side to side in an urgent fashion. When her eyes welled up, he forced a smile. "It's time to say goodbye, my dear."

"*No.*"

"There's no other way. You must go into hiding far away from here: Make a new life for yourself … and find a father for my child."

Livia kept shaking her head desperately, her eyes filling with tears.

"A group of Terrans are visiting Callisto," the confidant offered. "They won a contract to build a new space station for the Callistan government … rich, young men far away from home. I can take you there."

"Yes," the young senator said with a bittersweet zeal. "Terran men are *very* traditional—and gullible." He put his hand to her cheek and smiled. "Blend in with the Callistans: Change your name and don't let anyone know you're Europan."

"I can get her a forged identity," the confidant interjected.

"Yes," the husband nodded and turned back to his wife. "Find a suitor from an affluent Terran family … win him over as you did me. With your beauty and feminine wiles"—taking in her ice-blue eyes, striking features, and flowing, jet-black hair—"a young man so far away from home won't stand a chance. Let him think the child is *his* so he'll marry you—Terran men are like that. Let him take you back to Earth States where you'll be safe. No doubt, he'll use his family's influence to establish a Terran identity for you."

"Do you really want me to do that?" she pleaded, searching his eyes.

He hesitated, his face turning sober. "You don't have a choice. You're not only doing this for me, but for all of Europa. The Prime Minister can't take away the privileges and titles I earned for our family.

If I and the other resistance leaders are killed, our son may be the only hope against this rising tyranny. So take him to Earth … give him a Terran name … and a Terran life." Then he looked her squarely in the eyes. "But raise him to be *Europan*—and a noble at that—so that at the right time, he can come back here and fulfill his destiny."

The confidant, carrying her suitcase, had withdrawn toward the door. He gestured toward Livia. "We have to go."

The junior senator gazed longingly at his wife, who radiated such angst. So he brought her head to the curve of his neck and stroked her hair in a reassuring fashion. Feeling his own angst building within him as he held her close, the young man reached in and kissed her one last time—not easily parting from her. With a cracking voice, he said, "Go with him, my dear."

Livia held on to him for dear life, fighting as the confidant wrestled her out of her husband's grasp. Finally, she let go—though never parting her gaze from him. With the confidant still pulling her toward the apartment door, she cried, "I love you!"

"I love you too!"

Livia looked at him through tear-filled eyes from across the room. Finally—with the confidant still pulling her out of the apartment—the young woman left.

CHAPTER TWO

Emir Kern

"Lieutenant Morelli, we need more speed!" Captain Michael Gillen barked from his chair on the bridge of the *ESS Comanche*. His eyes kept trained on the bridge's view screen. Jupiter, a massive, brownish red-and-white marble-like sphere, loomed forebodingly in the sky over Europa set before him. Just then, the battle cruiser shook violently; pursuing Europan FW-190 fighters once again pounded the ship with artillery rounds. At the same time, energy blasts from Europan surface guns streamed narrowly past the warship. "—more dodging too."

"Yes, Sir," Morelli replied, wrestling *Comanche*'s trajectory controls as the ship ascended into the eternally black Europan sky. The subtle sharpness in the underling's voice betrayed his anxiety, an anxiety permeating the entire ship.

When the vessel shuddered once more, Michael glanced over at Tom Andrews in surrender: Volunteering the ship for the clandestine mission had been a terrible mistake.

The bridge crew feverishly worked their abrupt escape from the Galilean moon orbiting Jupiter, though fully convinced they would not survive the terrible ordeal. They remained unaware that fate would allow them an eventual, narrow escape. However, such foresight would provide little consolation: *Comanche* and crew would meet their demise just six weeks later while saving President James Mitchell from an Europan ambush. No, such knowledge belonged to the hand of fate alone.

Michael shook his head in frustration while studying the grim tactical readouts. Though anxious to find safety, he was more unsettled over how such dire circumstances had befallen his ship.

The Europans had caught *Comanche* executing a top-secret reconnaissance mission. The mission, which was in preparation for an eventual Allied invasion, had required *Comanche* to transport two Special Forces teams to and from Europa: a flight crew with a stolen Europan commercial transport, and a covert operations ground team— *Coverts*, as they called themselves.

Once delivered, the plan required the Coverts to infiltrate the Europan settlements to gather detailed military intelligence. The flight crew, flying the stolen transport on several low-level passes over the moon, would map the entire Europan civilization. *Comanche* would simultaneously monitor each team's progress and provide a quick escape, if needed.

The assignment was perilous indeed. However, neither the mission's peril nor the firestorm of Europan artillery was what disturbed the young commander so much.

No, something much worse had happened.

The mission had started out like any other assignment. Michael eagerly received the two teams aboard the warship the previous week. Despite the Covert's unusual, almost clannish behavior from the outset, he looked forward to working with them. Even meeting Maura Enzler, the Special Ops flight crew commander and former Centauri astronaut—the woman who tried to wreck Michael's exploration career on behalf of Gabriel Burke so long ago—was only uncomfortable the first few moments. The war had somehow put all those problems to rest.

The first phases of the mission proceeded as planned. Having slipped undetected through the formidable Europan home-world defenses several days earlier, *Comanche* had hidden in the shadows of a remote, newly formed ice lineae on the far side of Europa. The dispatching of the two teams into the main settlements using the stolen Europan transport had gone well too.

However, the mission quickly went awry.

Soon after their drop-off within the capitol city of Tyre, the Coverts disappeared from *Comanche*'s tracking systems. Predetermined communication checkpoints came and went. Maura Enzler soon notified *Comanche* that the Coverts were having technical difficulties.

The mission proceeded tenuously, as *Comanche*'s crew struggled to regain contact with the missing Coverts. The Coverts' disappearance also cast a suspicious shadow over the mission, for it seemed improbable that all of them could disappear from *Comanche*'s tracking systems at once. When Michael pressed Maura on the issue during subsequent communications, her explanations waxed inconsistent. Soon, the stolen transport started disappearing and reappearing from *Comanche*'s scanners too—and showing up in places not part of the mission plan.

That was when Tom Andrews found damning evidence against the Special Forces teams, evidence suggesting something far more sinister than the Coverts simply botching the mission. Just as Tom came onto the bridge with the evidence in hand, the Europan FW-190s showed up and chased *Comanche* from the ice lineae.

Watching his vessel now taking a pounding as it fled the surprise attack, Michael wished he had listened to Tom's many warnings about the Coverts.

"Recon transport still on course from the surface at full speed," Lieutenant Combs, *Comanche*'s tactical officer, announced. "We'll intercept in two minutes."

Michael hesitated to respond, watching instead the small tactical display to his right. The device showed *Comanche*'s aft gunners taking out the last FW-190s chasing his ship, leaving the Europan surface guns as the only immediate threat. He then turned toward Combs. "Prepare to execute our escape route the second they're docked—"

The young captain's shoulders fell dejectedly. Tactical showed an artillery round striking the fleeing transport far below. The computer-enhanced image went wild, listing off a myriad of strike effects on the tiny craft.

"Recon transport took a hit to its primary engine," Lieutenant Herschel, Michael's engineering officer, announced. "The vehicle is maintaining a parallel course to the surface, but it doesn't have enough power to ascend. I'm also detecting a fire infringing on the crew cabin."

"Lieutenant Morelli, re-plot your intercept course," Michael ordered.

Morelli nodded uneasily.

Comanche dove headlong toward Europa's surface. The details of the settlements below soon appeared. The black sky filled once more with artillery streaming past the plummeting vessel, and *Comanche* shuddered frequently and severely. After a long, rapid descent and a lot of artillery dodging, the warship assumed an uneven but parallel course alongside the distressed transport. Fire from escaping gases engulfed the whole stern of the craft, leaving a plume of smoke in the transport's wake.

The bridge went unnervingly silent amid the chaos.

"We've got a hard-dock," Herschel eventually announced.

Michael shot a commanding glance toward Morelli. "Get us out of here!"

With a quick nod, the young navigator piloted *Comanche* back into the star-filled sky. Engines firing at full power reverberated throughout the ship, and inertia pushed against the crew as the vessel picked up considerable speed. Artillery tremors faded with the rapidly increasing distance. However, *Comanche* still had a burning transport docked against its hull, while tactical displays spit forth imminent danger warnings.

Herschel, monitoring the transport, looked up at Michael. "The fire is breaching the transport's main fuel stores. We've gotta eject it before it blows us up with it!"

"Docking!" Michael called into his communicator. "Get those soldiers aboard now!"

The speaker crackled, and a voice emerged from the mayhem, "We're trying, Sir! Air pressure from the fire is jamming the hatch!"

"We don't have time! Blow the hatch!"

After an unbearably long moment, *Comanche* shuddered! Michael looked down at his tactical display, which showed the transport abruptly falling away from *Comanche*. The tumbling vehicle exploded into a fireball after barely clearing the warship.

"Flight crew and Coverts are safely aboard," Herschel sighed heavily.

Michael let out his own profound sigh as his ship sped away from Europa.

He enjoyed a short reprieve as *Comanche* outran its immediate threats. However, his anger over the Coverts' actions burned within him. Unable to contain himself any longer—and seeing a few more minutes break in the danger—the young captain stood up from his chair and waved for Tom to follow. "Lieutenant Herschel, execute the predetermined escape route. You have the bridge until I return."

Not waiting for an acknowledgement, Michael stormed off the bridge with Andrews in tow. He kept a determined pace and his face like flint while hurrying through the labyrinth of corridors. Eventually, the two men arrived at the docking level.

The whole area was embroiled in chaos. Smoke from the burning transport hung thick in the air, while *Comanche*'s docking crew fought to secure a charred emergency hatch covering. The Coverts and the transport flight crew—wearing filthy Europan military uniforms and very much in distress—lay scattered across the deck while coughing smoke out of their lungs. Arriving medics quickly tended to them.

Maura Enzler, leaning against the facing bulkhead and covered in soot, noticed Michael the second he had arrived. Her face turned pale when he trained his gaze upon her. She flinched: Maura flashed a desperate look at the Coverts. A few of them, noticing her gaze, looked at Michael in a similarly nervous fashion. Immediately, all eyes trained on the Covert leader.

Michael glanced at Tom, who nodded inconspicuously at him: they all looked as guilty as sin.

"Lieutenant Kern," Michael said, emboldened and coming to stand over the Covert leader. "What happened down there?"

Emir Kern remained bent over while coughing. He carried a faded green, military-issue satchel stashed tightly under one arm—the only gear salvaged from the burning transport.

"*Lieutenant Kern*," Michael repeated with more emphasis. "What happened down on Europa?"

However, Kern kept bent over and facing away from him. After coughing a few more times and appearing indifferent to everything transpiring around him, he finally—and rather sharply—replied, "What'd you think, *Sir*? We were on recon. What were *you* doing?"

Michael huffed. "You disappeared off the grid—all of you! You didn't initiate communication checkpoints either." He glanced suspiciously over at Maura Enzler before fixing his eyes on him again. "And Maura's flight trajectory proves you were near the palace—not where you were supposed to be. What were you doing there?"

Emir Kern stood up and turned around, shooting a quick, irritated scowl in Enzler's direction. The seasoned warrior's face remained flint-like before his superior, while his frame stood in defiance. "Captain, Special Forces have to improvise. That's just part of the job"—coughing a few more times—"And the Europans had a dampening field over the city preventing communications."

"Your communicators were *Europan*," Michael countered. "We detected millions of transmissions throughout the city. They could only block *your* signal if they knew who you were, where you were, what you were doing, and what frequency you were using." He paused, letting his statements linger for a moment. "What about the locators? Were they dampening *those* signals too?"

"No, Sir," Kern replied, taking his locator from his utility belt. He turned it on and handed it to Michael, showing him the device's *lack-of-signal* error. "They malfunctioned."

Michael paused cautiously. After a mere second in thought, he snatched a locator from another Covert's utility belt. Turning it on and watching the small device come to life, he declared, "This one's working."

Awkward silence fell over the whole group. Michael and Tom stared down the Special Forces team, while Kern kept poker-faced. Then Michael spotted one of the Coverts pleading with Kern by expression. Though the subordinate tried to remain inconspicuous, his look clearly said, *come clean!*

"What about *Comanche's position*, Kern?" Michael pressed, his anger uncontainable. "We kept out of sight for three days in that lineae without seeing *one* patrol. Then FW-190s come out of nowhere, as if they knew we were there."

"*Our* position got compromised too—same with Enzler. We thought you blew the mission."

Michael stared down the man, unimpressed. However, Kern's gaze was predictably cool and calculating—until Tom pulled a small, cylinder-shaped device from his pocket and held it out in his palm for everyone to see. At the sight, the Coverts looked at each other oddly.

"What about this?" Tom challenged. "I found it in your quarters."

Kern remained silent for a long moment while looking at the device. But then he dismissively replied, "It's just a spare piece of equipment we left behind. So what?"

However, his voice betrayed his wavering confidence.

"It's an Europan communicator," Michael practically seethed. "One that was programmed to broadcast a homing beacon. It activated just shortly before the Europan fighters showed up at the ice lineae. We had to have the device in hand just to figure out how to track its signal. Of course, I don't think the Europans had any trouble." Michael turned steely-eyed at Kern, and the whole Covert team shrunk under his gaze. "You purposely gave away our location. That makes you a traitor!"

"Or a spy," Tom heaped on.

"No," Kern shook his head in defense—rather unconvincingly. "We use that type of equipment all the time. It was probably left programmed from another mission."

"Captain to the bridge," the communicator on the bulkhead rang out, echoing with all the other call boxes throughout the ship and breaking the tense moment.

Shooting Kern a reproachful look, Michael went over to the call box and activated it. "What's the problem?"

"We need you up here, Sir," Herschel's voice called out. "The goons blocked our escape path. Destroyers will intercept us in five minutes. Another squadron of FW-190s is coming up from behind too."

"That can't be," Michael shook his head. "Those forward paths have been clear since they forced us out of the lineae. Where did the destroyers come from?"

"The goons were moving their ships around out of range of our passive scanners," Herschel's voice called out again. "—like they knew our escape plan."

Comanche shuddered from the first new wave of artillery, and Michael's gaze waxed as deadly as the incoming rounds.

"I guess somebody must have told them," Tom interjected, training a suspicious gaze on Emir Kern.

Though Kern's eyes widened in astonishment, Michael fumed.

"*What'd you do?*" the young captain seethed. Without warning, he grabbed Kern by the slack of his collar and slammed him against the bulkhead. Surprisingly, the hardened warrior cowered, emboldening Michael and his suspicions—enraging him too. So he slammed the Covert even harder against the bulkhead. "*What'd you do?*"

"Mike, we need to go to the bridge," Tom implored, pulling his friend away from the stunned Covert.

Michael reluctantly turned himself to leave, though not letting his piercing gaze avert from Emir Kern. Finally, the irate captain looked at one of the men on the docking team. "Put them all in the brig." Right before leaving, he turned once more to Kern—just as the ship shuddered violently. "*You've killed all of us!*"

Shortly afterwards, Emir Kern, his band of Coverts, and the Special Forces flight team sat huddled together in *Comanche's* brig. The ship shuddered violently and frequently as *Comanche* attempted an escape from the Jupiter region.

One of the Coverts looked at Kern. "I told you we should have disabled all the locators down on Europa."

"Maybe," the seasoned leader mused while leaning back against the bulkhead. He kept the faded green satchel close to him, and his expression was distant. "I didn't anticipate the fire on the transport before reboarding *Comanche*. I thought we'd have time."

"Just like you assumed *Comanche* would bug out when the Europans arrived?" another Covert shot back curtly. When the other soldiers nodded in support, he added, "They saw where Maura's team picked us up. They know we deviated from our orders."

"They're going to court-martial us," Maura Enzler lamented. "They've got my trajectories, proof you turned off your locators, proof your communicators were working, and the homing beacon—and don't forget my lame excuses for the blackout. The only thing they *don't* have is a full confession."

"And they're not getting it," Kern declared.

Maura shook her head. "It doesn't matter"—looking squarely at Kern—"I should have never let you *talk* me into it." She traded awkward gazes with him, and her face blushed when she realized the others were watching the private interaction. "We're all going to prison—probably receive death sentences too."

Another artillery round battered the ship somewhere in the distance.

"We're already dead," another Covert replied, holding on through the tremor "The Europans will pound this tin can to smithereens soon enough ... but we *should* be court-martialed."

"*And for what?*" another Covert shrugged his shoulders. "We failed."

Emir Kern stood up, surveying the dejected looks coming at him—giving them no quarter to sulk. "A lot can happen. Court-martial investigations take time, and all Gillen has are suspicions—but no real proof. Even the beacon doesn't prove anything. Gillen won't have the luxury of coming back into port for a prolonged investigation—not when this ship is needed on the front lines. Command won't leave us on the sidelines too long either."

Comanche shuddered again, causing Kern to make a quick grab for the low ceiling to steady himself. When the tremors stopped, he handed the satchel to one of his men. "Hide this for the next time." Upon seeing all of them looking at him as if he were crazy, he exclaimed, "That's right: There will be a next time. We won't fail either ... I guarantee it."

CHAPTER THREE

The Beast

The dark void of space shrouded the metallic leviathan as if waters covering the deep. To describe the structure as massive would have been a terrible understatement, for its size and complexity daunted even those who had constructed it—they simply referred to it as *The Beast*.

Hovering in the cold of space far from the light and warmth of the yellow sun—the sun itself only slightly more prominent than the myriad of stars draping the eternal night sky—*The Beast* remained estranged from the very solar system and people who had brought it into existence.

Its home was the darkness—the very intent of its builders.

A swarm of military ships, impressive in size themselves and bearing the markings of the mighty Europan Empire, buzzed around *The Beast* as if gnats. They delivered supplies and personnel to their much larger host, quickly leaving after completing their objective. The activity had gone on for days.

Eventually, the ships left, and the leviathan was once again alone in the dark void.

Without pause, *The Beast* sprang to life. Enormous fusion engines at its stern fired, and the structure lurched forward. *The Beast* was a ship—an immense ship at that! The mighty engines continued firing, slowly overcoming inertia and propelling the vessel forward at a modest pace.

The ship lumbered through the darkness, navigating through several broad turns to change course.

Once the vessel was traveling a straight course again, nodes protruding out of the leviathan's hull began to glow. These nodes, spread uniformly over the entire vessel and previously indiscernible from the complex array of protrusions, grew in brilliance. The nodes began interacting with each other; brilliant flashes of lightning-blue energy darted across the hull violently. Soon, the random flashes grew constant, flaring in symphonic chorus and cocooning the entire ship in shimmering, bright light.

With one final, blinding flash, the vessel disappeared as if it had never existed.

ONWARD

CHAPTER FOUR

Five Years of War

NEWSFLASH: Somewhere on Ganymede (July 29, 2510A.D.) – Battered Ganymede and Europan forces are receiving quite the thrashing from Allied invasion armadas, which landed on the Jupiter moon early this morning.

In a bold move fueled by recent tactical successes in the five-year-long conflict, Allied forces struck decisively against Ganymede strategic positions, though establishing a foothold away from the fortified capitol city of Achelous. Military representatives expect the intense fighting to continue for several days.

Allied commanders refused to comment on their strategy to bring the Galilean moon under Allied control. However, given the progress of the war, the weakening of Axis forces, and successful Allied invasions elsewhere, experts predict Ganymede will fall within seven months.

The full-scale invasion stood in stark contrast to the failed Europa invasion attempted last December, when Europan forces—scattered by the invasion—eventually regrouped and pushed Allied occupation forces into retreat. This happened despite the Allies gaining control of key Europan cities, including the capitol city of Tyre.

The people of the Inner Rim received news of the Ganymede invasion gladly but with prayerful concern. With Triton, Titania, and Callisto subdued—and Ganymede soon to be subdued—Europa will soon stand alone against Allied forces.

The end of the war is in sight!

———

The vast, desolate plain stretched toward the horizon, draped in darkness under a star-filled sky. Pluto—a dwarf planet at the edge of the solar system—hung prominently suspended in space low in the Charon sky, appearing in half-moon fashion over the irregular mountain range bordering the plain.

However, Pluto did little to illuminate the surface of the moon or the Europan settlements on the opposing horizon. Yes, Pluto lay far removed from Terrae Solaris' warm, yellow sun; the yellow sphere hung in the sky dimly, its size no bigger than a pinky fingernail viewed at arms-length. Pluto and its largest moon, Charon, existed as if orphans of the solar system.

And far from the epicenter of the ongoing war.

A myriad of lights appeared low in the sky from over the mountains in the distance. The specs of light varied in size; about thirty comprised the body of the swarm, while countless, far smaller specs crowded around them.

The specs grew larger as the swarm neared the plain. Deadly artillery fire, erupting from the Europan settlements on the opposite horizon, streamed toward the swarm. Return artillery shot back from the swarm in response, causing the black sky over the plain to light up as it never had before.

The swarm quickly morphed into a fleet of destroyers, battle cruisers, landers, and one-man Hellcat fighters. The fighters raced through the sky toward the Europan settlements with guns ablaze, while the cruisers came to hover just over the center of the Charon plain. Behind the cruisers, massive landers touched down onto the surface; the ships deployed landing anchors to attach themselves to the low-gravity moon.

With the sky full of angry, one-man fighters and cover fire from the battle cruisers, the massive landers began unleashing legions of space-suited soldiers, tanks, and the like. The entire landing area turned into a nebulous cloud of dust and laser fire, while the Allied armies advanced toward the settlement.

Though the battle had just begun, Earth States forces had successfully landed on Charon.

The young man, smartly dressed in his fleet uniform and bearing the auspicious rank of commander, made his way through the busy office complex. Earth States Military Command Center, located on Eratosthenes, the Moon, had become a very familiar place as of late to him. He too had become a familiar face within the prestigious organization. So the young commander went along, trading esteeming glances and saluting ranking officers in passing.

He noticed the spring in his step. However, neither the new morning nor enchanting memories of the previous evening caused him to move along so spryly. No, the young man realized that Command had become his new home. Never had he been more confident in his own abilities, while recent successes noticed by his superiors boded well for his career. All the brutalities of a terrible war had somehow worked in his favor.

Still musing over his turn of fortune, he finally reached his destination: an office set off from the bustling common area. A large desk guarded an impressive door on the far wall behind it, and a young, female secretary sat behind that desk.

"Good morning," she smiled, her eyes brightening at his appearance.

"'Morning, Sara," he returned the smile. The two traded coy gazes through a long silence, as if relishing a mutually shared secret. "Is he in?"

"Yes. Is he expecting you?"

"No, but I bring news he'll want to hear."

The young woman smiled daringly. "How do you know he doesn't already have it?"

"Because I made sure," he said, returning her playful gaze. He proudly held up a small reader chip. "It's right off the wire from the War Room."

She let out a subdued chuckle and nodded in the direction of the door. "Go on in."

Trading impish smiles with her while she announced him, the commander went through the doorway.

The large office behind the door spread out in lavish fashion. Behind a sprawling, wooden desk at the far end of the room sat an older man in an admirals' uniform.

"Here's the latest tactical report, Admiral Davidson," the commander smiled at his mentor, approaching the front of the desk and handing him the reader chip. He watched Davidson put the chip into the reader on his desk. The device activated, projecting a half-meter-square holographic image above the desk's surface. "Our forces arrived at Charon—three days ahead of schedule."

The old man smiled and leaned back in his chair while studying the report. "This is *very* good news, Commander Reece."

"It's just the first wave: three Earth States destroyers, twenty cruisers, five landers, and a single Martian fighter carrier. Nevertheless, they established a foothold. Once the rest of our fleet arrives tomorrow, we should secure Charon in no time."

"Let's hope it's that quick," Davidson looked up at his subordinate soberly. "This war has given us far too many surprises already."

Reece stood vigil over the desk, while his superior studied the details of the report. A quizzical grimace waxed over the young man's face. Though struggling against interrupting his superior, curiosity overwhelmed him. "Pardon me for asking, Sir, but I don't understand this offensive against Charon. Everything from Neptune to Pluto is out of the way. If we secure Ganymede and Europa first, the rest of the Outer Rim will fall without effort."

Davidson studied the young officer's reaction curiously. "Maybe it's in preparation for a flanking assault."

"None of those planets are in alignment now," Commander Reece countered. "Regardless, the distances would dilute our forces too much."

The older man smiled, clearly enjoying watching his charge process the discussion. "Then perhaps there's another reason. Most of the Europan prison camps are located on Charon. Don't you think our POWs deserve a rescue?"

"Certainly … but …"

"But what?"

"We bypassed other, more convenient prison camp locations," Reece hesitated nervously. "Charon must hold some sort of tactical advantage." He paused as a smile came over the older man's face. "What does Charon have to do with winning the war?"

"Nothing," Davidson exclaimed deadpan. "Nothing at all. The war *is* ending … just a matter of time."

"So what could Charon possibly offer us?"

The older man leaned forward, looking his subordinate squarely in the eyes. "Survival."

The commander stood over the desk, clearly dumbfounded and unsure of himself. Finally, he said, "I don't understand, Sir."

"It's better that you don't," Davidson replied. "—at least not right now." Then he reached for his communicator. "Thank you for delivering this report personally. Please excuse me, Commander Reece; I have some work to do."

Davidson worked the communicator on his desk, while the bewildered, young officer left and closed the door behind him.

The holographic tactical report hovering over the desk moved off to the side. Another screen appeared front and center, displaying the word *connecting* until an administrative aide appeared in the image. After Cyril and the aide exchanged greetings and small talk, the screen switched several times until a very stately, well-dressed man appeared in the display.

"Admiral?" the man greeted him.

"Good news, Mr. President: Our forces landed on Charon."

"Good," President Mitchell nodded. "Have you located him yet?"

"No, driving out the Europans should take a few days. Our prison camps will take a little longer to liberate. But we'll find him soon."

"You know what to do. I'll send out your transfer orders immediately. Don't hesitate … too much is riding on making this mission work."

Cyril nodded and waited for the President to close the transmission. He could feel a heaviness washing over him as he pondered what he was about to do.

Just as the executive reached to disconnect, he looked at Davidson oddly from the screen. "Cyril, I'm sensing some reluctance. You're not having second thoughts, are you?"

Davidson hesitated through an uneasy silence. Finally, he shook his head. "No, we're doing the right thing."

Major General Roland Moreau stepped into the docking terminal at Randt Medical Base, a military medical space station located somewhere deep in the Asteroid Belt of Terrae Solaris. Immediately, the clamor of bustling activity accosted his ears.

The hull of the *ESS Windsor*, a medical rescue ship that transported and treated wounded soldiers from the front lines, prominently filled what earlier had been the gaping hole of an empty docking collar. The vessel's large service hatchways lay open. Corpsmen and utilibots, supervised by nurses and doctors, carried a long train of gurneys with wounded out of the hatchways.

Making his way farther into the bay, the seasoned general watched the controlled chaos with much satisfaction. Though moving the wounded into the main hospital facilities was a formidable task, the crack team—having experienced too many trips to the front lines—executed the task flawlessly. A particularly boisterous female colonel with auburn hair stood in the center of the chaos, facing away from him and barking out orders to her team.

"I see you have everything under control, Colonel Ricci," Moreau announced over the din while approaching her.

Kara Ricci quickly turned around. Though no-nonsense and driven in front of her subordinates, Kara's haggard expression told the tale of a long, arduous rescue mission to the front lines. Her athletic frame had thinned somewhat from lack of a solid meal, while her blue eyes radiated the heaviness of the life and death decisions that circumstances had forced her to make. Nevertheless, she offered him a welcoming gaze. "General Moreau. This is a pleasant surprise—or is it a surprise inspection?"

"No," the middle-age man shook his head, sidling up beside her. Amid the chaos transpiring around them, the superior happily put aside military decorum. "I save surprise inspections for my less-than-stellar officers, Kara." Handing her a small reader, he smiled coyly. "Actually, I'm here to replace you. Here are the orders."

Ricci gave him an incredulous look before surveying the small screen. "I don't understand." Shooting him a playful smile, she asked, "What happened, Roland? You get demoted?"

"Actually, the orders are for *you*—not me," Moreau replied. "Command is recalling you immediately." When her expression grew more quizzical, he added, "I'm here because I don't have anyone else to replace you so quickly." Then he smiled. "All those times you busted my chops to spend more quality time in Surgical have come back to haunt me—you got your way."

However, Kara kept staring at the screen in disbelief, missing most of what the man had said. "Is this some sort of temporary assignment?"

"No. Command already authorized me to promote someone to replace you."

"That doesn't make sense."

"You've been chief of surgery for five years—a *tough* job. Maybe they figured you deserve a break."

"But the war isn't over yet. What about the final surges to occupy Ganymede? Or the invasion of Europa after that?" She gestured toward the train of gurneys streaming off the *Windsor*. "We'll have lots of casualties."

Moreau shrugged his shoulders. "They must have something more important for you to do."

Kara continued reading the screen. Actually, she read the orders several times. "I'm to report to *Fleet Operations* on Mid-Earth Station. That can only mean one thing." she sighed and went silent for a long moment. "At least I know who's recalling me ... but for what purpose?"

"I don't know," Moreau shrugged his shoulders again. "Whatever it is, they're impatient. The transport captain assigned to pick you up delivered the orders personally. You need to leave now, Kara. He's waiting for you in the main reception area." Then he added glibly, "I told you I was here to take over for you."

Kara looked back up at the older man, completely stunned. Then she gazed out onto the *Windsor*, particularly fixated on watching her team tend to the wounded. A pensive gaze washed over her face.

"I dreamed about this day for so long," she mused solemnly, still looking out onto the bustling scene. "I couldn't wait to get out of here … but *not once* did I ever think I'd be sorry to leave."

"You did remarkable work here," Moreau nodded and put a hand on her shoulder. "Countless soldiers owe you their lives. If it were up to me, you'd be a general by now."

"I owe a lot to my crew. Take care of them, okay?"

Moreau nodded. "You'd better go." He smiled and offered her a casual salute. "*Good luck*."

The small tavern clamored with excitement and celebration, jam-packed with patrons eager to put the long workweek behind them. A rainbow of neon lights washed over the entire establishment, though doing little to push back the darkness; music blared from speakers built into the walls. Frivolity was the theme of the evening—just like every evening—with the sour aroma of alcohol and the acrid smell of cigarette smoke hanging thick in the air. The bitter fragrances governed the dissipation, urging on various games of chance, meaningless competitive challenges, and pursuits of clandestine encounters quickly forgotten at first light. The place was a hole-in-the-wall establishment for certain, falling far short of the high moral standards characteristic throughout Earth States.

And Emir Kern was completely at home.

The lieutenant, garbed in the only set of civilian clothes he owned, sat with his chair tipped back against the wall while taking in the raucous scene. He recognized a few patrons from the military base just outside the small Earth town. However, except for his team scattered throughout the establishment, the patrons were forgettable faces.

Curran Zeidler, his second-in-command, sat opposite him at the table. They conversed infrequently while watching the pool table area of the bar. Two other team members, one named Mark Armstrong and the other Brent Tasker, were hustling two local patrons at a high-stakes game of pool.

When the game ended, Armstrong and Tasker collected their winnings. Just as they returned to the table where Kern and Zeidler sat, two other teammates hurried through the tavern's doorway. The soldiers, named Glen Volk and Eric Gunn, came to the table, boasting about a more interesting establishment down the street. After some back-and-forth jawing on the subject, Kern and his small team of emancipated soldiers left.

The clamoring tavern continued its revelry without the six Coverts.

Sitting alone at a table close to where Kern and Zeidler had sat was Cyril Davidson. Dressed anonymously in civilian clothing, the man nursed a drink in one hand and gazed toward the door. His reason for visiting the establishment that evening had just left. So quickly finishing his drink, the older man left a tip and gathered his things.

He waded through the crowded establishment and stepped out the door; a hot, muggy August night accosted him. Spotting the Coverts walking in the distance, he turned down the sidewalk in the same direction. His pace was slow and deliberate, though fast enough to maintain visual contact with them—

Someone accosted him from behind! The assailant spun him around hard into the brick wall behind him, and Cyril's back protested the pummeling! Emir Kern, keeping a tight grip on Davidson, came almost nose to nose with him. The soldier's face boasted the most foreboding expression.

"*Who are you?*" Kern shouted at him.

"I don't mean you any harm."

The other Coverts, who had acted as decoys, arrived. They surrounded the older man, giving Davidson his first up-close, unenviable view of the small team.

In some ways, the Coverts appeared motley and thrown together. With his flint-like expression and eyes ablaze with overconfidence,

Emir Kern stood out as the obvious leader. Curran Zeidler, on the other hand, remained mild-mannered and reserved at all times. He had a soberness about him too, almost in opposition to Kern. Muscle-bound Mark Armstrong and Brent Tasker were as impetuous as they were gargantuan. That left the smaller Eric Gunn and Glen Volk buzzing around the two as if sidekicks to their larger companions. This was especially true of Volk, whose baby face and small, wiry build betrayed him as the youngest of the bunch.

Yet the Coverts embodied everything so stereotypical of Special Forces soldiers too: They were brash, arrogant, held an obvious distrust of outsiders, and looked as though they lived by their own rules. They wore the telltale marks of men calloused by far too many deadly encounters. They had survived such peril by shear will alone—and contempt for anyone who might threaten the small team.

Cyril—an outsider for certain—had trespassed against the team by his skulking and eavesdropping.

"You were watching my team!" Kern shouted at him again. "I want to know why."

"If you let me go," the older man pleaded, "I'll explain." However, when that statement didn't soothe the lieutenant's anger, he added, "Let's not attract any attention."

"What do you want to do, Kern?" Mark Armstrong clamored, the man's oak-sized frame towering over his superior. The question—meant to intimidate their hostage—encouraged similar jeers from the other Coverts.

With one arm still pinning his captive, Kern searched Davidson's pockets.

"I'm the reason you're on leave," Cyril pleaded as Kern rifled through his wallet.

Upon finding and reading the older man's identification, Kern let go of him. "Back off guys, unless you want a court-martial." When his team behind him relented, he continued, "Should I salute, Admiral Davidson?"

"Certainly not—at least not here."

"So you have our attention," Kern said. "What do you want?"

"I need to speak with you, Lieutenant Kern," Davidson said as he finished straightening himself from the incident. "—alone please."

Kern studied him for a long moment. Eventually sighing, he turned toward his men. "Guys, go on ahead. I'll catch up later."

Reluctantly, the soldiers backed away and started toward another tavern far down the street. Every now and then, a Covert glanced back at Davidson curiously and traded whispers with the others. Davidson and Kern followed but walked at a much slower pace.

"I'm impressed you caught me observing you back at the tavern," Davidson smiled.

"You stuck out like a sore thumb," Kern replied glibly. "No one goes to a tavern in this part of town at this hour for a cup of tea."

"How did you know I was drinking tea?"

"Because you don't look like you drink anything else."

The older man smiled once more. "I'll keep that in mind."

As they walked down the darkened street, Kern studied him intently. "You look familiar.... Were you an actor? Because I could swear I've seen you on television."

"No, but I was on television—*once*. Before the war, I was the executive director for NSEA. The night before the Ceres Fleet Base attack, I announced our Alpha Centauri mission to the press."

"*That's it*," Kern nodded as the memories came back to him. "I remember turning you off."

"Not a fan of space exploration?" Davidson chuckled. When Kern shook his head dismissively, he added, "That's okay. Right now, I'm more interested in *your* accomplishments: thirty-five successful covert missions, all quite dangerous and no casualties. That's impressive."

Kern nodded sheepishly. "My men are very good—and very motivated."

Davidson took in the comment through a long moment of silence, and he studied Kern thoroughly. "But not as good or as motivated as their leader, who is quite exceptional." A calculating pause. "Of course, *his* record isn't without blemishes though, is it?"

The Covert fell silent under the man's intentional, rather omniscient gaze. Quickly growing impatient under the reproving look, he finally shrugged. "So why am I on Earth? We were about to start mission thirty-six when you transferred us here. We're just sitting on our butts while the war goes on."

"There *is* a reason."

"Then why all the secrecy?"

Davidson took a few steps while looking down the street. He watched the other Coverts disappear into the tavern far in the distance. "God gave me a pretty good intuition with people, if I can catch them in their natural element. Special Forces soldiers act differently around an admiral. I wanted to see you and your team on a more even playing field."

Kern remained silent for a long moment, his wary gaze betraying his concern. Finally, he asked, "Did we pass?"

"It's not an issue of pass or fail—but who you are and how you react."

"Then what's all this about?"

Davidson hesitated with a sigh. "I'm putting together a mission you'll be interested in."

Kern fixed his attention on the admiral. However, when the older man failed to continue, he grew a little impatient. "Must be something pretty big, given all the lengths you're going to."

"The interest in the mission's success goes as high up as you can imagine."

"Sounds too dangerous," Kern mused. "That's why you seem ready to *ask* rather than order me." He took a few steps before shaking his head. "I'm not interested in a suicide mission."

"It's not a suicide mission," Davidson assured. Then he shrugged. "It's definitely covert and as dangerous as anything you've already done, maybe a little more. But it's not the typical mission—much different parameters. *That's* why I'm asking. And you'll have to work with and take orders from another group that isn't Special Forces."

The lieutenant shook his head. "I don't work with anyone not trained in special ops."

"You will this time."

"And what makes you so certain?"

Davidson stopped in mid-stride and looked him in the eyes. "I know your history—your team's history. When I tell you what the mission is … *you'll* beg *me* to go." He let a rather intrigued Emir Kern ponder his words before adding, "But let's go where we can talk in private."

The tavern was only slightly less seedy than the previous tavern the Coverts had visited. Absent Kern, the soldiers hovered around the pool table with many of the local patrons. Armstrong and Tasker, brandishing cue sticks, interacted with two locals also holding cues. In play was an intense game of *Eight Ball*.

In the heat of the challenge, Emir Kern appeared and came to the table.

"Let's go, guys," Kern exclaimed over the din. "We have work to do." He turned to leave, signaling for the men to follow him.

"But Kern," Armstrong gestured to the two locals holding cues. "These gentlemen are showing us how to play pool."

Huffing impatiently, Kern walked over to a local holding the bet money. He took the money and handed it to the larger of the two locals playing pool. "You'd never win; trust me." This, of course, raised the ire of the Coverts behind him, for the purse included their wager as well.

"*You guys tryin' to hustle me?*" the gargantuan local protested to Armstrong and Tasker. A horde of other enraged locals—spurred on by the varying amounts of alcohol running through their veins—coalesced around them.

Kern took the irate local by the forearm, whispering in his ear while the man stared down the rest of the Coverts. The longer Kern talked to him, the more the man's expression relented. The local's face had also turned, a futile attempt to hide the pain Kern's grasp inflicted on his forearm. Finally, the local nodded in concession, causing his friends to move back from the standoff.

"Come on," Kern waved to his men while leaving.

Reluctantly, the team followed. When the six men made it out onto the sidewalk, Tasker turned to Kern. "What'd you say to him?"

"I convinced him that picking a fight with you guys would land him in the hospital."

"That's right," came from one of the Coverts behind him.

"If you were so articulate, why didn't you get our money back?"

Kern smiled. "Don't worry about the money. We've got another mission, and you guys will *never* believe what it is."

CHAPTER FIVE

Window Reflections

The young officer stood spellbound before the panoramic observation window in the banquet hall of the personnel carrier *ESS Tranquillus*, bathed in the brilliant blue light of the planet Neptune.

The twenty-nine-year-old felt low and insignificant in the presence of the grand sphere, for the massive planet hung in space as if paying tribute to some indomitable force. Its surface—a sculpted canvas, no doubt—lay shaded with darker and lighter variants of blue from pole to pole. In some places, the variants formed latitudinal bands; elsewhere, they appeared as large, irregular spots: immense storms driven by unimaginable winds. Sparse, wispy white clouds accented the blue. Yet the planet was alive and churning too. As if an approaching storm transfixing its victims by its beauty and power, Neptune loomed before him ominously.

The deck trembled beneath his feet, for the personnel carrier struggled to break the gas giant's formidable and unseen grip. Though the vessel was traveling at a tremendous speed, the planet's movement out of view was barely perceptible.

That was okay with him. Captain Michael Gillen happily lost himself in the grand sight. In fact, the planet's appearance was the high point of seven days aboard the vessel. Moreover, after three long years of confinement at a POW camp on Charon, Pluto's only moon, he preferred gazing at the spectacle as opposed to his prison cell.

Though the allure of the blue sphere had drawn him in, his thoughts remained far away. The respite *Tranquillus* provided had let loose a flood of emotions he had fought since his capture so long ago. Gazing at the magnificent sight, the young man didn't suffer under the gruesome images that haunted him day and night. He could lose himself for a short time in boyish dreams of adventure. He could put out of mind that *fateful* day three years earlier: the day he had ordered the destruction of the *ESS Comanche*, killing most of his crew. However, once the preoccupation ended, his guilt over letting so many men die would return.

And then there was his *own* near-death experience. Memories of passing into that cold darkness lingered within him. Michael fought those images most of all. When *Comanche* died, something inside him had died as well. He had left a part of himself on that bridge— something he could not get back. Not that he knew what that part was, nor was he aware of its presence before feeling the loss. Yet whatever he had left behind had been as real as any other part of him, and its loss left a gaping coldness he couldn't assuage.

Michael hoped returning home would let him feel normal once more.

Unfortunately, the trip aboard *Tranquillus* would be long and mundane. Traveling at a snail's pace, *Tranquillus* also frequently diverted course to pick up POWs from other, newly liberated prison camps. That was how they had arrived at Neptune. *Tranquillus* had just picked up a camp of female POWs from Triton, Neptune's largest moon.

Given all these factors, he guessed returning to Earth would take the greater part of a month, maybe even two.

While his thoughts churned uneasily within him, Michael felt a hand alighting on his right shoulder. A familiar voice greeted him from the left, and an arm wrapped tightly around him.

"Mike!" Tom Andrews, first officer from *Comanche* and long time friend, cheerfully greeted him.

"Tom!"

Michael instinctively bear-hugged his friend, not easily letting go of his somewhat gangly frame. Tom had thinned a bit, just as *he* had also lost weight because of meager rations while imprisoned. Tom wore his brownish-black hair longer than military standards required, making him look more civilian than soldier. His casual demeanor, jesting eyes, and permanent smirk—unchanged from whatever circumstances he had endured—only enhanced the familiar impression.

Michael had not seen Tom since that fateful day on the *Comanche* three years earlier. After waking up in an Europan medivac hospital, the young captain found Tom and the rest of the surviving crew gone. Chained to his bed, Michael spent the next month recovering. His captors told him nothing, except he was alive only because of their graciousness—and a stubborn, loud-mouthed, and impatient first officer. So in a way, Michael owed Tom for saving his life.

"You look much better than the last time I saw you," Tom smiled. He immediately caught a subtle, painful remorse lingering amidst the warmth of Michael's return gaze.

Not that Michael was aware of the heaviness in his expression. No, he was quite oblivious to it—but it was there nonetheless. In fact, Tom noticed that Michael carried himself as if his entire athletic frame struggled against some unseen adversary. His blue eyes, once ablaze with passion for adventure and accomplishment, now burned with the smoldering fires of whatever consumed him from within. Sadness inhabited his serious demeanor too. With such stark changes in Michael's demeanor, Tom struggled to keep his concern to himself.

However, Michael didn't notice Tom's reaction. Instead, he sighed, shaking his head while running a hand through his cropped, brown hair. "That's a day I'd like to forget. I thought I was a goner."

"So did I. We were lucky that Europan freighter showed up. Never thought I'd be so thankful to get captured."

Keeping the conversation light, Tom gestured toward the planet-filled observation window. "When I boarded at Triton—on the dumb luck you *might* be among the other POWs—I went to the first place I could think of." Then he laughed. "You had that far away, *I wish I could explore the universe* expression on your face."

Michael smiled, relishing the consolation that Tom's unexpected presence afforded. So he gestured toward an empty table nearby, and the two men sat down to enjoy their reunion. "So what happened to you after they split us up?"

"They sent me to Galatea. After two years of putting up with my troublemaking, the goons decided to move me to Nereid."

"*Nereid?*" Michael raised his eyebrows in surprise. "You must have caused a *lot* of trouble."

"You have no idea," Tom replied comically. Then he shrugged, "Not really. The goons tire real quick of prisoners trying to escape … that's all. It's their fault. If they had just kept us together, I wouldn't have tried to go off and find you so often. Anyway, en route, the transport became disabled and set down on Triton. They put me up temporarily at the women's prison, but the replacement ship never came. So"— shrugging his shoulders—"Here I am."

"A single guy in a camp full of women—*for a whole year?*"

Tom dismissed Michael's smirk. "I was in complete isolation the whole time."

By then, workers began arriving to prepare the evening activities. As happened every night, the Military Auxiliary turned the banquet room into a makeshift club, providing music, games, and refreshments. Attendance had been strong the week Michael came on board. However, with female prisoners aboard, attendance would surely skyrocket. In fact, early comers of both sexes already began showing up at the door.

Tom took the opportunity to call a serverbot over to order drinks.

"So, have you heard the rumors?" Michael inquired after the machine left.

"What rumors?"

"About the *Weightless?*"

Tom nodded *no*, surprised that Michael had even brought them up.

"Sounds pretty bad," Michael sighed. "Death counts into the hundreds of thousands—maybe millions; women and children rounded up with the men—whole cities eradicated in some cases."

"It doesn't surprise me," Tom replied cautiously, understanding the fine line he needed to walk with his friend on the subject. "But it's still unfortunate."

The serverbot soon arrived with their drinks. Tom raised his glass to propose a toast, gesturing for Michael to do the same.

"To getting out alive," Tom quipped with a touch of humor.

"And to those who didn't," Michael added with more soberness than Tom had intended.

The glasses ritualistically clanged, and the two men drank. Michael waxed pensive, though he attempted to hide his troubled thoughts behind a veneer of propriety. Tom, noticing his reaction, nodded and kept vigil with him through a long silence. Eventually, Tom shook his head with such an uncharacteristically sober gaze. "I can still see their faces."

"Me too."

They fell silent for another long moment.

"At least we saved the President," Tom offered. "So they didn't die in vain." He paused, lingering on the thought for some time. "Still, I didn't have to give the command to ram the destroyer. That makes me the lucky one—I guess."

The two sat awkwardly silent until Tom finally raised his glass again. "To the crew of the *Comanche*."

Michael met Tom's glass with his own and nodded. Once more, they toasted.

"Do you think they'll discharge us when we arrive home?" Tom asked, intentionally changing the subject.

"I think so."

This brought an immediate smile to Andrews' face. "*Great*.... I'm going to go to some resort on Mars and just get *lost* for a while." He pondered the thought for several moments with such satisfaction. "How 'bout you?"

"I just want to go home."

Tom smiled. "You don't realize just how lucky you are—living on Earth, that is." He smiled again and shook his head. "I could never afford the down payment on a condo. I'll have to go back to living on the Moon." He looked at his friend with an intentional but coy half-grin. "No, I'm gonna need a benefactor."

"Yeah, yeah, yeah," Michael countered dryly, picking up the veiled joke. "I'll rent you a room—courtesy of the Jonathan Gillen Benevolence Society." He chuckled, and Tom did the same. "Of course, you won't need the room if they revive NSEA."

"National Space Exploration Administration," Andrews recited with a false sense of grandeur, surveying the air sardonically. "*Nessie!* I haven't heard that name in a long time." Then his face went serious. "You aren't *really* thinking about exploring the stars, are you?"

"I *did* say I wanted some time off first."

"That's what I like about you, Mike," Tom smiled. "After all the turmoil this war has caused you, all you want to do is hop on a ship and set off exploring the stars." He paused amiably before offering a sympathetic though pessimistic turn of his head. "I wouldn't count on it. Rebuilding efforts will delay exploration until you and I are in rocking chairs."

Michael let his head and shoulders drop. "We were so close to launching before this war got in the way. If the goons had attacked Ceres Fleet Base three months later, we would be one-fifth of the way to Centauri by now." He shook his head and added, "It isn't easy giving up something you've dreamed about and trained for your entire life."

"Part of me still wants to go too…. Just be content that you made it as far as you did. Otherwise, you'll go crazy."

Michael nodded reluctantly, realizing he was entertaining some self-denial. He looked at the huge observation window and watched the last remnant of Neptune pan out of view.

By that time, the banquet hall teemed with enthusiastic men and women, all ready to put the war behind them. Emancipation ignited a high spiritedness the room had *never* seen. The band cranked out upbeat tunes from the corner, while impromptu couples danced on the dance floor. Others lingered at tables or to the sides, deeply engaged in conversation, games, and frivolities. Some gathered in large, pep rally-like groups, while others chose a more intimate setting. Occasionally, a couple attempted to slip away unnoticed.

Michael saw all this and turned back to his friend with a grimace. "Now this is *military intelligence*. We're going home at a snail's pace after years of detainment, and some genius decides to make this a co-ed cruise."

Tom nodded. Of course, as a bachelor, Tom certainly didn't mind. However, he shared his friend's unspoken concern that the war was straining many traditional ideals, ideals that were the heart and soul of the generation at hand. He also knew that—regarding matters of the heart—his friend's thoughts were far, far away. "Have you heard anything from Kate?"

Katey! Just the sound of her name filled Michael with longing. Telling his friend how much he longed for her would have been unmanly. "No,"—letting out a frustrated sigh—"Communication is restricted until we reach Allied territory again. The goons at the POW camp didn't allow us to send or receive messages either."

"Same way at our camp."

Tom stopped to sip his drink and then—a slightly perplexed look coming over him—stated, "Kate is why I can't understand your eagerness to jump back into exploration. You barely had a honeymoon … just stay home and make babies. That's what I would do—*well*, if I were you, of course."

Michael half-laughed. He always suspected that Tom held a secret attraction to Kate. It was how he interacted with her—a little flirty. However, Tom was above all things an honorable and loyal friend. So young Gillen took the comment the way Tom had intended.

"You know," Michael began, gesturing to a group of single women on the far side of the room, "I don't understand why *you're* not out there mixing it up."

"I'm just putting in some time with an old friend," Tom smiled. Then he grimaced comically. "It would be unfair not giving the other guys a chance."

The two men sat at the table, enjoying the music and conversing. This exchange went on for some time, for they had nowhere else to go.

"Gentlemen," a familiar voice eventually greeted them, causing the two men to look up at the officer coming over to the table.

"*Burke*?" Tom exclaimed, his eyes widening in surprise at the sight of Gabriel Burke standing over them. A quirky half-smile came to his face as he turned toward Michael, who looked similarly startled.

Staring up at the man, Michael's thoughts filled with memories of the bitterness, competition, and conflict from so long ago—a time that no longer mattered yet still manifested itself in the subtle uneasiness in Burke's expression.

Both Michael and Tom rose to greet their long-time acquaintance. However, when Burke waved them down, they shook his hand instead.

"So what are you doing here?" Tom asked curiously.

"This is my ship," Burke exclaimed, raising his arms wide and gesturing around glibly with his head. "It kept me out of harms way most of the war—a nice, easy assignment."

"That's good," Tom nodded, an awkward moment of silence following.

"Do you want to sit down?" Michael asked.

Burke half-waved his hand at his side. "No, thanks. I have a lot of work to do. But thanks—*really*." He hesitated. "I must apologize, Gillen: I meant to welcome you when you boarded—the other officers too. Unfortunately, other matters have kept my attention." Then he let out an uneasy sigh. "But I hope you found your private quarters satisfactory? I made sure you had the best accommodations possible."

"Yes, thank you," Michael replied. "Burke, you sure you don't want to sit down?"

"I can't. Unfortunately, this isn't a social call. I just received a communication from Command." He handed Michael a small reader he carried. "This afternoon, I submitted my passenger manifest to them. I immediately received back orders for the two of you. Command orders you and Commander Andrews to return immediately to Mid-Earth Station. Be prepared to leave within eight hours: They're sending a Thunderbird to pick you up."

Michael and Tom looked at each other quizzically. They took turns reading the orders displaying on the small device. The screen yielded no more clues other than what Burke had already conveyed. Nevertheless, the orders were clearly official.

"I have to return to my duties," Burke exclaimed, his body already turned to leave. "But if you need anything while you're still here, don't hesitate to contact me."

Sharing an abrupt handshake and a final, uneasy farewell with them, Burke quickly left.

"Wow," Tom mused, turning back to Michael when Burke disappeared. "Captain of a two-bit personnel transport.... Just think, Mike, if you hadn't beaten him out of the Centauri commander position, you might have ended up here."

Michael pondered the statement for a long moment, his pensiveness returning. "After everything that's happened ... I think he's the lucky one."

Reflecting an understanding gaze, Tom picked up the reader and surveyed the orders once more. "Do you know what this means?" He gestured comically with his eyes to the larger part of the crowded room. "All those single women are going to have to get along without me."

"No," Michael replied in a serious tone. "It means we'll be home within a week." He studied the reader in Tom's hand once more. "But why do they want to see *us?*"

The large common area in the Intelligence office on Earth continued its normal, deliberate pace. Located far from the main Intelligence centers on Mid-Earth Station and Eratosthenes—far from the frenzy of the ongoing war—the quaint workplace kept to a more casual routine. Personnel, mostly women with low-ranking insignias, staffed the many workstations laid out in a grid pattern, while officers' private offices lined the perimeter walls.

Brenda Reid sat at her assigned workstation, smartly dressed in her navy blue, Class-B military uniform. With shoulders slumping, the young, bleach-blonde woman labored through mounting reports and mindless assignments. Life had become terribly mundane, and no end to the work was in sight. However, she took consolation in the one bright spot in the office: her good friend Kate Gillen sitting at the adjacent workstation.

Noticing Brenda looking in her direction, the fetching twenty-nine-year-old glanced up with a warm smile. Then her brown eyes returned to the holographic screen floating in front of her. With perfect posture, a uniform gracing an enviable figure as if tailor-made, and long brown hair neatly up in a bun, Kate set the standard for the office. She worked hard too.

"Could this clock move any slower?" Reid lamented. She paused from working her reader. "Maybe I can get them to let us leave early."

"What?" Kate replied with a touch of sarcasm. "And miss filling out all these exciting reports? The whole war effort depends on us." Then she chuckled dryly.

"I think they make up this stuff for us to do—keep us busy for the sake of being busy."

After trading intentional glances, the two women raised their left hands into the air, ceremonially presenting their wedding rings to one another. "*Kept Wives Club*," they sarcastically exclaimed in unison. After a ritualistic pause, they brought their hands back down.

This caught the attention of the women working the nearby workstations, who repeated the rite, causing those nearby them to repeat it, and so on until the ritual rippled across the large office. This annoyed the few male workers sitting among the workstations, who had grown tired of the practice. Quickly though, the whole office returned to normal.

"Why are you so eager to get out of here?" Kate asked.

Brenda rolled her eyes and sighed. "Waiting for my leave is unbearable." She rested an elbow on the desk, bringing her chin down into an open palm to sulk. "They shouldn't schedule our leaves so far in advance. They should just come up to us the last day of the week and say, 'Surprise! You're on leave next week'."

"It'll be here before you know it."

The two females smiled at each other and returned once again to their work. After several long minutes, Reid noticed Kate feverously working her reader while wearing a determined look. Immediately, Brenda knew what Kate was doing, for she had witnessed the daily ritual for five long years. "*Again?*" When Gillen glanced over in an aloof manner, quickly returning to the holographic display hovering in front of her, Reid pressed, "Kate, why do you torture yourself? You've checked up on Michael every day for three years now. Every time, that screen says the same thing: POW."

"If I don't, I won't sleep tonight—not that I really do anyway."

The two went silent as Kate called up her husband's status on the Intelligence database.

"He's out of combat," Brenda assured. "And the Europans have to take care of him now that the war is turning on them. The war will be over soon … so just hang in there and don't worry yourself to death."

Kate remained fixed on the holographic screen, waiting for the exhaustive search routines to yield their results. "If only the Europans allowed us to send and receive communications … I could know he was all right."

"You know what you should do?" Reid asked, not giving up. "Why don't you go on leave with me next week?"

"That's impossible."

"Have your admiral friend pull some strings. You could use the break." When Kate glanced her way and raised an eyebrow as if intrigued, Brenda continued, "Come with me. My whole family will be there, and we have more than enough room for one more. It'll be fun."

But when Kate glanced back at the screen, her countenance abruptly fell—tellingly. Nervously watching the information spill onto the screen, she brought a hand over her mouth. Her eyes welled up too.

Reid's breath went cold in her chest. She remembered Kate having a similar reaction so many years before: the day Kate had learned of the *Comanche* destruction.

"What's wrong?"

Kate kept silent and her face twisted; the first few tears trickled from the corner of one eye toward her cheek. Brenda hurried over, knelt in front of Kate's chair, and took her by the hand. "Honey, I'm so sorry."

Kate's reaction caught the attention of some other women nearby, who also gathered around her workstation in support.

Reid gazed sympathetically at Kate, who read the screen repeatedly. Then Kate looked at her, and Brenda realized that her best friend's expression was different: not despairing, but as if a great weight was lifting from her.

"You don't understand," Kate began, self-consciously brushing her fingers across one cheek to wipe away stray tears. "Michael's name came up under the manifest of an Earth States personnel carrier named the *Tranquillus*." A broad smile washed over her face as tears of relief trailed down both cheeks. "He's been released!"

A horrified Emir Kern ran with all his might through the desolate street, though feeling as if he were moving in slow motion. The sky was felled dark with thick, choking black smoke. A forced night had descended upon the settlement, broken only by the fires burning throughout the crumbling structures around him. The haunting sounds of sirens in the distance filled his ears, while cries of agony came and went as he raced along.

Certainly, he had entered into the very bowels of hell.

Panting heavily as he ran, the Covert felt the oxygen mask over his nose and mouth giving way with each labored breath. Smoke worked in through the corners of the mask, choking him frequently. The device struggled to provide enough clean air, the strain only adding to his exhaustion. Yet desperation forced him onward into the darkness.

Kern glanced every now and then at his fellow Coverts running alongside and behind him. They wore the same dire expression, for they all shared the same terrible dread. Worse, everything still seemed as if it were moving in slow motion, forcing them to ponder what they might find ahead. They dared not look at each other too long, for their eyes betrayed an overwhelming and insuppressible fear.

Much too late and yet much too soon, the Coverts came to stand before the crumbling remains of an all too familiar structure. Traces of smoke trailed up into the air from gaping blast holes, though the raging fire that had consumed the sprawling building had long since extinguished. The structure remained hauntingly quiet and dark.

He gazed helplessly at the surreal sight, while the bitter truth shuddered through him as if a sledgehammer had hit him.

Suddenly—strangely—he walked alone through the charred rubble inside the darkened, barely recognizable structure. Smoke lingered in the air, while dim streams of light pierced the broken walls. Debris lay heaped everywhere, forcing him to wade through the charred rubbish.

The fire had thoroughly consumed the place.

Desperate cries began echoing far in the distance, coming one after the other and joining in morbid chorus.

The wailing cut him to the quick, for his turn was only a matter of time. Yet he held out a glimmer of hope that he might be spared.

Nevertheless, his search must continue.

Looking around, he found nothing familiar. No, not even the overall layout of the destroyed place was recognizable. Perhaps he was in the wrong building—no, that was merely a desperate wish. So he stumbled around haphazardly, trepidation building within him the whole time.

Turning a corner, he swallowed hard. An odd pile of debris lay heaped against the far wall. With a fear he had never known building within him, he stepped toward it; his labored breathing under the oxygen mask quickened as he neared.

Coming to stand over the pile, he strained at the darkness to discern the charred pile's origin. Perhaps part of the ceiling had collapsed there—no, once more a fleeting wish. With no flashlight and only a few streams of light penetrating the room, the man knelt and stared intently at the pile. Mocked by a terrible fear, he waited for his eyes to adjust.

He swallowed hard once more as the malformed debris took a morbid but familiar shape in his mind. His chest heaved as if splitting apart, and his face twisted painfully; fists clenched in angst at the terrible sight!

Suffering under a merciless anguish, the tormented man felt a terrible rage spark within him. Just like the fire that had consumed his surroundings, the rage spread fast and to every part of his being. It burned hot—consuming him cruelly.

Emir Kern sat straight up in bed, a thousand terrible emotions washing over him! He struggled to catch his breath while laboring over his terror.

He had been dreaming.

Finally coming to himself, the battle-hardened warrior sat uneasily in the darkness. He put his palms to his eyes, rubbing away excess water that had gathered during the nightmare. He would never call them tears—not even alone and to himself.

Sighing, Kern reclined back onto his pillow. With his mind awash in the terrible thoughts engendered by the nightmare, he put his hands behind his head and stared hopelessly up at the ceiling. He had come to hate the nights because of that day so many years ago—because of his failed opportunity on Europa three years earlier to put his mind at rest.

And as he lay there, the tormented man resolved that his new opportunity—the new mission Admiral Cyril Davidson had dropped in his lap—would not end the same way.

CHAPTER SIX

Mid-Earth Station

The small, two-man fighter—a P-15 Cobra—appeared as just a tiny dot against the vast, cold emptiness of space. The Moon, which had earlier loomed large behind the Cobra, had grown significantly smaller. The fighter was moving fast, causing the grey-white sphere to recede into the background. At the same time, Earth grew in prominence as the fighter neared it.

Inside the tiny craft, Michael Gillen piloted while Tom Andrews navigated.

The cockpit was unusually quiet, just as it had been for some time; their journey from the *Tranquillus* near Neptune had been long and unpleasant. The Cobra, the last of eight separate transports they had used, had served as home for twelve straight hours. Enduring cramped quarters, unrelenting companionship, and fatigue, the two men quietly but impatiently awaited the end of their journey. The enthusiasm of their reunion, just five days earlier, had temporarily vanished.

An indicator light on the console came to life.

"There's the proximity marker," Tom announced.

Michael adjusted the Cobra's flight path and speed to conform to military landing protocol. Immediately, the craft began to slow, pressing the two men forward against their safety harnesses.

Several minutes later, a new dot of light appeared prominently within the star field, just slightly in front and to the right of Earth. The white speck grew larger as the fighter sped toward it, eventually morphing into the irregular, cuboid-like shape of Mid-Earth Station.

As the fighter neared, the station increased in magnitude. Soon, countless smaller specs of light appeared, buzzing around the space station like gnats. These were warships coming and going. Intricate surface details soon materialized from the station's smooth, grey surface, revealing docking ports, communications antennae, gunnery towers, and the like.

Just before the enormous structure engulfed the Cobra, Michael gazed at the Earth: *Home!* The beautiful, marble-like sphere beckoned him seductively, and he fought the temptation to turn the fighter in its direction. Duty called—for the moment.

Mid-Earth Station, over five hundred cubic kilometers in size, quickly filled the entire field of view.

A voice crackled over the communicator, "Delta Bravo Two-Four-One, we confirmed your landing orders. Disengage self-navigation."

"Finally," Tom sighed.

Michael nodded and disengaged his controls.

For a moment, the craft drifted freely. Then, another indicator light on the console flashed, signifying that the station's flight operations had seized control of the craft. With a series of turns and maneuvers, the fighter quickly descended, becoming a mere dot moving against the grey surface. Another moment later, the tiny speck of light disappeared as it was swallowed up into the belly of the beast.

The small car raced along the busy thoroughfare on Mid-Earth Station, darting erratically among all three lanes while dodging and passing slower traffic. If the station's traffic management system were controlling the vehicle, Michael Gillen might have felt more at ease. However, his driver, a young ensign with an untamed look in his eyes, preferred the excitement of an old-fashion stock car race. Michael was convinced the driver had a death wish.

"Don't worry, Sir," the ensign shouted over the harsh din of traffic noises. "I drive this access way fifteen times a day … haven't killed anyone yet."

"With driving like this, you should fly fighter jets," Michael sarcastically exclaimed. He tried straightening his windblown hair, but the open-air cabin made such an effort futile.

"No, Sir," the ensign dismissed, once again changing lanes and barely dodging another vehicle. "They put you too close to the action. I'll serve out my time here."

Michael graciously smiled as the ensign's driving jostled him about. "I think my friend back at the personnel residences got the better part of the deal." Realizing that his attempts to persuade the ensign to drive more cautiously were not working, the young captain turned his gaze to the scenery rushing by.

He had forgotten just how impressive Mid-Earth Station was. As one of the largest freestanding military bases in Terrae Solaris, the structure rivaled many cities on Earth. The cavernous thoroughfare was one of the more densely populated areas of the station. High overhead stretched a simulated topaz sky, while the recreation park to his right boasted a number of grassy, rolling hills with surrounding woods. Structures crowded around the thoroughfare, creating a bustling town. Of course, the open area was just one of many similar environments.

Minutes later, the vehicle turned off the highway and down a narrow access way. After winding through an intricate layout of secondary roads, the transport screeched to a halt in front of a large operations complex.

Michael quickly exited the car, letting out a thankful sigh when his feet hit the ground.

After watching the transport speed away, he turned around and gazed at the building standing before him. He thought it odd that Command had summoned him to the complex: The structure wasn't the typical place executive officers normally hung their hats. Rather, the building appeared to be some sort of low-level fleet operations complex.

The travel-weary captain also surmised that docking facilities were not far off.

He made his way into the building and through a series of checkpoints. Armed guards kept watch everywhere, and the number of admitted personnel thinned with each checkpoint. Upon reaching a common area deep inside the structure, Michael smiled: Cyril Davidson appeared from the opposing side. Davidson returned the greeting from across the room with his own friendly smile. Coming face to face in the center of the room, the two men engaged in a long, close handshake.

"Mike," Davidson welcomed him with a glimmer in his wearied eyes, "It's good to see you again."

"Hi, Cyril," Michael smiled back, studying the man's face as they shook hands. Five years of war had not treated Cyril kindly. Subtle lines etched his face here and there, and his cropped hair had grayed considerably. The heavy burden of his position had thinned his face too. Certainly, he looked older than his middle-age years.

Cyril, still locked in a handshake with Michael, put his other hand on his shoulder and looked him in the eyes. "I was devastated when I heard about the *Comanche*. You and your crew were always in my prayers."

Michael fought recoiling at the statement, desiring not to ruin the reunion over his disdain for such superstitious thinking. After all, such genuine compassion radiated toward him from the old man's eyes— something he desperately needed. So the young man accepted the sentiment graciously. He also put on a brave face, for Cyril mentioning the tragedy had sparked that same nagging vulnerability within him.

Cyril saw through his façade and nodded sympathetically. Putting his arm around the young captain, Davidson guided him about. The two men started down the corridor from where the admiral had first appeared.

"Mike, nothing I can say about *Comanche* will console you; the grief you carry is the burden of a captain…. But everyone in the command chain who knows what happened is grateful. The President is *especially* grateful. He wants to honor *Comanche* when the time is appropriate. You'll never know how much your sacrifice contributed to the war effort. Had the Europans captured or killed him, we would have lost the war."

With much reluctance and an unnerving silence, Michael took in the remarks as the two men continued walking.

"What about Katey?" he intentionally changed the subject. "Is she okay?"

"Yes. She's where we agreed: still on Earth and working in Intelligence. We keep her busy enough so she doesn't worry about you. She knows you left Charon, but she doesn't know you're here. I arranged leave for her to coincide with *your* leave so you two can be together. Of course, we have a couple more days of work ahead of us."

"I'm glad she's okay," Michael sighed. "I haven't stopped worrying about her for five years." After a long pause, he decided to change the subject again. "So why am I here, Cyril?"

The admiral smiled. "It's good to see you haven't lost your curiosity."

Davidson led him past two armed guards and down an adjacent corridor. Coming to a stairwell, they descended several flights and through a doorway into almost complete darkness. Though trying to adjust his eyes to the dimly lit walkway, Michael barely saw his old friend walking next to him. However, the long echo of their footsteps told him everything: They had entered some huge open structure, probably a dry dock.

"Mike," Cyril's voice echoed in the darkness, "What would you say if I told you they were about to reactivate NSEA?"

"I wouldn't believe you."

Davidson chuckled and then shouted to the environmental controls, "Lights!"

The immense chamber washed over in bright utility lighting. Just as Michael was about to shield his eyes from the glare, he beheld the unusual ship sitting on its moorings prominently before him. Every other concern quickly faded away.

By military standards, the vessel was quite small: only about three hundred meters long and eight stories tall—ten counting the moorings suspending it above the deck. Its black metallic hull ran sleek like a racer, and the ship housed three oversized fusion engines at its stern. Gun turrets jutted out from all sides, though fewer in number than military standards required. Protrusions of docking devices, maintenance interfaces, and the like were much more simplified. An unusual array of nodes dotted the hull's surface.

Michael gasped at the profound implications: The vessel was a long-range mission ship.

"She's beautiful," he sighed, his blue eyes sharply fixed on the vessel. "Where did she come from?"

"The Europans—at least the design."

"*Europans?*" the young captain grimaced. However, his child-like curiosity over the odd ship was uncontainable. "What are these node arrays?"

"That will take some explaining," Cyril began, watching his friend marvel over the vessel. "About a year ago, we had a fleet en route to Enceladus. Without warning, a small group of Europan ships came out of nowhere—and I mean *nowhere!* They were fast and did a significant amount of damage—and gone before we could even aim our weapons. This happened several times over the next couple of weeks. No one could explain it, and I can tell you that we were concerned.

"When our armies launched the first assault wave on Europa three months later, our troops came across an abandoned dry dock and research facilities. There these phantom ships just sat. Apparently, they had become disabled, and their caretakers fled as our troops advanced. It took a little while to unlock the ships' secrets, but eventually we figured out that the Europans had discovered Slipstream propulsion."

Michael gazed slack-jawed at the vessel. Slipstream propulsion theoretically achieved faster-than-light speeds by *slipping* between the fabric of space—much like how a stone skips across the surface of a pond. The theories had existed for years. Ben Morris, astronaut and propulsion engineer for the scrapped Alpha Centauri mission, had indulged himself in the elusive concept. However, most pundits considered the theories wild speculation and fantasy. The technology became fodder for children's comic books—and yet there the technology sat.

Michael approached the ship, wishing to run a hand over the vessel's sleek hull. However, because the ship sat high up on its moorings, he simply began walking the length of the vessel. His eyes remained fixed on every detail as he walked.

"So this thing *really* goes faster than light-speed?"

"Yes, but not the way you're thinking," Cyril replied. The admiral conveyed what he understood about Slipstream technology.

While explaining the concepts, the older man noted a glimmer forming in the young captain's eyes.

"How fast can it go?" Michael inquired, struggling unsuccessfully against appearing too enthusiastic.

"It's limited by exponential power requirements as you go faster. However, it's magnitudes faster than anything you could have imagined five years ago. Instead of taking twenty-four years to travel the four-light-year distance to Alpha Centauri, this ship can take you there in two years—less at maximum power."

"Wow!" Michael stopped dead in his tracks and went slack-jawed. "I think the universe just got smaller. No wonder why you couldn't catch those other ships."

"Correct," Cyril affirmed. "The Europans developed the technology four years ago. However, the engines were too massive for even their largest warships. It took them until last year to shrink the equipment to the right size. By then, they had lost too many warships and had run out of resources. So they finished four prototypes. But if they had perfected the technology sooner, we would all be speaking Europan right now."

Michael stepped back and stared at the magnificent contraption. Images of him standing on an alien planet under an alien sun danced about his thoughts teasingly. He could see himself garbed in a pressurized suit just outside a landing craft on some distant world, looking down at his first footprint in the dusty soil. Behind him, his team emerged in pressurized suits from the landing craft. They studied the surroundings in awe. An Earth States flag affixed to a pole lay in his gloved hand; the perfect place to plant the flag sat just a few meters away. And though the incredible journey to the distant star signified a great accomplishment, one question remained: Would the landing site on this alien world someday lie at the center of a bustling metropolis, perhaps even hosting a museum dedicated to honoring the feat?

Of course, he also hadn't forgotten that he stood in a military complex, listening to top-secret information during a raging war. "Cyril, are they *really* serious about reviving NSEA?"

Davidson hesitated. "For the right mission ... *yes*."

Michael, feeling a knot forming in the pit of his stomach, paused cautiously. "And what mission would that be?"

"Let's head to the observation deck for a better view of this thing," Cyril gestured, leading him toward a slew of ramping walkways. Taking his first step onto the walkway, he continued, "Today is your day for secrets, Mike.

"When our forces captured Tyre nine months ago, we learned that all the Europan Council leaders died in a suicide pact; their bodies were burned, and all command records were destroyed. A man named Carus ran the entire Europan war effort from an unknown location—well, until they forced us to abandon Europa. No one questioned the official story, given the evidence. However, rumors surfaced that Aurelian Galerius and his generals had not only survived, but had escaped."

"Escaped to where?"

"The rumors remained just that," Cyril replied, ignoring the question. "After all, the Europan forces scattered throughout the Outer Rim kept pressing us. But we kept hearing rumors about a large-scale project: material orders, orders for laborers, and anecdotal tales from civilians.

"Then, we found the evidence: records, confirmations by captured ranking officers, designs, etc.... The Europans constructed a massive generation ship with Slipstream capabilities—loaded it with military assets and personnel, scientists, terraforming equipment, and supplies too. When the war took a terrible turn against him two years ago, Aurelian Galerius used the ship to escape to 18 Scorpii."

Following his mentor up the walkways, Michael raised his eyebrows at the comment. 18 Scorpii was a star system forty-six light-years from Terrae Solaris. Its sun was similar to that of Solaris' sun and had five major planets. One planet was very similar to Earth, at least as much as scientists could determine from such a great distance. Though 18 Scorpii was the first choice for a deep space exploration mission, it was too far away for the technology constraints at the time. However, the ship sitting before him had no such constraint.

"Do we care that Galerius escaped?" Michael ventured. "The farther away the better, right?"

"It's very complicated."

The two men arrived at the observation deck, and Michael surveyed the magnificent ship sprawled out before him. Though relishing the sight, he feared where the conversation was heading.

"I assume you've heard about the *Weightless* genocide?" Cyril asked. When his young subordinate nodded uneasily in the affirmative, he continued, "It's worse than the rumors suggest … and the surviving *Weightless* want Galerius brought to justice." Davidson paused, his shoulders dropping and his gaze pleading. "Mike, we have a lot of Outer Rim rebuilding to do when the war ends … and we don't have the money." Unbearably, the older man hesitated once more before finally blurting out, "*So* … we are conducting discussions with Mos Thieren—"

Michael let out an indignant huff. He shook his head in disbelief, feeling his breath go cold in his chest and his stomach sour. He felt numb too.

Cyril, seeing the disdainful scowl, offered a conceding half-shrug. Nevertheless, he pressed forward. "Thieren will help fund much of the post-war rebuilding—but only if we bring Aurelian Galerius back for trial." He put a hand on Michael's shoulder and looked him in the eye. "We need *you* to bring Galerius back."

Michael turned inconsolable.

"So," he began cynically, stepping away just a little, "You want me to travel forty-six light-years, kidnap a powerful tyrant out from under *all* his security forces, and bring him back for trial?"—his eyes sharpening—"You're crazy if you think I would agree." After a long pause, he shook his head dismissively. "Besides, by the time Aurelian Galerius stands trial, Mos Thieren will be long gone."

"Mike, the *Weightless* want assurance that justice will prevail over this genocide, that they aren't on the verge of extinction. Thieren is willing to pay a hefty price to secure that assurance, and *we* have a lot of rebuilding to do in the Outer Rim. If we don't secure Thieren's funds, Terrae Solaris will eventually collapse.… Your country needs you … the *President* is personally asking for you."

Michael turned and leaned on the railing, fixing his gaze on the exploration ship and sulking through a long silence. Eventually, he huffed and shook his head once more. "I'm not sure I can help the likes of Mos Thieren … too much history … too much bad blood."

Davidson's gaze pleaded that much more. "Your skills and training make *you* the only one qualified to lead the mission. Mike, I need your help."

Michael's skin crawled at the inevitable. Cyril had backed him into a corner. Aside from appealing to his patriotism, the man's appeals resonated on so many inexpressible levels deep within. Had anyone else asked, Michael would have easily resisted. However, Cyril—a surrogate father, a friend, a confidant, a man so much like his brother David— was the one asking him. He saw the desperation in the old man's eyes, and the expression completely unsettled him. Though Michael looked back at him as if to plead, Cyril's own pleadings cut deep. He sighed heavily, astonished at what he was about to do. "Who do you have in mind for the crew?"

"We enlisted a Special Forces team for the capture, but your flight crew is the Centauries: Kara, Ben, Phil, Tom, and Kate."

"*Kate*," Michael threw his hands into the air, recounting how much effort he had expended to keep her safely out of the war—*Katey*. His insides churned gruelingly. "I can't put her in such peril."

"I don't want you to, either, Mike. She's like a daughter to me. But I know you would never leave her behind either."

"Does she know?"

"No. We already asked Kara, Ben, and Phil. They'll do the mission if you agree. Tom knows nothing, but I'm sure you can convince him. As for Kate, you can discuss it with her."

Michael turned back to the larger part of the dry dock. The exploration ship lay stretched out before him, beckoning him seductively. A new age of exploration was upon mankind, and his destiny as an explorer called to him. Not that the mission itself held any appeal. No, if anything, the mission objective—and whom he was helping—filled him with disdain. Neither would he be the first human to step foot on those worlds. Nevertheless, 18 Scorpii awaited him. Perhaps such an opportunity would never come again.

"I'll commit only if Kate agrees. If not, find someone else."

"Agreed," Davidson offered an understanding smile. "Get some rest. Tomorrow, we meet with President Mitchell."

Michael's jaw dropped, and he searched his mentor's face nervously—incredulously too. "You're kidding, right?"

"I don't kid about such things. You're going to have to meet Mos Thieren too."

Predictably, the young man's trepid expression waxed into a scowl.

"*Lord Carus,*" the Europan subordinate called, catching sight of the leader and his entourage making their way down the adjacent corridor of the Europan Command Headquarters on Europa. He quickened his pace as the small group came to a stop and turned around. All eyes fixed on him.

Carus, standing impatiently amidst his aides, boasted all the regalia denoting his position as sovereign ruler of the Europan Empire—at least what was left of it. However, the thin, calculating man merely held such a title by proxy, the honor granted him by Aurelian Galerius himself just before his departure to 18 Scorpii. In the absence of the ruthless dictator, Carus found his high position frequently challenged by those availing themselves of the opportunities afforded by the current turmoil. Of course, Carus could be ruthless too.

The subordinate quickly came to stand before the sovereign. Though holding titles of nobility and a high position himself, the man nevertheless fixed himself in obeisance to the leader. He held out a reader to him. "Here's something you should see immediately."

Carus, his eyes heavy from a long day of holding the frail empire together, reluctantly took the reader in hand and activated it. A half-meter-square holograph appeared in the air over the device, displaying a picture of the Earth States' deep space exploration vessel sitting in its dry dock on Mid-Earth Station.

"We just received new intelligence from inside Earth States," the subordinate said. "This is a picture from a secured dry dock on Mid-Earth Station. Look at the configuration."

"Yes," Carus mused, watching the underling point to the Slipstream nodes adorning the vessel's hull. "Not an unpredictable move on their part. What's the consensus?"

"Not much is known at this point, my Lord. All we know is that the ship is near-ready to launch."

Carus studied the picture for some time before shaking his head. "We know enough just from the picture." He pointed to the ship's hull, accidentally scattering some of the pixels floating in the air. "This ship is far too under-armed for any type of strategic assault on our home world."

"And its size denotes large fuel cells and storage bays."

"Enough for a long voyage," Carus exclaimed, receiving agreeing nods from the subordinates gathered around. "No, this ship is destined for 18 Scorpii"—looking around at the underlings—"We can't let it launch."

The subordinate cleared his throat nervously. "But what about our long-standing orders from Lord Galerius?" When the sovereign's eyebrows raised and every onlooker's expression turned awkward, the man begged, "—I mean … this one ship *can't* be a threat. Shouldn't we concentrate on defending our home world from invasion?"

"Who says we can't do both?" Carus replied, uncharacteristically gracious. He boasted a rather omniscient expression. "Besides, hasn't our intelligence also reported the Terrans engaging Mos Thieren in discussions?" His eyes turned steely. "This ship's appearance is no coincidence. No, we have to consider this ship a threat to Lord Galerius himself. That's why we can't let it leave the solar system."

The subordinate paused, carefully crafting his response. "Stopping the ship will be difficult. Terran home space is well insulated from a direct attack. Our forces remain scattered too."

"*Scattered* may just work to our advantage this time," Carus mused, lingering over the comment. "Still, you're right about the difficulties. That's why we must work this threat on all fronts…. Put as many operatives as we can spare on this; find out every detail: launch schedules … people involved … *the crew*—everything. Let's see if we can't worm our way in and frustrate them at every turn."

"It shouldn't be too hard," the subordinate nodded. "Much of their pre-war deep space program was public knowledge. No doubt, many of the same parties are involved—and we had operatives among those people."

"Yes," Carus smiled. "—and their military too." Once more, the man lingered over his statement. "Perhaps stopping that ship won't take grand heroics after all. But if we find that a direct attack is the only way to stop the ship … we'll do that too."

CHAPTER SEVEN

Visit to Eratosthenes

Twenty-nine-year-old Michael Gillen anxiously sat in his seat aboard Cyril Davidson's personal transport, waiting for the craft's arrival into the capitol city at Eratosthenes, the Moon. Cyril sat in the next seat over, just as he had done the entire flight from Mid-Earth Station. Having repeatedly stressed the importance of the upcoming discussions ad nauseam, the older man simply offered a reassuring look to him every now and then.

However, nothing consoled the young captain. No, Michael had ventured far out of his element, and he filled with trepidation over what would soon take place. Though meeting President Mitchell was daunting enough, his stomach tied itself into knots at the thought of meeting Mos Thieren face to face. Desperately seeking a diversion of thought, Michael gazed out the window to his left.

The transport, still traveling hundreds of kilometers out and over the Moon's surface, flew over Southeast Mare Imbrium into its landing pattern. He beheld a spectacular view of the entire region. Sunlight streamed in from the east, casting crisp shadows over the western slopes of the

Montes Apenninus mountain chain. The mountains and craters, such as Autolycus, Archimedes, and Timocharis (all hosting cities named the same), rose up in contrast against the dark grey plains of Mare Imbrium bordering the region.

When the transport descended into the shadows of Crater Eratosthenes minutes later, the window filled with a billion tiny lights. Though most of the sprawling city lay buried deep beneath the Moon, surface structures nevertheless spread across the entire sixty-kilometer-wide crater. Traffic crowded a network of roads snaking throughout the city, while the sky swarmed with transports and military craft coming and going. At the center of all the bustling activity sat the capitol center itself, located within the rocky prominence at the center of the crater.

Michael watched as the transport executed an approach pattern toward the capitol center. Though the entire, sprawling habitat lay underground, a transparent ceiling level with the Moon's surface gave quite the view into the grand, earth-like setting far below. As the transport neared, he could see below him the towering Congress building (which protruded through the habitat's transparent ceiling), all the various other government buildings, parks, roads, commercial districts—and of course, his destination: the Executive Mansion.

The mansion sat prominently above most of the city on a series of grassy, step-like plateaus. Its marble and granite, Palladian-style architecture—complete with Greek-style columns supporting a center portico, arched window, and the like—made it a timeless palace boasting of the grandeur and accomplishments of the Earth States people.

Michael sighed, realizing that turning back no longer remained an option.

Following Cyril through the final security checkpoint in the Executive Mansion complex, Michael took his first step into the opulent main hall—and gasped at the sight before him.

The hall—the size of a small amphitheatre—overwhelmed him with its French Victorian architecture. Bluish-grey marble floors spread far and wide, while massive, white Corinthian-style columns stretched to the vaulted ceiling five stories above. Marble statues, plush red curtains, expensive furniture, and artwork adorned the interior and gave the hall a renaissance feel. The whole area was abuzz with personnel going about their official duties, while armed guards anonymously kept watch.

He took a deep, uneasy breath. Nothing about the place alleviated his sense of being out of his element. Rather, the sensation intensified with each step.

———

Coming to the end of the bureaucratic formality surrounding his arrival, Michael sat alone in a small side room off the main hall in a plush, antique chair. Cyril, needing to attend to some business prior to the discussions, had left him there a short while earlier. So the young man nervously stroked the velvet armchair fabric while fighting the urge to fidget. Time plodded along in deliberate fashion, causing each passing moment to intensify the suspense welling up within him.

The door opening broke the unnerving silence.

"The President wants to meet with you privately before the actual meeting," Cyril announced, coming into the room and letting the door swing open.

Michael could bear sitting no more. He sprang from the chair and straightened his uniform once again.

A busy procession soon appeared at the far side of the main hall outside. Spotting the leader's grayish-brown hair bobbing up and down in the midst of the group, Michael instinctively snapped rigid; nausea built in the pit of his stomach. Davidson, still beside him and in a more casual stance, leaned in toward him.

"*Mike,*" he whispered, "*Relax.*"

Michael readjusted his posture in an attempt to appear more settled. Yet he remained more than rigid within, putting the large Corinthian-style columns in the main hall to shame.

The tightly packed group fanned out upon nearing the room, and President James Mitchell emerged. Michael saw that the man's larger-than-life persona was not a fabrication of television. No, Mitchell was stately in appearance, having a natural grace and charisma that beckoned respect.

He radiated an assuring confidence and swagger beyond that of a mere man, while in his blue eyes lay a sense of deep conscience and conviction. In the presence of such a great man, the young captain was tempted to bow.

Without missing a step, the President swept into the small room. Michael and Cyril saluted. An assistant following behind the leader shut the door, leaving the rest of the group outside.

"Captain Gillen, I'm President James Mitchell," the leader said, flashing an assuring smile and extending a hand toward him. "It's an honor to meet you."

Michael responded—nervously fumbling through the motions—and the two shook hands. "The honor is all mine, Mr. President." The young man stood awestruck in the presence of the leader. Though the beneficiary of Mitchell's gracious and cordial demeanor, Michael suddenly felt the words on his tongue evaporate.

"I apologize for rushing you around like this," Mitchell said, bridging the awkward pause. "I know you were just released from an Europan prison camp last week. Is everything okay?"

"Yes, thank you. I'm glad to be home again."

"That's why we worked so hard on your release," President Mitchell replied. After a heartfelt pause, he continued, "You have my sincerest thanks for what you did three years ago. I don't know what would have happened if the Europans had captured me."

Michael once again fell speechless. Eventually, he managed to reply, "It was an honor, Sir—and an honor for my crew as well."

"Don't get me wrong," Mitchell began. "I'm eternally indebted to everyone who helped me: the *Eris*, the *Dorn*, the *Pyroscaphe*, the *Trafalgar*, and of course the *Comanche*. Nevertheless, I owe *you* special thanks: My transport captain told me of your heroism and cunningness. You should be very proud."

Michael stumbled for the right words. The distinguished hero stood before him, lavishing him with praise—an unbelievable experience! Cyril looked on as if a proud parent too. Suffering under his own humility, Michael finally eked out, "It was an honor to serve you, Mr. President."

President Mitchell nodded respectfully, letting the moment pass before his expression turned sober and businesslike. "I understand that you haven't yet given us your final answer on 18 Scorpii, correct?"

"I gave him a week to decide," Cyril chimed in, watching Michael stumble for a reply.

"That's understandable. For today, let's assume you'll agree. That'll make the meeting easier. But think through your answer thoroughly: 18 Scorpii is the key to securing Mos Thieren's funding of our postwar rebuilding efforts. Without rebuilding, the whole system will collapse." He paused for effect and looked Michael squarely in the eyes. "So I desperately need your help once again."

Michael responded with an affirmative but uneasy nod.

President Mitchell moved in closer and put his hand on his shoulder. "Michael, do you understand why you're here?"

"Not really, Sir."

"We need to win Thieren over. I know you're the best candidate to lead the mission, but he doesn't. Given your relation to Jonathan Gillen, Thieren will be very suspicious. I want you at that table, looking him in the eye. Persuade him that you're sympathetic to the *Weightless*—and one hundred percent dedicated to bringing Aurelian Galerius to justice. Can you do that?"

Michael swallowed nervously. Truthfully, he hated Mos Thieren more than he hated Aurelian Galerius. The meeting was the perfect opportunity to put Thieren in his place too. Nevertheless, duty called, and he regrettably nodded in the affirmative.

"Good. Now, I want to give you a word of advice: Mos Thieren is an incredible *wind bag*." He cracked a brief smile before turning sober again. "With you in the room, he will be at his worst. Now, everyone on my side of the table knows you're the best man for the job, and we will hold to that point. But don't let Thieren drag you into a debate; don't lose your composure. Just let him say what he feels he needs to say, okay?"

"I think I can do that, Sir," Michael said reluctantly and in complete disbelief that he was agreeing to such a request.

"I'm glad," the President sighed. "If I were you, I'd knock his teeth out."

Just then, the door opened halfway, and an aide popped her head in through the small gap. "Mr. President, Mos Thieren just arrived." Upon seeing the leader nod in acknowledgement, the young woman once again disappeared.

Michael felt his trepidation washing over him at the woman's words. He also knew his reaction was more than apparent.

However, President Mitchell, smiling encouragingly at Michael, ignored his flustered reaction. Instead, he nodded for the two men to follow him. "Okay, let's go get 'em."

At the President's lead, everyone left the room.

The conference room on the Executive Mansion's operations floor was not what Michael Gillen had anticipated. Compared to the majestic, renaissance-style chambers on the floor above, this room—really, the whole floor—imparted a much more practical mood. A broad oval table for no more than fifteen people sat in the center, while workstations for aides lined the corners. Directly above the table, a bulkhead descended from the ceiling, supporting an overhead console of operations equipment. Presentation screens, holographic generators, and the like cluttered the walls.

Michael occupied the far right seat on one side of the table, nervously waiting for the discussions to begin. Cyril Davidson sat to his left, while President Mitchell sat in the middle of the table on the same side. Flanking Mitchell was Gael Pariseau, Chancellor of the Republic of Western Mars, and Antonin Seres, Prime Minister of Mercury. Several other leaders, including Marius Fiske, Chancellor of the Republic of Eastern Mars, attended the meeting remotely, represented by holographic images. Aides to the leaders operated the consoles lining the corners.

Michael realized he was completely out of place among the austere group.

Mos Thieren had yet to arrive. Mitchell and the other Allied leaders had already greeted the *Weightless* activist in a private ceremony earlier, a ceremony Michael was thankful that he did not have to attend.

While Thieren and his entourage were settling into their quarters somewhere in the mansion, the leaders chitchatted. The conversation revolved around solar weather, sports, and family activities. Michael found that ironic: He never envisioned world leaders discussing such trivial matters.

When the conference room doors opened, the whole tenor of the room turned dark; Mos Thieren, enigmatic leader of the *Weightless*, appeared. The gaunt, ashen-skinned man with a characteristically thin, disproportional body structure—a typical *Weightless*—floated into the room toward the table. Several other *Weightless* cohorts and aides, appearing in similar fashion, followed him through the door.

Thieren, his advancing age more than apparent, resided within a gravity-neutralizing field projected by a device worn at his side. Michael relished the irony: After years of Thieren's rhetoric against pro-gravity contingents and Jonathan Gillen, Michael's first glimpse of the man came by the means of the same technology he denounced.

However, Michael quickly tensed up. He had never seen a *Weightless* in person before. All of them floated within zero-G fields as if ghosts on a haunt, though radiating far less charm and warmth. He wondered how merely having a semblance of a head, torso, arms, and legs qualified something as human, for he detected no signs of humanity among their strange, disdaining faces.

Thieren floated to the center of the opposite side of the table. The Allied leaders, previously radiating a light demeanor, stood up and gave polite but uneasy attention to the activist. The same uncomfortable tension reflected back from the other side of the table too.

Thieren stole a glance in Michael's direction; everyone noticed. The *Weightless* quickly turned back toward his hosts to defuse the attention he had drawn. However, the Allied leaders looked at each other tellingly—at Michael too. Falling under their conspicuous gazes, Michael winced: The discussion would ultimately turn toward him.

"Mos," President Mitchell greeted the *Weightless*, "I trust you found your quarters satisfactory?"

Thieren nodded appreciatively, and a round of small talk and ceremonial pleasantries ensued among all the leaders. Thieren clearly relished being the center of attention.

Michael sickened at the respect given to the political parasite. When Chancellor Pariseau addressed the *Weightless* leader as *Representative Thieren*, Michael wanted to sneer. *How did this scoundrel rate such a respected title?* he thought. Quickly, though, the young man realized he needed to keep his emotions in check. Otherwise, he would never last the whole meeting.

President Mitchell gestured to everyone, causing his side of the table to sit back down. Thieren and his floating followers sidled up to the opposite side, which had been left without chairs (for the *Weightless* had no need to sit). With both parties shooting awkward gazes at each other, the tenuous meeting commenced.

"I've heard a lot of talk from your representatives of late," Thieren warned the Allied leaders, jumping ahead of the agenda, "—a lot of promises assuring me that the perpetrators of this genocide against my people will not go unpunished. That is a most necessary step. But let us be clear: The *Weightless* have had problems *all over* Terrae Solaris. If we are going to prevent more atrocities, we need to get to the root of the problem—racism.

"For far too long, the people of Solaris have shunned my people. You view us as second-class citizens. Contempt for our wealth—our reward for making Solaris what it is today—remains rampant. We need you to diffuse this hatred ... to ensure that the special needs of my people are met."

Michael realized that Thieren had already checkmated the entire Allied leadership. Any disdain for such a man—if indeed he really was a man—fell victim to the *Weightless* genocide and the Allies' desperate need for his money. History had dealt Thieren a formidable hand, and he would play it for all it was worth.

"We *share* a common goal," President Mitchell nodded at Thieren, undaunted. "But the impacts of this war will extend far beyond the last artillery round. The *Weightless* aren't the only group threatened by extinction. Our whole way of life will collapse if the Outer Rim isn't stabilized soon."

He waved to an assistant to activate the holographic projection system. Immediately, image after image of the war-torn Outer Rim took its turn on the prominent display.

The Earth States leader surveyed the room. "I know we've all seen these images far too often, but the realities of this crisis are serious: Offensives into Axis territories have left Triton, Titania, and Callisto destitute. Ganymede and Europa will soon follow. Take a good look at them"—a long, intentional pause—"Circumstances are dire. Without us rebuilding habitats and economies, the whole Axis system of government will collapse. We'll have anarchy, and the same conflicts and genocides will arise again."

Mitchell paused, letting the importance of the initiative sink in across the room. Then he turned quietly to his aide. "Bring up the cost summary."

A simple fact sheet replaced the Outer Rim desolation pictures on the screen. The chart showed rebuilding costs and contributions promised by each faction. Thieren's pledge overshadowed all other contributions.

Michael recoiled at Thieren's unimaginable pledge. However, he also realized that the pledge was merely a portion of his wealth. Yes, the man wielded control of a vast *Weightless* fortune.

"Obviously, the pledges don't cover the entire rebuilding costs," Prime Minister Antonin Seres commented to Thieren. "However, they provide enough investment to fuel sustainable economic growth."

Thieren, indicating his familiarity with the concepts presented, waved off the analysis. Instead, he lashed at them with concerns over details he claimed the leaders had glossed over. For the next forty minutes, the leaders debated the proposal. The conversation ebbed and flowed, with the emotional tone vacillating significantly.

Thieren's responses were cool and calculating. He became frustrated and withdrawn any time the proposal failed to meet his expectations. Fear of him withdrawing his pledge forced concessions. Thieren then accepted each concession in a way that set up his next demand. Michael realized the deal would cost the Allies plenty.

Only at the end of the long discussion did Thieren turn the least bit congenial.

"Of course," Thieren half-smiled, languidly floating in his zero-G field as if immersed in water, "My people are eager to help the rebuilding efforts. With your nations providing materials, we have some latitude on labor costs."

"So do you agree with the reconstruction plan?" Mitchell asked.

Thieren paused several moments in thought, letting the Allies stew in his hesitation. "The program is acceptable."

A collective and unintentional sigh swept across the conference room.

"Of course," Thieren continued, "I will distribute the *Weightless'* pledge incrementally, as construction and social programs hit their desired milestones."

Michael lamented the statement. He realized Thieren would wield influence over Terrae Solaris politics for the next decade—probably two.

"And we haven't finalized our discussion on Aurelian Galerius."

The President directed Thieren's attention to Cyril Davidson. "This is Admiral Cyril Davidson, Program Director for the 18 Scorpii Project."

Cyril stood up and went to the front of the room. Using a series of charts, Davidson took Thieren through the entire forty-seven year itinerary: flight plans, strategies, capture scenarios, project unknowns, risks, and the like. Despite interacting with Davidson the entire way through, Thieren remained unsatisfied.

At the end of Davidson's presentation, the *Weightless* turned to President Mitchell. "I see no guarantee that Aurelian Galerius will be brought back for trial."

The President paused cautiously. The Allies had reached a critical moment.

Changing his approach, Mitchell leaned in toward Thieren as if reassuring a long-time friend. "Mos, I can't give you that guarantee. Deep space travel is inherently dangerous; the covert nature of this mission only increases that danger. We have no control over Galerius, his health, or a number of other factors that will determine success."

"That's not good enough," the *Weightless* impatiently replied, garnering supporting nods from the other *Weightless*. He stole a quick glance at Michael before turning back. "I'm making a long-term investment here. I need to give my people assurances—not wishful thinking. If Galerius doesn't stand trial after what I've invested, history will make me out to be a laughing stock."

Amid the nodding of every head on the *Weightless* side of the table, President Mitchell huffed. "Mos, I'm just being honest with you. Given the undertaking's complexity and span of time, how could I possibly give you such a guarantee? I can only guarantee you we've dedicated every possible resource to make it happen."

Yet Thieren remained floating within his zero gravity field, still very much unsettled.

Mitchell paused thoughtfully. "Mos, this mission's success may be inconsequential in the end—I know you don't want to hear that, but it's the truth." He gazed across the table at all the *Weightless*, refusing to be cowed. Just his confident expression repelled the other *Weightless'* skeptical reactions. Even Thieren shrunk back a little. Emboldened, Mitchell gazed at them beseechingly. "The future of our solar system and its inhabitants—*Weightless* or otherwise—depends on rebuilding. *That* is the benchmark of our success."

Thieren's face waxed over dejectedly; Mitchell had backed him into a corner.

Though the Allied leaders radiated polite facades, Michael could tell that they celebrated inwardly. The odd-looking *Weightless* had nowhere to go; nowhere, that is, until he glanced at Michael—and with such a gleam in his eye.

Thieren turned to President Mitchell, though keeping Michael in his peripheral vision. His face waxed over like flint. "Do you know what the *Weightless'* biggest problem is?"

He paused for effect, watching the leaders cower under his newfound boldness.

"Our problem," he declared, "is gravity! Gravity holds one man bound to the earth. But another man, in a more glorified state, is loosed and free. The bound man hates his condition and sees the free man—and hates him. Yet when given the chance to follow the free man, the bound man despises that he must follow and not lead. So he chooses to stay bound—to gravity."

Michael cringed under the man's bloviating. He saw a similar discontent on President Mitchell's face—from the other Allied leaders too. The *Weightless* was taking the conversation down a precarious path.

Thieren continued relentlessly.

"We *Weightless* are no longer viewed as humans. I'm sure some in this room feel that way now. But we *are* human—and more! Yet because of gravity, we are treated as second-class citizens. Because of gravity, we are despised. Gravity gave Aurelian Galerius his platform. Now, millions of my people are dead—all because of gravity!"

Michael felt the hairs on the back of his neck standing on end.

"Most of Solaris' inhabitants live where natural gravitational fields don't exist," Thieren continued his rant. "Yet we *Weightless* are a minority among *humans* bound to artificial gravitational fields.

Our problem isn't gravity itself, but rather the man who betrayed his own people—Jonathan Gillen."

Michael cringed. His worst nightmare was coming true. He sat alone, for no one said a word in his defense. Rather, everyone remained awkwardly silent.

Thieren turned to Michael. "Tell me Captain Gillen, how is it that the one thing I really want from this deal—Galerius' capture and prosecution—depends on a descendant of the man who caused the problem in the first place?"

Michael fell speechless as all eyes turned to him. He knew Thieren was baiting him, looking for an excuse to withdraw from the deal. So he replied rather obtusely, "I don't know what to say."

Immediately, the young man cringed at his stupid remark.

"Perhaps you consider this mission a chance to make amends for all the hurt your great grandfather inflicted on Solaris?"

"My great grandfather was just an inventor. He never intended to cause a division."

"On the contrary," Thieren retorted. "I knew your great grandfather. Though I was very young, I remember him working side by side with my grandfather. Jonathan Gillen couldn't leave well enough alone. As he constructed his first gravitational field generator, my grandfather warned him of the dangers his experiments posed. But Jonathan Gillen didn't listen—not that any of the Gillens I ever knew did."

Michael kept silent before Thieren. As he took in the leader's calculating gaze, he could feel the anger welling up within—as well as the temptation to launch into his own verbal assault. Yet he was silenced by his own promise to remain silent. All he could do was sit there and listen to the man's ranting. However, he didn't realize that he had folded his arms in front of him and wore a brooding expression while doing so.

"Truth hurts sometimes," Thieren said dryly. When Michael remained silent, the *Weightless* looked at him oddly for a long moment. "Do you know why you Gillens have had so many problems even among your own people?" When the young man kept silent again, Thieren pressed, gesturing to the Allied leaders, "You see, these men don't carry with them the same stigma that you carry. The solar system has changed so much over a few generations. I'm sure most of them have a distant *Weightless* ancestor in their family tree—someone they don't ever mention in *polite* company."

He looked Michael in the eyes. "But you don't have that luxury. When people see you … they *know* Jonathan Gillen was a *Weightless*— before he submitted to genetic reengineering, that is."

"So?"

"You see…"—gesturing to himself—"…you have more in common with *this side* of the table than what you might ever want to admit."

Michael kept silent, though his anger continued welling up within him.

"That's right," Thieren mused, relishing Michael's silence. "I'll bet you even keep many of the *Weightless* traditions. I know Jonathan Gillen observed our holidays long after he became *human*—long after he had permanently hurt the very people who gave him his chance in life."

Thieren fell silent through a long moment, keeping his eyes fixed on Michael. When Michael only brooded that much more, Thieren added, "Not that your great grandfather's efforts to embrace the culture he abandoned made up for the damage he did. No, he thought weightlessness was a curse! He betrayed his own people for his own selfish vision, and *he* is to blame for the atrocities as much as Galerius." Thieren paused, looking him straight in the eyes. "So, what are *you* going to do to make amends?"

Michael fumed.

Though he tried concealing his anger, everyone beheld his dour expression. President Mitchell's instructions to remain calm repeated in his mind. Yet Thieren was ripping apart the Gillen name in front of the entire Allied leadership. The faces of his brother David, his father, and his mother—victims of the *Weightless'* hatred of the Gillens— rose prominently in his thoughts; they cried out to him for vindication, and Michael so wanted to launch into his own verbal assault.

"Tell me, Captain Gillen," Thieren pressed mercilessly, "Do you hate the *Weightless* as much as your great grandfather?"

The Allied leaders looked at Michael conspicuously.

The young captain kept silent. His anger turned to despair. Circumstances levied on him a guilty verdict; he stood condemned— condemned over events that played out long before he was born.

To him, this meeting was *his* personal atrocity; the Gillen name fell into disgrace that moment, and the dignitaries wouldn't defend him. His own president could only help at the price of unraveling the deal. Michael's fate was certain: The Gillen name falling into disgrace was the price of reconciliation, the price of accepting Thieren's pledge.

Thieren stared him down tellingly from across the table. The old man's relishing grin betrayed his intentions to the whole room: He was moving in for the kill. "Do you hate *me?*"

Michael's despair turned to disgust.

The room fell silent. Anxiously, everyone awaited Michael's response. The Allied leaders cringed at the disdain washing over his gaze. President Mitchell's face—indeed, everyone's—pleaded for grace and understanding. Nevertheless, the hate swelled within him.

"*Very much indeed!*"

Had Michael scanned the room, he would have witnessed the agonizing looks on the dignitaries' faces. No matter, the young officer stared steely-eyed at his nemesis.

Thieren paused for a moment, sizing up Michael. From his peripheral vision, he noted the defeat in the Allied leaders' expressions.

Oddly enough, Thieren laughed—laughed heartily. "Finally, someone who's not afraid to offend me with the truth!" He looked around the room chidingly before turning back to Michael. "Tell me, Captain Gillen, will you *really* bring Aurelian Galerius back to justice?"

"*Yes.*"

"Why?" Thieren asked with a skeptical look on his face.

Michael paused, returning the leader's formidable gaze with his own steely-eyed expression. "Because it's my duty."

Thieren gazed at Michael amidst the gaping stares of the stunned dignitaries. The room kept deadly silent as the two men stared down each other.

Then Thieren laughed again. Turning toward President Mitchell, his mouth cracked the most affable grin. "Okay… let's do the deal."

Chapter Eight

Homecoming

Michael Gillen sat back in his seat among the other passengers riding the land transport, calmly watching the heavily wooded, plush green terrain pass by his window. The sight soothed his tired eyes. Earth, unique in so many ways, was unparalleled throughout Terrae Solaris in its beauty.

Michael struggled to keep himself upright, for he was terribly exhausted. Though his frame wanted to slither into his seat, years of military service prevented anything but a pathetic interpretation of a slouch. So he kept good posture, quietly enduring the soreness radiating through his muscles. No matter, having grown self-conscious of the esteeming glances from the civilian passengers, he didn't want them to see him slump.

The woodland scenery rushing past the window cast a strong persuasion over his troubled mind; its simplicity charmed him, and he longed to lose himself in the sight. However, the events of the previous day at the capitol troubled him deeply.

He longed to remember that day with fondness; he wanted only to remember standing before President James Mitchell—*his hero*—as the noble leader lauded him with praise. However, Michael had no such luxury. No, memories of those glorious moments had fallen victim to the dreadful meeting with Mos Thieren. Michael shuddered each time the encounter played out in his mind. Each time, the humiliation cut him deeper.

Even then, the ethereal faces of his deceased father, mother, and brother—all assassinated by *Weightless* sympathizers—pleaded for vindication from their senseless deaths. Other fallen relatives cried out to him too. Yet he remained silent before Mos Thieren and his accusations. He had betrayed his family's honor for the sake of duty, and the Gillen name once more fell into disgrace—all in the presence of the court of Allied leaders.

Michael gladly fled what he considered to have been an unintended ambush. Even 18 Scorpii, forty-six light-years from Earth, no longer seemed far enough away.

But Thieren's question played repeatedly in his head: *What are you going to do to make amends?* Despite his loathing of the *Weightless* and their despicable leader, Michael wanted the schism between *Weightless* and normal humans to end, for the decades-old conflict fueled disdain for the Gillen name throughout Solaris. The turmoil needed to end; someone needed to fix the rift before future genocides brought the *Weightless* to extinction.

But *he* wasn't that person.

However, another scenario played out in his thoughts too. Perhaps 18 Scorpii was his chance to redeem the Gillen name with the *Weightless*: that butcher *Aurelian Galerius*—what a prize for a *Gillen* to bring back to them! He marveled at all the wonderful possibilities. Perhaps such an opportunity was worth the disgrace of the previous day. Perhaps fate had dealt him a chance to redeem *himself* too.

Yes, he *needed* to accomplish the 18 Scorpii mission.

The young man's musings ended when the transport's engines powered down. The large vehicle glided to a stop directly in front of his home.

As he looked at the familiar homestead, images of Katey filled his every thought. He relished seeing her surprise when he unexpectedly came through the door. He could feel her nestled in his arms again;

he longed for her embrace; he longed to see five unbearable years of separation slip into memory.

If only he didn't have to tell her about 18 Scorpii.

However, such concerns fell into obscurity as he anticipated the imminent reunion.

Grabbing his duffel bag, Michael eagerly navigated his athletic frame up the narrow aisle. Upon receiving one last round of esteeming glances from the civilian travelers, he graciously tipped his cap to them. When he reached the exit, the automated operator opened the doors. With a spring in his step, the enthusiastic, young man hopped down onto the dusty ground; the afternoon sun struck his face pleasingly.

He turned and watched the transport speed away and disappear around the curve in the road. The hum of its engines faded until only birdsong remained. Then he darted across the road, coming to stop at the foot of the stone walkway to admire the sight.

Home.

The underground house lay hidden from the edge of the road. Instead, the walkway meandered through a lush landscape of gardens and small trees. The path disappeared into the dark shade of an alcove of trees at the base of a hillside, the hillside itself quickly cresting and running down into a shallow valley hidden on the other side. Within the alcove lay a rustic, stone entrance set into the hillside, which led to the main dwelling below the surface.

He hastened up the path and into the alcove of trees toward the doorway. A small gardenbot was working in the alcove just off the path. Shifting his duffel bag to the other shoulder, Michael inadvertently swung the heavy bag right into the machine, sending it tumbling headlong into the flowers. After righting itself, the device let out several disapproving beeps at him before continuing its work.

Showing no sympathy for the accosted machine, Michael came to the doorway and passed a hand over the security sensor. The door swung open, and the travel-weary soldier disappeared into the structure. He descended the adjoining stairwell, finally stepping into the foyer on the main floor. After dropping the duffel bag and setting his officers' cap down on the foyer table, he let out a long sigh.

It was good to be home!

Far from the opulence of the Executive Mansion, the house radiated a warm and inviting charm. Stone flooring covered the main halls, while the doors and moldings throughout were stained wood. All the colors were earth tone, while the furnishings remained simplistic and conservative. False windows equipped with image generators replicated the outdoor scenes found above ground. In fact, the foyer and main hallway lay bathed in bright sunlight. Other than descending the stairwell, one would never know that the home lay underground.

However, the house was unusually quiet with no sign of Katey anywhere.

Just as Michael was about to call out her name, he caught himself: He wanted to see her surprised look. He also wanted to catch her off guard—a playful, ongoing competition the couple had engaged in during their long courtship. This time, Michael had the upper hand.

However, Katey wasn't anywhere near.

Not giving up, he started a clockwise search of the house. The main rooms were desolate: the great room, dining room, and kitchen. They were neat as a pin, as if no one had lived in them for some time; same for the den. The sound of background music, Katey's staple accoutrement, remained disturbingly absent too. Of course, he reckoned that perhaps she was napping or on the phone. So he searched all the bedrooms and baths—nothing!

With anticipation welling within him mercilessly, the young man executed a more thorough search of the house. He did this several times, expanding his search to include the garage. Each time, he grew more desperate; each time, he refused to believe the irrefutable evidence; and each time, he arrived back at the foyer alone.

Almost in a panic, he searched both the front and back yards. He even ventured into the woods. However, the wilderness remained silent and still; only a dripping faucet on the outside shower greeted him. Making another pointless search of the house upon re-entry, he once again arrived back at the foyer alone.

Katey wasn't home.

Sighing in defeat, Michael dragged himself to the couch in the great room and fell backward into its overstuffed cushions. Every muscle went limp in reaction. Though exhausted from the trip, he smarted at his own stupidity: He should have never tried to surprise her.

From the couch—a penalty box of sorts—Michael gazed out at the surrounding wilderness through the large observation windows. A shimmering, deep blue lake in the distance lay nestled in the valley, surrounded by woodlands. The tranquil view captivated him, while the atmosphere in the room kept exceedingly calm.

With nowhere else to go and fatigue beckoning him to sleep, the defeated, young man laid his head back. The tranquil wilderness lulled him into a stupor. The longer he watched, the heavier his eyes became. His mind wandered aimlessly for the first time in days, and his eyelids pushed closed against his will; his whole body fell limp, and he sank ever deeper into the overstuffed cushions; sleep enveloped him seductively—

A violent shudder jolted Michael awake! His eyes shot open wide in panic!

However, a relieved sigh quickly followed: Katey had jumped onto him and was sitting astride his lap.

She was dripping wet and wearing a loosely draping, grey shower robe. Her long, brown hair, combed back nicely, drenched the top of the robe, while water beads on her legs and bare feet soaked into his uniform. However, her crowning feature that moment was the smirk on her face that said *got'cha!*

For the briefest moment, time stood still. Just the sight of her took his breath away. Even just out of the shower, she was drop-dead gorgeous. Her form rose up over him like a living statue, inhabiting an elegance and mesmerizing grace. The tattered robe did nothing to diminish her slender but feminine figure. Rather, her beautiful form blossomed out of the old garment as if pushing off its cocoon. The fragrance of exotic flowers from her wet hair wafted before him pleasingly. Delicate shoulders called out for his embrace, and her neck and mouth beckoned to be kissed. Her shimmering brown eyes— unfathomably deep pools in which he could lose himself—invited him warmly, giving him a glimpse into her girlish spirit too.

"Catch you off guard?" she offered with a half-grin. A warm smile followed. "*Welcome home.*"

He gladly accepted defeat from the woman who searched him with her eyes. "Hello, my bride."

The playfulness of the moment passed, and the two fell spellbound into each other's gaze. Her bittersweet smile radiated five years of incredible longing for him—the fear, the trials, and the sleepless nights too. Michael felt himself reflecting back to her much of the same angst, for her anticipating smile waxed over endearingly. He savored the rare, intimate exchange, knowing that his time apart from her was finally over.

Michael Gillen was finally home.

The young couple spent the next several days commencing the beginnings of a long-awaited and belated honeymoon. Each day, the sun would rise and set; the moon followed its course through the night. Clouds sometimes passed overhead, sometimes yielding their rain while other times simply yielding to the sapphire sky above. A rare vehicle passing by sometimes broke the silence, and people went about their business. However, whatever transpired around it, the Gillen home remained quiet and off to itself.

The woman in her early thirties sat alone at the bar, nursing a drink between her hands. Though sporting a fleet uniform with captains' wings affixed to her collar, she wore her shoulder-length, black hair down against regulations; her officers' cap was noticeably absent too. With her eyes soberly fixed on the drink in front of her, she sat with shoulders drawn in and her face boasting an unwelcoming sulk. So the clamoring patrons of the out-of-the-way establishment, located somewhere on Mid-Earth Station, kept their distance.

"Hi, Maura," Emir Kern greeted her while sidling up into the empty seat to her left. The hardened warrior radiated an uncharacteristically boyish smile. "It's been a long time."

Maura Enzler, less than impressed by the man's appearance, looked at him for the longest time. Finally, she grimaced. "Just when I had cleared my reputation from that reconnaissance mission on Europa—you show up again." She took a sip of her drink, keeping intentionally to herself. "Where's the rest of your team?"

"They're on Earth enjoying leave."

"I thought you guys traveled in packs."

Kern watched her watch her drink. Hoping to spark some familiar dialogue, he replied, "And I didn't think you hung out in such *seedy* places."

She looked up at him and rolled her eyes. "Give me a break. I just got off a long shift and needed to unwind." Seeing him relishing her reaction to his teasing—and suffering under his intentional charm—she finally cracked a sardonic smile. "Some things don't change."

A serverbot interrupted the conversation and took Kern's order.

"So, Emir, what are you doing here?"

Taking his drink from the serverbot, Kern rather shrugged. He surveyed the activity in the bar, avoiding her suspicious gaze. "*Well ...* I'm on leave ... it's the first time I've been back from the Outer Rim in years ... and I heard you were in the area. I thought I'd drop in and see how you were doing—catch up on old times."

Maura once again turned to her drink. "You tell *me* how I'm doing. I haven't run a Special Forces mission since Europa."

"At least we didn't get court-martialed—just as I predicted."

"I'm not so certain that would have been any worse," Maura sighed, looking at him again. "I really miss my old job."

"Yeah," Kern mused, his eyes waxing over warmly while silently recounting old memories. "Those fifteen missions we shared were exciting—*harrowing*, but nevertheless exciting." He fixed an intentional gaze upon her. "I miss working with you."

Maura fell silent and looked into her drink as if far away. Her eyes churned uneasily for the longest time. Finally, she looked at him with a withered smile. "But not the way I *want* you to miss me, huh?" Her gaze waxed over sadly. "You can be so manipulative sometimes."

Emir Kern fell silent as he took in her troubled expression, letting his own gaze soften. "I'm sorry for that."

Maura said nothing for a few tense moments. She just kept staring at her drink. Finally, she mustered enough courage to look at him again. "So what are you *really* doing here?"

"*Okay*," Kern shrugged. "... I need your help again."

"That's what I figured."

"But this time, I can help you too," he offered, watching her shake her head in disbelief. "What would you say if I told you I could get you back into Special Forces *and* deep space exploration?"

The statement certainly caught the young woman off guard, causing her to look at him abruptly with eyes wide. The surprise came not so much from the Special Forces opportunity he had dangled in front of her, but from the deep space exploration comment. After all, she had burned every bridge as a former Centauri astronaut, and the war raged on—NSEA no longer existed anymore. Her expression once more turned incredibly dismissive. "Are you serious?"

"Yes, I've been assigned a very special mission requiring someone with both of those qualifications."

"*Really?*"

"Maura, I'm completely serious."

"A mission *outside* Solaris?" she asked with a fading skeptical eye against his brimming confidence. "A long mission, right?"

"Yep."

She fell silent while taking in his assuring smile. "How can that be?"

Kern's boyish charm returned. "The question is: Are you interested?" He watched her ponder his question. When her skeptical gaze faded, and a glimmer returned once more to her eyes, he added, "I'm not saying I can guarantee getting you aboard ... but if I *could* ... you get back everything"—his charm gushing—"and we can work together again. What do you think?"

She winced at his overt eagerness, and her expression predictably fell sober. "I think the only thing you care about is that green satchel you've got stashed somewhere"—looking down reprovingly at his chest pocket—"... and what you've got stashed in that pocket." When his face betrayed his guilt, she turned steely-eyed. "*It's in there, isn't it?*"

The two traded awkward looks through a long silence.

Finally, Kern took a sip of his drink, fixed his gaze upon her, and shrugged affably. "Look, I'm leaving for good soon ... I thought you might want to come along."

"You're manipulating me again," she lamented while shaking her head. "—just as you did to get me to help you on the Europa mission. *Once bitten, twice shy* you know."

"It's just part of my charm," he replied, smiling against her chiding gaze. "So what do you think?"

Maura looked into her drink once more, her face filling with the many emotions churning deep within. Mostly, her expression betrayed her fear: fear of the opportunity before her, the fear of a lost opportunity—the fear of choosing wrongly. Her mind raced faster than she could keep up. Finally, she found herself looking up at him again. "So where are we going this time?"

"This isn't the place to talk details," Kern smiled, standing up and gesturing for her to gather her things. "Let's go somewhere private where we can talk."

Maura stood up, gathered her things sitting off to the side, and let him lead her through the crowd to the exit. "I've heard that before too."

Curran Zeidler sat alone at a table in the corner of the very forgettable bar, watching the rest of the Covert team—absent Emir Kern—extract money from the locals in a high stakes game of pool. Armstrong and Tasker played, while Volk and Gunn watched in support close by. The scene had played out so many times that month, for they were still waiting to deploy to 18 Scorpii.

The young man tired of wasting his precious leave. He longed to return to the glory days, when the team inhabited a more edifying lifestyle; when they didn't frequent such seedy places, trying to forget all that had happened. Nevertheless, the Coverts were his family. He would keep vigil with them for as long as the madness possessed them.

Emir Kern suddenly appeared at the bar's entrance.

"Where've you been?" Zeidler greeted him as the man made his way over to the table.

"On Mid-Earth Station," Kern beamed with pride while sitting down. "I found Maura." He waved off a serverbot approaching the table to take his order. "We had a nice, long talk."

"I would have liked to have been a fly on the wall listening to *that* conversation."

"Well guess what," Kern cracked a smug grin. "She agreed to go to

18 Scorpii if I can get her and the rest of her flight crew on the team."

"*Can you?*" Zeidler half-heartedly asked, humoring his superior and his wild ideas. "Did you let Davidson know they're available?"

"Absolutely not. He'd court-martial me for sure if he knew I spoke to anyone about the mission. I'll ask him first. Once he agrees, he can ask her himself. Maura won't let on that she already knows."

Commotion erupting at the pool table caused them to look in that direction. The two locals playing pool fumed at Armstrong and Tasker—a normal twist in such a game. Kern turned back, confident that his team remained in control.

Zeidler kept deep in thought for a long moment. "Why are you trying to secure your own flight team for 18 Scorpii? You don't even know who Davidson has in mind."

"I know *exactly* who he chose," Kern countered. "Gillen and the rest of those astronauts." When Zeidler grimaced, he added, "Who else would the former head of NSEA pick for a deep space mission?" He looked around cautiously before continuing, "I spoke to our friend Jimmy in Intelligence: Command recalled all of them from the Outer Rim. They're all on extended leave like us—except for the propulsion engineer; he's still on active duty on Mid-Earth Station."

"I still don't understand why you're going to such trouble."

"18 Scorpii is our *last* chance to set things right," Kern declared. "I won't let it go. Maura and her team will do whatever we ask. But Gillen will only get in our way, just like he did back on Europa three years ago."

"You won't persuade Davidson to make the switch," Zeidler shook his head. "He's invested in the Centauries."

Emir Kern fell deep in thought, finally shaking his head in agreement. His gaze waxed forebodingly dark too. "We'll *force* him to make the change."

Unexpectedly, Kern stood up and headed for the door.

"Now where are you going?" Zeidler called to him.

"I have to take a trip."

"To where?"

"Back to Mid-Earth Station—other places too. I'll call when I need you and the team."

Watching the seasoned warrior leave, Zeidler shook his head in disbelief.

CHAPTER NINE

Differing Viewpoints

Michael Gillen sat on the wooden steps off his back deck, leaning against the railing for support. He was clothed in nothing but a linen sheet from the bed, the wardrobe that had provided him the quickest and quietest escape. With Katey fast asleep, he had decided to come outside rather than wake her with his tossing and turning.

Her unexpected slumber gave the twenty-nine-year-old his first chance to enjoy the outdoors. He had forgotten just how breathtaking was the view from his deck. Wilderness spread out before him: pristine woodlands and water as far as the eye could see. He breathed a little deeper now and then, savoring the pleasing fragrance of unspoiled wilderness air. With the faint sound of birdsong in the distance, the place provided complete solitude—an escape from the cares and troubles of life. Though having seen many spectacular sights throughout Solaris, Michael considered his backyard to be his most favorite place of all.

The sun had recently set below the trees on the horizon, replaced by an increasingly prominent full moon suspended against the darkening sky. A few stars appeared in the fading blue. Though the day had been summer-like, the approaching fall season put a biting nip in the evening air. Michael kept the sheet fast around himself, regretting his choice of dress.

The young man gazed far off, and his thoughts remained distant. His last three days at home immersing himself in his wife's attention had been blissful. Michael relished having her all to himself on the belated honeymoon. If only he could go on like this forever.

But that was the problem: He couldn't. Michael owed Cyril Davidson an answer to the 18 Scorpii mission. He regrettably realized that his decision to go—and it was firmly set in his mind—would take him far from the tranquility of the lake house.

Yet he purposefully allowed the elation of their reunion to put out of mind the true reason for his arrival home. He feared the discord the subject might bring. Katey was delightfully ignorant of the pending decision, but he had to tell her soon.

The door behind him opened. He turned to see Katey groggily emerge from the kitchen doorway, letting the door slam shut behind her. Interestingly, she wore the exact same attire as him: a single, white bedsheet. However, he thought the impromptu outfit looked much better on her.

Suddenly, all his concerns faded into the ether.

"Twins!" she exclaimed comically.

Crossing the porch and sitting down on the steps close to him, Katey draped herself over his shoulder and locked her arm around his—as much as the bedsheets wrapped around them allowed. Michael smiled warmly. With the two settling in under the advancing night sky, a perfect evening of stargazing awaited the young couple.

She watched him peer into the sky at the brilliant full moon. Then she smiled, "If you ever lived there, you wouldn't be so impressed with it. I wasn't."

Michael smiled at her once more before returning his gaze skyward. As the chill set into her, Katey snuggled even closer.

"This is so wonderful," she sighed in delight. "I wish it would never end."

He almost missed her statement, mesmerized instead by the soft tone and delicate cadence of her voice.

Katey lifted her eyes dreamily skyward. "I remember so many nights out here…. Whenever worrying about you got the best of me, I would come outside and just look up at the stars. Somehow … it made me feel connected to you."

Pushing an arm out of his constricting bedsheet, Michael nestled her in his embrace. He savored her warmth against the chill of the night. With her head resting under his chin, the flowery fragrance from her hair wafted pleasingly before him. She was a feast for his senses. So he sat on the wooden porch with her in his grasp, taking in the coming of nightfall over the hushed wilderness—

Abruptly, his conscious goaded him: He needed to tell his wife the truth about his arrival. He could no longer filibuster out of the unenviable task. So with night draping itself over the landscape, Michael desperately searched for the right words—*and the courage*—to break the news to her about 18 Scorpii. Though he just wanted to blurt it out, his tongue tied within his mouth each time. But duty called. So taking a deep breath—

"Michael, don't you have something to tell me?" Katey looked up at him. Her tone was deliberate and beckoned for reassurance.

A thick tension rose into the night air. Michael suddenly found himself at the mercy of the court. The moon became his judge, the stars his jury, and Katey—the prosecution! He smarted at his own stupidity, realizing her surprise greeting three days earlier should have clued him in. "*You know?*"

"Nothing specific … but I've heard the rumors about NSEA. Cyril called me about a month ago too; he was more curious than normal. I also know Command recalled all the other Centauries from the Outer Rim, and you're home a month ahead of schedule." She paused for effect. "It didn't take me long to realize something was up."

Michael filled with regret, and he hung his head. "I'm sorry. When I arrived home, I didn't want to spoil the moment … but we kept having such good moments."

"That's why I didn't ask you until now … and I'm not sure I really want to know why you're home so soon"—taking a deep, anxious breath—"but what is it?"

Hesitantly, Michael divulged the 18 Scorpii secret. While he described the mission in detail, Katey listened intently. Darkness fell completely during the exchange. Though the weight of keeping the secret lifted from him, he also saw the concern mounting in her expression. Neither did her reactions resonate with his attempts at persuasion. Instead, she grew more distant. By the end of the explanation, his emotions had become a jumble of nervousness and relief.

An awkward silence fell over the young couple.

Though Katey remained sitting beside him, just a smidge more distance lay between them. She wrestled both hands up and out of her bedsheet to her face, propping up her elbows on drawn-in knees while resting her head in her hands. Rubbing her temples, she stared ahead as if far off for the longest time. With an eventual, heavy sigh, she turned her head side to side and lamented, "That's insane."

"That was my first thought too."

"Michael, you've got to tell them *no*," she pleaded, searching his eyes. She pulled the slack at the top of her sheet fast around her neck to fend off the cold. "You spent two years on active duty, three in an Europan prison camp—and you almost died saving the President! You did your part for king and country."

"Things are bad, Kate. If we don't agree to the mission, they're going to get worse."

Her eyes pleaded even more. "But you *just* came home."

Michael labored a long moment under her imploring gaze.

"We'll be together," he offered eagerly—too eagerly. "We can finally do what we trained for—*together*."

Kate huffed, looking away from him—leaning away too. "I don't care about exploration anymore."

"I can't believe that," he said, recoiling with raised eyebrows. "You were more than eager to set off for Alpha Centauri."

"18 Scorpii *isn't* the same thing."

"It's not that different either."

Katey looked him in the eyes soberly. "I'm not the same person that I was five years ago."

"But space exploration is your chosen career."

Averting her eyes, she looked far away into the darkness at nothing in particular. "Things change."

Michael paused, completely at a loss for words. He kept watching her stare off into the distance, her eyes avoiding his. She seemed so serious, and that really bothered him.

"You can't mean that," he finally pleaded.

That was when Katey looked back at him scornfully.

"Really, Michael?" she chided. "*You* of all people shouldn't be surprised. You're the one who cloistered me away for five years, while you put yourself in danger on the front lines."

The young man realized he had made a tactical faux pas.

Katey continued indignantly, "I trained the same as you. When the war started, I wanted to go with you. I wanted to prove myself, just like you, Tom, Kara, and the rest of the Centauries did. I wanted the sacrifices my grandmother made for me to mean something— something she would have been proud of. But you didn't let me. No, you went behind my back and made a deal with Cyril to put me on that desk job. You *wanted* me to stay here."

Before he could respond, she scowled. "Well, you got your wish: I stayed back here like the good little *newlywed housewife*, worrying about you—waiting for your return so my life could start. Now, you want me to go off on an *insane* mission!" She huffed, "I don't want that stuff anymore. I want a normal life ... to be a wife ... to have children someday—and you shouldn't be so surprised."

The young woman dropped her head in frustration. Michael sat beside her, dumbfounded—feeling smaller too. Nevertheless, the urgency of the mission hung over him.

"Kate, we don't have a choice," Michael persisted. "The whole system will fall apart if this mission doesn't happen. They personally asked for you and me—the whole Centauri team." He hesitated before continuing, "And bringing Aurelian Galerius back to the *Weightless* is a once-in-a-lifetime opportunity ... I can finally clear my family's name—*our* name."

Kate looked up at him, aghast! "*You already made up your mind. You're not asking me, you're telling!*"

She kept eye to eye with him, the indignation mounting until she fumed. Michael's silence and culpable gaze didn't assuage. Worse, his stoic reaction only made her fume that much more.

"I won't go!" she declared, pulling the bedsheet around her as taut as she could make it. Her exasperated gaze lingered through a long silence. When his determination withered under her reproach, she added, "Michael, you can't possibly think we'll make it back alive."

He bowed his head, searching for some way to defuse the argument. Yet he had no more appeals left in his arsenal. In fact, her reaction meant she understood the mission completely. So instead, he let a long silence pass.

"We're in this together," he eventually offered, his voice steady and reassuring. "If you say *no*, they can find someone else.... We'll stay here and watch the sun go down every night."

Of course, he really didn't mean it.

"What if I say *no* right now?"

"You won't. You won't reject doing something you know is right just because of my stupidity."

Katey bowed her head for the longest time, avoiding his pressing gaze. Finally, she looked back up at him. "I need some time to think about it."

"Okay."

"When do you have to give them an answer?"

"In about three days."

She chuckled scathingly while shaking her head in disbelief. After a long moment of silence, she flashed him a reproving grimace. "At least *this* time you're not planning on leaving me behind."

An uneasy silence fell over them, save the sound of crickets chirping against the night.

From her unenviable place sitting beside him, Katey stung at the disappointing revelation. She stung at Michael's impertinence more than anything. However, while wallowing in self-pity, she remembered all those evenings spent longing for him to return—waiting for him to come home so their new life could finally start.

And there he sat.

The young woman realized she had a choice: She could stay angry and hurt over what had just happened, letting it ruin their reunion for days or weeks to come. *Or,* she could put her indignation and pride aside for the time.

The choice was hers.

"When I first moved in here after you left," Katey began, gazing out onto the moonlit lake with a rather quirky look on her face, "I wanted to go for a swim—you know how much I love to swim."

"Yeah?" he replied cautiously, taken back by her sudden change of demeanor. He noticed that her defiant grip on her bedsheet had loosened too.

"I decided to wait until you came back. I wanted to share the moment with you—to support you from afar too."

"*Okay...,*" Michael replied, still cautious.

"Well, I've lived here five years now ... and *not once* have I swam in the lake." She flashed him a coy but determined gaze. "But now that you're here, tonight's the perfect night." She sprang up and dashed down the steps, the edge of her bedsheet dragging behind her.

"Now?" Michael called to her from where he still sat, for she was already well on her way down the obscure path. "But it's chilly out here." He jumped up and followed, though moving along with much less enthusiasm (for he hated swimming). He smarted at the cold, damp ground pushing against the soles of his bare feet.

"Yeah, but the water's warm," she called back. "*Come on.*"

She rushed well ahead of him, quickly disappearing into the thicket. Even after reaching the tree line, Michael strained to see her: The thick canopy of branches overhead obscured the moonlight, making the rest of the path very dark. Fortunately, he could see traces of her white bedsheet darting about temptingly against the darkness.

"How 'bout tomorrow instead?" he pleaded, picking up the pace to catch up with her. "It's cold."

"*It's cold?*" her voice echoed from afar, taunting him. "*What kind of explorer are you?*" Her voice echoed from even farther away. "You're asking me to go forty-six light-years away to chase a mad man. All I'm asking for is a dip in the lake. Stop being such a *wimp* and work with me!"

By then, Michael was running through the thicket to catch up with her. Carefully navigating the darkness to protect his bare feet from the cold, rough path, he wondered if Katey really wanted to swim. He considered that maybe his bride was doing this as a sort of revenge: to keep the belated honeymoon going while sticking it to him because of the mission. Yes, that was it! Regardless, he winced at the thought of hitting that cold water.

Michael sighed in relief when Katey stopped just short of the lake. He continued approaching her, hoping the cold had changed her mind. However, as he neared, the young man realized the darkness had played a trick on his eyes. Reaching the place where he thought she had stopped, he found Katey's white bedsheet draped over a tree branch. Then in the background, he heard a splash against the hush of the night.

Michael dropped his shoulders in defeat.

Conceding that his wife had made up her mind, he reluctantly hung up his bedsheet beside hers. The cold night air bit at him even harder. With a solitary shiver, he proceeded to the water's edge.

A moment later, another splashing sound broke the night air. Against the moonlit surface of the lake, the silhouettes of two people could be seen frolicking about the water.

The commercial transport flew out of the approach channel and into the bustling terminal deep within Mid-Earth Station. With the bay full of other transports coming and going, the craft nimbly maneuvered through the air around the obstacles. Coming to the end of its journey from Earth, the vessel sidled up gingerly against Docking Platform 24B. With a *hiss* from its stabilizers, the transport came to rest.

Passengers for the return flight waited behind queuing barriers, watching service personnel and utilibots spring into action. A gangplank lowered into place, while flight attendants inside the vessel opened the main hatch. Arriving passengers emerged from the transport, looking around and getting their bearings.

Among them traveled a very determined Emir Kern.

Upon exiting the transport, he glanced around while heading toward the exit. Kern studied the terminal thoroughly. After completing his work on the space station, he would head right back to Earth.

Deep into the fifth night of his arrival home, Michael stared up at the grey, shadowy ceiling of his darkened bedroom. He had been deep asleep for quite some time, and the fogginess obscuring his mind made him consider that he might be dreaming.

The young man wasn't sure why he was conscious. Certainly, he was exhausted from the previous day's activities: swimming in the lake, hiking the wilderness trails near the homestead; and of course, spending lots of alone time with his wife.

Katey lay snuggled against him on his left, fast asleep and facing away. He thought that odd: She normally slept with her head nestled in the crook of his neck, her body tightly against his, and one leg draped over his legs—a little uncomfortable for him but pleasing too. Perhaps she had tired of latching onto him all night. No matter, the warmth from her skin radiated into him nicely.

Gaining consciousness against his wishes, he realized something had awoken him. *But what?* He passively scanned the lifeless room— nothing. Finally, he heard the faint sound of a single sob and the drawing in of a breath. Then the room fell silent once more. Over a long moment, the unsettling sound repeated. He cringed! Katey was weeping.

Frozen in place by the haunting sound, Michael stared nervously at the ceiling. Her crying wasn't a deep, emotional outburst, though steady and consistent nonetheless. Desperately, he searched for the right course of action. However, as a clueless newlywed, the young man remained trapped in his frozen stupor. The dreadful sound persisted, cutting him deeper each time.

"Are you all right?" he very cautiously called.

Silence hung in the air for the longest time. Eventually, Katey sighed. "… just thinking about things: what to have for dinner tomorrow … whether I should replace the drapes in the guest room … whether I should take on a clandestine mission forty-six light-years away—just the normal stuff."

Though marveling at her sense of humor, he remained silent and unsure of himself.

"Do you remember the first thing NSEA looks for in an astronaut candidate?" she said, still turned away from him and looking into the darkness. "—someone with no roots…. That's us … you, me … Tom …

Kara…. None of us had roots when we signed on, and we bought into the persuasion that our destiny lay somewhere outside Solaris."

Because she continued weeping, Michael turned and draped himself around her; he stroked her hair reassuringly too. However, he couldn't see her face, for Katey remained turned away from him. Given the tense atmosphere in the room, he found that more than acceptable.

"That's why they think they can ask us to do this mission," she exclaimed, still sobbing. "They prey on the sense of destiny that *they* engendered in us."

"You're not the only one feeling imposed upon. Tom wasn't too happy either when I told him about it. He'll go if I go. Still, he would rather pass on it."

"That's why they asked you first," she lamented—rather scornfully. "It's the *Centauri family* thing: If they persuade you to go, the rest of us follow along blindly."

Michael fell silent under the recrimination.

"The war changed me," Katey exclaimed, still facing away and staring into the darkness. "When you and the other Centauries shipped out, I had no one to confide in anymore. When you were captured, I didn't know what to do. So I began laying down roots for the first time: at work … in the city … I'm even good friends with Mrs. Ricker across the road."

She turned and looked into his eyes, keeping herself within his reassuring embrace. Her eyes pleaded. "That's what I want now: I want a *normal life*…. I want to greet you when you come home from work. I just want to be a wife … to have children someday."

Her pleas cut him deeper than her weeping. He understood her desires. Deep down, he wanted those things too. However, fate seemed determined to deny such a wish—as did his conflicting motives.

Katey, seeing the familiar look in his eyes, turned away from him again and brooded. A long moment passed. Finally, she took a deep breath. "That's why I have to take this mission."

Michael's head practically spun off his neck at the double take. Surely, he had misheard her. "What did you say?"

"I can't believe I'm saying it…," she shook her head in disbelief, mostly ignoring him. She let a long moment of silence pass, and she trembled ever so slightly. "But I have to take this mission."

Michael lay stunned beside her, wishing to gaze upon her expression to see if she was serious. "I don't understand."

"Your whole family died at the hands of *Weightless* sympathizers, as did a lot of your distant relatives. The Gillen curse affects me too; there's no way to insulate myself from it." She sort of choked up, "What if something like that happened to *our* children—or me or you? We have to end the cycle. That's the only hope for a normal life."

Michael gulped nervously. Gently turning her face toward him with his fingers, he searched her eyes. "*Are you sure?*"

She searched him back that much more, the trepidation heavy in her eyes. "Yes. Call Cyril tomorrow ... tell him *yes*."

"Okay."

The couple went gravely silent for another long moment.

"How much time do we have?" Katey begged, wiping the tears from her eyes.

"They gave us a month before we report to Mid-Earth Station. Four to five months later, we launch."

"We've got three weeks then," Katey resigned, her eyes still full of tears and her face welling up with emotion. "Let's make the most of it." Taking a deep breath, the young woman grasped at him and began kissing him passionately—desperately.

Benjamin Morris—*Ben* to his friends—stood shaving in front of his bathroom mirror in his apartment on Mid-Earth Station. Though one of the most innovative propulsion scientists in Earth States, perhaps all of Solaris, the thirty-three-year-old enjoyed nothing more than an old fashion lather-and-straight-razor shave.

Between two long strokes of the razor against his face, Morris glanced at his open travel bag sitting just left of the sink. His travel passes sat atop the personal effects heaped inside. Assured once more, he returned to his morning ritual. Of course, the absent-minded man looked over frequently, for this day was not the day to misplace things.

No, the trip he was about to take was far too important for such delays.

Morris looked forward to the short journey to Earth. He would finally meet up with Michael Gillen, hopefully Kate Gillen too. He hadn't seen his former mission commander in five years. They had parted company shortly after the war started, just after NSEA canceled the Alpha Centauri mission.

Michael wasn't aware he was coming for a visit, so Ben's arrival would be a great surprise. In fact, no one knew he was leaving the research facilities on Mid-Earth Station, something the engineer had intentionally planned. With an uneventful weekend ahead, the Slipstream propulsion expert could slip out unnoticed, thus alleviating all the hassles associated with his departure.

Before long, Morris admired his clean-shaven face with much satisfaction. Setting down the straightedge razor on the sink, he took a towel in hand and wiped away the residual lather. Now, he needed to dress.

What sounded like a door opening and closing somewhere in the empty apartment caught his ear. He looked at his watch, noting the time had come for his daily cleaning service to arrive.

"Hello?" he called out and waited for a response.

None came.

"Hello?" he called out louder, for the old lady was quite deaf.

Again, no response.

He took a few steps into the dimly lit hallway. Not a sound emanated from the rest of the apartment. After glancing into the bedroom, Morris went down the hallway into the living room and dining room. The place remained completely still, and the front door was locked.

He laughed at himself. Years of living alone hadn't solved his weakness for imagining things, the character flaw becoming a daily occurrence lately. Home was just too quiet for him compared to the lab. That was why he employed a cleaning service rather than using an utilibot.

Needing to hurry to make the transport, Morris labored back to the bathroom to retrieve the travel bag. He planned to close the bag and carry it to the doorway, ensuring not to forget it when he left.

However, he immediately noticed that his straightedge razor was missing from the sink.

He huffed at himself, realizing he must have absentmindedly carried it to somewhere in the apartment. Without the razor, he couldn't close the travel bag. So he turned into the hall to search for the razor. Starting down the narrow passage—

Ben gasped in terror!

The assailant waylaid him from behind! The violent blow knocked the wind out of his lungs! An arm whipped around his forehead, seizing him—*bludgeoning him*! The assailant painfully twisted Ben's head back as if playing with a rag doll; Ben's whole body followed complicity until the scientist stretched backward and off balance!

In a split-second, Morris fell prey to the intruder.

Twisting about in futile defiance, the former Centauri watched his straightedge razor come up in the assailant's other hand! He saw the attacker's flint-like face reflecting off the deadly metal. Certainly, the intruder has chosen the razor over whatever other devices he had brought with him!

"*No!*" the helpless man barely choked out, flailing about within the assailant's merciless hold.

His pleas were to no avail. The assailant plunged the razor toward him with deadly precision, cutting a deep trail across the Centauri's throat.

Sunlight pierced through the Gillen kitchen window on Earth. Time was fast approaching the late afternoon, and the light cast long shadows on the rustic deck outside. Farther off in the distance, long shadows also stretched across the overgrown clearing at the base of the tree line, as well as parts of the lake surrounded by tall foliage.

Michael and Kate appeared from the shadowy tree line at the edge of the clearing, making their way up the pathway toward the house.

Adorned in swimwear and dressing towels, the belated newlyweds followed the path in an erratic and carefree manner. They behaved like schoolchildren, playfully flinging a beach ball at each other and goading one another with lighthearted provocations, all the while laughing and smiling.

Today was Michael's tenth day at home, and they celebrated with a customary dip in the lake. With much resolve, they had put the impending mission out of mind, choosing instead to enjoy each day as it came.

The mirth intensified as they neared the house. The frivolity was a means to an end, and the sparring of towels replaced the clash with the beach ball. They moved about briskly, as if gladiators zealous to defend their honor. Lighthearted shrieks and laughter rang out as they exchanged blows.

A hovering gardenbot, which was cutting the grass, found itself caught between them when Katey ducked around it for cover. Suffering under some abrupt jostling and the cracking of wet towels dangerously close to its sensors, the startled machine recoiled and sped off to safety.

The sparring and provocations reached a pinnacle at the foot of the steps. Katey darted up the steps toward the kitchen door, all the while laughing and saying something about Michael "... *getting beat by a girl!*" Michael, in close pursuit, followed her eagerly through the entryway.

Just inside, Kate froze in terror! Michael stopped just short of barreling into her. Seeing her terrified gaze at the far side of the kitchen, he turned and beheld three very foreboding-looking, armed men standing there.

Suddenly, the young couple realized how isolated they were from the rest of the world.

CHAPTER TEN

Family Reunion

Kara Ricci walked down the access way of the multi-thousand-family residence complex in Mons Hadley City, which lay buried deep beneath the Moon's surface in the Montes Apenninus mountain range. With the coming of evening, the lighting had dimmed throughout the entire common area.

Since arriving earlier that day at the Mons Hadley Fleet Base, Ricci had snaked her way through the city to its residence complexes, through this particular residence complex, and to the obscure and secluded passage in which she traveled. Coming to the door of a very familiar single-family home, Kara's journey ended.

However, she couldn't bring herself to ring the doorbell.

No, the thirty-one-year-old stood before the door, her courage withering whenever her finger neared the sensor. She labored through the small crisis for some time. Finally realizing that the knots tying in her stomach would not go away, Kara took a deep breath and rang the doorbell.

Several unbearable moments later, the door opened. A well-dressed man, who was at least several years her senior, came to stand warily in the open entryway.

"Kara?" he eventually brought himself to say. He gave her the once-over in an odd sort of way, causing the young woman to squirm self-consciously. "What are you doing here?"

"Hi, Pete," she smiled uncomfortably and took a deep breath. "Can I see her?"

He spanned his arms across door jam through a long, uneasy moment. Just as he turned toward the inside of the dwelling to call someone, a woman came up from behind him. Wearing her auburn hair up conservatively and carrying herself the same, she inhabited the typical Earth States housewife persona.

"Ciao, Sorella," the woman greeted her dryly. "È stato un molto tempo."

"Ciao, Tijah," Kara answered anxiously. "Ho ottenuto appena indietro dalla guerra."

Silence fell over the three for a long moment. After trading conspicuous glances with her husband, the woman gestured to her, "... You may as well come in."

With an uneasy sigh, Kara disappeared with the couple into the dwelling.

The eight-year-old girl, brimming with uncontainable excitement, bounced about on the floor in front of the living room coffee table. She matched wits against the interesting woman sitting on the couch, whom her parents had introduced as *Zia Kara* (Aunt Kara). The stakes were high: bragging rights over winning the game laid out on the table before them.

The youngster preferred someone her own age as an unexpected guest that evening. However, Zia Kara would more than do. Long, beautiful auburn hair draped her shoulders, just like her mom's— when her mom wore it down. Zia Kara conversed with her in the same language her mom did when they were alone (for the girl's father still struggled with his wife's native language). Moreover, unlike her mother and father watching restlessly in the background, the newfound aunt was a refreshing change from most adults: more than happy to meet her, smiling constantly, not boring, and wanting to interact with her all evening. Zia Kara played games too.

She was fun!

With the spin of a dial and the flickering of lights, the automated game enthusiastically declared the winner.

"Ho vinto, Zia Kara!" the young girl exclaimed, jumping up and smiling.

"sì, io vedo quello!" Ricci replied with a broad smile.

After a brief celebration, the young girl exclaimed, "Installiamolo anchors. Gli mostrerò come vincere."

"It's time for bed, Mia," Pete called as he came into the room. "Just like I told you a half hour ago." However, Mia started resetting the game for another round. So garnering a more commanding tone, Pete recited one of the few phrases he knew quite well, "Mia, esso sono tempo di andare dormire."

The young girl turned to her mother to plead, "Mom, can't I stay up just a little longer? I need to show Zia Kara how to win the game."

"You should go to bed," Kara said sympathetically, looking up to her parents in solidarity. "I've kept you up late enough already."

After a brief, unsuccessful negotiation, young Mia begrudgingly complied. She gave a goodnight hug to Zia Kara, because the woman asked for one. After bearing up under a very prolonged and emphatic hug—for Zia Kara wouldn't let go—the young girl did the same for her mother. Then Mia took her father's hand, and the two started up the stairs. From the first step, the young girl showered him with one comment after another—all spoken in her mother's native tongue.

The two women traded a quaint smile, relishing watching Pete try to keep up with the stream of words gushing from the young girl.

Kara went over to the pass-through counter in the dining room. She picked up the cup of coffee that Tijah had set out for her earlier. Turning and leaning her slender frame against the counter and taking a sip, she watched young Mia disappear with her father up the stairs.

"She's gotten so big since I saw her last," Kara said in the strange tongue with a warm smile. Now that Pete had left them alone, the two women could converse in their native language, just as they had done since they could remember. "She's becoming quite the girl—so beautiful and a bundle of energy."

However, the comment was more of a filibuster.

"You used to be like that," Tijah smiled back to be polite, though wearing an uncomfortable expression. She finished putting a recent picture of Mia into the locket in her hand. Closing the locket, she handed it back to Kara. "Here you go. I left Mia's baby picture behind her new picture."

Tijah took a sip of the beverage sitting next to her, while Kara hung the locket back around her neck. The jewelry disappeared when Kara flipped it behind the neckline of her shirt. Then Tijah looked toward the stairwell. "She never stops going. Pete will be up there a long time trying to get her to sleep. She has to think that it was *her* idea to go to bed."

The two women laughed quaintly. However, when their gazes turned uncomfortable, both sipped their beverages to break the mounting awkwardness.

"Kara, you should call first before showing up at the door," Tijah reluctantly warned. "Every time you just drop in like that, Pete gets nervous."

"I'm always afraid you'll tell me not to come," Kara lamented with a slight sharpness in her voice. She folded her arms in front of her too. "I don't exactly feel welcome, you know."

Tijah's expression chided. "I'd never keep you away, Kara. You're the one always going off on some adventure." She let the comment sink in through an uneasy moment. "And I know why.... It's all because of *him*, isn't it?"

"You don't know what you're talking about," Kara fumed—more than embarrassed too.

Tijah shook her head incredulously. "You remind me so much of Mom." She ignored the reproachful gaze Kara immediately shot back at her. "Mom always followed her heart at the expense of family. I can still remember the day she gave us all up to follow that *man*—as if he were any different from Dad or the rest of those men. ... She just *left* all of us there in that shelter and never looked back. You were too young to remember, but I'll never forget."

"I remember *too*."

Tijah looked Kara firmly in the eyes. "Kara, you have a family *right here* who loves you … who wants to be a part of your life—someone who *should* be a part of your life. You don't need to go off and follow *him*."

"You know it's more complicated than that," Kara sighed. "*Remember the war?*"

"What about before the war?" Tijah countered. "You didn't have to go into exploration. That was all about you following him." Seeing Kara's shoulders fall dejectedly and her head drop likewise, she pressed, "Is it all worth it, Kara? Your career and all those grandiose adventures? Don't you ever regret it?"

Kara looked up, her eyes welling up a bit. "Everyday." She labored over the probing comments—her embarrassment too. Just when she thought the exchange couldn't get worse, she cringed: An all too familiar, cynical smirk washed over her sister's face.

"I remember the broadcast announcing the Centauri mission," Tijah appeared to relish while sipping her beverage. "How that Davidson fellow made such a big deal about *him* with that *Kate* woman … announcing their engagement to the whole world—how they were going to be married when you reached Alpha Centauri." She sighed and shook her head. "… And you just stood behind them, smiling like any other well-wisher—*knowing what you knew*—while they became darlings of the media." When Kara sulked in silence, Tijah heaped on, "That was the saving grace of the war starting the next day. The fine people of Earth States wouldn't have been so enamored if they knew what Michael Gillen had done."

"You don't know what you're talking about," Kara retorted. Realizing that staying any longer would be a grave mistake, Kara huffed. She put down the coffee cup, pulled out a reader disk from her pocket, and handed it to her. "Here. Now I've kept my promise to you."

Tijah studied the reader's contents intently, barely noticing Kara gathering her things behind her. The housewife's eyes went wide; her face waxed over in remorse too. She abruptly turned around to Kara with such startled concern. "*You sure you want to do this?* This isn't what I asked for. I just wanted—"

"Yes, this is what I want," Kara declared, though a touch of lamenting inhabited the words.

Tijah stared down at the reader, astonished. "You must have some very influential friends," The more she read the documents, the more prominent her remorse grew over lecturing her sister. That was when she realized Kara was hurrying up the main hall toward the door. She pursued, arriving just in time to block the opening door with her forearm. "When will you be back?"

"I won't."

"*But why?*" Tijah pleaded, still keeping the door from opening. "Stay this time."

Kara looked at her sister, seeing empathy radiating from her for the first time. "I can't. That's why I gave you the reader."

Once again, there was silence. When her sister reluctantly let go of the door, Kara opened it to leave.

"Off to save the world again?" Tijah smiled quaintly.

"Something like that … *goodbye.*"

Just as Kara started through the door, Tijah grabbed her arm. "Kara, I know I'm the prying older sister"—offering a pleading gaze—"but whatever you're going off to do … *find yourself.* Don't come to the end of your life, only to regret that you wasted it chasing all the wrong things."

Kara, surprised by the gesture, looked affectionately at Tijah—her *sister.* For the first time in her life, she relished the returning gaze. So she hugged her, not easily letting go. Finally shooting Tijah a sentimental smile, Kara disappeared out the door.

As the door shut behind her, Kara hurried down the abandoned corridor. With each step moving her farther from the modest dwelling, she labored with the sense of loss and regret washing over her. She fought back tears while lamenting the thought of never returning. She despaired over her life, despaired over how the life her sister wanted for her had already eluded her.

She made it to an isolated area in the residence complex. With no windows or doors from which prying eyes might spy on her, Kara fell prostrate against the wall there and wept miserably.

She cried for some time, keeping her arms wrapped over her head to hide her face. No matter, the late hour made the habitat mostly deserted.

But then, a hand alighted on her shoulder. She cringed; embarrassment immediately washed over her. Her despair had garnered the attention of a sympathetic passerby. Taking a futile moment to compose herself, she turned around to greet the concerned citizen—

Kara gasped! Her eyes filled with fear! Standing over her were three suspicious-looking men brandishing weapons.

The small band hurried through the darkened plaza on Mid-Earth Station. The time was just past nine at night. The area, reminiscent of a small town square, remained subdued by virtual nightfall. An occasional street lamp broke the night, accentuating the shadowy canopy of leafy tree limbs suspended overhead. Most of the shop windows along the perimeter were dark and empty; the atmosphere, still and silent. Few people moved about the area, save the security staff monitoring the contingent moving through the square.

Michael Gillen kept Kate wrapped within the protection of one arm. The couple followed the lead security officer, Lieutenant Buhl, toward the unassuming back entrance to the 18 Scorpii Operations complex. Two other security escorts followed closely behind.

The young couple, laboring to continue, still reeled from stumbling upon the security detachment back at the lake house on Earth. Their faces remained drawn over the shocking and tragic news of Ben Morris' death. Worse, the perpetrators had probably targeted them too; thoughts of imminent danger—and being blissfully ignorant of it—struck them with fear.

"My back is *killing me*!" Kate grumbled, the tiredness in her eyes and the edge in her voice readily apparent. She reached around, put her fist against the small of her back, and stretched, using her arm as a lever. "I forgot how uncomfortable military transports can be."

Michael nodded sympathetically, though receiving a sharp gaze in return. He didn't know how to interpret her irritated expression. She was either looking for support or venting her frustration over the mission. He realized at that moment that the voyage might be a *long* one.

The small band reached the back entrance to the 18 Scorpii complex. The detail guarding the door yielded the entryway, and the group slipped safely into the structure.

Everyone breathed a collective sigh of relief and continued down the corridor.

The long passage soon opened into a vestibule. A lavish, unattended reception desk sat watch there, while a marble sculpture exhibit sat against the opposite wall. Plants surrounded the exhibit, and a railing fenced off the whole display. Accent lights from the ceiling bathed the sculpture in warm light, adding a touch of sophistication. The exhibit was likely a remnant of the complex's original civilian function, for such lavishness fell out of place among the stoic, military atmosphere of the 18 Scorpii project.

When they entered the vestibule, an all too familiar voice called out.

"Mike! Kate!"

They looked up in anticipation, their faces brightening. A larger-than-life Tom Andrews appeared from an adjacent corridor. His characteristic smirking demeanor complemented his very casual attire. Though fatigue was apparent in how he carried himself, Tom enjoyed the attention given to him by his escorts. In fact, he almost appeared regal as security led him into the vestibule.

"Tom! Welcome back!" Kate exclaimed as the three met in front of the sculpture exhibit. She reached around his somewhat gangly frame to hug him.

Tom readily followed through by lifting her up and swinging her around. "Hello, Sunshine! You're a sight for sore eyes." Not readily setting Kate down, he extended a hand to Michael. The two, shaking hands, traded quips about their long trip from the Outer Rim two weeks earlier.

But Kate interrupted by reaching in and taking Tom's face in her hands. She pulled him close and kissed his cheek. Keeping eye to eye, she radiated an almost painful gratitude. "Michael told me you saved his life.... *Thank you.*"

When Tom fell silent and blushed awkwardly, she smiled, kissed his cheek once more, and let go.

"Of course," Tom tried to recover, overtly comical and smiling at her, "Saving Mike's life wasn't one of my finer moments. I blew my chance to get this *lug* out of the way so I could sweep you off your feet."

"Don't let him con you," Michael interjected. "He only saved my life to get into the good graces of the Jonathan Gillen Benevolence Society."

"*Oh*, you're still lookin' for that room, *huh?*" Kate flashed him a coy half-smile, more than familiar with the running joke.

Tom bore a comical, false humility. "Sometimes, the only way to survive is off the charity of others."

"I can understand that," Kate reciprocated dryly, continuing the mood with a half-smirk. "After all, I've *kinda* been on that program for the last five years."

The six security officers had distanced themselves from the trio, allowing the moment and socializing among themselves. Still, Security intended to deliver them to the awaiting conference room. Though Michael noticed they were growing impatient, he couldn't have cared less.

"So how was your leave?" he asked Tom.

"Interrupted!" Andrews replied, a little indignant but still humorous. "After a very long trip to Mars, I finally settle into the resort. Just as I'm starting to enjoy myself"—gesturing at his escorts standing off to the side—"These guys show up and muscle me out of there!" Then he shrugged. "At least I got time off. How 'bout you two?"

The belated newlyweds, both blushing, stumbled for a reply.

Tom recoiled, more than a little embarrassed. "*Ahhh* ... I shouldn't have asked."

"No ... *no...*," the couple said somewhat together, trying to reassure him.

Then Michael stumbled, "We had a ... *great* time."

"... *Ahhh* ... *yes...*," Kate added, also stumbling over herself and her face a healthy shade of red. "Everything went"—cracking an unintentional but coy half-grin—"... *swimmingly.*"

An awkward pause followed. Tom suffered through the couple trading discreet but playfully gazes. Lieutenant Buhl saw the pause and seized the opportunity. "Sirs, you're expected in the briefing room."

Giving a collective, surrendering sigh, they followed Buhl and the other soldiers down an adjoining corridor. The trio walked arm in arm: Kate in the middle and the two men flanking her. This deliberately slowed their pace, which irritated their escorts. However, they didn't care; the *three musketeers* were together again.

Tom glanced down at Kate. "So, Sunshine, I see he conned you into doing this mission too."

Though she didn't say anything, the look on her face said everything. Michael tried not letting them notice him noticing her reaction.

"Too bad," Tom replied, his humor fading. "I wanted you to put your foot down. I can't: Technically, he's still my commanding officer." His tone abruptly turned serious. "We should have our heads examined." Then he looked at Michael even more soberly. "I heard about Ben … such a terrible way to die."

Silence lingered in the air as the three pondered the tragic news.

"It could have been any of us," Michael replied. "—maybe all of us if Security hadn't acted so quickly."

"Do they know who's behind it?" Tom inquired.

"You know as much as I do. I don't even know who's going to replace him."

"Whoever it is, they won't be good enough," Andrews acknowledged. "Morris was the best."

"Maybe Ben was the lucky one," Kate added out of nowhere.

A brief moment of silence fell as the trio pondered their imminent future. During that moment, the entrance to the conference room came into view.

"Unfortunately, you may be right, Sunshine," Tom replied. "This mission has disaster written all over it." He let out an unsettling sigh while shaking his head cynically. "I still can't believe we agreed to do this."

Michael kept silent as they approached the door. He could see that Tom had much more to say on the subject, as did Kate. However, the time for protesting had passed. The tragic loss of Ben Morris was more than enough to bear at that time, so they resolved by vote of expression to drop the subject.

"By the way, *Captain*," Tom began, "What did you name the ship?"

"The *Endurance*," Michael replied. When Tom grimaced, he added, "You know … *Shakleton* … the early twentieth century Trans-Antarctic expedition."

"*I know my history.* Wasn't that ship crushed in the ice before sinking to the bottom of the sea?"

Michael acknowledged with a nod but then countered, "It was a great expedition."

Tom, having a superstitious bent, returned an incredulous smirk. "You named it after a ship from ill-fated expedition?" Turning to Kate. "*That's* a good omen!"

The small band reached the end of the corridor, which opened into a common area adjacent to the main conference room. The security officers fell away, directing their charges into the conference room.

When Michael, Kate, and Tom slipped into the conference room, smiles washed over their faces. Standing near the front of the room was the rest of the Centauri family: Kara Ricci, Phil Marcotte, and David Tashjian. Tashjian, backup engineer on the Centauri mission—the apparent replacement for Ben Morris—was a haunting reminder of Morris' absence.

Immediately, the three other Centauries saw the new arrivals. With smiles washing over them too, they met the trio halfway to the door. The long-awaited reunion commenced. Hugs and handshakes traded back and forth amid more smiles and quaint *hellos*. Confusion in small order reigned as everyone greeted everyone else, and idle conversations crisscrossed the small circle in mayhem. Michael gloried in the gathering. To him, they were family; he was the big brother. Five years of separation couldn't impede that closeness.

"Hi, guys!" Kara smiled over-enthusiastically at Michael and Kate, seizing her chance to greet the young couple with a bear hug.

"Kara!" Michael replied just ahead of Kate.

"Michael, *I'm so relieved you're safe*," Kara gasped, still locked in the hug with them and keeping hold. "When I heard about the *Comanche*, I—"

"You okay?" Michael interrupted, noting a bit of heaviness in her expression. His concern also masked his desire to avoid an awkward conversation about the *Comanche*'s destruction.

"Yeah," Kate picked up the questioning, surveying the subtle hints of frustration in Kara's demeanor. "Is everything all right?"

"Mike's right, Sis" Tom greeted Kara with a nod from outside the small circle. Watching her eyes brighten at the familial greeting—for Tom had called her *Sis* since their NSEA days—he wrapped an arm around her supportively. "Is something wrong?"

Kara turned sheepish and rolled her eyes. "Everything's fine ... It's been a *long* day." She shrugged self-consciously. "I visited my sister earlier."

"Oh," Michael, Kate, and Tom, who were more than familiar with Kara's jaded family history, said almost in unison.

"That's more than enough for one day," Tom mused, receiving a round of mutual nods from the whole team.

"I got to see my niece though," Kara perked up. She pulled the heart-shaped locket from the neckline of her shirt, opened the cover, and held the youngster's picture out proudly to the couple—to Tom too. "Look how big she's gotten."

"Looks like a bundle of energy," Tom quipped from the side.

Michael and Kate admired the picture, nodding approvingly. Focusing on the picture, neither noticed Kara watching their reactions—particularly relishing Michael's expression in an odd sort of way.

"I'll bet she's quite the handful," Kate smiled.

"Yeah, she's—"

"Captain Gillen," a man's voice—a familiar but unrecognized voice—interrupted from behind Michael.

Facing away from the door and preoccupied with the reunion, Michael had missed the arrival of the six Special Forces soldiers. So he turned around—his smile immediately fell. Tom, who had also heard the greeting by the vaguely familiar voice, turned too—same reaction as Michael.

Immediately, the blissful reunion ended, felled silent by Michael and Tom's slack-jawed gawking. Standing before Michael was Emir Kern and the other Coverts.

"It's been a long time," Kern quipped sardonically against the stunned expressions.

"Yes," Michael replied, attempting to hide his complete disdain for the man. "Yes, it has."

CHAPTER ELEVEN

Briefing

"Cyril, I need to talk with you," a rather flustered Michael Gillen exclaimed, practically barging into Cyril Davidson's office in the 18 Scorpii complex on Mid-Earth Station.

Cyril, leaning over his desk and in a hurry to leave, briefly glanced up at him. He barely noted his protégé's perturbed gaze. Instead, the older man continued rifling through the materials on his desk. "Hi, Mike. They told me that you, Kate, and Tom had arrived. Now that everyone's here, we can start the mission briefing and get everyone settled in ... *oh*, and I'm glad to see that you're safe too. I should have said that first."

"I'm not sure I *am* safe."

Davidson abruptly stopped his rifling and looked up at him. "What are you talking about?"

"You didn't tell me the Special Forces team for this mission is Emir Kern and his men!"

Falling under Michael's sharp gaze, Cyril paused tellingly. Then he sighed in surrender. "I was hoping you were past that."

"You're kidding, right?"

The two men traded anxious looks through a long silence.

"The Europa Recon mission was a dangerous mission," Cyril finally replied—and rather uneasily. "The investigation cleared Kern and his team of any wrongdoing or negligence." However, when Michael remained unsettled, he added, "Let's go have the meeting first. You'll see that Kern is very much on board for this mission."

As the two men faced off across the desk, Kara Ricci hurried through the door.

"Cyril," she interrupted, her face betraying her concern, "We need to talk about the cryogenics calibration schedule for the Coverts."

"Let's talk about it in the meeting."

Michael, still fixated on Kern's presence on the mission, didn't acknowledge Kara's remark. "Cyril, no one investigating the Europa mission took my testimony—Tom's either. Emir Kern lied about what happened on Europa. I don't feel safe with him and his men working alongside my crew."

Kara shot Michael a quizzical glance before turning back toward Davidson. "The Coverts may be in trouble themselves. Medical Support scheduled the Coverts for two five-day calibration sessions; protocol calls for three."

"Didn't Medical tell you the technology was updated?" Davidson probed, more than impatient and starting toward the door.

"Yes, but—"

"So then you know we only need two calibration sessions now," he replied, abruptly waving her and Michael toward the door. "We can discuss all this in the meeting to everyone's satisfaction."

However, neither Michael nor Kara moved, forcing Davidson to stop too.

"But Cyril," Kara pleaded, "Twenty-three years is an unprecedented time under cryogenic suspension. The cryogenic processors need as much data as possible to predict how everyone's physiology will react to the process. We should *over calibrate* ... do three sessions just in case."

Davidson shook his head. "We don't have time. Ben's assassination forced us to move up the schedule." He hesitated, nervously taking in their attentive gazes. "You now launch in three months."

Both Michael and Kara's mouths dropped.

"That's crazy!" Michael gasped, his concern over Kern evaporating for the moment. "We can't do all the prep work in such a short time."

"I agree," Kara added.

"Yes, we can," Cyril countered. "We learned a lot from the Centauri mission, and you'll be safer if you launch." Once more, he gestured for them to leave. "So let's go to the conference room where we can discuss it. Time is wasting away."

Just then, David Tashjian appeared through the door. "Cyril, I just saw the launch schedule. Why aren't we testing the Slipstream propulsion system?"

Davidson sighed, clearly regretting how everything was proceeding. "We tested the propulsion system inside and out, David. It's calibrated."

Emir Kern came into the office just then. However, no one noticed. Michael, Kara, and David were too preoccupied with Cyril's statement to care.

"But none of the crew has worked with the Slipstream technology," Michael pleaded, more astonished than before.

"We scheduled simulation training," Davidson assured.

"Maybe the Slipstream field will affect the cryogenic processors," Kara heaped on. "We should check that out too."

Cyril, visibly annoyed, fought his mounting impatience. "Can we just *go* to the conference room? I have a whole team of experts ready to answer your questions."

"Admiral Davidson," Kern greeted with intent and ignoring the older man's pleadings, "I know Captain Gillen—"

"*Commander* Gillen," Michael corrected him curtly. "Flight crew designations will follow NSEA standards."

"But everyone maintains their military ranks too," Cyril clarified.

Kern shrugged. "*Fine*. I know *Commander* Gillen has concerns about working with my team. I suggest letting the Centauries out of this mission—I'm sure they don't want to go anyway. I know of a suitable Special Forces flight team we can use."

"That's crazy!" Michael fumed. "You need astronauts."

Davidson nodded in agreement. "Kern, this isn't the time to discuss this."

"But my team *has* long range exploration training," Kern pressed, watching their faces wax over curiously—warily too. "Maura Enzler's the captain. She was one of the original Centauries, right?"

Stunned silence fell over the room. Michael, Kara, and David went slack-jawed.

Seeing the Centauries' reactions, Cyril put his hands up and looked crossly at Kern. "We're not going to discuss it now." When Kern mounted a defiant gaze as if to continue, the older man's eyes sharpened, and he pointed an accusing finger at him. "And don't think I don't know what you did! Nobody pulls rank on me!"

The comment hung in the air for a short moment, and the three Centauries traded quizzical looks. So Cyril turned to the larger group. "*Everyone* ... go to the conference room. We'll discuss your concerns *there ... please!*"

After a defiant standoff, Michael begrudgingly turned and followed Kara, David, and Kern to the door. But Cyril grabbed his arm from behind and held him back.

Waiting until after the other three had left, Cyril finally spoke. "Mike, I know you have a lot of concerns—"

"That's an understatement."

The older man acknowledged with a reluctant nod. "But I need your support in front of the rest of the team." He shook his head. "This is a dangerous mission, a complicated mission that won't get off the ground if everyone keeps going down this path. I need you to make the rest of the team comfortable with what we're trying to do."

"But *I'm* not comfortable, Cyril."

"I understand," Cyril reassured, putting a hand on Michael's shoulder. "But given what happened to Ben, this mission is in danger every day we *don't* launch. Thieren may also withdraw his pledge if he thinks his investment is in jeopardy."

"You want me to just *ignore* the risks?"

"No, just do what you've always done ... *trust me.*"

"What about Kern? He's already causing trouble."

"It's too late to replace the Coverts," Cyril shook his head. "You'll have to work with him." Upon seeing him remain unconvinced, the older man pleaded, "Seriously, have I ever let you down?"

Michael suffered under Cyril's imploring gaze for the longest time. Though returning a pleading gaze of his own, the young man felt himself falling victim—*once again*—to his mentor's persuasion. He was really beginning to abhor that all too familiar sensation.

"No ... no, you haven't," he conceded. "In fact, you have this uncanny ability to make sure things work out." He paused, looking his mentor in the eyes and sighing. "Okay ... I'll give you my support. I'll even try to work with Kern. Just don't expect any miracles."

Davidson nodded, and the two men left the office.

The crew quarters section of the *Endurance*, dry-docked in the 18 Scorpii launch bay, remained quiet. Lighting in the main corridor was scant, indicative of the late hour. A solitary utilibot with ten or more claw-like arms hovered about the area, quietly performing its duties. Less than an hour earlier, the place had hummed with the sounds of the 18 Scorpii crew settling into their quarters. But once more, everything had returned to its subdued ambiance.

A weary Michael Gillen appeared at the corridor entryway. He yawned as he walked, simultaneously rubbing his neck. The long evening of meetings, preceded by an even longer day on Earth and an abrupt departure from Earth, had taken its toll on him; he just wanted to sleep. However, the day wouldn't end until he had completed the unenviable task ahead of him.

He labored down the darkened corridor past the entrance to his quarters. At the end of the passage, Emir Kern's quarters sat with the door open. Light streamed out of the room, illuminating the area just in front of the entrance. He could see Kern inside, facing away from the door and unpacking his belongings.

"May I come in?" Michael greeted Kern as he came into the doorway.

The lieutenant turned and flashed an irreverent smile at him. "*Gillen*. I'm not surprised. Sure, come on in. You can help me unpack."

Michael shut the door behind him. Making small talk to delay the inevitable conversation, he said, "I'm surprised you're still unpacking."

"I had to tuck my crew in for the night—read them a bed time story too."

Michael feigned a polite smile, keeping his disdain for the man's sardonic, disrespectful humor to himself. Kern studied the pile before him, pausing as if considering what to do next. While doing that, the man ran a hand through his short, brown hair, exposing touches of grey hidden underneath the top layer of hair.

Kern was young, only five or six years Gillen's senior. He appeared older, though not just because of the advanced graying. No, Kern's brown eyes seemed haunted and wearied. An occasional scar adorning his face and arms—souvenirs of past hostilities—gave him an unnatural ruggedness. His permanent sneer hinted of a boyish charm underneath, though his calloused exterior cowed the more affable demeanor.

"I should welcome you to my humble home," Kern quipped. "It's not much: small and drab. I don't even have a window. It's not the kind of place I expected to spend the next fifty years."

"True," Michael replied, struggling against the uncomfortably close distance between him and the Covert. "But they spared no expense on your cryogenics chamber. That's where you'll spend most of your time."

Kern's face waxed over in displeasure as he opened one of the storage drawers. "You mean those glorified coffins? I'm not too thrilled about being turned into a popsicle. Of course, I'm sure you *astronauts* are looking forward to it."

Michael said nothing in response.

"Where are my manners? I should offer you a drink."

Kern quickly scanned the jumble of items, even searching the storage drawers he had already filled. When the bottom recessed drawer yielded him success, he pulled out a bottle and two glasses.

Michael's eyebrows went up at the sight—not at the bottle and glasses, but at the faded green military-issue satchel already lying tucked away in the drawer. He had seen the satchel three years earlier: Kern had carried it off the burning transport from the Europa reconnaissance mission. It was the only equipment salvaged from the transport—Kern and the satchel were inseparable. From the time Kern and his men entered the *Comanche's* brig, the satchel had disappeared (though Michael never made Kern aware he was looking for it).

Oddly, the Covert activated the locking mechanism after closing the drawer.

Kern, not even noticing Michael's curious gaze at the drawer, opened the bottle and handed him one of the glasses. Though the Covert carried out the actions with complete hospitality, Michael felt an undercurrent of tension swirling about the cramped quarters.

"I was saving this for the long trip," Kern exclaimed as he filled the two glasses. "But I'll just ask that pretty little assistant they assigned me to get me a replacement." He raised his glass to propose a toast, and Michael hesitantly responded. Of course, both men kept their drinks close, as if toasting across a chasm. "To fifty years of accrued hazard pay, all thanks to Aurelian Galerius ... or should I say *Mos Thieren?*"

The two men feigned a sincere toast.

After an awkward moment of silence, Kern said, "I'll bet you never thought we'd cross paths again—or at least hoped we wouldn't."

"Something like that."

"And judging by the expression on your face, I suppose you're still upset about our little encounter three years ago."

"Do you blame me?" Michael replied sharply. An uneasy moment followed. "But I'm more concerned about that stunt you pulled earlier this evening, when you requested Enzler's team to replace my team."

"That was no stunt. I don't have time to nursemaid a bunch of civilian astronauts. I need experienced Special Forces personnel."

Before Michael could respond, Kern waved him off and turned to his belongings. The two remained silent while he continued unpacking. The Covert took some of his clothes, opened the recessed drawer—giving Michael another look at the satchel—and packed the clothes inside. Once again, the man closed the drawer and activated the locking mechanism.

"Based on what happened on Europa three years ago," Michael began, picking back up the train of the conversation, "I'm not sure you know what you need."

Kern paused and looked straight at him. "We completed our mission. That's what counts."

"And you almost got my whole crew killed."

"No one told you to stick around when the Europans showed up. You should have bugged out, just as the plan called for. Every other captain in the fleet would have left."

Michael felt the same indignation from three years earlier overcoming him. "That's not the point. If we're ever going to work together on this mission, I need to know what happened while your team was down on Europa."

"Are we going to go over this *again*?" Kern grimaced. "I told you what happened: The Europans detected us—that's it. The investigation *you requested* cleared my team. You need to accept that dangerous missions go bad sometimes."

Michael shook his head dismissively. "You may have buffaloed Command, but I know you lied to me about what happened. Until I know the truth, I can't trust you."

Kern shrugged and took another sip from his glass. "What could you *possibly think* happened that day?"

"I'm still trying to figure it all out," Michael admitted. He began pacing the small room in a deliberate fashion. "But without warning, you Coverts disappear off the grid; communications go silent. Then later, we find evidence that you and your men are near the palace—fifty kilometers from where you were supposed to be. Finally, we find an active homing beacon in your quarters—just as the Europans show up."

"What are you saying?" Kern asked, his face turning dour.

"Maybe you're a spy," Michael quipped, watching him boil. Relishing the Covert's reaction, he added, "It wouldn't be the first time a Special Forces operative played both sides. Perhaps you're even *Trajan*, the infamous Europan spy sent by Aurelian Galerius himself to bring down Earth States. Isn't that the legend?"

Kern said nothing.

"Maybe you're just incompetent," Michael shrugged sarcastically. After an effective pause, he added, "But I think it's simpler than that: I think you had your own agenda on Europa. You abandoned your primary mission. That's why Enzler's team picked you up so far from where you were supposed to be. Maybe you've got some sort of side business—something to supplement your lieutenants' salary. Maybe you're mixed up in the Europan black market. I'm sure your covert duties keep you in Europan territory enough to carry on such activities."

"You think?" Kern sneered with a heavy impatience in his voice.

"Yes," Michael replied. "But one thing is certain: You gave away *Comanche*'s location to the Europans. *Comanche* became a decoy to keep the Europans preoccupied while you carried out your real intentions."

Kern fumed. His face became like flint. "You'd better be able to back up a statement like that."

"I guess it doesn't really matter anymore what happened three years ago," Michael assured. "I'm more concerned with what's ahead of us. Regardless of what Davidson thinks, I don't trust you. I won't let you endanger this crew the way you did with the *Comanche*."

Kern laughed cynically. "That's funny. Wasn't *Comanche* destroyed six weeks after our little encounter?" He looked Michael straight in the eyes. "I'll leave killing your crew up to you. You're so much better at it."

This time, Michael fumed.

Kern relished his small victory for as long as the opportunity allowed. Just as Michael was about to explode on him, he interjected, "I *know* why you're here confronting *me* instead of Davidson." An intentional, irritating pause. "I'll bet Davidson already refused your request to kick me off the mission. I'll bet he ordered you to work things out with me."

"So?" Michael seethed.

"Do you know how I know? Because when I went to him privately to ask him to replace *your team*, he told me the same thing. I even tried calling in some favors—none of which worked."

Silence hung in the air for a moment.

"I guess we're stuck with each other then," Michael snipped.

"I guess so," Kern replied, steely-eyed. He stared down Michael until eventually relenting with an affable smirk. "The flight crew and responsibility for the voyage are yours—I surrender those points. You outrank me too, so I'll extend to you all the courtesies that come with that privilege. After all, we're still on the same side—no matter what you believe." However, his words rang hollow. Then his steely-eyed stare returned. "But when my team goes into action on 18 Scorpii, don't get in my way like you did on Europa. Keep your people out of my way too. And don't tell me how to do my job."

Kern opened the door and motioned to him. "Now excuse me: I have an appointment at eight hundred hours to be turned into an ice cube. Good night, *Commander*."

Michael stood his ground and returned Kern's condescending gaze. After letting out an indignant huff, he left, shutting the door behind him.

Finally alone, Kern sighed and let his shoulders fall. He took his glass in hand and stared toward the door with the most troubled expression. Sips from the glass accompanied his churning thoughts, until only generous swigs from the bottle would do.

Trading the glass for the bottle, Kern sat down on the bed and imbibed a mouthful of the drink. He leaned back until half-reclined against one elbow, brooding silently. Growing increasingly frustrated, he reached into his chest pocket and pulled out a tattered photograph.

His gaze immediately fell under the power of the image, and he stared at it with incredible longing. A relishing glimmer formed in his haunted eyes, pushing away some of the darkness that inhabited him. The man even appeared happy for the briefest moment. However, darkness once again washed back over him, and his face twisted bitterly. The tortured gaze waxed more severe as the terrible emotions swelled within him, so much so that the drink no longer assuaged the maddening emotions—

Kern sent the bottle flying across the small room! The container crashed violently against the bulkhead, spilling the beverage everywhere and spreading shards of glass across the floor.

Frustrated and even more exhausted than before, Michael proceeded through the entryway to his quarters. The door shut behind him, and the room darkened. He paused for a second, allowing his eyes to adjust.

Katey lay in bed, fast asleep and curled up under the covers.

He carefully walked over to the desk where his evening meal sat waiting. Though he picked at the food half-heartedly, all he wanted was to put the tedious day behind him. So he slipped off his outer garments and climbed into bed next to his wife. When he delicately kissed her on the cheek, Katey groggily turned and draped herself over him as if he were a pillow.

"How'd it go?" she eked out with her eyes firmly closed and still half asleep.

His whole body went limp. "Let's just say that it's going to be a *long* trip."

Gently touching his face in a consoling manner, she fell to sleep once more.

Quiet settled in once again on the quarters, and Michael lay in the darkness beside his wife. He studied the grey shadows on the ceiling, anxiously waiting for sleep to subdue him. After all, training started early that next morning.

Yet the discussion with Kern weighed heavily on him, and he replayed the conversation repeatedly in his mind. Though exhausted, Michael realized that he might be staring at those shadows for quite some time.

Chapter Twelve

Preparation

"Adria," Kara Ricci called across the cryogenics test lab in the 18 Scorpii complex on Mid-Earth Station. She stood dressed in physicians' scrubs, hovering over Mark Armstrong's closed cryogenics chamber. The lifeless Covert lay within the chamber, still deep in suspension. When Adria turned, she asked, "Can you please check on Kern? He should be at *First Waking* soon."

Six weeks had passed since Kara's arrival at Mid-Earth Station. Launch preparations for the 18 Scorpii mission had gone tenuously.

She and Adria, a middle-age physician from the launch support medical team, were reviving the Coverts from their second five-day cryogenics calibration session. Once complete, Kara could put the dreadful suspension process out of mind until the actual launch, still over six weeks away.

"Ah ... sure," Adria replied, stepping in the direction where Kern lay. She stopped mid-stride. "But I thought you wanted to oversee *First Waking* with each of them?"

By then, Kara had turned around. She intently studied Mark Armstrong's vital signs on the medical readout to his left. "I did, but Armstrong developed an arrhythmia. I want to find the cause."

"You worried?"

"Not immediately," Kara shook her head. "It's going away as fast as it appeared—you know how difficult the body responds to being revived." Then she paused in thought. "He didn't develop the symptom on the first calibration session." Another long pause while her face twisted quizzically. "If only I had one more calibration session, I could ensure the computers have adjusted for the anomaly. Unfortunately, a third session is out of the question, thanks to you support engineers."

"I had *nothing* to do with that decision," the brunette waved her hand dismissively. "As far as I'm concerned, we should calibrate everyone eight times instead of two—you Centauries too."

"I'm not worried about *us*," Kara half-laughed. "We've been frozen and thawed so many times, our DNA has freezer burn. It's the Coverts I'm worried about."

Adria nodded, and the two women went about their work. Kara studied Armstrong's readouts, while Adria checked on Kern, who lay unconscious on the table of his open cryogenics chamber. Wires and tubes covered the man's body, though most remained concealed by the sheet draped over him.

"Kern won't be conscious for a while," Adria exclaimed matter-of-factly. "His brain functions are still coming online." She looked over at Kara busily working the medical computer beside Armstrong. "By the way, watch out when Armstrong comes to. He gets handsy when disoriented—groped me a bunch of times the last *First Waking*. I had to re-sedate him."

"He's a little handsy even when awake," Kara grimaced, briefly turning around to look at her. "I prepped him for both calibration sessions—groped me both times. The meathead must fancy himself to be a real ladies' man."

After sharing another mutual grimace with her peer, Kara turned back and engrossed herself in the arrhythmia anomaly. The room went quiet while both women carried out their work. Just as Kara began making progress on the curious anomaly, a sudden commotion erupted behind her. She turned in response and looked across the room.

"Emir, lie still!" Adria pleaded while struggling to subdue a very disoriented and agitated Emir Kern. "Emir … you're safe."

Though far from conscious, Kern nevertheless flailed about. He was mumbling unintelligibly through labored breaths. Extreme weakness accompanied this stage of revival, so the petite woman easily kept him on his table—though the strength he mustered impressed her too.

"You'll hurt yourself!" she pleaded again, still wrestling with him.

The man's eyes reflected back some sort of undeniable madness.

"What's wrong?" Kara asked, still across the room. Though tempted to assist Adria, she remained by Armstrong's chamber.

"I don't know … he should still be out. Nothing looks right!"

"Try to calm him."

"*I'm trying*…. I can handle him, but he's going to hurt himself."

Kara kept vigil by Armstrong's chamber. However, the commotion kept distracting her from his fading arrhythmia problem. She watched Kern's resistance against Adria mounting too. No matter how much her smaller colleague struggled to subdue him, the Covert remained in his agitated state.

"Look at his brain activity," Adria finally exclaimed, struggling to keep her gaze on the medical monitor. "It's all over the place—must be some sort of psychosis. I'm going to have to reboot his brain functions."

"No, don't do that," Kara pleaded. Realizing she needed to help her peer, the young woman started across the room. "We might have problems reviving him that way. I saw that side effect a couple times."

Arriving at Kern's table, Kara studied the readouts while Adria continued struggling. "That's no psychosis. He's *dreaming* … looks like some sort of night terror."

"*Can't be,*" the brunette strained. Steadying her small frame against Kern's increasing jostling, she looked closer at the complex readouts. "*You're right* … but that doesn't make sense. We *haven't*"—the man suddenly flailed out of her grasp, forcing the petite woman to seize him even harder—"haven't restored enough brain functions for him to be dreaming."

Realizing the Covert's increasing agitation was overwhelming her companion, Kara took hold of Kern's wrists and immobilized him. "Go get a sedative."

Adria went for the drugs across the room.

Kara, wrestling Kern's thrashing arms, looked down at the struggling Covert. A painful, tormented gaze reflected back from the unconscious man. When his eyes randomly trained on hers for the briefest moment, a dreadful sensation shot straight through her. She winced terribly, trying to shake off the icy shivers racing up and down her spine. The feeling lingered much longer than she could bear it.

Coming to herself, the young woman once again subdued the Covert. "Emir"—surprisingly, the man's eyes trained on her—"Lie still…. It's okay…. Trust me."

The possessed man gazed back at her. Amazingly, his arms relaxed within her grasp, eventually falling harmlessly to his side. However, the Covert's eyes kept fixed on her. When Kara offered a reassuring smile, the man's eyes rolled closed and his head dropped to the side.

Kern was unconscious again.

"Wow!" Adria exclaimed, arriving and holding a hypodermic of sedatives in her hand. "What'd you do?"

"I don't know," Kara shrugged. "Nothing you didn't already do."

Both women gazed at the hypodermic in Adria's hand. Then they turned back to a very lifeless but healthy Emir Kern.

"Do you think he can explain it to us when he wakes up?" Adria asked.

"I don't think he was ever awake to know…. You'd better give him the sedative, just in case."

Kara watched her colleague administer the medicine, unsure of what to make of the incident. She looked back at Armstrong's medical readouts displaying across the lab on his monitor. Letting out an abrupt huff, she shook her head. "*Great*, now I'll never know what caused his arrhythmia problem."

The back lawn of the Executive Mansion on Eratosthenes, the Moon, sat subdued in the sober quiet of a commemoration service. A small crowd of visitors filled thirty rows of white chairs facing the podium, while dignitaries watched from two rows of chairs behind the podium. Everyone listened respectfully as President James Mitchell stood and gave the address.

The ceremony honored the lost crews of the *Comanche* and the other ships that had saved the President so long ago. However, the details of the tragedy remained masked behind an official cover story, for whatever had drawn the President to the asteroid belt was still top secret. After all, Earth States was still at war.

Though every ranking officer who survived the onslaught attended, Michael Gillen and Tom Andrews were the only ones not from the *Executive One*, the President's transport. Michael had learned just that day that he and Tom were the only known survivors from the *Comanche*.

From her place in the visitors' section, Kate Gillen sat between Kara Ricci and Tom Andrews. Next to Tom sat David Tashjian, flanked by Phil Marcotte. Though the stately leader delivered a moving address, Kate glanced frequently at Michael sitting with Cyril Davidson among the dignitaries.

Though proud that Michael was receiving such a high honor, Kate lingered over the remorse seeping out from behind his polite demeanor. He sat alone among the dignitaries, while the President recounted the heroics of that day. When the President called him to stand to his right at the podium, Michael's face only waxed heavier. With a false graciousness, the young man labored through the praise lauded on him.

Michael had spoken very little to her about the tragedy—always changing the subject when the issue came up. Kate so wanted to hold him as he stood before the leader. Her face must have betrayed her angst, for Kara took hold of her hand and smiled reassuringly at her.

Finally, the President placed an ornate medal around Michael's neck. The leader stepped back and saluted him.

Kate sighed in relief. The ceremony was almost over.

Some time after the commemoration ceremony, Michael Gillen and Cyril Davidson walked across the grass in Capitol Square Park. Neither man appeared in a hurry to traverse the grounds, nor were they walking toward any particular destination. Instead, the duo was intent on enjoying a day off from the grueling 18 Scorpii launch schedule.

Michael took in with much satisfaction the Earth-like setting of the capitol city, which fell completely out of place on the Moon. The open-air habitat stretched for kilometers in all directions. The transparent ceiling of the massive structure, over two hundred meters above him and level with the Moon's surface, emitted a rich sapphire distortion field, replicating the look of an endless blue summer sky. Filtered light from the sun overhead streamed in, warming the entire area and completing the visual.

For all his senses could tell, he was in a beautiful park set in the middle of a bustling city on Earth. Towering maple and oak trees lined the park's perimeter, while statues, fountains, and the like lay scattered throughout the grassy landscape. A healthy crowd of tourists and locals enjoyed the park, serviced by vendor carts spread throughout. On the park's perimeter and working outward ran a system of busy streets, which were fed by a network of access tunnels. The tunnels connected the capitol to the rest of the Eratosthenes settlement. Smaller buildings crowded within the bustling thoroughfares, yet giving way to the grand government buildings lining the perimeter of the habitat. The air hummed with the muffled sounds of city noise in the distance.

The two men continued their stroll, keeping their hands tucked into their pockets and chatting as they went along. A security detail inconspicuously followed.

"I wonder where the others went?" Michael mused.

Davidson nodded his head toward the commercial district to the east. He smiled, "I expect Kate and Kara have laid siege to one of those shopping malls. David and Phil said they were going sightseeing, and Tom … *is Tom*. Who knows what that guy is up to?"

"I hope they stay with their security details."

"Don't worry," Davidson replied. "This town's secure. With the President's own security watching us and some caution exercised, everyone should be safe." He smiled again. "Just don't tell the Coverts we took you off Mid-Earth Station."

Well behind them lay the grand Executive Mansion from where they had come. Directly ahead in the distance, set prominently above ground level on a large, lavishly adorned plateau, lay the congressional building. The elaborate structure towered majestically through the transparent ceiling, its crowning dome visible through the sapphire distortion field.

"So you've met the President twice now," Davidson observed. "Is it getting mundane yet?"

"I'm still at a loss for words when he talks to me."

"He's just a man like you and me … just has a more important job."

Michael gazed down at his new medal hanging from his neck, embarrassed to be wearing it in public—even wearing it at all. However, taking the medal off would have dishonored the long-gone crew of the *Comanche*. "I'm glad the schedule allowed for the memorial service. All those men who died protecting the President deserve public recognition."

"And even those who survived," Cyril gently reminded him.

The young man nodded. "Why was I the only one to receive a medal?"

Davidson paused in thought for a long moment. After walking a few steps, he said, "Tom talked to me before we left Mid-Earth Station. He told me he didn't want to be recognized. He said he had his reasons, so I honored that request."

"I would be dead without his efforts. He's the real hero in my opinion."

Cyril kept his gaze far ahead at the beautiful scenery. Michael waited for the older man to impart his typical wisdom. However, Cyril said nothing. In fact, the young man sensed the slightest hint of irritation from him.

"Such a tragedy impacts everyone differently," Cyril eventually replied. "Tom is dealing with it in his own way."

The two men continued their stroll in silence.

Michael's face waxed oddly. Eventually, he turned to the older man. "Cyril, I'm trying to keep an open mind about 18 Scorpii"—his expression turning—"but I'm concerned about how we're proceeding."

Cyril intentionally took a few steps and replied, "Mike, I know you want real-time testing with the Slipstream drives, but we tested and calibrated the prototype countless times before you arrived."

"What about the launch schedule? We would have never launched the Alpha Centauri mission so quickly."

"Alpha Centauri was our first deep-space launch," Cyril reassured. "Despite never launching, we learned much. We took that knowledge and refined our procedures." He watched Michael spin the conversation uneasily in his mind. When the young man remained apprehensive, Cyril put his arm on his shoulder. "Mike, you live every day with the memories of what happened to the *Comanche*, and you fear repeating such a tragedy; that's understandable. But I think that's why you're concerned too."

Michael gazed back at his mentor tellingly, though his concern persisted. "You keep telling me to trust you—and I do…. But my crew is looking for assurance that everything is okay. Every time I concede another point to you, they become a little more dubious—you're putting me in the middle."

"The *Centauries* certainly trust you," Cyril looked him squarely in the eyes. "So you're not telling me the one *real* concern you have, right?"

"Okay, fine," Michael replied after returning the older man's insistent gaze. "The *big* problem is the Coverts—but don't dismiss my other concerns. You told me to work out my problems with Kern, but that won't happen."

"You may want to ask Kara to help you with him," Cyril offered, seeing the predictable but quizzical grimace come over Michael. "Kern responds to her for some reason—more subconsciously than anything."

"Really?"

"From what I've seen so far," Davidson mused. "And you know my intuition—not that Kara gives him the time of day." After letting him ponder the statement, Cyril continued, "Kern's a warrior by nature: Push him, and he'll push back harder—Kern *always* has trouble with his commanding officers. But approach him with a softer, more vulnerable, *feminine* appeal—and he doesn't know what to do."

Michael pondered the disturbing thought for a long moment. However, he shook his head glibly. "It's not that—I can handle Kern in a conflict. *I don't trust him*; I don't trust any of them."

"I don't disagree with you there," Cyril sighed. "I always breathe a little easier when they go under cryogenic suspension—until they're thawed out."

"Then why don't you stand up to the oversight committee?"

Davidson sighed once more. "Well, Mos Thieren likes them—better than you, I might add." He let the statement sink in to his protégé for a moment. "One of their first missions after the war started was rescuing Mos Thieren's daughter out from under the Europans' noses. Her rescue was quite the slap in the face to Aurelian Galerius, who was holding her to influence Thieren. Thieren was predictably grateful to the Coverts."

"So Kern went to Thieren to get us kicked off the mission?" Michael probed. "The night we arrived, I remember you warning Kern not to pull rank on you. Is that what you meant?"

"It's better that you don't involve yourself in the politics of the mission," Cyril waved off the discussion as they walked. "Just know that the Coverts are good at what they do—probably the best team we've got—and Thieren knows they're motivated. I couldn't kick them off the mission if my life depended on it."

"But if you don't trust them—"

"You think it's *easy* recruiting teams for deep-space missions?" the older man cynically chuckled. "Alpha Centauri was hard enough; remember the problems you guys had at the beginning?" He paused for effect. "No, you're just going to have to go out on a limb this time—just as I did for your team so long ago … put some trust in them."

"That doesn't sound reassuring."

Cyril smiled, "Then maybe you should try prayer." Upon receiving quite the sour grimace from Michael, he added, "Prayer changes things. It always works for me."

Michael shook his head, rebuffing the intentional and playful jab from his mentor. Cyril knew him better than anyone did, save perhaps Kate—and Kara before her. Michael respected him tremendously, for the older man had become a surrogate father. Moreover, given the man's flair for religion, Cyril also reminded him—very fondly too—of his deceased older brother, David.

Upon hearing the comment, Michael's thoughts filled with memories of David again.

David had been the most fervent religious person Michael ever knew, bordering on the fanatical—not that he knew too many religious zealots. David carelessly threw around terms like *sin*, *faith*, and *Jesus Christ* to anyone, never caring whom he offended. And what had it profited his older sibling? Despite unwavering integrity and charity toward others, David ended up dead—killed by the very *Weightless* people he had gone to help.

What a gaping hole the loss inflicted on him. Despite David's annoying religious zeal, Michael nevertheless hero-worshipped him. David had been a wonderful brother: always more than generous, always more than protective, and always the type of person Michael wished to become—religion aside.

Then he was gone.

No, David's tragic death steeled the young man's resolve: Whatever benevolent god the older Gillen had claimed to worship, David's death was proof to Michael that God didn't exist.

So Michael politely put up with what he considered Cyril Davidson's only real character flaw: his religiousness. However, Cyril was less impertinent. He professed his own faith without calling out Michael's hostility toward religion. Neither did he carelessly throw around a lot of *religious* words. No, Cyril was always positive, never contentious, and never acting as if his faith was the only truth. Michael found that disposition much more comforting and encouraging.

"You know that's not me—never was," Michael smiled at him cynically. "Never will be, either."

Cyril just smiled back at him. "Good thing *one* of us doesn't see it your way."

The time was late into the night on the *Endurance*, which still sat dry-docked on Mid-Earth Station. Twenty-nine-year-old Michael Gillen stared up at a shadowy ceiling. This particular view of his quarters had become a familiar sight. After six tedious weeks of launch preparation for 18 Scorpii, Michael had dreadfully memorized every shadow adorning the grey surface.

Katey lay snuggled close to him, fast asleep.

Seeking refuge from his churning thoughts, he turned toward her and caressed the outline of her form against the covers. Quickly mesmerized by her beauty and angelic appearance, Michael desired to wake her, to recapture just part of those ten precious, intimate days they had spent at the lake. However, waking her would have been unfair. She would perceive the gesture as opportunistic too: a convenient diversion that didn't interfere with his increasing preoccupation with the mission. Knowing she would have been right, he softly kissed her cheek and turned back to the much less alluring view of the ceiling.

He put his hands behind his head on the pillow, surrendering to the concerns over 18 Scorpii spinning madly in his head.

He tried consoling himself with the positive aspects of the mission. After all, the launch support teams had declared *Endurance* ready to launch, completing final Slipstream propulsion tests, onboard systems calibrations, fueling, and provisions stocking. Of course, they would perform a final check in another six weeks, just as the schedule dictated.

However, nothing could assuage his overall concerns about the mission. No, Michael would churn the thoughts repeatedly until wearying himself to sleep—

An alarm suddenly blared against the quiet!

Instinctively, he jumped straight up and out of bed. Kate, bleary-eyed and still half-asleep, sat up too.

"What's *that*?" she asked. "Some kind of malfunction?"

"Sounds like the defensive systems."

Kate tiredly put her hand to her head, still in a fog and cringing at the irritating alarm. "But I haven't even activated scanning and tactical. It *has* to be a fault."

Yet the alarm kept blaring.

"It's the feed from the station's defensive systems," Michael replied while opening the door and stepping out into the corridor. "I think the station is under attack."

"That doesn't make sense," she exclaimed. Finally coming to herself, she jumped up and followed him. "It's too late in the war for any serious attack here."

The rest of the crew, still dressed for bed and wearing the same bewildered look, gathered in random fashion in the corridor. Bed head was the norm.

"What's going on?" Tom yawned.

"I'm not certain," Michael replied, starting down the passageway. "I'm going to Launch Control."

Michael set off down the corridor. The entire crew—Centauries and Coverts alike—followed closely behind him. Speculative comments traded back and forth as they hurried.

The small band made their way through the ship, noticing the *Endurance* coming to life. Lighting throughout the ship brightened from normal nighttime levels, while computers and support systems methodically powered up. The faint hum of fusion engines coming to life echoed from deep below—an unnerving sound.

Finally, Michael and crew reached the gantry connecting *Endurance* to the dry dock. From this vantage point, they witnessed a flurry of activities transpiring in the launch control room.

Michael, Tom, and Kate looked at each other soberly.

Davidson, accompanied by several mission directors, hurried toward them from the opposite end of the gantry. The man's uniform appeared disheveled, as if he had dressed in a hurry.

"Cyril, what's going on?" Michael called.

The admiral labored toward him, visibly unsettled. "An Europan armada breached Mid-Earth's outer defenses. Their trajectory will bring them in close proximity to this complex. They're ignoring ammunition and fuel depots on the other side—some of the more vulnerable targets." Then he hesitated, looking Michael straight in the eyes. "They're here for you and the *Endurance*."

"We're too deep inside the station to be at risk," Phil Marcotte stated.

"Don't count on it," Kern warned. "Look what the goons did at Ceres."

Davidson looked around as if gazing at all of them at once. "*Endurance*'s location is *exactly* why it's vulnerable. The launch channels are fortified, but this complex lays shallow to the top of the station—it's vulnerable to bombardment."

"So we move the ship to safety until the danger passes?" Michael asked.

Davidson hesitated nervously. "No, we want you to launch."

Immediately, Cyril received twelve stunned expressions in return.

"That's crazy!" Michael scoffed, his team behind him nodding in agreement. "We're still in prep mode."

A debate ignited—a heated debate. The *Endurance* crew voiced their objections, while the mission directors behind Davidson countered in like fashion. Chaos reigned throughout the exchange.

Summarily, Cyril waved his arms, felling everyone silent. "This armada is dangerous! They'll concentrate all efforts on *this* dry dock.

They could land as many as ten thousand foot soldiers…. You're in danger if you stay." Then he turned to Michael. "I hate to do this, Mike, but I *order* you to launch."

Michael stood there, torn. Opposing allegiances clashed in his conscience. His instincts as mission commander fought his sense of loyalty to his old mentor. Cyril's pleading for trust echoed uneasily in the young man's head.

Davidson anxiously waited for his young protégé's reply. The rest of the 18 Scorpii team anxiously waited too; Michael sensed the mounting apprehension behind him. No doubt, they wanted him to refuse the order. After quite a long pause, he turned to David Tashjian. "David, go fire up main propulsion."

Though Cyril and the mission directors sighed, the whole *Endurance* crew went slack-jawed.

"We came out of suspension only a couple days ago," Kern protested. "We haven't had a chance to train."

"And the Slipstream generators need time to come to full power before we can jump," Tashjian added. "We'll be sitting ducks if we launch now."

"I'll make sure our ships hold the armada at bay so you can get away," Davidson interjected.

"Michael, do you really think we can leave so *abruptly*?" Kara pleaded. "We should retreat and come back when it's safe—just as you suggested."

The rest of the team, especially the Coverts, nodded in unanimous agreement.

"You're in danger if you come back here," Cyril held his ground. "Ben's assassination and the arrival of that armada prove the Europans will do anything to stop you."

Michael, pondering those words briefly, turned to the team. "David, go oversee the engine power-up. Kara, if you are all set on Medical, go help him." Though tempted to shrink under his team's stunned— and very justified—reactions, he had his orders. So he turned to Phil Marcotte. "Phil, bring up Navigation. Start programming coordinates for the jump into the Slip." Then he turned to Emir Kern. "Kern, place your men in the gunneries and coordinate a defense so we can escape."

However, everyone just stood there in defiance.

"Go!"

Reluctantly, the Coverts, David Tashjian, Phil Marcotte, and Kara set off toward the *Endurance*, leaving Michael, Tom, and Kate standing there with Cyril.

"I know we're all set on Stores and Systems," Michael said, turning toward Kate and Tom. "So fill in during the escape where you think you can be of help." He gestured toward the ship. "Let's go." Immediately, he turned toward the *Endurance* to leave. Tom and Kate followed suit—

"Mike," Davidson grabbed his shoulder to stop him, causing Tom and Kate to stop too. "Don't turn the ship around. If you can't Slip, then outrun the armada to the nearest friendly base. Once you activate the Slipstream, don't disengage; don't maroon yourself needlessly."

Michael nodded soberly.

"Take care," Davidson said, throwing his arms around Michael and Kate. He gave a regarding glance toward Tom, who stood behind the couple. "Tell the rest I said goodbye."

They exchanged embraces and parting sorrows, though quickly because of the urgency. Finally, the trio headed toward the *Endurance*.

"Go with God!" Davidson called out as the three explorers disappeared into the ship. "My prayers are with you."

CHAPTER THIRTEEN

Early One Morning

The 18 Scorpii team had no time to lose: *Endurance* needed to get underway immediately.

Phil Marcotte and Curran Zeidler staffed *Endurance*'s bridge. Marcotte manned the main navigation console, though he intermittently fiddled with the Slipstream trajectory controller next to him. Curran Zeidler, acting on Kern's instructions, positioned himself at Tactical. Neither man paid notice to the bridge's consoles automatically coming to life.

When Michael, Kate, and Tom rushed onto to the bridge toward their stations, Michael immediately noticed Marcotte straddling both consoles.

"Phil," he called, pulling up behind his command chair, "Man the Slipstream controller instead: We'll need you dedicated to updating the trajectory coordinates as the armada forces us to change course." Then he turned to Andrews. "Tom, can you to steer the ship?"

"My pleasure," Tom quipped, replacing Marcotte at the navigation console. "I always liked piloting anyway."

Michael activated the intercom. "David and Kara, what's the status on propulsion?"

"Fusion reactors are still initializing," came Tashjian's voice over the speakers. "They'll need ten more minutes until we can fire the engines. It's too early to know about the Slipstream drives, but they're still within normal operating parameters."

"Notify us immediately when the fusion engines are fully online," Michael replied. "Kara, take over mooring controls. As soon as we're under power, release the moorings. Don't delay one second."

"Got it!" Kara's voice crackled over the speakers.

With launch preparations progressing as well as could be expected, Michael decided to sit down. He came around his command chair to take his place—

His self-confidence withered within him at the sight of the chair. He paused nervously, quickly surveying the bridge to see if anyone had noticed his hesitation. Fortunately, everyone remained preoccupied with his or her work.

Memories of the *Comanche* destruction suddenly flooded his mind. Seeing the faces of her long-gone crew, the young man fell victim to the images. Nothing during the launch prep had hinted at the deep-seated fears accosting him. Nevertheless, Michael couldn't bring himself to sit down in the chair.

He didn't know what to do.

Michael remained transfixed by the chair and the haunting memories it conjured up. Tom, Kate, Phil Marcotte, and Curran Zeidler kept working unaware. However, one of them would eventually notice his reluctance. The economies of leadership prohibited such hesitation, especially at such critical moments.

"Commander, my men are all ready on the gunneries," Kern's voice came over the loudspeaker.

For the first time since arriving at Mid-Earth Station, Michael was happy to hear the Covert's voice. "Good, but let's hope we won't need your services."

"Agreed," Kern replied before the speaker went silent.

When Michael glanced back up, he noticed Kate watching him from her station. Though she didn't say anything, the young man recognized her concerned gaze. He realized his anxious posture betrayed his reluctance to sit down. Kate was catching on to his current crisis, and the others would too. So taking a deep breath, Michael forced himself to sit down in his chair.

Nevertheless, the strong emotions lingered.

Several minutes later, Cyril Davidson's voice came over the intercom. "*Endurance* crew, you need to get out of here!"

The bridge trembled from Europan artillery blasts hitting the station far above. Everyone paused at the foreboding rumbling, looking up and around while trading uneasy glances. Their expressions were telling: The Europans were systematically bombarding the station from above—drilling a hole into the station to get to them. Soon, the deadly artillery blasts would reach the 18 Scorpii complex.

More motivated than ever, the small crew frantically worked their escape. Detonations soon rolled in like ominous thunder. Tremors increased in intensity each passing minute, shaking *Endurance* violently. Michael, watching dust-like debris begin to fall around his ship, surveyed the bridge: The tremors were growing in intensity faster than his crew was executing the launch.

"Cyril's right," Michael exclaimed, having also opened a channel to Tashjian and Ricci in Engineering. "We have to leave *now*."

"Fusion reactors were cold just a short time ago, Mike," Tashjian's voice warned over the speaker. "If you fire the engines before the reactors finish the start-up sequence, you'll have unpredictable results. Just give me a few more minutes."

"The dry dock is coming apart," Michael warned. "Kara, release the moorings *now*."

A moment passed where nothing changed. The crew looked at him uneasily, while the view screen filled with raining debris. After much too long of a wait for the anxious commander, the mooring indicators turned green.

Michael looked over at Andrews sitting behind the helm. "Tom, get us out of here."

Taking a deep, uneasy breath, Tom powered up the engines. *Endurance* trembled erratically as the fledgling-like ship strained to lift itself off its moorings. Europan artillery blasts from above tore the dry dock bay apart as it did so. The vessel wobbled something fierce while lifting itself into the air. The crew—holding on for dear life—watched Tom struggle to keep her steady. With much effort, the ship came to hover tenuously above the deck of the dry dock.

"David," Michael called into his communicator. "Keep on those engines."

No response followed.

Endurance teetered dangerously out and away from the gantry and support structures, pitching while clumsily rotating its three-hundred-meter-long hull ninety degrees toward the launch channel. Barely accomplishing the turn, the ship labored toward the narrow launch channel.

Michael oddly relished the unsteady rhythm surging through the ship from its engines, finding the sensation a welcome change to the tremors from the deadly artillery blasts. However, he also longed for the pulsating rhythm to turn steady, a sign that the engines had fully initialized, thus making the ship's flight controllable.

Debris continued falling throughout the dry dock, the damage intensifying each moment. Michael watched it rain down on the ship's navigational shields from his tactical display. The miniscule pieces disintegrated upon impact with the field, while the larger debris repelled away from the hull. Fortunately, the debris so far was simply too small to be a threat, for the navigational shielding wouldn't protect the ship from anything sizeable—at least at power levels allowable within the confines of the space station.

"Tom, don't be bashful," Michael pleaded. "Floor it!"

Andrews reluctantly complied, pushing the ship as much as was tolerable for such narrow confines. However, the vessel labored to gain any measurable speed.

A powerful concussion washed through the ship! The dry dock bay rocked fiercely; deadly artillery rounds had exploded several levels above the bay. Michael winced as the tremors surged through him. Though not having hit the 18 Scorpii launch complex directly, the blasts nevertheless compromised its integrity. The upper level supports above the dry dock began buckling.

The bay was collapsing.

Michael looked over to Tom, who struggled to keep *Endurance* on course as it neared the narrow launch channel.

"Why don't they deactivate the gravitational fields?" Kate pleaded as more debris rained down around the ship.

"They can't," Michael replied. "The station uses a single field generator for this entire region. Shutting it off would affect the habitat areas—probably our defensive too."

Just as the nose of *Endurance* passed into the launch channel, the whole dry dock bay shook violently once more! The tactical computer to Michael's right beeped frantically at him! The explosion breached the dry dock complex, compromising the overhead utility armature suspended just above the launch channel entrance.

The massive metal armature, boasting an array of cranes and sizeable machines, teetered precariously over the *Endurance* as the ship passed underneath it. Each shudder from artillery strikes above pulled on the armature's overhead supports. Should the armature fall right then, the enormous piece of debris would crush much of the ship—maybe even rip *Endurance* in two, just as had happened to *Comanche*.

Michael—having no time to bark out an order—shot a frantic look to Tom, whose face had waxed over in horror. Andrews anxiously pushed forward on the accelerator controls.

The vessel feebly accelerated—not fast enough! The damaged armature swayed precariously while *Endurance* passed underneath it. Finally, the armature could no longer hold. It tore away from its supports, falling toward the vessel's propulsion system; the steady rhythm of fusion engines coming to speed suddenly surged through the deck! *Endurance* leapt forward into the channel with renewed vigor, barely clearing the falling debris.

Inside the 18 Scorpii launch control room overlooking the disintegrating dry dock bay, Cyril Davidson and the launch controllers watched *Endurance* barely escape certain destruction from the falling mass. The entire room, which sat within the bay, shuddered when the massive debris struck the deck far in the distance. Debris rained down in increasing frequency and mass, causing the room to quake violently. The small group traded anxious looks.

The entire bay was crumbling—threatening the control room too.

"We're done," Cyril exclaimed, herding his team toward the exits. "Let's get out of here before we're buried under the collapse!"

With its fusion reactors fully engaged and the former danger well behind, *Endurance* sped dangerously fast down the narrow launch channel. Reaching open space would take another minute.

"Ready to bring up navigation and defensive shields to full power," Zeidler announced, receiving an approving look from Michael. "We're clear for launch."

"Mid-Earth's rotation puts us one hundred and eighty degrees in the wrong direction for the Slip," Marcotte noted from his Slipstream controller console. "We'll have to double back across the station."

"We can use this to our advantage," Michael nodded, studying his tactical monitor. Then he turned to Andrews. "Tom, the Europans erred by concentrating their attack from above. Once we clear the channel, dive below the station and run along her belly. We'll use the station as a barrier. We may also escape detection until we're out in the open. Then he turned to Kate. "Communicate the plan to our ships. Have them set up a blockade on the other side."

Endurance rocketed out of the launch channel as if a bird of prey taking flight. Earth hung majestically in space before them on the view screen—a sanctuary far removed from the chaos engulfing Mid-Earth Station.

The vessel rolled starboard while diving in an arcing pattern to reverse course, causing the beautiful planet to roll and pan away in opposition until once again gone. Having caught a brief glimpse of the elusive but magnificent sphere—*home*—Michael and Kate shared a brief but remorseful gaze.

Quickly completing the maneuver, *Endurance* raced along the underbelly of Mid-Earth Station, picking up considerable speed. Michael, feeling inertia pushing him hard against his chair, relished the adrenaline surge over the increasing speed of his charge. *Endurance* was no slouch! The young commander reckoned it could outrun almost anything, and he could use all the speed the ship could muster.

The vessel soon cleared the protective shadow of the station, heading up and out into open space—

Tom knee-jerked the navigation controls in panic! Proximity alarms wailed! An Europan destroyer, hidden by Mid-Earth Station's scanning signature, suddenly filled the entire view screen! The formidable vessel, traveling in the opposite direction toward the station, lay directly in the path of the *Endurance*! Tom's abrupt course change turned *Endurance* away from the mammoth—but the lumbering destroyer veered in the same direction too! *Endurance* and the destroyer were still traveling on a collision course!

As the massive destroyer grew larger in the view screen, Michael gripped the armrests on his chair; shear horror covered his face. Everything was happening all over again—just like on the *Comanche*!

Michael didn't need to bark an order. Tom wrestled the steering controls to change course once again. The nimble ship acted as if by sheer instinct, darting starboard while ascending steeply—but the clumsy destroyer once again turned in the same direction! *Endurance* was coming underneath the destroyer's bow as it turned, and the two ships were arcing right into each other.

The crew morbidly beheld the ever-increasing close-up view of the destroyer. Tom wrenched the navigation controls back madly, and the ship began skimming the destroyer's hull. Every docking port, communications antennae, gunnery tower, and a host of other surface details on the destroyer's hull came up incredibly large on the view screen—with each successive feature larger than the previous as the two ships closed in on each other!

Finally, *Endurance* cleared the stern of the formidable obstacle. The view screen once again showed nothing but star field.

Taking *Endurance* through several graceful acrobatics to return to its original trajectory, Tom sighed in relief. Kate, Phil Marcotte, and Curran Zeidler did too—

But Michael looked at him desperately! "*Change course!*"

Tom had erred! With the surprise encounter over, Tactical showed the destroyer's guns training on the *Endurance*. The destroyer didn't disappoint. Immediately, deadly artillery rounds streamed by as the destroyer turned to intercept. *Endurance* rocked under the vicious artillery, and Michael grabbed hold of his chair to steady himself.

Tom atoned for his mistake by rapidly changing course, thus eluding weapons fire as *Endurance* sped away from the destroyer.

"We got lucky," Zeidler exclaimed. "No damage to report."

"I won't make that mistake again," Tom looked around the bridge sheepishly. He shot an affable gaze at Phil Marcotte, who would struggle that much more to adjust the Slipstream coordinates. "Sorry."

Marcotte just nodded and kept working.

Looking into his tactical display, Michael watched the Allied battle cruisers approaching from behind. *Endurance* sped along with abandon out of the main combat zone, so the friendly cruisers turned and engaged the Europan destroyer. The much smaller cruisers would continue to engage, putting themselves in the line of fire. Just as *Comanche* valiantly protected the presidential transport so many years before, the cruisers would protect *Endurance* to the end.

Though breathing a sigh of relief, Michael knew the Axis armada would not give up so easily. Surely enough, swarms of small, red dots appeared on his tactical display, racing toward the *Endurance*.

"FW-190s!" Curran Zeidler called out, heralding the arrival of the Europan one-man fighters. "Fifty or so! About seventy-five of our Hellcats are in pursuit."

"David," Michael pleaded into his communicator to Engineering. "We have two squadrons of FW-190s on our tail. We need to jump as soon as Phil locks in the coordinates. You ready?"

"No," Tashjian's voice came over the loudspeaker. "The Slipstream generators are fully active, but it will take twelve more minutes to build up enough energy to jump."

"By that time, they'll inflict enough damage to keep us from jumping at all."

"Sorry, Mike," Tashjian's voice once more filled the bridge. "You're just going to have to hold them off."

"Okay," Michael surrendered, looking around the bridge. "Let us know the second we can jump." He turned to his navigator. "Phil, will you have the coordinates locked in by then?"

Marcotte, looking somewhat frazzled by Tom's erratic navigating, rather laughed. "Sure ... but let's try to minimize course changes."

Tom nodded in an unconvincing manner.

Michael looked at his tactical once more. FW-190 fighters were the only Axis ships capable of keeping pace with the *Endurance*. They would try cutting off *Endurance's* escape path, slowing it down so that the warships could intercept. He couldn't allow that. Though the FW-190s were easy targets for the pursuing Allied Hellcats, they could inflict serious damage to the ship.

"Kern," Michael called into the intercom, watching the horde of fighters approaching, "We'll need your help keeping the FW-190s away from the Slip nodes on the hull."

"No problem," Kern replied through the loud speaker.

"Tom," Michael looked over at his friend, "Don't let them cut us off or slow us down."

Andrews nodded.

A minute later, FW-190s engulfed the *Endurance*. A hailstorm of artillery rounds lit up the immediate area around the hull. FW-190s strafed the ship, each one closely pursued by at least one Allied Hellcat. The Hellcats fired mercilessly at the FW-190s, joining *Endurance's* guns in keeping the FW-190s at bay. However, the immediate area around the zigzagging ship became one confusing mess.

Michael watched his shields taking a terrible pounding.

Not too long into the assault, ten FW-190s suddenly broke away from the main conflict. They sped well ahead of the *Endurance*, veered back around in sequence, and charged the *Endurance's* fore section in a precarious game of chicken. Tom struggled to dodge the charging fighters and their deadly artillery rounds.

Michael looked over at Phil Marcotte, who labored at programming the Slipstream jump coordinates into the controller. "You okay?"

"Under the circumstances, yes," Marcotte replied, still working feverishly.

However, Marcotte's expression didn't ease Michael's concern.

A thousand near misses with fighters and artillery filled the ship's view screen. *Endurance* raced through space, gaining more speed and swimming in the mayhem accosting it. Tactical showed the slow but steady demise of the Europan FW-190s, whose risky maneuvers to stop the ship made them vulnerable to the Hellcats' guns.

However, Michael couldn't relax: *Endurance's* shields continued weakening under the assault, especially in the forward sections.

Michael anxiously looked at the tactical clock, noting that twelve minutes had passed; he had still received no word from his propulsion engineer. So he activated his communicator. "*David, where's—*"

"We're *Go* for the jump!" Tashjian's voice interjected, much to Michael's relief.

"Okay, Phil, it's all yours."

Marcotte's expression didn't encourage. "I need thirty seconds. Tom, keep us steady or I can't make the jump."

"I don't think we have thirty seconds."

Tom was right. Tremors on the *Endurance* grew more severe, and the shields were weakening. Soon, the blasts would start tearing into the ship's hull. Worse, more FW-190s joined in on the tactic of charging *Endurance's* fore section.

Andrews' patience lasted only fifteen seconds into the wait. A single FW-190 far ahead of *Endurance* turned and raced back toward the ship on a collision course. Energy blasts spilled from its guns, buffeting *Endurance's* shields.

"*Where are the Hellcats?*" Michael shouted, watching the FW-190 charge his ship. He activated his communicator once more. "Kern, destroy that fighter!"

"Will do," came the lieutenant's voice over the loudspeaker.

The rogue fighter raced in on an unchallenged path. Though two Hellcats were flying in from the sides to intercept, they wouldn't neutralize it in time.

"We're going to hit!" Tom pleaded to Marcotte.

However, Marcotte remained cool and unwavering—perhaps just preoccupied—as he programmed in the last trajectory changes. "Don't move."

The fighter grew increasingly larger in the view screen and missile-locked on the *Endurance's* nose. Only seconds remained until the tiny craft would collide with the ship.

"Go!" Marcotte yelled.

Simultaneously, *Endurance's* artillery pierced the rogue fighter, causing the FW-190 to erupt into a ball of flames. Yet the debris from the craft still lay in the path of the speeding *Endurance*.

Somewhere deep in the heart of the vessel, David Tashjian tripped the Slipstream engines.

From the vantage point of the Allied cruisers far behind the *Endurance*, the conflict looked as if a swarm of killer bees chasing their prey. Smoke engulfed the exploration vessel, and debris from destroyed fighters littered its wake. Laser blasts flashed in the nebula of smoke like lightning strikes. However, with one blinding flash of light, *Endurance* disappeared as if it had never existed.

"*What was that?*" Kate gasped while jumping up from her chair.

The rest of the bridge crew came to their feet too. Everyone looked around warily, following the mysterious echo of metal-striking-metal moving through the ship. Though the sound quickly faded away, the eerie sensation it left behind didn't.

The bridge went silent.

The moment *Endurance* had jumped into the Slip, a violent shudder reverberated through the vessel. The strange sound came from the fore section—the same direction as the oncoming fighter debris.

"Maybe it was just the normal Slipstream transition," Marcotte ventured cautiously. "They *did* tell us to expect some bumps."

"No," Curran Zeidler countered. "That felt more like chunks of metal hitting the ship. We must have struck the fighter debris."

"And that could mean damage," Michael added. "Zeidler, see if you can get a tactical damage readout."

Zeidler complied, turning his complete attention toward the console in front of him. Kara and David soon arrived, having also heard the sound. One by one, Kern and the rest of the Coverts arrived too, boasting to each other on their kills as they came onto the bridge.

Zeidler finally looked up and shook his head. "I can't be sure. There's no internal damage, but I have no way of knowing if anything has compromised the outer hull. The Slipstream field makes us blind. I can't even tell if the Slipstream nodes have been damaged."

"David, can you find anything wrong with the Slipstream?" Michael asked.

Tashjian took up position over one of the controller stations. After working the controls and studying the display, he shook his head. "No, all indicators show the field stable and within normal operating parameters. We're traveling two times the speed of light, just as expected." He shook his head again while looking around at his crewmates. "But that sound couldn't be good. We have to find out what it was before proceeding."

"We keep going," Michael exclaimed, watching their concerned expressions reflecting back at him. "That's Davidson's order."

"But Cyril didn't anticipate this latest problem," David pleaded. "If something damaged the Slipstream nodes, we could be in trouble: We might fall out of the Slip five light-years later and become stranded; we might be traveling wildly off course. Who knows what other scenarios are possible? Shouldn't we go a day or two out, disengage, and inspect?"

"Those things could happen anyway," Michael mused. Then he sighed. "We don't know anything's wrong. In fact, the field controllers aren't registering any problems. With only a creepy feeling as evidence, we keep going."

"He's right," Kern added—much to Michael's surprise. "It's too dangerous going back in any scenario."

The whole bridge went silent while everyone traded uneasy stares. Emboldened by Kern's unexpected support, Michael went deep in thought as he sat on the edge of one of the controller stations.

"We may as well just throw our launch schedule away," he eventually said, looking around. "Normally, we would enter cryogenic suspension in twelve hours, but that isn't going to work. Let's do a three-day shakedown of the entire ship." He looked over at Tashjian. "David, you have three days to find anything in the Slipstream requiring us to turn back. But if the ship checks out"—turning his gaze back to the rest of the crew—"We enter cryogenic stasis on day-four. Kern, your team needs to help on the shakedown."

"I disagree," Kern replied. "My men need to train for our part of the mission."

"Sorry, but once the mission is underway, training goes real-time."

"The Covert Ops part isn't underway," Emir Kern countered. "You should at least give us additional time to train before going into stasis."

Tom shook his head purposefully. "Stores and auxiliary fuel get saved for when they're needed."

"And with such an abrupt departure," Michael added, "We need your help on the shakedown. Let's get to 18 Scorpii first. We'll set aside extra time for training when we arrive."

Though Kern remained silent, he nevertheless shot back a disapproving gaze. His team traded irritated glances with him too.

Ignoring the Coverts' dissatisfaction, Michael looked down at the ship's chronometer. "It's three hundred hours. Let's start eighteen-hour shifts immediately. So … if there are no questions, let's go to work."

The crew began leaving one by one, less than eager to start their work. Tom, realizing he had no other recourse, stretched to shake off the night's fatigue. Right before he left, he turned to Michael. "Mike, this is an historic day: the launch of the first Earth States interstellar vessel. I'm glad we dressed for the occasion."

Michael glanced down at his attire before surveying the crew. He half-chucked at Tom's remark. The entire crew was still dressed in their nightclothes. He, in particular, still wore his boxer shorts.

Kate Gillen knelt in front of an open service panel in a utility corridor somewhere aboard the *Endurance*, which was speeding away from Terrae Solaris at twice the speed of light. Holding a scanning unit in one hand over the exposed navigational field regulator inside the wall, she worked a servo-wrench in the other in an attempt to calibrate the mechanism. Occasionally, the young woman would trade quips with Tom Andrews and Kara Ricci, who were working on equipment inside the many open service panels throughout the short corridor.

It was still the morning of the first day of the three-day shakedown.

Though many long hours of work lay ahead, Kate found herself in an unusually good mood. The panic of the ship's harrowing departure from Mid-Earth Station had passed, leaving behind all the cares and troubles that had plagued her since first hearing the name *18 Scorpii*. The ship, racing between the folds of space, acted as a bubble of sorts— as if nothing existed beyond the powerful Slipstream field enveloping the ship. Yes, the voyage was proceeding like just another exploration mission—at least for the moment.

But more than anything, her closely knit Centauri family surrounded her once again. Their presence—particularly Kara and Tom's—made her tasks enjoyable and her world complete. The corridor brimmed with familiar conversation and laughter; in a way, she was home again. The work was a fine change of pace too. Having left her demeaning clerical job far behind, she was finally fulfilling the destiny she had worked so hard to achieve.

"How's everything going?" a rather haggard Michael Gillen asked, appearing through the hatchway and interrupting the lively conversation.

"Maybe we should ask *you*," Kara replied, standing up and turning her attention to his unsettled expression.

"Coverts giving you a hard time?" Tom added.

"Yeah, I've been working with them for hours. Aside from not knowing what they're doing, they're that much more uncooperative. So I came down here for a break—to check on everyone else too."

"Everything's in order," Tom offered as he handed him a reader used to track their progress.

Michael studied the display, nodding occasionally in satisfaction. Abruptly, a quizzical look came over him, and he turned toward Kate. "Aren't you supposed to be inspecting Systems right now?"

"I came down here to help Tom and Kara," she paused from her work on the regulator. "I heard they were having problems, so I thought I'd lend them a hand."

"But what about Systems?"

"They're fine, Michael. Other than a couple more minor things needing checked, Systems inspection is done."

"That's pretty fast," he replied with an incredulous gaze. "You sure you followed the procedure?"

"To the letter—*and then some*," she said, the slightest irritation resonating in her voice. Turning back to the scanner in her hand and taking the servo-wrench once more to the regulator, Kate resumed her calibration work. As she performed the fine adjustments to the device, she could feel Michael watching her from where he stood.

"How's it going?" he asked, coming to kneel over her as if supervising her work. He appeared rather animated and more than ready to jump in and help.

"I'm almost done calibrating this regulator"—turning the wrench and watching the readings change on the scanner—"It was a little off-spec ... just a few more adjustments."

"*You know what you should do?*" Michael begged, his hands hovering eagerly near the wrench in her hand.

"*Yes, Michael; yes, I do.*"

However, he grabbed the wrench—and the scanner too. "These regulators are a little quirky."

"*I know,*" Kate implored as Michael pushed his way in and took over the calibration procedure. "You taught me ... remember?" Though she tried to seize the tools from him, her husband persisted. "*Michael.*"

"Just let me help you with this one adjustment," he offered to smooth over the tension—unsuccessfully. He gestured for her to look at the scanner. "Look at this vector right here. Now if you just..."

Shaking her head in frustration, Kate stopped listening to his words—a chiding really. Neither did she watch his possessed expression as he finished her work. She didn't look at him at all, for the young woman was too embarrassed. Upon noticing Kara and Tom trading awkward looks with one another, she blushed. Perhaps it would be a long voyage after all.

... *Michael Gillen suddenly found himself on the bridge of the* ESS Comanche, *sitting in his command chair and wearing his Class-B officers' uniform. He wasn't sure how he had gotten there.*

No matter, the bridge was in complete chaos, and his officers—Andrews, Sloane, Perez, Donne, Morelli, Combs, Herschel, and Pavia—all had the same horrified look on their faces. The vessel quaked under one artillery strike after another. Tactical showed the cruiser coming apart piece by piece, the hapless victim of the Jupiter-Class destroyer.

Comanche *was dying, and the President's transport was still in trouble!*

Instinctively, Michael barked out orders, orders that did no good. No, the ship was still coming apart, and the President's transport would be helpless to defend itself once Comanche *was gone. With no other recourse, he heard himself giving that fateful order.*

Time moved in slow motion. Comanche *and the Europan destroyer ran along side each other, sparring to the very end. The navigator veered the ship toward the destroyer, attempting to ram it. But as the destroyer veered away in response, the damaged Earth States cruiser began shooting past and ahead of the destroyer—losing its only chance to ram.*

A reactor breach warning blared over the confusing din.

Michael saw the navigator's telling expression looking back at him. Instinctively, the subordinate understood his wishes without him ever saying a word. Before Michael could rethink the order, Comanche *came to a dead stop in front of the speeding destroyer.*

Captain Michael Gillen looked at the faces of his crew shrouded in imminent death—because of the order he had given.

But they weren't the same faces! No, men like Morelli, Herschel, and Combs were gone. The faces staring back at him in horror were the Centauries: Phil, David, Tom, Kara—Kate! They wore 18 Scorpii mission uniforms. The bridge was not the Comanche's; *no, he was on the* Endurance.

And the destroyer was still on a collision course!

The bridge shuddered violently as the speeding destroyer bludgeoned Endurance's *mid-section, cutting through it as if the ship were made of paper. With a violent jolt, the structure around Michael ripped apart. Equipment flew through the air. A fireball erupting on the port bulkhead engulfed one of the Centauries.*

The bridge was coming apart violently …

—in the blink of an eye—

… Michael found himself trapped in the rubble once again, his side bleeding profusely. He looked around at the dead bodies of the Centauries—his family—scattered among the wreckage. Kate's lifeless, bloodied face stared accusingly at him from out of the rubble!

Michael sat straight up in bed in the dark, gasping for breath! A heavy sweat ran down his face! Panicking, the young man clutched the gaping wound at his side—nothing. His shirtless torso remained unharmed, save the bumpy scars from the injuries he had sustained so long ago. No, he was sitting up in bed in his darkened quarters aboard the *Endurance*. Everything was peaceful.

He had been dreaming.

From where she lay next to Michael, Kate awoke to his sudden movements. At first, the thick, disorienting fog of sleep kept her still. She watched him sit with his head in his hands, while she faded in and out of consciousness. However, upon realizing Michael wasn't lying back down—and that he was also acting rather oddly—the young woman quickly came to herself.

She remained silent and still through a long vigil, watching him nervously stare into the darkness. At first, she wondered why he was even awake. The first eighteen-hour shift had done in the entire crew, Michael included.

Nevertheless, her husband wasn't lying down and going back to sleep.

"Are you okay?" she whispered, putting a hand on his closest forearm. She felt him trembling ever so slightly.

He remained silent for a long time and kept staring ahead.

"Michael, what's wrong?"

Still nothing.

"Michael, please tell me what's wrong."

Finally, he blurted out while shaking his head, "I can't do this."

"Can't do what?"

"This mission…," he exclaimed in desperation. "*I can't do this mission….*" The shaken, young man went silent for another long moment, appearing as if he were trying to gather himself—rather unsuccessfully. "This mission's starting out just like *Comanche*—only worse. I think I made a terrible mistake."

The statement—his fear—hit her like a sledgehammer.

Katey labored to a sitting position, keeping close behind him and just to his left. Because he was leaning forward away from her with his head in his hands, she couldn't see his expression. She didn't want to either: Pondering the dangerous mission and Michael's uncharacteristic lack of confidence, she was too scared to look at him.

Katey kept vigil with him through the long silence, also keeping a reassuring hand on one of his shoulders. However, she brimmed with anxiousness, and she desperately wanted to help him. So she draped herself affectionately over his torso, nestled him in a warm embrace, and let another long moment pass in silence.

Though Michael remained unsettled, his trembling soon passed. Her embrace had appeared to soothe him, which emboldened her to continue.

So in a slow and deliberate fashion, Katey began gently caressing his torso; delicate kisses alighting on the nape of his neck followed. With each passing moment, the young woman's doting grew increasingly intentional and overtly amorous. Michael kept staring ahead and still, though he put one arm affectionately across her legs as if enjoying the attention. At least that was what she thought. After all, she still couldn't see his expression—

He suddenly pulled away from her, stepping out of bed and ruining the moment. The romantic music playing in Katey's thoughts abruptly stopped.

"Where are you going?" she asked self-consciously as he started to dress. Had Michael not been so fixated on whatever thoughts raced through his mind, he would have noticed her smarting from his rejection of her advances.

"I'm starting my shift early," he replied, pulling a shirt over his torso.

"You shouldn't. You look exhausted."

"I'll be fine."

Katey watched her husband dress, very much taken back by the possessed expression covering his face. Finally, she beckoned, "Why don't you stay here … *with me?*"

"I have a lot to do," he replied matter-of-factly, still completely oblivious to her advances. He opened the door, letting the dim light from the corridor wash into the small room.

"But it's the middle of the night."

"I can sleep in cryogenics."

Katey watched helplessly. Michael nodded at her and disappeared out into the corridor. The door to the room closed, and the young woman sat on the bed alone and in the dark. She stared in disbelief at the door for the longest time. Finally surrendering, she fell backward onto her pillow and stared up at the shadowy ceiling. Letting out a long sigh, she replied to the empty room, "But not with me."

CHAPTER FOURTEEN

En Route

Kara Ricci stood in front of the food processor units in the crew common area, finishing a big yawn. Leaning against the tall, built-in service table, the young woman stared vacantly into the food preparation unit making her breakfast. She wasn't in a hurry. After all, another grueling eighteen-hour shift awaited her.

She perked up a little when Kate Gillen dragged herself into the room. Immediately, Kara noticed the absence of Kate's normally glowing demeanor.

"Good morning," Kara greeted her, to which Kate barely nodded. "You're up early."

"Yeah," Kate sighed, laboring a grimace. She sidled up next to Kara and began preparing her breakfast. "I've been up for a while ... couldn't sleep."

"Not tired of space travel already, are you?" Kara quipped, flashing a comical smirk. When Kate rebuffed the humor, she returned to watching the food preparation unit. Eventually, she asked, "Where's Michael?"

"He's why I couldn't sleep," Kate grimaced again. However, upon noticing Kara's raised eyebrows and suggestive gaze shooting back at her, she added, "I *mean* … he got up early to work on the shakedown." She kept to herself for a moment, becoming pensive. Then, looking at Kara, she said, "Since our arrival at Mid-Earth Station, all he ever thinks about is the mission … and I mean *all*."

Kara nodded supportively.

"He hasn't slept much either."

"He has a lot on his mind," Kara offered, watching her fix a cup of coffee.

"True … but you know Michael."

Kara nodded her head again, and the two women went silent.

"I don't know," Kate finally shrugged while keeping her gaze on the coffee cup. "When he was younger, he was reckless … *now* … he's obsessive. It's the same old character flaw—as if he's regressing."

"Maybe it's not the same. I saw a lot of officers at the medivac base in the war. Losing men under your command is traumatic … Michael lost *hundreds*."

Kate pondered the thought for a long moment. "I know. I'm *trying* to understand … but he's not making it easy on me. Yesterday, he checked up on everything I did; second-guessed me the whole time— you *saw* what he did with the navigational field regulator. *He drove me crazy*." She returned her pensive gaze back to the coffee cup for the longest time, stirring the spoon ad nauseam.

Unable to bear the churning in Kate's eyes very long, Kara replied, "You and Michael are still newlyweds."

"*So?*"

"So you're still adjusting to one another. This mission is going to make that adjustment much more difficult … especially given what Michael is dealing with right now."

Kate pondered the statement while still gazing into her coffee. Her face turned rather bitter. "I never wanted any of this, Kara. I just wanted a normal life."

"I didn't see anyone pushing you on board this ship," Kara chided. "But you still have the opportunity to make the most of it. Do the right thing … *just be there for him*. Don't let him obsess over the mission;

don't let your dissatisfaction over the mission get in the way either. Given what happened on the *Comanche*, you're going to have to be the sensible one." She let the comment sink in and then smiled, "*Or …* talk him into turning the ship around and going home. I can use the rest."

Commotion erupted in the outer corridor, causing the two women to look. The Coverts barreled through the common area entrance, bringing the dull roar with them. They were certainly ripe from some sort of rigorous workout. Worse, they brimmed with macho bravado—over and above their normally brazen demeanor—causing Kara and Kate to trade uncomfortable stares with each other. As the soldiers pushed each other around sportingly, an utilibot passing through barely escaped an unintentional pummeling.

"Don't linger here too long," Kern shouted over the banter, following his men into common area. "We've got a lot of work to do on the shakedown."

A round of disapproving moans rose defiantly into the air.

"Can't you get us out of the shakedown?" Volk pleaded.

"Yeah," Armstrong huffed, swaggering his sizeable frame. "Are we Coverts or *techies?*"

"Pipe down," Kern warned but then turned as if speaking to the two women. "I guess for the time being, we're techies—thanks to our glorious *Commander Gillen.*"

Kate, still facing away from the Coverts, shot Kara a telling look, picked up her things, and quickly left.

Watching Kate walk out—and offended at the Covert leader's impertinence—Kara huffed. She spun around, folded her arms in front of her, and stared them down. "There are worse things than being *techies …* like marooning the ship halfway to 18 Scorpii. Keep *that* in mind when you're doing your job." Flashing them one last reproachful gaze, Kara turned back around and began fixing herself a cup of coffee.

Though she couldn't see them, the Coverts traded irreverent and gawking looks to brush off the chiding. However, Kara's unshrinking defiance had caught Emir Kern's attention.

"So get used to it, guys," he added sarcastically while sidling up beside Ricci. Turning and leaning back against the serving table, he watched her prepare the drink. He also ignored her obvious disdain for him being so close.

"This mission will force us to do things we've never done before." Then he half-laughed. "Maybe the Centauries will return the favor and help us out on special ops."

Pausing to let a quick round of jeers pass, Kern looked intentionally at Kara. "How 'bout you, Doc? You ready to pick up a gun? Ready to kill people?"

Kara looked him in the eye, clearly unimpressed at the man's humor. "I couldn't do that."

"You think killing people is easy for *us*?" he countered. Then he paused for effect. "Someone has to. Otherwise, the wrong people die."

"I'll leave that to you," she replied. Pointing to the medical insignia on her uniform, Kara added, "I'm on the *other side* of that equation."

"Sometimes you have no choice. Sometimes it's either you or the other guy. You telling me you'd let the other guy live?"

The young woman fell silent, wishing she had left with Kate. She wasn't sure why she *hadn't* left either. Worse, Kern fixed his unflinching gaze upon her, and she felt herself fidgeting about nervously. Despite her rebuffing, the Covert wasn't going away.

She hated that smug, overconfident grin. To her, Kern was less of a man and more of a stereotype: no different from the Europan armies who had kept her operating tables full throughout the war. So with her resentment of him swelling within her, she exclaimed, "I've learned just how precious life is. If I ever took a life, I know I couldn't live with myself." Then she turned steely-eyed. "How do *you* live with *yourself*?"

Flashing one last cold stare in his direction, the young woman picked up her coffee cup and left the common area.

Emir Kern remained leaning against the serving table, ignoring the jeers from his men. Intrigued by her fiery insult, he watched her until she disappeared from view.

Michael Gillen awoke from a sound sleep into a sitting position in bed. He looked around the darkened quarters. The chronometer indicated that the time was very early in the morning of the fourth day since leaving Mid-Earth Station, and Katey lay fast asleep beside him. The previous day, the young mission commander had declared the three-day shakedown of the *Endurance* complete. With all systems functioning properly, he gave the crew the morning off before entering cryogenic stasis.

However, he still had much to do.

Gingerly stepping out of bed—carefully watching his sleeping wife for signs of stirring—he quickly and quietly dressed himself in the darkness. Upon completing the task, he grabbed his reader sitting on the desk and turned toward the door.

"What are you doing?" Katey's unexpected voice jolted him from behind.

Quickly composing himself, he turned to see her propped up on one arm under the covers. Even in the dark, he could see her intent gaze fixed on him.

"I thought I'd get an early start on the day."

"*Oh really?* I thought everything was done."

He held up his reader almost apologetically. "I just need to double-check some things before we enter stasis—just to make sure. I'll be back soon."

"You never come back soon," she chided, swiveling herself into a half-sitting position on the bed. "What do you have to do?"

"Just some things."

"Like what? Maybe I'll help you. Do you have a list I could see?"

Suffering under her dubious expression, Michael cautiously and reluctantly activated the reader. The device projected an exhaustive list of tasks into the air before him. The entire darkened room glowed in the odd light of the display. To his surprise, checkmarks appeared beside each item on the list, accompanied by the time they were completed (all registering the middle of the night), comments about inspection results, and any other necessary information he would want to know.

"That's right," she exclaimed, taking in his stunned reaction awash in the display. Her eyes beamed with pride. "After you dragged yourself into bed late last night, I got up and completed all of them—I just knew you wouldn't rest until you did everything three times."

"I don't know what to say," he shook his head while studying the list. However, his face waxed over with the same obsession she had beheld the previous three days. "You know what? Let me just go check some of the bigger items myself. I'll come back real quick." Deactivating the device—the room darkening again—he turned toward the door to leave.

"*No, Michael,*" she warned, getting out of bed and grabbing his arm. In the very dim light, she caught him noticing the rather elegant nightgown adorning her form. Still, his preoccupation with leaving remained. "I'm not going to let you do this."

"I'll be right back," he assured while passing his hand over the sensor—yet the door didn't open. So he tried again—nothing. It wouldn't budge at all. That was when he turned and beheld Katey's relishing grin.

"What's wrong?" she taunted him. "Door won't open?"

"Just open the door please."

She just shook her head defiantly.

"Please open the door."

"No, Michael," Katey said, backing him against the door with her hand. "I gave up my last night so that we could be together today. Short of a fire, that door won't open for either of us until it's time for my cryogenics prep." She stepped back and folded her arms in front of her reprovingly. "Do you know this *whole ship* runs off the systems I maintain?" After staring him down, she added, "That's right ... the great Michael Gillen has to depend on *me*. How scary!"

Watching her stand there with such a reproachful gaze, Michael withered. His obsessive expression waxed to remorse, and his frame fell limply against the door. Letting his head fall, he said, "I'm sorry. I know I've been such a pain the last several days."

"Yes, you have. And I can't help but noticing that half the items on your checklist are things I worked on. Why's that?"

He looked up at her, his face betraying the same concern as the night of his dream. Then he shrugged, "... *I don't know.*"

"Don't you trust me?"

Michael fell silent under her gaze, his face only waxing more helpless.

Katey relented with a sigh. She put her arms around his neck and searched him with her eyes. "Michael, I'm really trying here." Her eyes pleaded with him through a long silence. "In six hours, I step into my cryogenics chamber. Let's not ruin our last day together, *okay?*"

Michael took in her reassuring expression, eventually nodding in surrender. After sharing a moment to reaffirm their newfound truce, he said, "That gown isn't exactly regulation."

"It's the same one I wore on our wedding night—the last occasion we didn't have much time."

"I thought it looked familiar."

"I've been waiting for you to wake up and notice—too bad I had to go to such extreme measures." She took his face in her hands and kissed him, draping herself over him intentionally as he leaned against the door. "So do you still want that door open?"

"What door?" he smiled, taking in her shimmering eyes for the longest time. Abruptly, he recoiled—and with such a quizzical look. "Can you control all the locks on the crew deck, just like you did with the door?"

"Michael, I control everything."

Cryogenics Lab One on the *ESS Endurance* was awash in steady but subdued activity, giving it a hospital-like feel. Temporary privacy barriers surrounded each of the twelve cryogenics chambers, which lay arranged in two groups of six in pinwheel fashion. Another group of cryogenic chambers, which were designated for Aurelian Galerius and company on the return voyage, sat lifeless off to the far side of the large room. Indiscernible conversations abounded from where Kara Ricci was preparing the Coverts—absent Emir Kern—for stasis.

Michael stood in the corner of the privacy barrier surrounding Kate's open cryogenics chamber, helping her prepare for the pending procedure. Scant traces of conversation from the Coverts leached over into the small area, though the couple ignored the bits and pieces they could hear. They chose instead to make the most of their short time together, before Kara arrived to prep Kate for stasis.

While Michael folded her discarded garments, Kate hopped up onto the table, lay down, and pulled the warming blanket tightly over her. Resting her head on the temporary pillow, she stared up warily at the sarcophagus-like shell suspended from the ceiling. Its robotic surgical arms, IV tubes, and sensors dangled menacingly toward her, reaching out as if relishing the start of the gruesome cryogenics procedure.

"I hate looking up at that thing," she exclaimed.

He didn't hear her. Still folding the garments, Michael quietly pondered coming to this point in the mission. His gut told him they should have never left the dry dock. However, his gut had no vote in the matter. No, the three-day shakedown had finished without one deficiency surfacing. Despite his better judgment, *Endurance* was on its way to 18 Scorpii.

He soberly pondered Kate's upcoming stasis—his too. The *Endurance* crew would spend twenty-three long years in stasis—something unprecedented in human history. Knowing the long-term effects on the human body remained purely conjecture, Michael wondered if he would ever see her alive again.

Regardless of the dreadful thoughts running through his head, he resolved to remain light-hearted and reassuring in Kate's presence.

Michael handed the folded clothes to an awaiting utilibot. The hovering machine carried the garments up and over the privacy barrier and disappeared from sight. The sounds emanating from it quickly faded away.

"How are you doing?" he smiled while sidling up to her.

"*I'm cold*," Kate smiled back, keeping wrapped in the blanket so that not even a bare shoulder was visible. Her gaze betrayed her trepidation. "It's going to get a lot colder too."

"At least Kara will go easy on you," he said, remembering his past calibration sessions. "She always treats my prep like payback."

"You probably deserve it."

The two shared a quaint laugh, though Katey's smile barely cracked through her anxiousness. So Michael brought himself close to her. "I'm sorry again for the way I acted."

"Don't keep apologizing," she replied. Flashing a coy smile at him, she added, "Besides, you more than made up for it this morning." A wink followed, and the young couple lost themselves in each other's reflection. Katey, in particular, radiated the most relishing glow. "I wish we could spend one last evening at the lake."

Savoring the sparkle in her eyes, he replied, "Just keep that thought in your mind. Before you know it, we'll be back there again. I promise."

Katey hesitated, a little bit of the energy fading from her eyes. "And then it's off to the next exploration mission."

Michael's silence betrayed his thoughts.

Abruptly, Kara's voice broke the air from the other side of the lab. "For the last time, Armstrong!" she shouted. "Stop it!"

Michael and Kate looked curiously at each other. They kept silent, choosing to eavesdrop on the heated conversation.

Jeers directed at Armstrong rose into the air from the other Coverts, the taunting spread across where their cryochambers lay. A rather heated discussion followed between Kara and Armstrong, though Michael and Kate couldn't discern most of what they said. However, Kara's impatience was more than apparent. A few moments later, her voice broke the air again.

"Look, Armstrong," she warned, "Cryogenics is complicated. If I can't concentrate, I may make a mistake." She paused and then added threateningly—suggestively too, "Which *part* of you do you not mind working when you wake up?"

Though the other Coverts made off-handed, rather crass comments, Armstrong fell silent. Michael and Kate continued eavesdropping, eventually hearing Kern's voice as he came into the lab. Kern chided his wayward team member, bringing an abrupt silence to that side of the room.

"I'm okay, Lieutenant Kern," Michael and Kate heard Kara assure him. "I'm running a little behind schedule right now. Please go to your chamber and get ready. After I finish his physical, I'll come over and do preliminaries on you—give me five minutes. Then I'll come back and put Armstrong under."

Upon hearing Kern comply and walk to his chamber, Michael leaned in closely to Kate.

"*I have to go do what we discussed,*" he whispered. "*Did you change the computers?*"

"*Yes,*" she assured him in the same tone. "*When the lights come on, change their setting to twenty-three percent, then seventy-two percent, then forty-six percent.*"

"I've got it. Don't let Kara start until I return."

Giving Kate a quick, reassuring kiss, Michael quietly stole away.

Michael Gillen, followed by Tom Andrews, quietly slipped into Emir Kern's quarters in the crew section of the *Endurance*. Immediately, the lights came up in response. Tom shut the door behind him. Radiating a bit of anxiousness at the possibility that Kern might unexpectedly show up, Michael recited the lighting sequence changes Kate had given him. The lights dimmed and brightened accordingly.

When the lights dimmed to forty-six percent illumination, several clicks broke the air; the security indicators on Kern's recessed drawers changed from red to green.

"Leave it to Kate," Michael quipped proudly.

"Yep, she's a whiz at Systems," Tom replied as Michael knelt and opened the large drawer just above the floor.

Michael pulled a faded green military-issue satchel from the drawer and looked at him. "Do you recognize this?"

"No."

"It's the same satchel Kern carried on board the *Comanche* three years ago. The Coverts abandoned all their equipment to escape the burning recon transport—but Kern held onto this as if it were a life preserver."

"If it were something suspicious, he wouldn't have let you see him bring it aboard."

"He didn't know I had noticed it three years ago."

Still kneeling, Michael meticulously opened the satchel and looked inside. Both of them gazed at the contents in stunned silence.

"*Incendiaries?*" Tom eventually said. After another long pause, he looked at Michael. "Why would he bring firebombs for this mission? They have no practical use."

"I don't know."

"And why would he keep incendiaries here and not with the rest of the munitions?"

"To keep us from knowing about them," Michael declared, studying the cache of charges. His face filled with an indignant strain, and he looked up at his friend soberly. "At least we know he's up to something. We just need to figure out what—and we need to do it carefully."

Twenty-nine-year-old Michael Gillen sat in front of Kate's sarcophagus-like cryogenics chamber. Her lifeless body, immersed in preservative gel deep inside the chamber, continued succumbing to the power of the dreadful process. Only the medical monitors above gave any clue as to her condition.

He hated watching his wife shut down like a defective computer. Nevertheless, he had promised to keep vigil over her until the very end. As the monitors tracked her slow descent into the death-like state, he longed for her transition to complete successfully. Then he could stop worrying—and submit himself to the same dangerous process.

"I'm back," Kara greeted him, appearing from the main entryway. She made her rounds to each of the other chambers, carefully assessing each person's status. Satisfied with their progress, Kara came over and inspected Kate's monitors. A quick scan of the data yielded another look of satisfaction. With nothing needing her immediate attention, she pulled up a chair and sat down close to him.

Though haggard from the long day, Kara relished the moment. Michael's vigil gave her a chance to sit down one on one with him—for the first time since long before the war. Not that the young woman minded Kate always being part of their conversations; not at all. It was just *different*.

"I can't wait until this day is over," Kara sighed and slumped back in her chair. "This cryogenics stuff really unravels me."

"Is that why I heard you yelling earlier?" Michael asked, recounting the commotion earlier between her and the Coverts.

Kara rolled her eyes in disbelief. "Oh, *that*…. Yeah, I kinda lost my cool."

"What happened?"

"Armstrong got fresh with me!" she exclaimed, though quickly relenting with a sigh. "I should have expected it: He did it during both calibration sessions—recovery too. What is it with those meatheads? It's like they never saw a female doctor before."

"I'm surprised he got to you. I always thought you were unflappable."

Kara pointed in the direction of the Coverts' chambers. "I had *a lot* on my plate. Tasker and Volk came in late, putting me behind schedule. I had three different preps to do at once. Marcotte and Tashjian had just reached *Stage Two*—you know how critical that is."

"Yeah, I do. Those Special Forces guys always pick the wrong time to get out of line." Then he smiled. "Don't let it bother you."

She sighed once again. "At least it's almost over. Tom just finished the transition, which didn't take him long—faster than anyone else. Kate's the only one left, and she's almost through *Stage Three*."

Kara noticed Michael watching Kate's monitors, his worried expression returning. Seeing his gaze lingering on the readouts, she decided to lighten the mood.

"Of course, she's not doing as well as earlier *this morning*," she began, quickly getting his attention. "When I examined her during the prep, I noticed her endorphin levels were unusually high." Then she smiled suggestively. "At least I know how you two spent your free time this morning." When Michael blushed, Kara laughed at his embarrassment and added, "I'm glad to see you two made up."

He nodded in the direction of Kate's chamber. "She made us make up."

"Well, Kate always was the sensible one."

Michael shook his head in disbelief. "I didn't even know we were fighting."

"Hence my comment about Kate being the sensible one," Kara smiled again. "Let's face it, Michael: Once you start obsessing over something, you retreat into your own little world. You can't do that with Kate."

He gazed at Kate's chamber sitting before him, his face waxing pensive. "Do you think she really wants to be here?"

"*Who does?* Do *you* really want to be here?"

"Good point," he shrugged haplessly. But then he rather grimaced. "Sometimes, she really surprises me—mostly when she's concerned about me. But other times … I feel like I have to watch everything she does. I just don't think her heart's in this mission."

"*Michael*," Kara chided. "Where in the world did you get the idea you need to babysit Kate?" When he fell silent under the recrimination, she put a reassuring hand to his shoulder. "I know you're worried about the mission, but you're wearing two hats now: Commander *and* husband.

Don't confuse those roles. Kate is a capable woman; you don't need to protect her anymore. At the same time, she needs to know that you're there for her too."

"I know," Michael surrendered. However, Kara's comments completely baffled him. "This mission has me *so* frazzled. We should all have our heads examined for agreeing to do it."

"Maybe *your* head," Kara laughed and began gently stroking his neck. "The rest of us are just following you." When he grimaced, she laughed again and added, "That alone certifies us as crazy."

Michael acknowledged with a self-deprecating nod. Then he folded his hands and stared down at the deck. "I should have refused this mission the moment Cyril asked me."

"Like *that* would ever happen," Kara rolled her eyes. Upon seeing him looking at her obtusely, she shook her head. "From the moment Cyril told me about the mission, I knew you'd accept—everyone did. This is your chance to clear your family name with the *Weightless*. That's why you're here; that's why the rest of us are here too … for *you*."

"I didn't know I held so much sway," he quipped, deflecting her comment.

"Don't let it go to your head or anything," she continued the banter. "I'm just here to make sure you don't do anything stupid."

Once more, he grimaced.

"Tom and Kate told me how obsessed you became with your tour of duty in the war," she admonished, though continuing the banter. Traces of seriousness began mixing with her comical demeanor. "You've wanted to clear your family name for a long time. So someone needs to keep you from doing something stupid—to protect the other Centauries."

"And that would be *you*?" he asked lightheartedly, noticing her increasing awkwardness.

Kara shrugged. "Hey, I kept you out of trouble over the years as much as anyone *could*. The last time I let you run off on your own, you almost died and spent three years in a POW camp." She shrugged her shoulders again, smiling self-consciously and averting her eyes. "Maybe it's not the whole Centauri team, Mike. Maybe I just need to protect you from *yourself*."

The two went silent.

Michael returned Kara's quirky and self-conscious gaze. Oddly, Kara had slipped and called him *Mike*—she hadn't addressed him that way since his sophomore year at the academy. Kara appeared to realize this, causing the moment to turn even more awkward. Then she realized she was still stroking his neck—he felt her hand recoil away. So to break the tension, he said, "Maybe you can help me out another way."

"What do you mean?"

"I think the Coverts are up to something."

The awkwardness drained from her face, and she sat up. "Like what?"

"I don't know. Tom and I found incendiaries hidden in Kern's quarters today. They were in a satchel Kern has carried since I first met him three years ago on the Europa reconnaissance mission."

"*Incendiaries?* Why would he need incendiaries for this mission?"

"He doesn't," Michael lamented. "And that's what's so troubling." The young man looked her straight in the eyes. "So I need you to help me find out what he's up to."

At the abrupt turn in the conversation, a rather incredulous if not dour grimace washed over her face. "How could I help you with Kern?"

"Cyril thinks Kern might respond to you better than me."

"But I don't even like the man."

"He didn't explain it; that's just what he said—and you know Cyril's instincts."

"Yeah," Kara folded her arms in front of her. "Kinda creepy."

"So will you help me?"

Kara rather shrugged and shook her head. "Sure ... *I guess.*"

Three succinct beeps from Kate's cryogenics monitor suddenly broke the air—the uncomfortable exchange too. Sighing in relief, Kara got up and examined the readouts.

"Kate's completely under," she declared. "Okay, Michael, now it's your turn." She stood up and went over to a storage unit. Pulling out a fresh white sheet, she threw it to him. "You know the drill. I'll meet you over at your chamber in a couple of minutes."

Kara Ricci's cryogenics monitor gave out three succinct beeps, indicating the successful completion of her suspension procedure.

The onboard medibot had carried out the procedure, for Kara obviously could not put herself under. However, Kara had chosen to perform her own physical and prep. She preferred suffering under her own bedside manner—poking and prodding herself—rather than leaving the prep to the unsympathetic machine.

The beeps heralded the end of a long day of suspension procedures. Just like the rest of the *Endurance* crew, Kara slept in the surreal, her lifeless body entombed deep within the chamber and immersed in preservative gel.

The end of her procedure did not go unnoticed. Not more than a few moments after the beeps sounded, the main computer shut down all lighting throughout the ship. Auxiliary systems followed the lighting; then life support, gravitational field generators, and utilibots shut down.

Within fifteen minutes, *Endurance* fell into as deep of a sleep as its crew.

Twelve cryogenics chambers sat in the darkness, carefully protecting their precious cargo. Only the indicator lights from the monitors broke the imposed night. The medical computers would patiently keep vigil, waiting for *Endurance*'s arrival at 18 Scorpii.

They would wait a long time.

Within one of the twelve chambers—and this chamber having no particular prominence over the others—Michael Gillen lay in the deepest of sleeps. His monitor showed no brain activity, none at all.

Neither did the device hint at the many thoughts troubling him since taking command: no thoughts of Katey and the danger he had compelled on her; no thoughts of the myriad of trifle problems complicating the mission; no thoughts of the *Comanche*, its long-gone crew, or the self-doubt those memories brought him.

There were no thoughts of Kern, who seemed to be an opponent rather than ally; no thoughts of Kern's real intentions for the mission—the ones he kept to himself.

There were no thoughts of the *Weightless*: how Jonathan Gillen had inadvertently made them the bane of Terrae Solaris, how they were on the verge of extinction; no memories of the Allied leaders staring him down, while Mos Thieren condemned the Gillen name.

There were no thoughts of the fates that were at stake: the Gillen name, the survival of the Allies—even Terrae Solaris itself.

No, for the moment he was at rest.

Or was he?

For when all that discernibly comprises a man is stripped away so he is no more than a cold lump of flesh, perhaps in the mind of his disembodied soul, the images haunting his thoughts come and go as mere shadows moving against the darkness.

Michael Gillen was in darkness, living among those shadows.

The dark, cold loneliness of space settled in on the intrepid vessel, a lifelessness and loneliness that would last twenty-three years. It sped along at more than twice the speed of light, barely existing as a blip between the folds of the distorted fabric of space. *Endurance* was between worlds, just as its crew existed between life and lifelessness. Precariously, both hung in the balance, as did the fate that awaited them forty-six light-years away.

THROUGH TIME AND SPACE

CHAPTER FIFTEEN

First Waking

"Michael?"

What is that? he thought.

"Michael?"

There it is again. It beckoned his attention. *Why? What does it mean? Just go away.*

"Michael?"

He realized the sound was a voice. Someone was calling him. *Yes! That's it!* He was Michael—Michael Gillen! And the voice was ... *Kara's.*

"Michael?" Kara softly called again.

Michael found himself lying in darkness for some reason. Exhaustion pressed in on him as if a millstone, while every nerve in his body cried out for relief. Nausea filled his gut, and a crushing headache pounded him. Worse, a thick cloud of confusion permeated his mind. He needed to sleep—actually, he wasn't sure what to do.

"Michael?" she called again.

The young man opened his eyes. Blinding light accosted him as if an axe splitting his head in two. Through blurry vision, he barely made out Kara's silhouette standing over him. She held his right hand in hers too, though he hadn't realized it until catching sight of his hand. The young man also saw a medibot hovering well behind her. However, he didn't know what it was.

Where am I? he thought with uncertainty washing over him.

"Don't talk," she warned. "You're much too weak."

Her instructions came as a relief. With his tongue swollen, his throat like sandpaper, and a dreadfully bitter taste in his mouth, he would have found talking too much like torture.

She continued, "If you can understand me, squeeze my hand." She smiled encouragingly when he obeyed. "Do you know who you are? Squeeze once for *no* and twice for *yes*."

What a silly question, he thought. Nevertheless, he squeezed twice. Surprisingly, the muscles in his hand cramped at the simple exercise.

"Good. Do you know *where* you are?"

No, he didn't, and that was what he found so unsettling. He didn't know why he was there either; he needed to think. However, the urge to sleep fought him all the way, while the pain and nausea fought both his urge to sleep and his desire to concentrate. The disorientation was maddening!

Michael looked around as best as he could, desperate to know the answer to her question. Hanging suspended from the ceiling above him was a large piece of equipment with surgical robotic arms, tubes, sensors, and the like—a complicated and menacing piece of machinery! He was lying on some sort of table; countless sensor wires stuck to his skin, while tubes ran in and out of his body. He wore nothing but the bedsheet that barely covered him. He was cold too.

Did I have surgery? he thought. Though unable to remember what or why, he resolved to give her an answer—and fast. So he squeezed her hand twice again.

"Good. It's going to take awhile for the cryogenic suspension effects to wear off."

Her comment brought him back to himself! Yes, he had gone into cryogenic suspension—must have survived it too! *Whew*! He was on the *Endurance*. His mission was to travel to 18 Scorpii to capture Aurelian Galerius. Moreover, in what seemed as quick as the blink of an eye, twenty-three years had passed.

His commanders' instincts quickly set in. Fighting against his formidable condition, he strained to sit up. However, Kara easily pinned him to the table by pushing two fingers against his chest. The young man sighed in frustration, realizing his athletic physique may as well have been made of jelly right then.

"Lie still," she gently ordered him. "There's no reason to get up. *Endurance* is safe. We came out of the Slipstream yesterday. Navigation confirms our arrival at 18 Scorpii. We're safely hidden in the sun's Kuiper Belt. Passive scans show nothing but dust and ice particles for millions of kilometers. The main computer restored life support to all levels, and all systems are functioning properly."

Michael relented and went limp. He smiled up at her, as if to say *good job!*

"I know you're in a lot of pain," Kara said, working his medical monitor. "So here's something to make you sleep while the effects wear off. See you in a little while…."

With the ship safe—and feeling the strong persuasion of powerful drugs entering his blood stream—the young man lacked the power or desire to resist. So Michael fell unconscious once again.

Michael Gillen stumbled into the cryogenics recovery room, laboring halfheartedly to an empty bed. He carried a strand of wires and tubes that protruded out from under his recovery gown. Having reached his destination, the groggy, disheveled man lowered himself onto the mattress, which elevated at the head. Sighing painfully in relief and tolerating the strange, unpleasant, cryogenic-induced smell emanating from his skin, he let his body sink deep into the padding.

After sounding off some feeble moans in protest, he hooked the wires and tubes into the adjacent medical monitor. The machine came to life—emitting several head-splitting beeps—and displayed his vital signs. The device also began pumping medicine and nutrients into his IVs. With nothing to do but wait for his strength to return, he closed his eyes to sleep once more.

Four hours had passed since his first encounter with Kara Ricci, something cryogenics physicians called *First Waking*. Since then, he had remained sedated, while the cryogenic processors continued bringing his body back to life. Fifteen minutes earlier, he had stirred. That was when Kara got him up, made him dress (though the recovery gown really didn't cover much), and made him begin the long process of recovery. Days would pass before he felt completely normal.

"If I look as bad as you, I must be pretty bad," he heard Tom Andrews weakly exclaim from the adjacent bed.

Michael had failed to notice his friend reclining there—failed to notice anything really. Therefore, he surveyed his surroundings. Emir Kern and Curran Zeidler reclined in their beds across the room. Everyone was unkempt and in a stupor. The other beds sat empty, indicating Kara was still resuscitating the others. A small medibot attended to the recovering patients, hovering about while performing many mundane tasks.

Just the sight of Kern brought to his mind the hidden incendiaries.

"Did you get the number of the train that hit me?" Michael strained, looking at Tom.

"I know what you mean," Tom replied with the same apathetic stare. "If my symptoms were from something I had done last night, I would *never* do that again."

The four men labored through the slow process of recovery. Their demeanors gradually changed over time, mostly due to the medicines surging into their veins from the IVs. Tom and Michael conversed infrequently, while Kern and Zeidler did the same. However, scant conversation traded between Centauri and Covert. Rather, each time Michael glanced over at Kern, he simply pondered the incendiaries locked away in the man's quarters.

Some time later, Kate stumbled into the room, disheveled and having that same apathetic stare.

"Kate," Michael called out weakly, soon followed by Tom. Though too weak to radiate a proper response, he was overjoyed to see her again.

Kate ignored him. Holding her recovery gown fast around herself while juggling the handful of wires and tubes, she staggered to a free bed, reclined, and hooked her wires and IVs into the monitor. Once situated, she flashed Michael a reassuring glance and closed her eyes.

In time, David Tashjian and Brent Tasker followed suit.

"Is everyone happy?" Kara Ricci quipped upon entering the room much later. The recovering crew greeted her with ambivalent stares. Sympathizing with their condition (for she had felt the same way the previous day), she ignored their reactions and proceeded to make her rounds.

"What's the status of the others?" Michael asked.

"I revived Volk and Marcotte about an hour ago," she stated, checking vital signs as she went along. "They passed their *First Waking* test. I put them back to sleep while the cryogenics wear off. They should be in here before you know it. I revived Gunn into *First Waking* ten minutes ago. He ignored my instructions not to talk. He gave me his name, rank, and serial number." Then she chuckled. "He just went back under. Armstrong is still in transition."

Kern's eyebrows went up. "Didn't you start reviving Armstrong before Volk?"

Kara, similarly concerned, nodded. "He's not responding to the initiation programs as well as the rest of you."

"Is that a problem?" Curran Zeidler inquired somewhat anxiously.

"Marcotte had the same problem," Kara replied, walking over to examine Tasker's monitor. "People don't always resuscitate the way the calibration sessions predict. Sometimes we have to adjust. I'll let you know."

"Please do, Doc," Kern said.

Ricci acknowledged with a nod, though abruptly turning her gaze toward Tasker. The man appeared more lethargic than before; his face was pale too. Coming to stand over him, she studied him intently. "How do you feel?"

"Worse than earlier."

"Your vital signs are healthy," she exclaimed, examining the monitor but watching him labor over his condition from the corner of her eye. "I think your medication doses are off slightly."

She worked the recovery settings on his monitor while instructing the medibot hovering behind her. Then she turned back to him. "You should be okay in a little bit … I'll check on you in fifteen."

Tom piped in, "With twenty-three years of cryogenic suspension, I'm surprised any of us feel as good as we do."

From where he lay half-reclined in his recovery bed, Michael watched Kara's face wax over oddly at the comment. Though she tried keeping inconspicuous and preoccupied with her work, her face betrayed some sort of concern. When he kept his gaze curiously fixed on her, Kara appeared to notice him watching her. Her face grew even more anxious. He looked around at Kate, Tom, and David. They had noticed too, for they traded uneasy glances with him.

Kara shrunk under the unwanted attention—turned away and tried to remain nonchalant too. However, nothing concealed her mounting awkwardness.

"Kara," Michael called to her from his bed, "What's wrong?"

"Nothing," the young woman tried to assure. Her gaze grew more self-conscious, even catching the attention of the Coverts.

"*Kara*," Tom persisted.

"Just worry about recovering," she exclaimed, forcing a rather feeble *I'm the doctor so listen to me* expression.

However, the recovering Centauries didn't relent.

"*Kara*," Michael shot back. "*What's going on?*"

Though Kara reflected a defiant gaze, everyone's insisting stares remained.

"*Fine*," she huffed. "We weren't in stasis twenty-three years. It was more like ten years."

The whole room fell silent. Everyone sat in his or her recovery bed, stunned and confused—Michael more than anyone! After all, Kara had given him the *all clear* five hours earlier. Were they really at 18 Scorpii? Was something else wrong?

As he had done earlier at his *First Waking*, the young mission commander strained to get up.

"Stay there!" Kara chided him from across the room. Begrudgingly, he relented. "That's why I didn't tell you at first. I'm sorry, Michael, but your recovery is top priority right now. We can deal with our problem later."

Everyone traded anxious looks.

"But you said the ship was okay."

"I didn't lie to you. It *is* okay: The ship is stable. We *are* at 18 Scorpii. I checked the navigation system five times, and I verified it visually to the star maps. But we were only in the Slipstream 3,747 days, a little over ten years—not twenty-three years."

"Our speed calculations *couldn't* have been off by two hundred percent," Tashjian declared, though not as confidently as the late Ben Morris might have. "maybe ten to twenty percent—*but never two hundred.*"

"The Slipstream controllers didn't record any anomalies," Kara added. "I checked—"

"Maybe someone programmed the drives incorrectly," Kern launched an obvious accusation at the inexperienced David Tashjian.

Kara spoke up again, "But the—"

Tom cut her off, immediately coming to Tashjian's defense. A rather heated debate—mostly a mud slinging contest—ignited between Centauries and Coverts. While Michael listened to the feeble banter (for they were all still weak from the cryogenic aftereffects), he saw the grave concern on Kara's face and realized the awful truth.

"We're missing the point!" he shouted, felling the room silent. "If we arrived in less than half the time, then we were traveling twice as fast." All eyes went wide as the recovering crew realized the *true* problem. "Fuel usage increases incrementally as you go faster." He looked at Kara with much concern. "Kara, how much fuel is left in our reserves?"

"That's what I was trying to tell everyone…. We only have enough fuel for one or two light-years at the most."

"*We're stranded?*" Kate gasped.

Michael's heart withered within him as Kara nodded soberly. Somehow, he had marooned his crew. Perhaps he missed something on the shakedown; perhaps something else had eluded his attention—something he should have caught. Surely, agreeing to launch so abruptly from Mid-Earth Station had been a grave mistake. He also regretted not personally double-checking his final list of inspections the morning prior to entering stasis; he had let himself become distracted.

His crew reacted no better. The debates and mudslinging erupted all over again. Amidst the subdued chaos, Kara pleaded for everyone to calm down. However, the recovering crew ignored her. Everyone, unsettled over the difficult circumstances—and suffering under the side effects of cryogenic suspension—fell victim to the discord Kern had sparked previously. Tashjian was the target of choice with the Coverts, while the Centauries came to his defense. The Centauries and Coverts lashed out at each other reproachfully—all but Emir Kern.

No, Kern remained surprisingly calm. When Michael noticed, the hidden incendiaries in the man's quarters once again came to mind. However, the observation was a fleeting thought, for the young commander had more immediate concerns to deal with.

Michael kept silent amid the accusations and arguments crossing the room, desperately searching for some sort of solution. Unfortunately, only one option—one very unappealing option—existed.

"Don't forget about the Europans!" he shouted against a pounding headache, felling the room silent again. "No doubt, they have more fuel than we could ever need. We'll steal it from them."

He received mostly skeptical gazes in return.

"David," Michael continued, trying to appear unfazed, "When you're recovered, find out what happened to the Slipstream drives. Kara can help you once she's done in Medical. As for the rest—"

The medical monitor on Kara's belt suddenly blared. Kara looked down at the device—her face waxed over in dread, and she tore out of the room.

Everyone traded anxious looks.

"*I'll bet it's Armstrong*," Kern finally exclaimed, abruptly pulling out all his wires and tubes from his monitor. Zeidler and Tasker, their faces waxing over in panic, immediately followed suit. The Coverts rushed out of the room like a shot, while Michael, Tom, Kate, and David succumbed to the same morbid curiosity.

Michael led Tom and David in the unimpressive footrace toward the door. However, he lost his lead upon catching sight of Kate out of the corner of his eye: She stood on unsteady legs beside her bed, even holding on to the mattress to keep herself balanced.

"You okay?" he asked, quickly coming over and taking her weight upon himself. He strained, for the young man was still rather weak too.

"This is really embarrassing," she lamented, holding fast to him. "I made it in here earlier all by myself."

"Maybe you should stay in bed."

"No," she shook her head. "I just came off my IVs too quickly; that's all. Help me go see what's happening. I'll come back and hook myself in later."

Keeping her firmly in his grasp, Michael practically carried her toward the frantic sounds. They caught up with the rest of the crew in the cryogenics lab—now awash in confusion and chaos. Kara stood over Mark Armstrong's cryogenics chamber, feverishly working the medical computers. A surgibot hovered on the other side of the chamber, following Kara's urgent instructions.

The young physician wore the most dreadful look on her face.

Though Armstrong remained deep within his cryogenics chamber, the medical monitors showed the telltale signs of his critical condition. Alarms blared, while the displays overflowed with data describing his dire condition. The man's vital signs and brain activity grew increasingly erratic. If Kara didn't stabilize him quickly, the man would die.

The Coverts, visibly distraught, looked on intently. They stood as close as they dared, while the Centauries stood behind them, nonetheless concerned.

"*What's wrong with him?*" Kern pleaded.

"It's his heart," Ricci replied from her place standing over Armstrong's chamber, not taking her eyes off the unenviable task before her. "His vitals are all over the place."

The nerve-racking commotion persisted, spurred on by alarm after alarm. Volk and Marcotte, still suffering under mild sedation at their suspension chamber tables, stirred at the ruckus. Though remaining on his table, Volk realized something was wrong with his comrade. So the man watched, crooking his neck to see while fading in and out of consciousness.

Kara grew increasingly desperate, for Armstrong's vitals continued their precipitous decline. Her face soon waxed over in frustration: The computers were reacting too slowly, making the complex machinery more of an obstacle than a help.

The man was dying!

She slammed her fist against the cryogenic processor's override trigger. The large apparatus hissed in protest, and the chamber's top shell shot up into its receptacle in the ceiling. Viscous preservative gel spilled out over the sides of the main chamber like thick syrup, for the cryogenic unit's pumps couldn't drain the substance away fast enough. Armstrong's sizeable body—covered in a thousand wires, tubes, and a ventilator mask matted within the gel—emerged from the mire.

Kara had no time to lose. She cut into Armstrong's broad chest with a powerful saw-like instrument. Blood spilled out, commingling eerily with the preservative gel that covered him. The assisting surgibot plunged a heavy, vice-like armature into the opening. Bones cracked as the machine spread wide the man's rib cage. Blood shot everywhere from a damaged artery, causing everyone to cringe at the gruesome sight.

Kara skillfully attended to the cryogenic-induced injury, desperately working to patch the artery. Blood erratically spurted into the air. Amid the mayhem, Kara noticed the telltale signs: the cryogenics had damaged the man's heart—probably beyond repair. Her breath went cold in her chest at the sight.

Regardless, she worked feverously to save the man.

Armstrong's vitals declined rapidly—far faster than she could intervene. Soon, his sinus rhythm flat-lined altogether.

The young doctor applied small defibrillator probes from the surgibot to the lifeless heart, forcefully jolting it. The surgibot took over her attempts to mend the damaged artery. Unfortunately, the damaged organ failed to respond to the defibrillator. She repeated the procedure, ignoring the desperate pleadings from the onlookers—her own mounting concerns too.

Despite her best efforts, nothing changed the grim patterns displaying on his monitors. Reluctantly, the young physician relented her fevered pace until stopping altogether. With a heavy sigh and a sympathetic gaze at the man, she threw down the instruments in defeat and waved off the surgibot.

Mark Armstrong was dead.

Desperate pleas from the shaken Coverts behind her accosted her ears. Kara paid them no mind right then. No, with her back to the unwanted audience, Kara looked down at the dead man for the longest time. The seasoned front-line physician, having seen death thousands of times, unexpectedly welled up. She fought the dreadful and unexpected emotion, pushing it down deep within herself.

Nevertheless, Kara was sick to her stomach over what had happened.

With one last glimpse at the man, Kara turned off the wailing alarms. The room went eerily quiet. "I'm sorry"—turning to the Coverts and fighting her own sense of dismay—"There's nothing more I can do."

The Coverts fell silent, their faces hapless and drawn in shock. Brent Tasker looked away and covered his face, while Curran Zeidler sat down and shook his head mournfully. Though Kern tried comforting his men, the soldiers remained inconsolable.

The Centauries stood behind them in silence.

"You've got to help him," Glen Volk called in raspy tones from where he lay on his chamber table.

Tasker turned around once more, pleading, "Yeah, don't stop!"

From where he stood behind the Coverts, Michael remained respectfully silent. The days he had mourned his family's deaths came to mind: first David's death and then his parents' deaths. He could see himself standing over their coffins, looking down helplessly at them—remembering the intense emotions swirling within. For the first time, he felt compassion for the soldiers.

He watched the Coverts labor over their loss, the intense side effects of cryogenic suspension only making their reactions worse. He quickly realized that they weren't in the correct state of mind to deal with such a tragedy. The situation could turn ugly fast.

"I'm sorry," Kara tried to console them—her own expression as heavy as theirs. "His heart was too damaged from the cryogenics."

The Coverts' twisted stares quickly turned to scorn.

"You didn't *want* to help him," Glenn Volk declared from where he lay.

"*What?*" Kara gasped.

"Everyone heard you threaten him at his prep," Tasker said.

"You *let* him die!" Volk heaped on.

"I was just keeping him in line," she pleaded with tears floating in her eyes. "I'd never do anything like—"

"*We don't believe you,*" Volk shot back. "*You let him die.*"

"Enough!" Kern warned, felling them silent. However, their expression remained filled with scorn. "Blame the medical support team back at Solaris—not the Doc. They were the ones who said we only needed two calibration sessions. Obviously, they were wrong." He turned to a visibly shaken Kara Ricci. "They don't mean it, Ma'am. None of us are quite ourselves right now." Then he turned to Zeidler. "I'll tell Gunn when he wakes up."

The room remained subdued in a dreadful silence. An emotionally crushed Kara Ricci—her scrubs and auburn hair saturated with blood and cryogenics gel—stood in the midst of the Coverts, accused. She trembled nervously while fighting back tears.

"Armstrong knew what he was getting into," Kern addressed his men. "He took the risk because of this mission's importance. Let's not let him down."

Kara Ricci sat alone at her desk in the medical lab, facing the wall and mindlessly leafing through medical procedures displaying on her reader. The task provided a much-needed diversion from Mark Armstrong's death. Still covered in cryogenics gel and dried blood, she couldn't escape the painful thoughts tormenting her. Neither did she understand why she felt so terrible.

Nevertheless, the incident had dealt her a crushing blow.

Upon hearing the lab door opening behind her, she perked up; hopefully, Michael had come to console her over the incident. She needed his counsel, for her emotions churned gruelingly within. Kate would do too.

"Ma'am?" she heard a cautious Emir Kern call, also hearing him take a single step into the room. "Are you okay?"

Her shoulders fell; she sighed and rolled her eyes too. Aside from Michael—perhaps Kate—the young woman preferred to be left alone. So she kept facing the wall, discreetly wiping her eyes with the tissue in her hand.

Kara didn't answer either. Instead, she stared at the holographic screen in front of her, though training her ears warily on the man's unwanted presence. Upon hearing several steps in her direction, she curtly replied, "*I'm fine.*" The footsteps stopped. "I'll go down to the recovery room in a minute to check on your men."

"No, Ma'am, that's not what I came to see you about—I'm sure they're okay…. I'm concerned about you."

"That's the second time you used the word *Ma'am*," she chided. "If you're looking for my mother, she's not here."

"I'm sorry, Dr. Ricci," he offered, "or *Kara*—if that's okay?" Though he waited for a reply, Kara didn't respond. "I'm sorry for what my men said to you. They aren't normally like that. I think it was the side effects of the cryogenic suspension."

"I'm sure that's what it was," she replied matter-of-factly, though discreetly wiping a few stray tears from her eyes.

"But are *you* okay?"

"I'm used to it."

Yet she knew her words rang hollow.

"It wasn't your fault."

"I appreciate your concern," Kara replied, fighting back the strong emotions welling up within her. "But it's not necessary." When Kern remained silent behind her—and realizing his attention was chipping away at her resolve to remain unruffled—she pleaded sharply, "*Please! I just want to be left alone.*"

Silence fell over the room once more. She sighed in relief upon eventually hearing his footsteps moving back toward the door—but then he paused.

"Okay, I'll leave you alone," he said sheepishly. "Just don't blame yourself."

Still facing the wall, Kara listened to the door open, a few more footsteps sound out, and then the door close.

She was alone again.

Michael Gillen, holding Kate's slender frame securely against him, helped his wife into the observatory lab on the *Endurance*.

The lights came up at the young couple's arrival. Like many scientific stations on the ship, the room lay cluttered with stacks of scientific equipment.

Both of them still wore unflattering recovery gowns and were rather unkempt. Kate, much weaker than her husband, kept the revealing garment fast around herself. However, Michael, using both hands to support his wife, had no choice but to let his gown hang loosely. Brisk air came at him from some rather vulnerable directions.

Fortunately, they were alone.

"We should have at least gotten dressed," Kate urged, lifting herself up the first step by tightening her grip on his shoulder.

"There's no time for that," he replied eagerly, pulling her along.

"I should still be recovering," she strained. "Kara would never let you take me out of the lab like this. We should probably check on her; she seemed really upset."

"She'll be fine. I'll get you back quickly too—I promise."

He patiently waited for his wife to navigate the few steps, keeping his arms securely around her to steady. Finally, the two made it onto the main floor of the lab.

"I feel like an old lady," she sighed, still holding fast to him. "I think the cryogenics scientists were wrong about us not aging during stasis. I feel more like thirty-nine than twenty-nine."

"Trust me," he said, giving her a rather suggestive once-over. "You don't look like an old lady."

Kate ignored the comment and concentrated on walking across the cold floor. She lamented not wearing slippers.

Michael led her over to a broad console table in the center of the room. He pushed aside the junk lying on top so she could sit down. With one last bit of help, the young woman came to sit on the edge of the table.

"That's cold even through the gown," she exclaimed with a shiver.

"You okay?" he asked while cautiously stepping back, more concerned about her balancing herself.

"Yeah. Can't we warm this ship up a little though?"

Satisfied that she wasn't going to tumble over, Michael stepped over to the outer bulkhead. "I turned the ship so we could get a real good view."

When he pressed an actuator near the corner, the blast shield doors slid away, revealing a large observation window displaying a magnificent star field. Michael, perking up noticeably, stepped back and sat down next to his wife—taking her hand in his too.

The two gazed at the spectacular sight.

"It's beautiful," Kate conceded. The comment, however, was more of a supporting gesture on behalf of her husband. She had accompanied him to the lab to be polite, for she felt completely miserable from the cryogenics. Her mind also remained awash in the many tragedies besetting the mission—and she wasn't sure how *he* had so easily put them out of mind.

Michael nodded, unable to find just the right words to describe the view. He had seen many star fields in his day. However, his excitement wasn't particularly due to the star field itself, but rather what lay within it.

The entire 18 Scorpii system hung suspended within the star field. In an effort to avoid Europan detection, *Endurance* orbited too far away to see the planets with the naked eye. The cold blackness of space filled the view, accented by the twinkling of tiny stars. However, a prominently larger yellow star lay in the center of the star field, its size about half the size of a pinky thumbnail at arms length: the 18 Scorpii sun.

As Michael gazed at the sight, problems with the mission simply faded into the ether.

"It's incredible," he finally said in awe.

Kate watched her husband linger over the magnificent view. A warm smile came to her face, and she relished the boyish glimmer forming in his eyes. She loved that familiar expression, for he always gazed upon the stars the same way he gazed upon her. She remembered the first time she had beheld that gaze: her first day at the academy when he hit on her during freshmen orientation. Despite rebuffing him, Kate knew right then she would someday marry him.

However, she hadn't seen that glimmer in his eyes since before he had left for the war. She had missed it too. Seeing the glimmer return, Kate realized just how much the war had affected him—just how much the mission pressed down upon him.

So she smiled once more and brought herself close to him. Michael responded by wrapping her in an affectionate embrace. With her head nestled under his chin, the young woman settled herself in for a perfect time of stargazing with her husband—just like the young couple had enjoyed back at the lake house so many light-years away, so many years before.

CHAPTER SIXTEEN

Working the Problem

Michael Gillen kept a determined pace down the empty corridor on the *Endurance*. Still early in the morning the day after Kara Ricci had revived the crew—fatefully losing Mark Armstrong—the young mission commander had much on his mind. However, concerns over capturing Aurelian Galerius weren't his focus then. Neither was how the Slipstream problems had marooned his crew far from home. No, he had a much more pressing problem to solve.

Coming to an intersecting corridor, he caught sight of Tom Andrews walking toward him from the other passage.

"Tom," Michael greeted the yawning Centauri as the two met. "I'm glad you're here. Can you come with me?"

"Sure. Where are we going?"

"To see Kern."

Tom chuckled while keeping pace. "Why do you want to ruin your day so early?"

"I don't have a choice," Michael replied, completely serious. He waited until an utilibot heading in the opposite direction passed. Then looking around to ensure they were alone, he said in hushed tones, "I've been thinking about the hidden incendiaries we found before going into stasis. Since we don't know what Kern is up to, we need to keep him off his game."

"How are you going to do that?"

"I think it's time to move up the schedule again."

Tom nodded, though looking at him quizzically.

They navigated the labyrinth of passages, going down several decks, until coming to the docking bay. Two transports, one much smaller than the other, sat facing away on the far side. A large, open area lay between the entrance and the ships, and the Coverts had gathered there. Immediately, the soldiers quit whatever activity had preoccupied them, and Emir Kern met Michael and Tom halfway.

"Good morning," Kern greeted them.

However, Michael remained business-like. "Kern, we need to move up the recon mission to the Europan settlement."

"Why?" Kern asked, standing up a little straighter.

"My team found the Europan settlement on Sco-II," Michael began. "—the second planet in the system. Pick two men and send them out in the *Quest*. Phil Marcotte can provide a detailed map of the system. Give them whatever else they'll need and send them off today."

Kern shook his head and put his hands on his hips. "*Today*? Sir, you promised we could train once we arrived at 18 Scorpii."

From where he stood behind Michael, Tom watched the exchange. The Coverts behind Kern traded astonished looks. Their faces also wore heavy with the strain of dealing with Mark Armstrong's death.

"Our low fuel reserves make us vulnerable," Michael replied. "Every minute we waste makes us that much more susceptible to detection. We have no choice but to accelerate the mission."

"But I can't train with half the team gone—not when I already lost one man."

Michael shook his head. "The recon data will help you too."

"Sir," Kern countered sharply, his defiance readily apparent, "We're in the middle of nowhere. No one's looking for us. We have no reason to accelerate the mission again—not like when we left Mid-Earth Station."

"That's your assumption. Sorry, but I've made my decision."

"Commander Gillen," Kern pleaded. "You've got to give us time to regroup…. We *lost* a man yesterday."

"I'll give you that time after the recon mission. Make sure your men launch today." He paused, watching Kern mull through his words. The Covert appeared at a loss, and his men well behind him looked at each other tellingly. So to put the issue to rest, Michael added, "Those are my orders."

Emir Kern watched Michael Gillen and Tom Andrews turn and head for the hatchway. With no more appeals left, he called out mockingly, "*Yes, Sir.*" Huffing one last time, he turned around and endured the many, dubious stares reflecting back at him from his team.

Kara Ricci sat alone in one of the work labs on the *Endurance*. A reader sat on the workstation before her, emanating a half-meter-square holographic screen above the tabletop. The projection stood out rather prominently, for she had set the lights in the small room to low.

The young woman leaned in toward the screen, intently watching the contents change while performing complex calculations on the data. Yet her back protested something fierce, and her straining eyes begged for sleep. Though the hour was late, sleep would only come after she completed her work.

Kara was okay with that. The intense analysis kept her mind off Mark Armstrong's death. Though two days had passed since the fateful incident, Kara remained deeply upset. The troubling images of watching the man die lingered in her thoughts

Just then, Emir Kern appeared at the work lab entrance. Holding a cup of coffee and boasting a rather smug grin, he casually leaned against the doorway. Kara immediately regretted not shutting and locking the door.

"Hi, Kara. You busy?"

"I'm helping David Tashjian with the Slipstream investigation," she replied, briefly glancing at him before returning her gaze to the screen.

"Probably a good thing. That guy needs all the help he can get."

Kara stopped her work and glanced curiously in his direction. The man wore a rather cynical expression. "You don't like David very much, do you?"

"We're stranded here because of his propulsion system problems," Kern rather scoffed—though not at her. "It's more about disliking incompetence."

"But we don't know he did anything wrong."

"Yet," Kern asserted. He fell silent for a long moment as she returned to her work. "How's it going?"

"Gruelingly slow."

After watching her for a few moments, Kern sauntered over and held out the cup of coffee to her. "I thought you might want this."

"Thanks, but you didn't need to do that," she replied, keeping focused on her work—very much intentionally.

"It's *just* the way you like it."

Kara gazed at him oddly—skeptically too. He appeared sincere, even insistent. So the young woman humored him by receiving the offering. She took a sip. A sigh and a savoring pause betrayed her surprised satisfaction. She even brought the cup close and breathed in the drink's steamy aroma. Her face waxing more affable, she looked up at him. "How did you know how I take my coffee?"

"I'm observant."

She nodded before taking another sip. "It's just what I needed."

"Too bad it only tasted like real coffee ten years ago."

Kara lifted up the coffee cup as if making a toast. "Welcome to the space program."

As the two smiled at each other, Kara felt herself relaxing. The unwanted distraction didn't seem so bad anymore. "To what do I owe this act of kindness, Mr. Kern?"

"*Mr. Kern?*" he protested comically, cracking his flint-like, calloused exterior. "If you're looking for my father, he's not here."

"Okay," Kara rather blushed, remembering her terse comments to him two days earlier, "To what do I owe this act of kindness, *Emir?*"

"That's better," the Covert smiled, unexpectedly pulling up a chair and sitting down. "I just thought you needed a cup of coffee."

Though trying to appear relaxed, he squirmed a bit in the chair—quite an odd sight for the normally overconfident man. "And I wanted to make sure you were okay. You were pretty shaken up the last time we talked."

"I'm okay."

Yet even she realized that her words rang hollow.

"I'm happy to hear it," he smiled, as if more of a polite gesture than an acknowledgement.

Nervously returning his gaze, she abruptly averted her eyes back to her work. She caught him watching her out of the corner of her eye as she continued her analysis. Oddly, he appeared as if mustering his courage.

Finally, he pulled something from his pocket and held it out to her. "I want you to have this."

Kara looked down at the elaborate medal lying in the palm of his hand. The ornament was far from some simple trinket, and she immediately recognized its rare value. Admiring the medal and imagining what the soldier had done to earn it, she looked up at him quizzically. "I don't understand."

"It's a peace offering—for the valiant efforts you made trying to save Mark Armstrong's life."

She recoiled. Her face waxed pensive too. "I can't take it."

"I'm not even sure what I did to receive it," he replied glibly. When Kara flashed him a skeptical look, he added, "Besides, I've got plenty of medals."

Yet she remained troubled.

Emir watched her reluctance. Finally realizing he had no other recourse, the man leaned in as close as politeness allowed. His face went serious and his voice lowered. "Kara, these medals are the only thing I own." He paused intentionally while taking in her withering gaze. "Mark Armstrong was very important to me—*he was family*. You need to know just how much I appreciate your efforts."

Kara labored over the sentiment, her eyes betraying her angst over Armstrong's death.

"Life is precious," she eventually said, her voice cracking tellingly. Then her eyes welled up. "Mark came into my lab perfectly healthy. He didn't deserve to die that way."

Emir gently placed his free hand over the hand she rested on the workstation. Ignoring her flustered reaction, he offered, "Sometimes, medals are awarded even when things didn't go the way we wanted them to. But it doesn't mean that the efforts weren't heroic."

With the gentlest touch, he turned her hand over. Keeping hold so that her hand lay cradled within his masculine fingers, Emir gingerly placed the medal in her open palm. With the same free hand, he closed her fingers over the medal, closing his own fingers over hers. "I want you to have this. And I'm not letting go until you agree."

Kara remained in her chair, her hand with the medal cradled protectively within Emir's assuring grasp. Fighting desperately to keep from falling to pieces in front of him, Kara gazed up at him, completely unsure of herself.

"Simulator code?" Michael Gillen winced at David Tashjian and Kara Ricci—flashing an odd gaze at Kate too. "You've *got* to be kidding."

The entire *Endurance* crew—save Brent Tasker and Glen Volk, who were on their way to Sco-II for reconnaissance—stood around a projection table in one of the science labs. Rather than displaying an intricate model of the ship's propulsion systems, the device instead projected timeline statistics and computer readouts: evidence David and Kara had gathered to explain *Endurance's* arrival at 18 Scorpii thirteen years earlier than expected.

"I'm certain," Tashjian replied. "The problem is simulator code."

Michael sighed deeply, making a vain attempt to suppress his angst over the statement. The young commander, overwhelmed by the mounting problems confounding the mission, regretted ever coming out of cryogenic stasis.

Simulator code was programming placed into *Endurance's* computers for training purposes. This programming allowed the flight crew to train while never leaving the dry dock. Launch protocol required the removal of that code prior to launch.

Kara reluctantly chimed in, "We confirmed our findings with Kate, Michael. The *Endurance* is riddled with simulator code."

Michael turned a doleful gaze in his wife's direction.

"It's true," Kate rather squirmed. "When the engineers prepped the ship for launch, they loaded the controllers with live code. But the version they loaded still contained some of the training code. Diagnostics was running a simulation almost the whole time we were in transit."

Everyone pondered the devastation that such a problem could have caused—all but Emir Kern. No, the man's flint-like demeanor never changed.

"And to think that we were only concerned with *Endurance* hitting the FW-190 debris," Phil Marcotte added.

Tom, hoping to defuse the mounting tension, chuckled at the thought. "Are we sure we're even here? Maybe this all is a simulation."

Michael grimaced, glancing conspicuously at Kate before turning back to the larger group. "We're lucky to still be alive." Then he turned to Tashjian. "David, I don't understand: It seems improbable that a rogue simulation could run concurrently with real-time operations and *not* be detected or cause problems."

"We were lucky," Tashjian nodded. "The simulation's intent was to test our reaction to the exact same problem: first, increasing speed to four-point-six times light-speed; second, increasing fuel consumption proportionally; third, intercepting and nullifying all traces of the problem in the ship's computer. It was a conflicting stimulus test: the controllers versus the main computer."

Tashjian continued, "Thirty days into the flight, the Slipstream controllers detected a slight anomaly in the Slipstream field. It sent the information to the main computer, which initiated the diagnostics program. The type of anomaly required a certain routine, which unfortunately had the simulation code embedded in it.

"From that point on, the simulator ran real-time, changing speed and fuel parameters. The navigation computer recalculated our entry-point back into real space. Once we jumped out of the Slipstream and the field was no longer active, the diagnostics program shut itself down, wiping out the simulation routine. Everything returned to normal, as if nothing had ever happened."

Michael gazed at the analysis hovering over the table before him. The scenario seemed completely absurd despite the credible data.

He took no comfort from the explanation either. He looked over at his wife—*the Systems expert*—sharply before returning his attention to the larger group. "You're sure about this?"

David, Kara, and Kate nodded in the affirmative.

Michael shook his head in disbelief. Everyone watched the consternation building within him over the disturbing revelation— how the man's dismay radiated toward his wife.

"Let's move forward," he said, turning to Kate. His voice betrayed a subtle impatience. "Purge the simulator code from the system. You'd better start now, since you've got about a billion lines of code to inspect."

After flashing one last displeasing gaze in her direction, Michael huffed and set off out of the lab and down the corridor. A thousand thoughts raced through his mind.

"Michael," he heard Kate calling to him from behind and hurrying to catch up. Reluctantly, he stopped and turned just as she came up behind him.

"Don't you have work to do?" he inquired sharply.

"What's wrong?"

"Everything," he lamented, though desiring not to continue the discussion. "Just start pulling the simulator code from the system. Let's not have any more *unforeseen* problems, okay?"

With an indignant look in his eye, he started to turn and walk away. However, Kate grabbed him by the arm and pulled him back around. Her expression pleaded with him. "Michael, you don't think this is my fault, do you? You know how quickly we left Mid-Earth Station, right?"

"Kate, you had three days during the shakedown to inspect the computers. You *know* what simulator code looks like … you should have looked for it."

"I did."

"Obviously not good enough!"

Kate fell under his reproachful gaze. With an all too familiar feeling of inadequacy building within her, she pleaded with him that much more, "*Michael*, I'm doing the best I can."

"I'm not so sure about that," he regrettably heard himself blurt out.

Kate's expression turned scornful. "What's *that* supposed to mean?"

Michael remained silent, just as his conscience begged of him. However, his dissatisfaction over what had happened—though he was trying to bury the feeling deep down inside—swelled within him. Regrettably, he felt his mouth opening once more. "If you didn't want to come on the mission, you should have said *no*. But you're here, so work this mission like our lives depend upon it—because they do!"

"*What?*"

Michael stood over her, bearing the brunt of her outrage. Yet at the same time, he fumed over her failure with the simulator code—increasingly so each moment. He didn't care that so many other things had gone wrong too. He also couldn't see that those other failures, combined with his fear of the *Endurance* meeting a similar fate as the *Comanche*, imposed a sort of temporary madness upon him. Though the young woman had erred with the simulator code, her biggest mistake was finding herself in the wrong place at the wrong time.

That was when Michael snapped.

"Systems are *your* responsibility!" he pointed an accusing finger at her. "I can't carry you like I did back at NSEA. You need to do your job the way NSEA expects you to." Though he saw her shrinking under his reproach, he couldn't contain himself. "We're marooned forty-six light-years from home—on the doorstep of people who will *kill us* if we're found!" He tried to restrain himself—a futile effort. "And it's *your* fault!"

Devastated, Kate watched him abruptly turn and walk away from her. The young woman's eyes welled up, and her lips pursed. Just then, the rest of the crew spilled out of the science lab, causing her to turn self-consciously toward the wall. Certainly, everyone had heard what he had said to her. She felt their awkward gazes from behind as they passed by. Finally finding herself alone, Kate stood in the corridor, letting her tears work their way down her cheeks.

Kate Gillen labored alone down the dimly lit corridor. The narrow passage was one of the most isolated parts of the *Endurance*, leading deep into the bowels of the ship. The familiar hum of the fusion engines came prominently from above.

With her mind still heavy from Michael's accusations and her eyes puffy from crying, she labored to the end of the dark corridor and opened the utility room door. Stepping in, she surveyed the modest place. A line of utilbots hung affixed in their holding bays on one wall, while a single computer console sat at the far end of the room. A stale flavor hung unpleasantly in the air too.

She approached the console and let out a heavy sigh. The condemnation she had received earlier from Michael played repeatedly in her mind, and she fought the urge to agree with him. The place reminded her of so many other obscure work bays at NSEA, places she had kept herself hidden while struggling with the many challenges she faced—trying to be as good as the other Centauries.

However, wallowing in self-pity would not remedy her mistakes. So Kate activated the console, determined to know how she had missed something as obvious as simulator code.

The planet Sco-II hung peacefully in space, prominently affixed against the pitch-black canopy in half-crescent form.

The majestic sphere resembled Earth in many ways. The planet's vast, brownish landmasses stretched across its surface, broken by less prominent, deep blue patches of ocean. Wispy, white clouds hung in its nitrogen and oxygen rich atmosphere, giving the planet a marble-like appearance. Sco-II was as massive as Earth, overwhelming the speck of light approaching it.

Though appearing as a mere speck of light against the planet, the terra-tanker was one of the largest commercial vessels ever created. In reality, the ship was a tanker in name only, actually carrying its cargo on the outside along its narrow, claw-like frame. The ship was part of a fleet of tankers circling in a long, extended orbit around the planet.

The fleet, part of the Europan terraforming operations, delivered water to Sco-II. Platforms high in orbit over Sco-V, the fifth planet in the system, mined water from the giant planet. Gathered in large, comet-like masses, the water shot through the 18 Scorpii system in the form of ice. The fully automated tankers would capture the cargo, convert it to a liquid, and ensure its safe delivery into Sco-II's lower atmosphere.

Within centuries, Sco-II would have oceans as vast as Earth.

The terra-tanker—prominently marked with the designation A141-7—lumbered toward the planet, weighed down by immense, heaving spheres of water. The liquid, enough to fill several large lakes, surrounded the tanker on all sides. Only the very nose and engine sections were visible. Even less visible on the underside of the vessel was an imperceptible dot: a small, two-man reconnaissance craft.

Brent Tasker and Glen Volk wearied of their journey aboard the *Quest*. Eight days of close quarters, miserable food, lack of sleep, and the threat of Europan detection had taken its toll. Both men had grown irritable and impatient for their quarters back on the *Endurance*. Of course, returning required another eight-day trip back to where the ship lay hidden—and they needed to complete their mission first.

The sound of an old bell ringing twice came from the instrument panel.

"Tasker," Volk called after opening his eyes and surveying the dimly lit cockpit, "Where's my bread ration from dinner?"

Tasker lay reclined in his chair with his arms folded, eyes closed, and head turned away. The cockpit chair barely accommodated his sizeable frame. "It was sitting there the whole time you were sleeping. So I ate it."

"I was saving it for later!" Volk declared, preparing his instrument panel for the upcoming task. "That's it: Tomorrow, I get the pick of your breakfast ration."

"I'd give away the whole breakfast in payment for you bathing. You're really starting to stink up the cockpit."

"You don't smell too good either. Remind me of a farm, you do." After a long silence, Volk sighed. "How do we get stuck doing these missions?"

"Kern," Tasker lamented. "We're the best, and he knows it—not that I'm too happy about that right now."

"You'd better get ready for the upcoming recon," Volk interjected, still checking the control panel before him. "The scanners show no other ships in the area so far, save the tanker itself. Do you think we'll get through undetected?"

"I think so. These tankers are completely automated. As long as we don't interfere with their operation, we should be okay. No one pays attention to terra-tankers anyway. Just like back—"

"Look alive," Volk cut him off. "We're coming into the approach."

Tasker snapped to the ready, joining Volk in working the equipment in front of them. Assigned the task of mapping Europan settlements and defenses, they had a whole planet to chart and only one pass to get it right.

"I wish we could see the planet," Tasker lamented. "I hate doing this when we can't see the actual target."

"Just pay attention to the scanners."

Falling into the shadow of the grand sphere, the terra-tanker began the long process of circling Sco-II. The vessel would continue descending toward the planet's surface, reaching its perigee on the opposite side. At the appropriate moment, it would release its cargo into the atmosphere. The terra-tanker would then slingshot around the other side and speed back out into open space.

They monitored the scanners as the ship passed over the planet's surface. The displays showed a single Europan main settlement, which lay on the opposite side of the planet. The rest of the screen remained unimpressive, save a rare outpost here and there: surveillance towers, mining, and industrial facilities dotting the surface. Mostly, the planet was a barren rock.

"The terra-tanker deactivated its navigational shields protecting the cargo," Tasker announced.

Sco-II's broad, darkened surface rolled before them on the scanning displays. Just as the Tanker came into the light, the Europan settlement appeared on the horizon: a singular, prominent, brownish-green circle adorning the planet's northern hemisphere.

"Look at the settlement's coloring," Tasker pointed to the display. "That can't be natural."

"No, it isn't. Thousands of square kilometers of self-sustaining forests and wilderness, complete with diverse vegetation and animal life? While the rest of the planet is a barren rock? The Europans must be terraforming the planet."

"It'll give us lots of places to hide," Tasker quipped. "—and look! Isn't that some kind of automated terraforming machine on the perimeter?"

Volk nodded in agreement.

Just as detailed data on the settlement began pouring across their screens, the terra-tanker released its cargo of water. The water spheres burst, inundating the *Quest* and quickly turning to ice. The scanners went wild in response.

"I can't see a thing!" Tasker fumed.

"It'll clear. Just do what you can."

The settlement far below continued rolling toward them. However, the scanners offered only garbled and distorted images that faded in and out.

"I'm gettin' nothing," Tasker lamented, "If this doesn't clear, we'll have to repeat the mission."

"Don't worry; it'll clear in time."

Volk was right. Just as the terra-tanker came over the settlement's zenith, the vessel hit the atmosphere. A fiery plume engulfed the tanker, burning away the surrounding ice and water. When the automated terra-tanker readjusted its navigational shields, the fiery plume dissipated; the vessel effortlessly slipped through the atmosphere.

The scanners returned to normal.

"Okay!" Volk celebrated. "Let's not miss anything."

The settlement—over fifty kilometers in diameter—was a sprawling city interspersed with regions of thick vegetation. The inhabited areas were in different phases of construction, almost delineating the sections of the colony.

"Wow, it looks as if they've been here fifty or sixty years," Tasker said, slack-jawed. "—maybe a century, taking into account mining and terraforming throughout the system."

"But the data shows that the oldest buildings are no older than nine years," Volk replied, studying the information streaming across the screen. "That means they arrived here much faster than the mission directors thought."

"Look at the population estimate!" Tasker interjected. "Two and a half million people: thirty percent adult, seventy percent children under eighteen—fifty percent of the total population under ten years old! They left Terrae Solaris with less than half a million people."

The two men looked at each other oddly. Finally, Volk shrugged his shoulders. "Population growth initiative?" he studied the readouts more intently. "You know what? The population estimator isn't counting anyone in that main construction zone or in that habitat outside the settlement's perimeter." He worked the scanner controls for several moments. "Those add up to about eight hundred thousand. Why weren't the estimators picking them up?"

The two men zoomed in the scanner images much closer on those areas. Unfortunately, the images of the people never focused enough to discern the distorted images.

"Must be some sort of interference," Volk mused. When he moved the scanner to an adjacent part of the settlement to compare, his mouth dropped and his eyes opened wide. "... *what in the....*" The man crumpled his brow and brought his face close to the screen. Tasker followed suit. "That's not good."

The young Europan ensign sat at his control station in the Terra-Tanker Controllers Complex, located somewhere in the Europan settlement on Sco-II. Taking his eyes off the screen in front of him, he surveyed the unremarkable activity transpiring throughout the operations floor. Half of the controllers, mostly older men, sat at their stations in a stupor. One really old man was actually asleep with his arm propping up his head.

He returned his eyes to the screen—nothing. The computer plotted the orbit paths of the automated terra-tanker fleet circling the planet. Much to his chagrin, everything remained in perfect compliance. So he dropped his chin into an open palm in surrender. He sighed. Sometimes, his job was incredibly boring.

A flashing icon suddenly appeared on the screen, catching his eye.

The ensign—Ensign Tighe—sat up in his chair and peered eagerly into the display.

The icon appeared next to a terra-tanker streaming away from its perigee orbit. The tanker—Tanker A141-7—was ascending out of the atmosphere after dropping its cargo. The icon indicated a minor deviation in its ascent trajectory. Nevertheless, it *was* a deviation.

The young man worked the controls, thoroughly examining the tanker's log. The more he looked at the tanker's progress through its last orbit, the more his face waxed over musingly. Finally, Ensign Tighe smiled.

"Interesting," he exclaimed to himself, celebrating the very unusual and disturbing finding.

CHAPTER SEVENTEEN

Mission Meeting

"Tasker and Volk are back," Eric Gunn interrupted, coming into the science lab on the *Endurance*. "I'm downloading the reconnaissance data now."

"Good," Michael replied as he stood with Curran Zeidler and some of the *Endurance* crew around a large, three-dimensional holographic projection table. He turned back to Zeidler. "So what were you saying?"

Zeidler turned once again to the map of the 18 Scorpii system projected over the table. The three dimensional map showed every detail of the system. He pointed to the orbit paths of the countless terra-tankers, which circled in a long, extended oval around Sco-II. "Once we get this close to the planet, we can use the tankers to hide our final approach—just as Volk and Tasker did with the *Quest*." He followed the orbit path all the way in to Sco-II with the end of his pointer, veering off to the planet at the closest point of the orbit path. Bringing the pointer to hover just above the northern pole, he added,

"Then we just follow the magnetic field of the planet all the way to the pole. The rest of the way to the base camp site is academic."

"True," Michael nodded with the rest of his team. "—assuming we ever get close enough to Sco-II without being detected. After all, the *Aurora* is bigger than the *Quest*, making it more detectible to Europan scanners."

"We'll have to see if Kern has any recommendations on our approach plan."

"Where is he?" Michael asked, a touch of irritation in his voice.

Zeidler simply shrugged. "He said he'd be here."

Just then, Kara came through the doorway to the lab, closely followed by Emir Kern. Their arrival together appeared more than simply coincidental, thus drawing quizzical looks from Centauri and Covert alike. Nonchalantly, the two took up positions on opposite sides of the holographic display table.

"Kern," Michael greeted him. "We're planning the approach to Sco-II. We need your input."

"What's the problem?"

Zeidler took him through the plan that he and Michael had crafted. They didn't last five minutes into the discussion before Brent Tasker and Glen Volk barged into the lab. Though both were exhausted, disheveled, and a little ripe, their anxious expressions caught everyone's attention.

"You need to see the data we brought back," Tasker exclaimed as he and Volk came up to the projection table.

"In a minute," Kern cautioned. "We're in the middle of something here."

"You'll want to see this," Volk pressed. Without waiting for permission, the young man inserted a reader disk into the presentation unit. The 18 Scorpii map disappeared, replaced by an automated map of the Europan settlement. The massive circular construct engulfed the whole table.

"Wow!" Michael gasped, taking in the complex display. Everyone else expressed a similar surprise. "It's not exactly the makeshift settlement we thought we'd find."

Despite many of the surface details remaining obscured because of the distance, the settlement contained a labyrinth of structures, transit roads, utilities, industrial complexes, and the like—too many details to take in all at once. Agricultural areas lay on the periphery. Where the infrastructure was incomplete, the computer enhanced to demonstrate a projected final look. Labels floated over various points of interest here and there. Key statistics hovered in one corner of the map: population estimates, structural completion date estimates, and the like.

"At least it'll give us the opportunity to blend in with the overall population," Kern offered. Then he looked at Volk and Tasker. "So do you have any idea where Galerius is holed up?"

Volk pointed to the northwest quadrant of the settlement. "We've located what looks to be a government complex in *this* region of the settlement, complete with a palace complex. That's our best guess. However, this appears to be a temporary situation."

He zoomed in on the center of the settlement, which grew to fill the entire table. The landscape was an irregular circle in form, lying within the rocky bluffs separating it from the surrounding settlement. It had natural and manmade water features throughout. Most of the infrastructure remained incomplete, making the razed area appear barren. Nevertheless, large foundations rose up from the dusty surface.

"We think this is the intended capitol center," Volk exclaimed. "The large foundations suggest opulent palaces and administrative buildings in the future." He fiddled with the projection controls until a simulation of the projected city appeared. "The final complex will rival anything in Terrae Solaris."

While the rest studied the simulation of the capitol city in awe, Michael looked oddly at the image. Though the smallest details of the picture were blurred, thousands of tiny dots lay scattered throughout the construction site. Though resembling people, the forms appeared slightly out of proportion. Pointing to the odd specks, he asked, "What's wrong with these details? Is it just the lack of focus making them so big?"

Volk perked up. "That's what we thought. Unfortunately, this is the best view we have. We had the same problem with a habitat located outside the main settlement too. The computers can't enhance the visual data for some reason."

"We did have some technical problems involving the terra-tanker," Tasker interjected.

"That's the problem with using passive scans," Kern sighed, looking at Michael. "They never give you enough information—and active scans give you away." Then he turned back to Volk and Tasker. "Is this everything we needed to see?"

"No," Volk replied. "We'll have a serious problem soon." He panned the presentation to another section on the periphery of the capitol.

Michael stood up a little straighter. "That's not good."

Thousands of newly constructed warships sat packed together in long rows. The rows stretched across the entire display, which was still from a high aerial perspective. A partially constructed tower sat in the center, boasting a network of conduits connecting the tower to the ships.

"We count three thousand," Volk said. "This fleet will be operational within two months. The tower in the middle is a fueling cell. However, the ships are landlocked at this time, since the fueling tower isn't finished yet. We detected fleet training activities close by too. Every ship has a Slipstream drive."

"Three thousand warships with Slipstream drives could give the *Endurance* a real run for its money," Michael mused. "And with our depleted fuel reserves, they wouldn't have any problem catching us."

"At least we know where to find fuel," David Tashjian interjected.

"And how to transport it to the *Endurance*," Kern added. "We'll steal a fueled ship, fly it to the *Endurance*, and refuel."

"A little dangerous though," Tom replied.

Kern looked at Michael, his eyebrows raised. "We can do it, but you're going to have to give us time for training and planning."

"I think everyone's missing the point here," Michael said to the whole room. "We have two months before those ships are operational. That means we have to complete our mission and leave by then." He lingered on the picture of the fleet for a moment. Something caught his eye again. Though unable to verbalize the feeling in his gut, years of military experience told him something wasn't right. "Why are there so many different types of ships?"

"It *is* an odd configuration for a fleet," Tom Andrews agreed.

"Yeah," Michael continued. "What possible tactical advantage does it offer?" Though he looked around the room, no one offered a theory. So he turned to Emir Kern. "Kern, can you and your men look into this?"

"Mike, we figured it out!" David Tashjian exclaimed, coming into the science lab on the *Endurance*. Kara Ricci followed closely behind him. David had a spryness in his step and a relishing grin on his face. The interruption rather irritated the Coverts, who were in the middle of a discussion with Michael and Tom.

"Figured out what?" Michael inquired curiously, barely catching Kara trading inconspicuous looks with Emir Kern. The Covert rather softened during the exchange, even cracking a subtle grin in her direction. Once returning his attention to the larger group, Kern's face waxed back to his normal, calloused gaze.

"The reason for the odd Europan ship designs," Tashjian replied.

Everyone in the lab perked up, especially Kern and his team. After two days of searching for an answer to the same question, the Coverts were stymied. Their analysis and design theories, prominently displaying on the three-dimensional presentation unit at the center of the room, remained fraught with inconsistencies.

"Then let's hear it," Tom quipped.

With Kara taking up position beside him in support, Tashjian inserted a small reader chip into the presentation unit. The Coverts' analysis disappeared, replaced by architectural designs of the Europan warships. The designs displayed smallest to largest.

"Here are all eight unique ship designs," Tashjian said. "There are three thousand ships—or three hundred and seventy-five sets of eight. We know they are sets, because the ships sit grouped as such and not by ship type, which is more conducive to efficient docking designs."

"We know that," Emir Kern countered.

Tashjian continued unfazed. "Every warship has an infrastructure that ensures maximum strength and balance. However, *these* ships have redundancies not normally found in Europan ships; they carry more weight as a result. This is very odd for battleships, which tend to have thicker armor plating instead."

"We know that too," Kern countered again, this time more impatient. However, the man remained less flippant than normal, as if he were restraining his reaction. He flashed subtle looks in Kara's direction. Challenging David meant challenging Kara at the same time. Of course, none of this went unnoticed by Michael.

"But did you realize *this?*"

At David's prompting, the computer moved the ship designs around until they lined up vertically. The redundant supports on each ship also lined up, and the computer connected those points using dotted lines. After an intentional pause, the ships coalesced like jigsaw puzzle pieces into a singular, egg-like shape.

Though Kern and his men waxed humble at the analysis, Michael and Tom beamed with pride at their companions.

"Good work, David and Kara," Michael stated. "Why'd the Europans do this?"

"It's the Slipstream technology," Kara offered.

"Yes," Tashjian nodded his head. "These ships have retractable Slipstream nodes built into their hulls. Every ship has the same size drives. This configuration allows them to combine eight separate Slip fields simultaneously. With the right calibrations, such a field would be extremely powerful and efficient—and fast too!"

The statement struck Michael like a sledgehammer. "David, how fast can this *pod* thing go—if it had to span a distance of forty-six light-years without refueling?"

"Fifteen to twenty times the speed of light—maybe more."

"That's fast," Curran Zeidler mused.

"No, that's dangerous!" Michael declared. "That puts this fleet within two to three years of Solaris."

Kara's gaze waxed over in concern as she watched Michael's wary expression. Nervously, she took hold of the two strands of the locket chain hanging from her neck, pulling the locket out from under the neckline of her shirt into her fingers while watching the discussion. Of course, she was unaware of her actions.

"The goons couldn't launch an offensive against Solaris from here," Tom shook his head. "18 Scorpii is too far away."

Michael remained unflinching. "That's exactly what they're doing! Worse, they have the advantage of surprise. No one in the Allied command chain expects such a move." He looked around the small group of Coverts soberly. "Aurelian Galerius didn't exile himself. He came here to regroup, to strike while Terrae Solaris remains bogged down in rebuilding efforts. The Allies are sitting ducks."

"The first place he'll attack is Earth States," David mused. "Take out the biggest threat first, and then Mars and Mercury will fall quickly."

"And that means lots of Earth States military and civilian casualties," Kara exclaimed with a churning expression. "We have to stop him."

While everyone pondered her words, Tom turned to Glen Volk. "Didn't your analysis show the Europans are within two months of readying their fleet?"

The room fell silent at the statement; telling glances traded back and forth.

"Our mission objectives have changed," Michael declared. "Our first priority is still capturing and taking back Aurelian Galerius. But before leaving 18 Scorpii, we will destroy that fleet." Standing up from the table, he flashed them an intentional look. "We leave for Sco-II in four days."

As Michael quickly left the room to tell the rest of the crew, Kern followed with the same determination.

"Commander," Kern called, causing Michael to stop and turn, "This mission change will require additional preparation."

"We don't have time," Michael stated, watching the rest of the Coverts sidle up anxiously behind their leader. "You'll have to improvise like the rest of us."

While his men traded incredulous looks behind him, Kern grew indignant. "Look, Sir, I held my tongue when you denied every *other* request to train, but this new objective requires thorough planning. *Three thousand ships to destroy!* You can't overlook the enormity of such a task!"

"In two months," Michael warned, "Those three thousand ships will be ready to launch an invasion against Earth States. We can't let that happen."

"But—"

"You have four days!"

Michael abruptly left, leaving behind a bewildered Emir Kern. Fuming, the Covert leader turned around. Gazing back at him was a unanimous round of dubious—even chiding—expressions from his team.

Work in the docking bay of the *Endurance* moved along at a slow, steady pace. The *Aurora*, a small transport the *Endurance* crew would use to travel to Sco-II, sat beside the much smaller *Quest* with its cargo hatch open. The Coverts—absent Emir Kern—were loading the craft for the next day's journey. Brent Tasker, Glenn Volk, and Eric Gunn carried supply boxes into the ship, while Curran Zeidler coordinated the effort.

"How's everything going?" Emir Kern called while coming through the bay's entryway. After shutting the hatch behind him, he crossed the short distance to where his men were working.

"We loaded all the equipment and provisions for the base camp," Zeidler commented, looking down at the reader he was using to organize the effort. "The land crafts and gear are loaded. Most of the guns and ammo are loaded too. A few more cases of ammo charges … and we're all set for tomorrow."

Tasker appeared from the open cargo hatch, returning from his umpteenth trip into the vessel. "I hope the Europans don't spot us. With all this ammo, one good shot and we turn into the best fireworks show in the system."

"That's a chance we'll have to take," Kern replied, taking Zeidler's reader and examining the inventory checklist on its display.

Glen Volk sat down for a quick break, inspiring his comrades to do the same. "It's gonna be tight in there with all these stores; quite the intimate setting for eight or nine days. I hope everyone's ready to get to know the Centauries real well."

A round of disgruntled sighs and groans rose into the air.

"Kern," Gunn pleaded, "Can't you make them stay back here on the ship?"

"I wish I could."

The soldiers looked at each other dubiously, though making sure they remained discreet. A rather coy expression came over Tasker.

"Yeah, I really hate those Centauries," he exclaimed with the slightest hint of sarcasm in his voice. "Especially Michael Gillen's wife."

Gunn fought a smile while shaking his head in mutual agreement. "Yeah, that Gillen guy sure doesn't give her any respect. I can't say as I blame him though."

"Kate Gillen's not so bad," Kern said, recounting the obvious discord between the couple as of late. However, his comment was merely a passing remark, for he was studying the inventory checklist on the reader.

"I'm not talking about Kate Gillen," Tasker countered. "I'm talking about his *other* wife."

"*What other wife?*"

"The other one … the one he treats like dirt."

"Who are you talking about?" Kern demanded impatiently, his mind preoccupied with a hundred other concerns.

"Well…,"—Tasker struggled against breaking up until finally blurting out—"You!"

The Coverts erupted into uncontrollable laughter, showering Kern with similar insults and jeers. Zeidler, sitting off to the side and smiling the entire time, remained much more reserved.

"You're not going to find it so funny on the planet's surface," Kern warned.

"Hear that, guys?" Gunn feigned a concerned look. "We'd better go tell Commander Gillen so he can put him in line again."

Though a few chuckles rippled through the small team, the joke had run its course.

"Why do you let that guy push you around?" Tasker chided, picking up another storage box and carrying it not too far into the *Aurora*. After setting it down, he reappeared again.

"Yeah, Kern," Volk added. "I never saw you so cowed before."

"*It's the doc*," Gunn piled on. "Kern's too *preoccupied* right now— not thinking clearly."

Though Kern returned a dismissive gaze, the rest of the Coverts nodded unanimously at each other.

"We should have seen that one coming when we first saw her," Tasker mused, picking up another box while still trading looks with his teammates. "I've got to hand it to Gillen; he really did his homework on us—figured out how to put you in your place."

"That's absurd," Kern shot back.

Volk, clearly dubious of his superior's assertion, counted off his fingers as if reading off a list of complaints. "He denied your request to let us train right after leaving Solaris. He denied your request to train before the reconnaissance trip—you stood there while he practically *ordered* Tasker and me to leave for Sco-II; you didn't say a word."

Kern stood his ground. "Once that guy makes up his mind, there's no changing it." Upon receiving some dubious return expressions, the man added, "He *is* the commanding officer—and in charge of flight operations. Besides, we can't draw attention to ourselves and risk playing our hand too quickly. Why do you think I've been so low-key?"

"But you let him add destroying that Europan fleet to our objectives without any additional time to prepare," Gunn countered. "You had a solid case on that one."

"Yeah, you said you would take care of the Centauries before we left," Volk piled on. "Obviously, you didn't follow through on your promise."

"So much for your *grand plan*," Tasker exclaimed sarcastically.

That was when Zeidler spoke up, "Has anyone considered that maybe the Centauries can help us? Sco-II's a big planet, and we're down to five now."

This drew some ire from the rest of the Coverts, Kern most of all.

"They're *not* helping us," Kern declared. "They *wouldn't* help us either."

Tasker smiled at Kern sardonically. "As if we really have a choice."

Kern, tiring of the abuse, turned steely-eyed. With a flint-like indignation washing over him, he stared down his men. Immediately, all of them cowered.

"Do you think I've forgotten why we're here?" he chided. "—or what I promised?" He let the comment linger through a long moment. "Do you think I've forgotten about Maddison ... or Nicholas ... or Anna? How 'bout *Mark*? He hasn't even been gone long enough to forget." He looked Tasker in the eye. "Brent, do you *really think* I've forgotten about *Rose?*" when the subordinate's expression withered and his head dropped tellingly, he flashed the same cutting stare at Volk. "How 'bout you, Glen ... do you think I've forgotten the last time I saw Jaden? Who could forget such a thing?" He scoured all of them with his bitter gaze. "Who thinks I don't hate going to sleep at night?"

The docking bay fell silent for the longest time, with the Coverts all hanging their heads.

"Look, guys," he offered, his expression relenting, "*Captain* Michael Gillen outranks me. This ship gives him his authority"—shaking his head—"but not for long. Once we're on Sco-II and the Centauries have to depend on us for their safety, *I'm in charge*. Then we'll do what we came here to do.

"When our chance on Europa fell through, I promised you another chance ... and here it is. Until the right time, we play along to keep the Centauries from getting suspicious ... but when we finally strike, Michael Gillen won't be able to stop us."

"I think that about does it," Phil Marcotte said to Michael Gillen, studying the navigations console display in front of him. "Any last suggestions?"

With Michael looking over his shoulder, he studied the miniature representation of the 18 Scorpii system on the screen. A projected trajectory path ran the outer perimeter of the system from *Endurance*'s current location. Once the path passed out of line-of-sight of Sco-II, it arced inward until taking up a close-orbit position behind the 18 Scorpii sun. The path to the ship's new position ran irregularly, in an attempt to minimize Europan detection risks. At the lower corner of the screen displayed the many parameters involved in programming the instructions.

"I can't think of anything else," Michael shook his head. He surveyed the bridge as if searching the air for something he had forgotten, only to shake his head once more.

"Okay," Marcotte said, committing the instructions into the computer. He turned around and shrugged. "So do you think the computers can really redeploy the ship without being detected by the Europans?"

"I don't know," Michael shrugged. "We've got the most advance navigation system ever designed for combat. Still ... I'd rather trust the intuition of a good navigator any day. The real question is whether we can get back to the ship if we have to escape Sco-II quickly. Despite what Kern thinks, I'm not sure the shorter distance makes us any safer."

Marcotte nodded in agreement.

The communicator at Michael's side issued an unobtrusive beep, just as it had done many times that day. With the crew in the final stretch to prepare to leave for Sco-II the next day, he had become a rather popular person. So he took the device in hand and surveyed the small screen. "I'll be back. I have to go see Kate."

"Where's *she* been? Did she fall off the ship?"

Michael simply shrugged and walked off the bridge.

A tired Michael Gillen made his way through the dimly lit corridor. The narrow passage was one of the most isolated parts of the *Endurance*, leading deep into the bowels of the ship. The familiar hum of the fusion engines came prominently from above.

His mind was heavy in thought. The three days of preparing for departure had passed quickly, and the crew still had much work ahead of them. Both the Coverts and Centauries were high above in the upper decks, preparing to leave for Sco-II the next day.

This excluded Kate, who had called him down to this particular diversion. She had made herself scarce since their fight over the simulator code. She wasn't even sleeping in their quarters anymore. Neither had he reached out to her. Given the tension between them, the young man was wary about confronting her in such an isolated place. Kate had a tendency to let her frustrations boil until finally exploding.

After reaching the end of the dark corridor, he opened the door to the isolated utility room. Inside, Kate worked the console at the far end, examining an utilibot hovering before her. Her mission uniform was a little dirty and her hair slightly unkempt, the telltale signs of the long hours she had spent in the dungeon-like room.

Concern covered her face.

Michael paused hesitantly, not relishing the imminent discussion.

"I got your message, as cryptic as it was," he greeted her, futilely attempting to look comfortable being there. "What's up?"

"Did anyone follow you?"

"No. Everyone's busy finishing preparations for tomorrow's departure."

"Good. Seal the door."

He complied, turning around to close the door. While activating the locking mechanism, he heard Kate's footsteps coming up from behind him; the hairs on the back of his neck stood on end in response. She was about to lay into him for his harsh comments so many days before. Gathering his courage, he turned back around to face her—

Kate waylaid him against the door, wrapped her arms around his neck, and locked him in a long, passionate, unrelenting kiss.

Taken back by the unexpected greeting, Michael yielded to his wife's amorousness—as if he could resist anyway. With each blissful moment, the young man felt himself unwinding from all the tensions plaguing him. The discord and resentment evaporated too. *Kara was right*, he thought as he kissed her. *Kate is the sensible one.* Of course, the thought stung terribly at his pride.

Reluctantly, he drew himself away from her ever so slightly. After offering a contented sigh, he smiled, "What's the occasion?"

Katey's face waxed over in deep concern once more. "Because this is the last time you won't be completely preoccupied with what I'm about to tell you."

He gazed at her curiously. "What are you talking about?"

"Someone tampered with the engines," she said softly but with desperation. "That's why we arrived early."

Michael turned incredulous despite Kate's seriousness. "David and Kara already found the problem. You agreed ... *right*?"

"That was before I found *this*," she replied, taking him by the hand and leading him over to the console.

Kate fiddled with the console, all the while pointing to the utilibot hovering nearby. The console's display scrolled through an activity log.

The log details displayed in reverse chronological order, stopping early on in the mission.

"I would have never found this," Kate began again. "But during the shakedown, I programmed all utilibots to log their activities to each other—just in case an utilibot's memory storage malfunctioned. I never told anyone—it was an unimportant detail.

"This is the E-1 utilibot, and the log is from *E-2*," she said, pointing to the screen. "Here, you can see that E-2 activated itself thirty days into the mission. I don't know why. E-2 has no record of these activities."

Michael glanced over at the E-2 utilibot hanging innocuously from its docking collar on the wall.

Pointing to a particular log entry on the screen, she continued, "*Here* is where E-2 changed the Slipstream speed and fuel consumption parameters to four-point-six times light-speed."

After pausing to let him absorb the data, she advanced the log almost all the way to the end. "When we came out of the Slip, E-2 reactivated and wiped out all traces of the changes on the main computer. It replaced the diagnostics routines with the version that had the simulator code. Then it altered the ship's logs to make it look like the simulator had run—but it never did! After that, it downloaded all sorts of rogue simulator code into the main computers to support the malfunction explanation."

"This is terrible," he said, staring at the irrefutable and troubling evidence. But then he let his head and shoulders drop in surrender. "I guess I owe you an apology too."

"Yes, you do," she replied, affording him more grace than he knew he deserved. "But now isn't the time." With a terrible dread washing over her face, she looked him straight in the eyes and declared, "We have a conspirator aboard."

Michael searched her sober gaze. "Are you sure someone didn't program this prior to launch? Then, it could have been anyone on the support teams."

"No," Kate shook her head. "Whoever did this reset E-2's memory shortly after we came out of hibernation—just to make sure no traces remained. You can see that in the log *here*." She paused, letting the truth sink into him. "This stuff is sophisticated. Whoever tampered with our systems is an expert."

"Kern," Michael seethed. "—*or* one of his men." Then his face lit up morbidly, as if realizing a dreadful truth. "Kern never wanted the Centauries along on this mission. He wanted a team sympathetic to *his* team—someone who would allow him to change the parameters of the mission, no doubt. If he's tampering with the ship, it means we're getting in his way." He mused over the thought uneasily. "An expert killed Ben Morris.... Perhaps we were too hasty in blaming the Europans." He looked at her soberly. "I think all of us Centauries are in danger."

"Because of the incendiaries you found?"

Michael nodded. "If only we knew what Kern was up to. But why would he strand himself just to arrive here so quickly?"

"But it's worse than that," she warned, changing the console to display the utilibot's instruction code. "Someone programmed E-2 to modify *Endurance*'s redeployment parameters. Shortly after redeploying to the other side of the sun—while we're on Sco-II—the ship will navigate itself *into* the sun. The saboteur even programmed mayday transmissions to us to make it look like some kind of fault." Again, she paused, letting him take in the dreadful news. "Someone's trying to scuttle the ship."

The room fell quiet through a tense moment.

"At least we know why Kern wanted the *Endurance* redeployed," Michael shook his head. Trading anxious looks with his wife, he realized he had completely underestimated Emir Kern. "But why would he want to scuttle the ship?"

"But what do we do about it?"

Michael stood there at a loss, betraying his quandary by a heavy and unresolved sigh. He stared at the disturbing display for quite some time. "Don't tell *anyone* about this—not even Tom or Kara. If Kern senses that any of us know, he might do something drastic, maybe even deadly."

"Okay, but what about the utilibot?"

Michael fell silent again, desperately searching the air for the elusive answer. Finally, he looked her squarely in the eyes. "If the Coverts want to destroy the ship ... we'll let them."

Early the next day—though the progression of days meant nothing in space—the *ESS Endurance* floated almost lifelessly in the dark void of space. The ship remained barely perceptible from the blackness encompassing it, for the yellow 18 Scorpii sun—just a mere dot against the eternal night sky—scarcely illuminated the vessel's black hull.

Two doors opened on the bow of the ship, and the soft glow of utility lights emanated from the formerly concealed docking bay. Moments later, the *Aurora* sprang from the bay, turning and accelerating toward the distant, yellow sun.

With little fanfare, the docking bay doors closed once again. *Endurance* came to life. As its fusion engines began to glow, the ship accelerated on a perpendicular course away from the much smaller *Aurora*, setting off toward the designated redeployment site on the other side of the 18 Scorpii sun.

Aurora, carrying the entire *Endurance* crew—Coverts and Centauries alike—sped off in the direction of the sun toward Sco-II. Though quickly coming to speed, the tiny ship's progress toward the planet was imperceptible. Therefore, the crew, filled with trepidation over the dangers awaiting them on Sco-II, settled in for a long and dangerous voyage.

CHAPTER EIGHTEEN

Covert Mission

The crew section of the *Aurora* remained dimly lit. Only the faint yellow glow from its instrument panels broke the night, leaving most of the *Endurance* crew shrouded in darkness. The atmosphere was uneasily quiet too. The steady hum of its engines resonated throughout the craft, broken only by scant conversation taking place up front.

Michael Gillen leaned over into the cockpit section of the transport, standing next to where Emir Kern supervised Brent Tasker and Glen Volk. Tasker piloted the transport, while Volk sat in the navigator's position to his right. Both, holding their breath and staring into their instruments, flew the transport dangerously close to the blackened terrain around them.

Nine days had passed since the *Aurora* had left *Endurance*, and the trip to Sco-II had been long and arduous. Aside from the natural dangers of space travel, the threat of detection remained a constant fear. Despite the Europans' relaxed security grid, the *Aurora* still had to proceed cautiously to avoid detection. Therefore, the small transport tediously worked its way from one place of cover to the next, making sure not to give away or reveal its presence.

At this moment, the *Endurance* crew labored through the most critical phase of the voyage yet.

Aurora was flying within thirty kilometers of the Europan settlement, though it was still ten kilometers from the designated base camp. The intended site was a cavern located within a remote canyon deep in the heart of a small mountain range near the settlement. Arriving at the base camp undetected required the *Aurora* to weave through the mountains, forcing Tasker to navigate the craft dangerously close to the jagged terrain.

As he pondered the dangerous trials ahead, Michael's stomach twisted in knots. Arrival on Sco-II marked the start of the covert part of the mission, and the young commander was out of his element. Worse, the need to destroy three thousand Europan warships complicated the primary mission: capturing Aurelian Galerius for extradition to Terrae Solaris.

He also couldn't stop worrying about the *Endurance*. The vessel was traveling somewhere in the 18 Scorpii system, redeploying to the far side of the sun. Yet if the ship strayed into Europan detection fields, they would quickly find themselves in danger.

However, the real danger stood close to him, very close indeed: Emir Kern!

Kern's tampering and intended sabotage of the *Endurance* enraged him; his hidden stash of incendiaries—somewhere on the transport most likely—worried the young commander. Yes, the rogue lieutenant hid his real intentions under a veneer of military protocol. He was unpredictable, even dangerous. If Michael intended to keep the Centauries alive, he would have to regard Kern and his men as renegades.

"Tasker," Kern warned. "Fly closer to the surface before you blow our cover."

Tasker grimaced, less than enthusiastic to pilot the craft any closer to the jagged terrain. Nevertheless, he pushed down on the elevation controls. The craft dove briefly until leveling out again, and the jostling increased. Everyone held on for dear life.

"I see the mountain configuration," Volk declared, looking into his scanners, "but I still can't locate our canyon—there's too many of them."

"Do what you can," Kern replied. "We can circle around if we miss it."

Tasker grimaced once more.

Kern turned to Curran Zeidler, who sat at a small tactical station just behind Volk. "Any hint that we've been detected?"

"None at all. I think the whole settlement is asleep."

"Good," Kern quipped and looked at Michael. "This might be our first break of the mission."

Michael nodded, though keeping his eyes trained on the *Aurora*'s navigation display.

The craft weaved through the terrain for some time, rocking back and forth as it maneuvered along. Michael and Kern swayed in similar fashion, keeping a tight grip on their restraints as they stood behind Tasker and Volk.

"There it is!" Volk exclaimed. "Straight ahead."

Just as Tasker began to steer the craft to fly over the final mountain, Kern interrupted. "Don't. Go through the canyon instead. That way, we won't stray into the detection fields."

Realizing the logic in his superior's direction, Tasker adjusted the craft's trajectory again. Still under the cover of darkness, the *Aurora* dove into the narrow canyon and snaked through the passage. The craft flew no more than several meters above the canyon floor. When the craft reached a prominence in the canyon, Tasker turned and banked the *Aurora*, sliding the vehicle to a full stop. The small ship, hovering a meter above the ground, faced the canyon wall.

Immediately, all eyes turned to the night scanners.

The rocky canyon wall boasted a cavern entrance capable of accommodating the *Aurora*. The cavern receded into the rock one hundred and fifty meters. Though the opening was comparatively narrow, the cavern swelled to a much wider oval-like shape about fifty meters in.

"Any sign of occupants?" Michael asked warily.

"None," Zeidler replied. "It's tectonically stable too."

"Back the ship in, Tasker," Kern ordered. "It'll make for an easier escape—should we need to."

Tasker spun the vessel around and reversed course into the cavern's entrance. The *Aurora* patiently squeezed backward through the jagged mouth of the cave. When the cave veered slightly, Tasker adjusted. Ninety meters into the cave, the *Aurora* came to rest on the rocky floor.

The *Endurance* crew had arrived on Sco-II.

The travel-weary vessel sat only a few minutes before its side hatch opened. Carrying flashlights and brandishing pistols, the Coverts and Centauries—wearing heavy jackets—emerged one by one from the hatchway. The Coverts led the way, surveying the surroundings while fanning out into the chilly cave.

Michael, taking in a healthy dose of Sco-II air at the open hatchway—noticing the cave's musty smell too—stepped down onto the hardened ground.

He paused to look down at his footprint, which barely registered in the scant dirt covering the ground. Memories from years of dreaming about this moment flooded his thoughts. His mind filled with his boyish visions of realizing such an historic moment in exploration: what setting foot on an alien world would mean to humanity, what a grand destiny he would fulfill. He laughed as his flashlight remained trained on the imprint; the moment seemed so anticlimactic!

"Let's start making camp," Emir Kern commanded, more than eager to secure the site. "Tasker and Gunn, set up the blackout netting in front of the ship: wall to wall. Don't let a single beam of light in or out. Zeidler and Volk, start unloading the ship. Once the netting is up, erect the lighting system behind the *Aurora*; we'll set up a command post there."

"Centauri crew," Michael called out to his team scattered about the cavern, "Let's help unpack the provisions."

Kern nodded appreciatively. "Until my men are done, can you have two of your people watch the entrance? I don't want to get caught unaware."

Michael nodded and then gestured to Marcotte and Tashjian listening close by. Immediately, the two men started toward the cavern's entrance.

Making camp proceeded quickly. While the rest of the crew began unloading the gear, Tasker and Gunn went just ahead of the *Aurora* to drill supports into the reddish-brown rock walls.

"Lieutenant," Gunn called, looking at the bottom of his shoes. "This ground's a little muddy up here. Are you sure we won't get caught in a flash flood?"

Kern looked at him, unconcerned. "Our Centauri friends tell us this is the dry season, so we'll just have to trust them." Then he raised his hand flat out as high as his chest. "Of course, put in some extra supports about this high, just in case we have to put up netting to keep our gear from washing away."

Within an hour, the *Endurance* crew had transformed the cave into an exemplary operations post. Bright lights flooded the makeshift command center directly behind the *Aurora*'s stern, while the blackout netting in front of the craft kept the cave's entrance dark. Temporary sleeping quarters resided far in the back of the cave, where the uneven ground rose up two meters higher than where *Aurora* sat. To the left of the *Aurora* was a small land craft.

Kate Gillen emerged from the *Aurora*'s hatch, followed by Eric Gunn. The man, carrying a rather bulky piece of equipment, struggled through the hatch and followed her to the command center behind the ship. Michael Gillen, Tom Andrews, and Emir Kern, who stood leaning over a three-dimensional map of the settlement, noticed and looked on curiously. The other Centauries milling about saw too.

"Over there please," Kate pointed to a sturdy storage bin sitting off to the side.

The Covert labored with the heavy piece of machinery over to the bin. Setting it down on top of the bin, he let out a formidable sigh.

"Thank you," Kate smiled, causing Gunn to nod sheepishly.

Watching her activate the device and fiddle with the controls, he asked, "So why do you need it out here instead of leaving it in the ship?"

"It'll work better here," Kate replied, keeping focused on the display. Of course, she had just told a white lie. In reality, she preferred working out in the musty cavern rather than confine herself in the *Aurora*. Nine days of eleven people traveling in cramped quarters had turned the air inside the ship rather ripe. She didn't know how long the environmental controllers would take to fix the problem.

"So what do you have to do?" Gunn asked while watching over her shoulder.

"*Endurance* will signal us once it finishes redeploying behind the sun," Kate replied, fiddling with the device. "It will transmit on a secured carrier wave matching the sun's radiation signature—a signal the Europans won't easily detect. I need to reprogram the communicator to pick up the signal from the intermediary communications satellites we deployed and interpret it."

"If you have any trouble," Gunn offered, "You may want to ask Zeidler to help. He's good at that stuff. Plus, Kern already asked him to tap into the settlement's transmissions—so he'll need to use the device too."

"I'll keep that in mind," Kate smiled.

Tasker and Volk, appearing from the tents set up at the back of the cavern, walked into the command center area. Immediately, they caught everyone's attention, for both wore Europan military uniforms. Kern had assigned them the unenviable task of surveying the settlement. The assignment was mainly reconnaissance: Locate Aurelian Galerius and find out how to capture him.

The crew gathered around curiously.

Michael winced at the sight, though not because of their uniforms. Rather, he still smarted from losing a debate with Kern earlier. He had requested that Tom accompany Tasker and Volk to the settlement, hoping to keep an eye on the two Coverts. Tom was eager to go, for he found the cavern an unpleasant place to wait. However, Kern insisted that the two men go out alone. Quite the heated discussion ensued. Despite his ability to pull rank, Michael relented. He realized he needed to proceed carefully, especially given Kern's hidden agenda. Regardless, losing the point to Kern smarted terribly.

"How do we look?" Tasker gestured comically at his wardrobe.

"Good enough to shoot," Kern replied matter-of-factly. "You two ready to go?"

"Yep," Volk replied. "Everything's loaded into the land transport."

"Good! You have three hours before dawn. That's enough time to get to the settlement and find a place to set up. Don't hurry yourselves;

don't get caught needlessly. Check in if you can, but don't compromise the mission. Zeidler gave you two weeks of supplies. That's enough time to find Galerius and figure out his routine. Remember: We need a predictable ambush point."

"Got it," they almost said in unison.

After the Coverts exchanged parting pleasantries, Tasker and Volk hopped into the land transport, powered up the small vehicle, and sped out of the cave. Zeidler and Gunn held the blackout netting back to let them through.

The crew dispersed. However, Kern walked with Michael to the mouth of the cave. Both men watched the nimble craft speed into the darkness. When it finally disappeared into the night, Kern turned toward Michael. "So far, so good."

The door to the *Aurora*'s lavatory opened, and a rather pensive Kara Ricci stepped out into the dimly lit and deserted crew compartment. Having taken advantage of the anonymity of the abandoned craft, Kara wiped the remaining tears from her eyes and composed herself before heading toward the open hatch—

She jumped and gasped for breath! A shadowy figure lurked out of the way, sitting in the passenger's seat in the corner against the lavatory wall.

"*Michael!*" she moaned, putting a hand to her heart while laboring to catch her breath. "*Don't scare me like that.*"

"Sorry," he replied. "I didn't mean to." Noticing her fright rather than her puffy eyes and drawn face, he added, "You okay?"

"I'll be fine."

Mostly recomposed, Kara finally took a good look at him. He didn't say anything. Instead, Michael just sat there rather anxiously, perturbed too. *Yes, he was anxiously perturbed.* He looked as if something pressing were on his mind. She realized he had come to talk with her alone. That was the only reason for meeting her in such an out-of-the-way place.

"What's up?" she asked.

He just shook his head dismissively. "Nothing … just needed a quiet moment. The Coverts are driving me crazy."

Though she half-laughed, the young woman knew her best friend was lying—at least about needing a quiet moment. His determined expression betrayed him. Yet he was waiting her out too. So remaining rather indifferent, Kara sat down next to him and smiled as if needing a quiet moment herself.

Inwardly, though, Kara desperately hoped he had come to console her—like Emir Kern had done. Mark Armstrong's death still deeply affected her—and for what reason she did not know. Since Michael knew her better than anyone did, she needed his friendship and unique perspective more than ever. Yet in all the busyness since arriving at 18 Scorpii, Michael had not asked her about the incident *even once*. Certainly, he must have noticed how much Armstrong's death had troubled her.

At least right then, he could make up for his oversight.

They remained quiet for a long moment, with Kara waiting eagerly for Michael to speak. When he just sat there, the young woman decided to help him along.

"Remember all those years we spent at the academy and NSEA?" she asked, putting her hands between her knees and relaxing into the chair. "—training for space exploration?"

Yeah," he grimaced, shaking his head and rolling his eyes. "It's nothing like I expected."

"That's what I was thinking too."

They shared a quaint smile before Michael continued, "So you and Kern are spending a lot of time together."

"Yeah, he's been really nice."

Is he getting the hint? she thought.

"So what do you two talk about?"

The young woman shrugged, though clearly grateful for the opportunity to prompt her obtuse friend a little more. "Mostly me, I hate to say. Ever since Armstrong died, Emir has been more than gracious."

"Emir?"

Kara looked at him oddly, quickly realizing Michael's preoccupied expression had nothing to do with her. "That *is* his name."

"Did he ever mention the incendiaries he's hiding?"

"No."

"What about our Europa recon mission during the war?"

"No, it never came up," Kara replied, growing increasingly frustrated.

"Did you ever ask him?"

Finally, Kara rather leaned away from him with a quizzical if not disappointed gaze. "No, Michael. *Why would I?*"

"So we can figure out what he's up to—just as I asked you to do."

She sighed and shot him an incredulous gaze. "I don't think he's up to anything."

"He is. Trust me."

The two fell silent for a long moment and averted their gazes out *Aurora*'s portholes—nothing but an unappealing rock wall in the view field.

"Michael," Kara finally offered, turning herself toward him and putting her arm up on the back of her chair—her hand extending partially across his chair. "I know there's bad blood between you two because of what happened during the war … but I think you're being overly suspicious." She leaned closer as if to plead. "He's really nice, once you get to know him." However, when his face waxed skeptical, she added, "Besides, do you really think he would tell me if he were up to something?"

"Cyril told me you could help," he fixed his gaze upon her intentionally. "And I see how he reacts around you. I *need* your help."

Kara sat looking at her long-time friend, conflicted—and saddened that his discord with Emir Kern had come to possess him so. Michael wasn't relenting either. Rather, he was intentionally playing on her sympathies—an indefensible tactic. He was so cavalier about it too. She decided that perhaps she could humor him. So with just a hint of sadness, she shrugged and rather shook her head in surrender. "What do you want me to do?"

"Talk to him about the mission. See if he'll tell you what he's up to."

"I doubt that will work."

"Then lie to him," Michael pressed. "Make him think you're dissatisfied with the mission—that you and I have had a falling out."

"Do you think that would really help?" she asked, though noting the irony that some truth lay in his statement.

"If you get *close* to him. Play on his emotions ... pretend to have feelings for him"—watching her wince at the statement—"Lie if you have to."

"Michael, don't ask me to do that."

The two traded contending gazes through an awkward silence. Finally, his expression steeled. "Kara, I'm not *asking*." He shot one last intentional look at her before getting up and leaving her all alone.

After he disappeared through the hatch, Kara whispered, "I'm fine, by the way."

"It's getting dark," Tasker said, leaning his oversized frame in toward his shorter companion. "The crowds are thinning too. Let's get off the streets and into our hotel room before someone stops us."

The two men strolled through the scenic Europan plaza, which sat surrounded by lush foliage. Still neatly dressed as Europan soldiers, they stood out among the bustling crowd of civilians traveling home for the day.

"So are we going to tell Kern that we deviated from the plan?" Volk asked.

"You feeling guilty about staying in a luxurious hotel room, while everyone else suffers back at the base camp?"

Volk looked around inconspicuously, ensuring that no one was eavesdropping from behind. "No, but checking in to a hotel room with assumed identities? A risky move. I'm sure they built the hotel so soon for Europan nobles needing a place to stay—not a couple of foot soldiers on leave."

"Tonight, *my friend*," Tasker put his hand on Volk's shoulder reassuringly while swaggering along, "We will enjoy a *fine* meal and then retire to the hotel's spa. This recon assignment will make up for sixteen days aboard the *Quest*—unless you prefer camping in the woods every night."

"But what are we going to tell Kern?"

"Hopefully, '*we found Galerius*'," Tasker shrugged. "After that, he won't ask about the mission." He paused while taking a few steps. "Of course, we have to find Galerius *first*."

"It's just the first day," Volk stated. He discreetly gestured to the bustling crowd of civilians around them. "And we're still a little removed from the command centers."

Tasker nodded. "I agree. Tomorrow, we'll work toward the palace and military centers."

"We'll have to be more careful."

The taller Covert smiled. "Maybe not. Look how lax security has been so far. This might be a cake walk."

"That's a good sign. That means that they haven't detected any of us yet."

The two men, still walking, looked at each other and nodded in agreement. Just as they started turning their attention in the direction of where they were going—they collided hard into something. However, the formidable obstacle was moving too, and the force of the collision sent the two Coverts tumbling backward onto the ground. Moaning at the force of the collision—and their embarrassment—the two men looked up.

Fear shot through them, and the two men recoiled in panic!

The odd-looking creature standing before them stared down at them menacingly. Though similar in form to that of a human, the creature towered almost four meters tall. Its mass was four to five times that of the sizeable Tasker, who easily fell into its hulking shadow. Its massive frame lay covered in thick, dark, creviced skin with matted hair all over. Thick muscles layered down its overly large arms and legs; the same with its torso garbed in rags. The creature's mostly bald head was of smaller proportion to its body, boasting a prominent forehead, sunken in eyes that brooded, and an oversized, rock-like jaw. The only sign of civility in the beast was a metal collar around its thick neck. The collar glowed as if some sort of restraining device.

The two Coverts gulped nervously at the sight of the smelly beast, whose eyes remained fixed on them. Any fears about attracting unwanted attention faded into obscurity. However, when a voice called from the crowd, the creature turned and followed. Tasker and Volk watched the beast push through the crowd until catching up and following the civilian. No one else paid them or the creature any mind.

"Now I know why the *Quest's* scanners couldn't enhance all those out-of-focus people on our recon mission," Volk mused as he stood up, his eyes still transfixed on the strange creature in the distance. "It didn't know how to interpret them—that *thing* certainly isn't human."

"And that means there's thousands of them all over the place," Tasker added, coming to his feet as well.

"More like eight hundred thousand. I'll bet they use them for defensive purposes."

"Probably," Tasker shuddered. "So let's make sure we don't get caught."

Lieutenant Kalb sat at his desk in the Europan Terra-Tanker Controllers Complex, located somewhere in the Europan settlement. He surveyed the busy operations floor spread out before him. The steady buzz of unremarkable activity continued unabated and with little fanfare—just like every day. So after rubbing his tired eyes, the aging shift supervisor turned back to the holographic screen hovering before him, more than eager for the end of his shift.

However, his shoulders abruptly fell: An eager, young ensign sidled up to the front of his desk. So he said, "Ensign Tighe, your shift's almost over. Shouldn't you be wrapping up so you can go home?"

"I wanted you to take a look at something, Sir," the young man with an untamed look in his eyes replied. He held out a reader chip for him to take.

Instead, Kalb leaned back in his chair and stared him down.

The ensign had a notorious reputation among the controllers group: He worked as if the whole Europan settlement's welfare depended on him. Though Kalb found this trait commendable, the ensign's eagerness and hyper-curiosity fell out of place in the bureaucratic organization. The organization typically employed aging servicemen finishing out long, unexceptional careers. Moreover, the fully automated terra-tankers mostly took care of themselves—the controllers were merely babysitters. However, the young ensign kept bringing needless issues to his desk, day after day.

Though Kalb wished the young man would simply go away, the ensign stood firmly planted across the desk. Finally sighing in surrender, the supervisor took the reader chip and inserted it into his own reader. The holographic display lit up with some sort of status log. "What's this?"

"It's the status log from Tanker A141-7. Twenty-five days ago, the onboard computers detected a slight anomaly in the tanker's orbit path."

"*Twenty-five days ago?*" the experienced supervisor scoffed. "Any problems since then?"

"No. But I—"

"Then why are we discussing a minor anomaly a month after it happened? These tanker computers are always picking up anomalies—they're programmed to deal with them too."

However, the ensign remained unfazed. "Something happened yesterday to trigger my concern … but let me explain the problem from last month first."

Sighing in reluctant surrender, the supervisor waved him to continue.

"Last month, the tanker's orbit deviated during its approach to New Europa. The deviation while approaching the planet was unremarkable, though detectible." He pointed to the specific data displaying on the screen. "However, during the tanker's re-ascent after dropping its cargo, its navigation computers increased power to its engines to account for a slight weight differential." Once again, he paused—more hesitantly this time. "I think a small ship piggy-backed the tanker on that orbit."

Predictably, the supervisor laughed. "That's a grand assumption. Maybe the containment field holding the water to the tanker remained partially engaged, keeping some of the cargo with it as it re-ascended."

"The computers reported no such problem. I found something else too."

Tighe encroached upon the supervisor. Leaning over his desk, he fiddled with the reader until another status log displayed. "When I found the anomaly with A141-7, I set up my computer to monitor for similar problems. Last night, Tanker B071-3 reported a similar weight differential on its approach—only the deviation was bigger."

"Did it also report the re-ascent problems?"

"No, but look what I found."

Once more, Tighe fiddled with his supervisor's reader. The status log disappeared, replaced by a brilliant picture of Sco-II's northern polar region. The computer enhanced the picture to show the planet's invisible magnetic field. A slight bulge in the field appeared high in the atmosphere. The bulge descended through the magnetic field, finally disappearing close to the planet's surface. Once finished, the picture looped repeatedly.

"I tapped into the weather monitoring systems," the ensign pointed to the moving bulge. "Shortly after the anomaly disappeared on tanker B071-3, the weather systems detected this variant in the northern pole's magnetic field—a variant attributable to the exact size of a ship that might have piggybacked B071-3."

When he changed the display again, the orbit trajectory of the terra-tanker superimposed over the image. The computer modeled a theoretical ship diverging from the hull of the tanker—when it was very close to the poles—and descending toward the planet, thus causing the bulge-like distortion in the magnetic field.

"I tried tracking its trajectory after it left the pole," the ensign added to the now-mesmerized supervisor. "But our monitoring systems aren't set up for that work."

The two went silent as the older man stared at the looping display.

"I'm very impressed, Tighe," Kalb exclaimed, not taking his eyes off the screen. "What do you think it is?"

"I don't know. Perhaps our military is doing something classified."

"I doubt it's the military."

"Then perhaps we have smugglers working a black market."

The older man pondered the analysis for a long moment. Eventually, he shook his head and sighed. "I would have thought we had rid ourselves of smugglers when we left Solaris. However, we didn't leave human nature behind. Maybe someone's making themselves rich without paying Aurelian Galerius his fair share of revenue—maybe not. Regardless, notify the military. Let them know someone is making unauthorized trips on and off the planet."

CHAPTER NINETEEN

Alien Planet

Emir Kern struggled to sit comfortably on the rocks just outside the cavern at the Sco-II base camp.

He didn't relish the coming of night or the long watch at his post. However, with Brent Tasker and Glen Volk already gone two days to scout out the Europan settlement, he had nothing to do but wait for their return—and keep watch over the camp, of course. That thought gave him no consolation: The scouting trip might continue for the next twelve days—twelve *long* days with the Centauries.

Kern surveyed the canyon before him, looking for any sign of movement. He kept watch at *Lookout One*, which sat just outside the cavern entrance. He could see Michael Gillen also keeping watch, positioned across the canyon floor to the west of the cave entrance. That was *Lookout Two*. Both posts sat draped in camouflage netting to hide their presence from the air.

He pulled his jacket tightly around himself, fending off the coming chill. Evening was falling. Shadows crept up the canyon walls as the

18 Scorpii sun slowly fell toward the horizon. Although nightfall would take some time, darkness was imminent. Then the watch would become a long, lonely one.

Just then, Kara Ricci appeared from the entrance to the cave, coming toward him. She carried a plate of hot food in one hand and a thermos in the other. The battle-hardened soldier sat up just a little straighter.

"Beware of strangers bearing gifts," Kara smiled as she came up to him and handed him the plate.

"Thanks," the Covert leader replied. A glimmer appeared in his eyes when she unexpectedly sat down next to him. Taking a few quick nibbles while enjoying his turn of fortune, he paused and said, "I'm not used to room service."

Just then, Tom Andrews appeared from the cave's entrance. Carrying similar provisions as Ricci, Andrews instead set off toward Michael Gillen far across the canyon.

"We thought you and Michael might be hungry," she replied as Kern watched Tom make his way across the rocky terrain.

"And you drew the short straw?"

Kara cracked a coy and aloof smile—a playful smile. "*Actually* ... I volunteered."

The man responded with raised eyebrows and an impishly suspicious tilt of his head.

"Well, Emir, since you volunteered to cover my guard-duty shift tonight—on top of yours—it's the least I could do."

"You shouldn't worry about returning the favor. If I'm not out *here*, I'm driving Gunn and Zeidler crazy inside." However, upon seeing Kara's incredulous gaze, he shrugged. "Call me old fashion, but I don't think women should have to do guard duty."

Kara held his gaze for a long moment and studied him shrewdly.

"What about Kate Gillen?" she probed, her mouth turning a curious half-grin. "I haven't seen you covering her shift."

He paused, taken back by the not-so-veiled interrogation. So pointing his head in Michael's direction, he said, "She's *his* problem."

After trading curious looks with her, Kern held up the thermos of coffee as a peace offering. When she nodded in acceptance, he gave her the thermos cup and started pouring the beverage. Steam wafted into the cold air over the cup before dissipating. "If you keep hanging around me like this, you're going to lose credibility with the other Centauries."

"I'll manage."

"Not worried about your reputation? It's pretty obvious they don't like us, especially Michael Gillen."

Kara shook her head *no*.

"If they banish you," he smirked, "You'll have to become a Covert."

Kara gazed at him for a brief moment, turning coy once more. "That wouldn't be so bad. Can you use a medic?"

"I hope not."

After sharing a quaint laugh, they went quiet and enjoyed the coming evening. Kara, feeling a change in the air in just the short time she had ventured outside, cinched up her coat and cupped her hands around the steaming hot coffee. Remaining close to Emir and gazing out onto the barren landscape, she was amazed at how quickly the man's presence had put her at ease, how comfortable she felt around him.

"So are you feeling any better?" he asked, clearly hesitant to bring up the question.

She continued looking out onto the chilly canyon as if losing herself in it. The sparkle in her eyes faded a bit too. Finally, she nodded her head soberly. "I still can't sleep though. I keep seeing his face in my dreams—*nightmares* really."

"I can relate to that … but you can't keep blaming yourself."

"I keep telling myself that it wasn't my fault, but—"

Kara abruptly went silent, chocking back the strong emotions.

Emir nodded sympathetically and placed a reassuring hand on her knee. She glanced back just briefly enough, taking in the sentiment. Then her gaze returned once more to the distant landscape ahead. She remained pensive, though leaning in just a little closer toward him.

"This is crazy," she finally lamented, her gaze remaining distant. "I saw *so much* death on the front lines, I vowed to do something different when my tour of duty ended." Then she smiled. "I thought pediatrics or obstetrics would be nice—something with children and babies." However, the smile quickly faded, and she shook her head in disbelief.

"But then Cyril Davidson asked me to join this mission. ... It's like I can't get off this crazy ride."

"So why are you here?" Emir gently asked, watching her struggle against welling up. When she shrugged despondently, he added, "You *shouldn't* be here. This mission is too dangerous."

"That's *exactly* why I have to be here," she nodded, looking across the way. "If he's here ... I have to be here too."

Kern looked to where Michael sat with Tom far across the canyon. "*Gillen?*"

"Not just him...," she shrugged to deflect his question. "*All* the Centauries are family—we tend to follow his lead though. But I've *kinda* been Michael's big sister all these years—kept him out of trouble." The young woman hesitated self-consciously. "Michael needs a chance to clear his family name ... and someone needs to keep him out of trouble while he does it." She waxed pensive and labored over the thought. Finally—as if convincing herself—she nodded. "... Someone needs to protect him."

Emir went silent for a long time, boasting a dog-like tilted head and crinkled eyebrows. His expression betrayed his shock and dismay over her comments as much as his concern over her laboring gaze. "But *who's* going to protect you?"

They traded uneasy looks through a long moment of silence.

"I'm protected," Kara offered, her face waxing over warmly. After unzipping the very top of her coat, she pulled out from under the neckline of her shirt the gold locket chain she wore. The medal Emir had given her after Mark Armstrong died hung from the chain, dangling next to the heart-shaped locket. She proudly held the medal up to him between two fingers. "I like to think of it as my lucky charm. I never take it off."

The Covert leader looked at the medal. Though nodding in acknowledgement, his gaze didn't change. "So you believe in luck?"

"*No* ... I believe in the person who gave it to me."

Curiously, the Covert fidgeted at the comment.

"That's not why I gave it to you," he replied rather brusquely. "You should stick to believing in luck."

"I'd rather not," she shook her head. As if searching his expression, she added, "Luck is too intangible—fleeting too.... I prefer a sure bet."

Emir's expression soured something terrible, and he looked out onto the darkening terrain. His reaction was so strong and so unchanging, Kara panicked.

"What's wrong?"

However, the man remained silent and withdrawn.

"Emir," she softly beckoned, putting a hand on his forearm. "What did I say?"

Suffering terribly under her imploring gaze, the man finally replied, "Don't say you believe in me."

"Why?"

"*Just don't!*" he chided harshly—his eyes suddenly wide upon hearing himself. Nevertheless, Kara recoiled away. "I'm sorry. I didn't mean to yell at you."

Kara watched Emir fall silent. The man even appeared somewhat awkward, maybe even choked up. She found it hard to tell what was going through his mind. Something had formed an impenetrable, calloused exterior around him. "I didn't mean to pry."

Taking in her anxious but sincere gaze, Emir Kern relented. "You're not *prying*."

"Then what is it?"

The man labored over a long moment. For the first time since she met him, Emir Kern actually appeared anxious, as if he were mustering his courage too. Finally, he reached into his chest pocket, pulled out a tattered photograph, and—cracking such a self-conscious expression—handed it to her.

Kara looked down at the worn image. Pictured in what looked like some sort of park were three people. Kneeling down in the center was a beautifully dressed young woman with auburn hair, smiling warmly. A toe-headed boy wearing a black suit and holding a toy stood wrapped in her right arm. A baby girl in the cutest white dress stood just in front of the woman, as if caught in mid-stride of an awkward step.

Kara couldn't help noticing how similar in appearance the woman was to her.

"That was my family—my pride and joy," he said, losing himself in the picture. His preoccupation kept him from noticing Kara's startled expression. He pointed to the woman in the picture.

"My wife, Maddison…"—moving his finger to the boy—"… Nicholas …"—and then to the baby girl—"… and Anna."

"You were married?"

He nodded.

"I didn't think Special Forces personnel led normal lives," Kara replied, trying to cover her shock.

"All the Coverts had families. We were stationed at Ceres Fleet Base long before the war. It was great—we were like one big, happy family. Their wives were like sisters to me; their kids, adopted nephews and nieces…. We did everything together…. The weekend barbecues were phenomenal too."

Kara looked at him curiously. While he gazed at the picture, his eyes shimmered with the most captivating gleam.

Abruptly, the warmth drained from his face.

"But then the Europans attacked the base," he said with an incredible heaviness, his words coming haltingly as he stared into the picture. "So I and my men went to help…. While we were out defending the base, the goons attacked our residences." He choked on the strong emotions. "Everyone died that day … our wives … our *children*…."—shaking his head wistfully—"It should have been us."

"Emir, I'm so sorry," she offered, looking down at the picture to avoid the pain radiating from his gaze.

"That's why I yelled at you. Despite all the great times we had on Ceres, my wife never wanted to move there. She was afraid of being so far from Earth States—and nervous about being so close to the Outer Rim. Nevertheless, I convinced her to go. Despite her reservations, she followed me." He laughed awkwardly as he stared at the picture. "That was her downfall … I was always off doing something I shouldn't have been doing … a career man to the end—doing things *my* way. I got in *so* much trouble too—that's why we were transferred to Ceres in the first place. Yet through all that, she kept telling me how much she believed in me." He fell silent and his expression waxed grave. "… And look how that turned out for her."

"I'm so sorry, Emir."

"This picture is the only thing I have left to remember them. Anna wasn't even a year old. If you look closely at the picture, you can see her taking her first step."

Kara watched him labor over the tragic memories. Though she desired to respond, the words evaporated from her lips. So instead, she leaned in closer to him.

Emir struggled to continue, "They suffered terribly too. The goons used firebombs"—chocking back something fierce—"... Everyone burned to death."

Though Emir quickly tried to compose himself, Kara nevertheless felt the torrent of emotions churning deep within him. The powerful emotions swept her away too. So she sat beside him in silence, keeping vigil and looking at the picture with him.

But another, more painful notion struck her. Emir had dropped his guard. Very intentionally, he had made himself vulnerable to her by recounting those memories—and she relished the gesture. However, she smarted that he had also revealed something that played right into Michael's suspicions. Kara had no choice but to follow through with Michael's orders.

"Is that why you're here?" she finally and reluctantly asked, setting up her real question. She took a deep breath, desperately desiring not to go any further. Yet her own curiosity begged her on as much as Michael's pleadings. "Is that what the incendiaries are for?" Though Emir suddenly looked up at her with such a startled expression, she continued, "For revenge against Galerius?"

Emir said nothing as he continued looking at her cautiously.

Kara returned his penetrating gaze, nervously waiting for his response. At once, she regretted telling him what she knew. Perhaps extending an olive branch with the question had been impetuous. Worse, Michael would be furious if he found out she had mentioned the incendiaries. Panicking, the young woman peered far across the darkening canyon to where Michael sat—he was looking at her too. Kara immediately felt her face betraying her guilt.

"So you know about them," Emir warily sighed. When Kara turned back to him with such an unsettled expression, he added, "I guess that means your good friend, Michael Gillen, knows about them too."

Kara smarted even more. Nevertheless, she couldn't take back her statements. "Michael was the one who told me. Is that why you're here, Emir? *For revenge?*"

He sat there in a brooding silence. Once again, she felt the strong undercurrents of his emotions. However, this time the sensation grew dark, even frightening. When he remained brooding, Kara pressed, "Incendiaries are a brutal weapon, and there's no other reason for you and your team to have them.... You want the man responsible for your families' deaths to die the same way they died.... And from what Michael told me about your time on *Comanche* and Europa during the war, you probably already tried this once—and failed, obviously."

"You have to admit," Kern quipped self-consciously, "It's the second chance of a lifetime." He remained brooding for quite a long time. Finally, he looked up at her. "But why are you telling me what you know?"

"I already told you—" holding up the medal around her neck again—"I believe in the person who gave this to me." She searched him with her eyes. "I don't believe you could murder someone in cold blood."

"I don't have a choice, Kara. I've wanted it for too long. It's the only reason I'm here."

"You can't *really* want something like that," she pleaded—hoped. "You wouldn't be able to live with yourself."

Emir looked at her soberly. His face still betrayed the darkness churning within. "Kara, I *already* can't live with myself."

"Have you noticed that Kara's been hanging around Kern lately?" Tom Andrews asked, gazing across the canyon at *Lookout One*. Ricci and Kern sat there underneath the camouflage, carrying on idle chitchat. She had just given Kern his food and was sitting and talking to him.

However, Michael Gillen was too preoccupied to notice.

"Ah, this really hits the spot," he sighed, taking a ravenous bite of his sandwich. "Thanks."

"Don't flatter me," Tom joked, annoyed that Michael had ignored his question. "Put it in my tip."

While the young man devoured his meal, Tom kept a suspicious eye trained across the canyon, though trying to remain as inconspicuous as possible.

"By the way," Tom said, still watching the two, "Kate just made contact with *Endurance*. It finished redeployment to the other side of the sun and everything is stable."

"Good," Michael exclaimed, his mouth half full of food. "Is she sure the communication wasn't detected?"

"She said something about matching the carrier wave to the sun's radiation signature, *blah blah blah* … so I think that's a *no*."

The young commander sighed in relief, quickly going back to enjoying his meal.

"I just don't like it," Tom eventually said.

"What?"

Irritated at his long-time friend, Andrews gestured discreetly toward *Lookout One*.

Michael peered over at Kern and Ricci, who sat deeply immersed in conversation. "Oh, that's nothing."

"Doesn't look like nothing to me."

"Kern helped her after Armstrong died," Michael replied, taking a sip of his coffee. "That's all."

However, Andrews remained unsatisfied at the explanation. "I don't like it."

Michael laughed. "Why? Are you jealous?"

"I love Kara *like a sister*," Tom grimaced. "I don't like her hanging around the likes of Kern. He's bad news." When Michael shot him a dismissive look, he retorted, "You might think it's innocent, but consider this: You're eating a cold sandwich, but Kara *cooked* for him. You know Kara: She doesn't cook."

Realizing the truth of his friend's words, Michael raised a suspicious eyebrow and looked across the canyon. Kern and Ricci appeared to be involved in a rather serious discussion, even sitting closer together. "You may be right, but that only plays to our favor."

"What do you mean?"

Michael finally put down what was left of his food. "She didn't go over there on her own. I sent her. I asked her to find out what he's planning."

Tom once again looked across the darkening canyon, watching Kara interact with the Covert and remembering seeing them together recently. "You may have just made a mistake."

"Why?"

Tom went deadly serious—something so unusual for him. "I see the way Kara looks at him." When Michael shrugged obtusely, he added, "I've seen that look before: It's the same way Kara used to look at *you* back at the academy—you know how that turned out."

"You're not saying she would betray us, are you?"

"No, but Kern is smart enough to know how to manipulate her."

"I'm not worried. Kara's smart, and she knows where her allegiances lie."

Tom shook his head incredulously at him. "You once told me I'm good at reading people. You need to start taking your own advice and listen to me."

"Don't worry about Kara."

"Right," Tom replied sardonically, "because Kara *never* does anything impulsive when she's attracted to someone."

The dagger-like comment caught Michael off guard. He watched Tom's admonishing—rather chiding—look for the longest time. Then he gazed across the canyon to where Kara sat. Just then, the young woman turned her head and looked at him. Curiously, even from such a great distance under the soft evening light, Michael could see the guilt washing over her face.

"*Kara,*" the young woman heard whispered to her through the fog of a sound sleep. She also felt an annoying hand upon her shoulder, shaking her. Lying in the makeshift bed, she opened her eyes to the familiar sight of her sleeping quarters at the base camp. The beige canopy of the tent—appearing dark-grey in the night—stretched out above her. A familiar silhouette leaned over her too.

"*Michael?*" she replied in a half-stupor and partially sitting up. "*What's wrong?*"

"Keep your voice down," he admonished in hushed tones. "I just got off my watch, but Kern's still out there."

"Yeah, he's covering my shift tonight."

"What have you found out from your conversation with him?"

Kara sat up, keeping the blanket over her. Struggling through the fog covering her mind and unprepared to answer his question—and feeling a tremendous sense of conflict washing over her—the young woman rubbed her face sleepily. Finally, she replied, "... Nothing really ... just a lot of small talk." However, she could feel her expression betraying her thoughts, for Michael looked at her dubiously.

"Kara, he's up to something ... and I think you know what it is."

She remained silent, returning his probing gaze with her own guilty look. Finally, she sighed. "The only thing I learned is that the Coverts had families before the war. They were stationed on Ceres when the Europans attacked the fleet base. While Kern and his men were defending the base, the Europans firebombed the residences. Their wives and children all died in the attack."

"That's all he told you?"

"Yes," she replied a little hesitantly, hoping he wouldn't cross-examine her any more. "But it's nothing really. Didn't Cyril give you their background?"

However, Michael didn't hear her. No, he was already deeply engrossed in the sobering thoughts churning in his mind. She knew what he was thinking: His thoughts focused on the incendiaries, on memories of Kern clutching that satchel after escaping the burning Europan transport so long ago, on memories of everything that had gone wrong while the Coverts were down on Europa—everything he had told her about his encounter with Kern. Kara didn't need Michael to tell her what he had realized: She already saw it in his face.

"He wants to burn Galerius alive," he declared with such disdain. "He'll kill him before we ever get a chance to take him back to the *Weightless*."

Michael went silent again. He remained fixated on the revelation, laboring over it. His gaze unexpectedly turned dark and foreboding—much like how Kern's face did when he recounted the Ceres Fleet Base attack. Whatever other thoughts passed through his mind, the expression scared her as much as watching Emir.

"Michael, what is it?"

He barely acknowledged her. "We're all in trouble."

"No, we're not. Emir wouldn't endanger us."

However, the young woman realized her comments fell on deaf ears.

247

"I've got to tell Tom," Michael exclaimed, still staring into the air. "We can't let him succeed." Then he turned to her once more. "Find out exactly what he's planning and keep me apprised. That's the only way to counter his threat."

"Michael, he *isn't* a threat to us."

His gaze turned suspicious. "Kara, don't let your feelings blind you."

Before Kara could appeal, Michael got up and left the tent. A cold chill from the cavern wafted in at his departure.

Kara listened to his footsteps fade away. She wanted to go after him, to persuade him that he had nothing to fear. But she knew such persuasion was futile. Yes, she had seen the obsession in his eyes. Finally, the young woman lay back down on the bed, put her hands behind her head, and stared up pensively at the tent's ceiling.

Brent Tasker and Glenn Volk, smartly dressed as Europan soldiers, nervously made their way down the crowded street in the Europan settlement. They kept mostly to themselves while negotiating through the busy area, though occasionally nodding to a passerby or saluting a ranking officer going in the opposite direction. They even smiled at some of the citizens, more than eager to fit in. After all, one wrong move could end their clandestine reconnaissance, resulting in consequences the two dared not ponder.

The time was late in the morning of the fifth day of their mission. Things had gone much better than they had anticipated. With a settlement full of Aurelian Galerius sympathizers and the Allies light-years away—or so the Europans thought—Tasker and Volk enjoyed almost free rein of the small city. Brazenly, the two Coverts breached key security points without much effort. After many successes, the two set their sights even higher: the palace complex towering over them.

"*This isn't going to work*," Tasker whispered to his shorter companion as they neared the entrance.

"It's worth a shot," Volk replied. "They'll just turn us away if we don't have the right authorization—we've made up convincing stories before."

"Or they'll let one of those creatures loose on us."

The two fixed their eyes on the palace entrance, hoping to look nonchalant. The targeted entrance was an obscure transport hub beneath the main palace. A land craft access ramp extended out of the structure, connecting the palace to the settlement's main road system. Sidewalks bordered the ramp.

They made their way down one of the sidewalks toward the entrance. The Coverts hoped that, by posing as service personnel, they could gain entry from the transport hub into the larger palace.

Coming so close to the gaping entrance that they could see inside, the two men abruptly stopped in mid-stride: A rather stern-looking security officer brandishing a rifle appeared out of nowhere.

"Don't move," the Europan warned, coming to stand an arms-length distance between them and the access way. Though the gun remained simply in a blocking fashion, both Tasker and Volk felt the hairs on the back of their necks stand on end as the Europan stared them down. Several other armed guards appeared throughout the area. Tasker and Volk suddenly realized their tenuous predicament.

"What's wrong?" Volk asked, hoping his shredded nerves didn't betray them.

Just then, a small land craft appeared from the entrance, navigating up the access ramp toward the main road. The security officer positioned himself between them and the transport. Tasker and Volk watched in astonishment as the open-air vehicle passed them. Four men rode in the transport: a driver, two guards, and—much to the Coverts' surprise—an old man sitting in the back seat.

The two looked at each other in stunned silence, watching as Aurelian Galerius watched them from the transport as he passed. The man's frail face cracked a warm smile, and he brought his hand up and waved at them. Ironically, Tasker and Volk found themselves saluting just to keep from drawing attention. Quickly, the transport drove away, and the whole area returned to normal.

"Thanks for cooperating," the security officer smiled, bringing down his rifle and walking away.

"Can you believe that?" Volk whispered after the Europan walked out of earshot.

"No."

Realizing that their assumed identities remained intact, Volk turned to his companion. "Are we still going into the palace?"

Tasker kept watching the transport move farther away. "Didn't we see him yesterday around this same time, just a little farther to the southeast? In the same car? Same lack of security detail?"

"Yeah, come to think of it."

"And didn't we see him coming back from the southeast the previous day? Only later in the day when we were closer to the capitol city construction site?"

"Yeah."

Tasker leaned in closer to his smaller companion. "This is the only place where we've seen any real security. Let's forget about getting into the palace. We need to find out where Galerius keeps going every day."

The *ESS Endurance* floated languidly in space, subdued under the prominent yellow glow of the massive 18 Scorpii sun it orbited. Having successfully redeployed to the other side of the star—well out of view of Europan scanners on Sco-II—its computers easily kept up with their responsibilities: maintaining the ship's position and status, ensuring communications capability with the *Endurance* crew so far away, passively scanning for any sign of trouble, and the like.

In a small utility room deep within the vessel, the E-2 utilibot hung lifelessly in its docking collar against the wall. The device, its many service arms drawn in close and all status indicators dark, had hung deactivated in its docking collar for some time. According to the maintenance schedule, the utilibot would remain that way for quite a while.

Unexpectedly, the small machine came to life. Lighting up like an ornament, the utilibot spun its flattened head around as it disengaged and floated out of its docking collar. The machine hovered in the center of the room for several long moments, moving each of its service arms as if stretching from a long nap and relishing its newfound freedom. Continuing to hover in the air, it listened to the special instructions playing deep within its logic circuits.

Confirming its orders one last time, the utilibot floated up through a portal in the ceiling to a service passage. The utilibot quickly disappeared into the passage and headed for the ship's main computer core. Once there, it would make the instructed parameter changes— changes the main computers would not relay to the *Endurance* crew so far away.

Michael Gillen sat with most of the *Endurance* crew gathered at the command center behind the *Aurora*. Of course, Brent Tasker and Glen Volk, who were on day-five of surveying the Europan settlement, were absent. Phil Marcotte and Eric Gunn stood watch at the lookout posts outside the cavern. Taking a quick break from their busywork that kept the day moving, the remaining crew was enjoying lunch at the table in the center of the area.

While eating and engaging in small talk, Michael noticed the irony of the seating. He, Kate, Tom, and David Tashjian sat on one side of the table, while Kern and Zeidler—the only Coverts present—sat on the opposite side. Most ironic of all was Kara, who sidled up between the Centauries and Coverts—between him and Kern really. Every so often, Tom shot Michael wary but inconspicuous glances while Kara and Emir Kern playfully interacted.

Unexpectedly, the communications console off to the side beeped frantically. Kate immediately went over to the machine while everyone watched.

"The *Endurance* is contacting us," she said after studying the device. She knelt and read the encrypted data streaming across its display. Everyone watched uneasily, since she appeared rather concerned. "*Endurance* is reporting a cascade failure."

"What's wrong?" Tom asked ahead of everyone else.

"The fusion drives misfired, interrupting its orbit," Kate replied. "The computer can't shut down the engines." Reading the display another moment, her eyes went wide. "The ship's headed straight into the sun!"

Silence fell over the entire crew.

"What happened?" Michael asked.

"I don't know," she shook her head while studying the readouts. "Maybe the ship was struck by a meteor or something." After studying the display through a tense moment, Kate shook her head again. "I can't tell ... but the sun's corona is already affecting the ship. We're already losing vital control systems."

From where they sat just a short distance away, the rest of the crew watched data from the *Endurance* streaming erratically across the communicator's screen. Kate began working the controls of the unit to send back instructions.

"Don't, Kate," Michael interjected. "You may give away our position." When a wave of quizzical if not incredulous looks washed over the small group, the young man added, "It'll take seven or eight minutes for the commands to reach the ship—assuming the ship could even execute them. Besides, what we're hearing already occurred that long ago. Whatever is *going* to happen has *already* happened."

"The computers have lost control of the auxiliary thrusters." Kate announced.

The entire crew haplessly listened as Kate sounded out the demise of the ship: hull temperatures rising, radiation breaching the shielding, critical support systems disabling, and the like.

Out of the corner of his eye, Michael watched Kern and Zeidler for any sign that might betray them as *Endurance*'s saboteurs. However, Zeidler appeared as troubled as the Centauries. Kern, on the other hand, never flinched at the troubling news. No, his face remained flint-like the entire time.

The transmission grew even more garbled as the disaster played out. Eventually, the transmission stopped altogether.

The *Endurance* was gone.

An uneasy silence filled the cavern for a long moment.

"I guess we don't need to worry about finding fuel anymore," David Tashjian lamented.

"Just finding a ship to get home," Kara added dryly.

"Kate, redeploy the communications relay satellites into the sun," Michael looked at her soberly. "We have no use for them now."

While Kate complied by sending out the instructions on the communicator, the command center remained unnervingly quiet; downcast stares became the norm.

"I'll go tell Gunn and Marcotte," Kern stated, standing up and walking toward the mouth of the cavern.

Heavy with trepidation, the crew began dispersing until only Michael and Kate remained in the command center. Michael sidled up beside Kate, who was still next to the communicator. The two traded uneasy looks. Kate turned off the unit and gave him a rather serious sigh. "I hope you made the right decision."

"Me too."

CHAPTER TWENTY

An Opportunity

Kara Ricci made her way across the broad canyon toward *Lookout Two*, enjoying the rare sensation of the 18 Scorpii sun against her face. Today was late into the fifth day since Brent Tasker and Glen Volk had left to scout out the Europan settlement. Strictly following Emir Kern's urgings to avoid leaving the cavern, the young physician was starting to go stir-crazy.

Drawing near to the lookout post, Kara spotted Michael and Kate Gillen hidden discreetly under the camouflage netting. Though Michael was attending the watch, Kara immediately realized he had instead immersed himself in his wife's attention. They sat close together, doting over each other playfully and enjoying the stolen moments. Kara even heard Kate giggling and shrieking every now and then.

Though happy for the young couple, Kara thought their behavior was a little odd: The base camp remained subdued under the devastating news of *Endurance*'s destruction.

When she cleared her throat intentionally, the young couple abruptly parted and tried to act nonchalant.

"Don't you just *hate* guard duty," Kara smiled devilishly while ducking under the netting. She received the pleasure of watching the couple attempt an awkward recovery from their embarrassment. Kate even blushed a little.

"Hi, Kara," Michael greeted her self-consciously as she sat down across from them.

Letting the awkwardness of the moment pass, she finally said, "Michael, I need to talk with you."

"I'll leave you two alone," Kate said, patting him on the knee quaintly and getting up.

"Please stay, Kate," Kara gestured. "This involves you too."

After Kate sat back down, Michael fixed his attention on Kara. "What's up?"

Kara hesitated for a long moment to muster her courage. Finally, she blurted out, "We need to slow this mission down."

Michael went sober, though the corner of his mouth twisted into an incredulous if not cynical smirk. "Why would I do that?"

She hesitated again. She knew she didn't have a good reason, at least not one that Michael would accept. No, her suggestion was merely an excuse to buy her more time, to put off what she foresaw as an imminent tragedy. "A peace offering to Emir." She watched him grimace at the mere mention of the man's name. "To let him and his men train for the upcoming missions."

"Kara, I intentionally accelerated the mission to keep him off guard."

"It will help us too," she pleaded, her fingers nervously playing with the locket chain under the neckline of her shirt. "This mission is flying at the speed of light—and for no reason. Too many things are going wrong: the Slipstream drive malfunction ... losing the ship ... *Armstrong dying*. No, Michael, you need to slow things down for the safety of the crew."

"Kern is our biggest threat," Michael huffed. "We have to keep him from killing Galerius so we can take him back for trial. *That* should be your focus."

The young woman gazed at Michael and Kate uneasily. Seeing his expression turning dark and Kate's wax over in support of him, she immediately smarted at ever telling him about the Coverts' past. Chills ran up her spine; she foresaw a foreboding future for the *Endurance* crew. "Michael, these Coverts are dangerous."

"That's why we have to stop them," he retorted, noticing she was clutching the locket around her neck in a nervous fashion. His eyes lingered on the locket, as if he had noticed Emir's medal hanging off the chain. So she discreetly concealed the decoration with her fingers. Michael continued, "I'm not letting them put us in danger like they did with *Comanche*—I'm *not* losing this crew! I'm also not going to let them ruin my one chance to clear my family name."

"We've lost too much already, Michael! We're stranded—*this mission is a failure!* We need Kern and his men on our side to protect us against the Europans. We'll need them to destroy that Europan fleet so it doesn't endanger Earth States—you still want that, right?"

"Yes."

"Then maybe you should let the Coverts kill Galerius," Kara reluctantly offered, immediately wincing at the indignant looks shooting back at her. "What's that *murderer* to us anyway? We can still bring his remains back to the *Weightless*."

Michael and Kate looked slack-jawed at each other.

"Take *what* back to the *Weightless?*" Michael rather mocked. "A pile of ashes?"

"*Kara*," Kate gazed at her with eyes wide, "I can't believe that *you're* advocating letting them kill someone in cold blood."

"I'm not—"

"And if we let Kern do such a thing," Michael piled on, "—we're dead!"

"That's absurd."

Kara watched the couple converse by mere expression. Once more, chills ran up her spine, for the two appeared as if knowing some sort of dreadful secret. Finally, Michael looked at her with such a deadly serious gaze. "Kern and his men are here to die."

Kara went silent at the incredible remark. She gazed at the couple— particularly Michael—searching for some sign of relenting from them. None came. Defiantly, she shook her head. "I don't believe it."

Once again, Michael and Kate traded curious looks before he turned back to her. "Kern and his men intentionally destroyed the *Endurance*."

"That was an accident."

"No, Kara, it *wasn't* an accident," Kate interjected. "We were wrong about the Slipstream drive malfunction too. Someone programmed the utilibots to alter our speed. The simulator code was intentionally loaded into the computers to cover up the tampering. They programmed the same utilibot to destroy the *Endurance* after it redeployed."

"That can't be," Kara exclaimed, her voice cracking a bit. Though trying to remain unflinching, the young woman's confidence withered. The dread of such a terrible revelation—and its more dreadful implications—washed over her too.

"I found the evidence myself," Kate asserted.

"No one else but you knows about this," Michael cautioned. "I'm telling you because you need to understand just how dangerous Emir Kern is."

"Maybe it wasn't Emir," Kara challenged rather unconvincingly.

Michael shook his head compassionately. "Kara, there's only one reason why the Coverts destroyed the ship: They aren't going home. They've lived on revenge for years—that's what probably made them so good at what they do." He watched the angst welling up within her. "This is the chance Emir Kern and his men have waited for: They exact their revenge ... and then go out in a blaze of glory by taking on the whole planet. Once Galerius is dead, we all die with him."

He went silent for a long moment, as she imbibed the bitter truth. Her head dropped, and she stared vacantly at the ground. "Then why did you let him destroy the *Endurance*?"

"Because otherwise, he would know we found out what he had done. And then the Coverts might kill us"—pausing hesitantly—"just like they killed Ben Morris."

Kara abruptly looked up at him again, her eyes filled with as much dread as disbelief. "You think they killed Ben?"

"I can't be certain. But Kern wanted his own flight team since the beginning. I think the authorities found Ben too quickly for them to carry out killing the rest of us. Once the mission got underway, Kern and his men needed us to get them here. But our value ends when they find Aurelian Galerius."

Kara remained silent for a long moment. "I'm not sure I believe that."

"Whether I'm correct about who killed Ben doesn't really matter right now," Michael replied, glancing at Kate for support. "What matters is that, with the *Endurance* gone, Kern knows we're at his mercy. That makes him comfortable. That gives us the room to counter his plans to kill Galerius—maybe even save the mission."

"How can you even care about the mission anymore?" Kara pleaded, her slender frame slumping back against the rocks and her face filled with angst.

"I won't let this chance to restore my family name slip away," he declared with an all too familiar obsession—perhaps worse than she had ever beheld from him. "Regardless, we stay alive by keeping *Aurelian Galerius alive*.... And I'm going to need your help to pull it off."

Kara, her spirit withering away, looked up at him curiously.

"Tasker and Volk are back!" Eric Gunn's voice echoed from the mouth of the cavern, breaking the subdued, early evening ambiance of the base camp inside.

Michael Gillen, Emir Kern, and Tom Andrews—all standing over the table in the makeshift command center behind the *Aurora*—immediately looked at each other in surprise. The three dimensional holographic map of the surrounding terrain suddenly became unimportant. Therefore, the three men set off toward the front of the cave, followed by the rest of the *Endurance* crew mulling about.

Before the eager team had gotten very far, the blackout netting draped in front of the *Aurora* pulled back, letting Brent Tasker and Glen Volk enter. Phil Marcotte and Eric Gunn followed closely behind, having left their guard duty posts to celebrate the soldiers' unexpected return.

"Gentleman, welcome back," Kern smiled at Tasker and Volk, slapping each of them on the shoulder and sparking a new enthusiasm among the whole team. "Everything okay?"

"Yeah," the two men almost said in unison.

"You didn't bring back any unwelcome guests?"

"And where's your land craft?" Michael added.

"Everything's okay," Tasker replied. "The land craft is out front."

While Kern waved for Marcotte to bring the vehicle behind the netting, a small reunion celebration commenced among the Coverts. With much enthusiasm, Tasker and Volk recounted the highlights of their trip, while Kern, Zeidler, and Gunn lamented about being stuck in the cave the entire time. However, the festivities took a serious pause when Zeidler mentioned *Endurance*'s destruction.

Michael watched Tasker and Volk's reactions closely, looking for signs that the two men weren't surprised at the news. Tom, who stood by watching with the other Centauries, glanced tellingly at Michael: He sensed that the two men were aware of the ship's sabotage. However, Michael couldn't sense such a reaction. If anything, he thought Tasker and Volk's reactions conveyed an appropriate level of shock.

Of course, Tom was always much better at reading people.

"You were only gone six days," Michael interrupted the reunion.

"The mission was a lot easier than we thought," Volk replied with a smile. "Security is lax. Even the command centers were approachable."

"I'm not surprised," Curran Zeidler mused. "They don't have any enemies here on Sco-II."

"They don't *think* they have any enemies on Sco-II," Kern corrected him with a gleam in his eye.

"We're not on Sco-II," Tasker interjected. "They call it *New Europa*. And the settlement is *New Tyre*."

"*New Europa*? *New Tyre*?" Kern pondered disdainfully. "Over my dead body." Then, putting aside the subject, he asked, "How far did you have to camp outside the settlement?"

The two men traded conspicuous glances. Volk, in particular, looked to his companion to answer the question.

"We found Galerius," Tasker exclaimed, watching Kern's expression change predictably. As if to filibuster any follow-ups to the leader's original question, he added, "And we found a place to ambush him."

The statement felled any pending comments, and the subdued atmosphere hanging over the base camp lifted as if a passing storm. Upon seeing Glen Volk proudly holding up a data disk, Kern waved everyone back to the command center.

The entire Endurance crew gathered in the command center behind the *Aurora*. Everyone fixed their eyes on the holographic display hovering over the main table.

The three-dimensional image at the center of attention was a map of an isolated area of the Europan settlement. A modest roadway snaked through the hilly and unpopulated terrain. Though the terrain ran thick with vegetation and undergrowth, the roadway cutting through was under heavy construction.

Zooming in on one small section, the display showed a place where the road curved on a gradual, northeasterly path. Two-thirds of the way to the east, another road—barely carved out of the rough hills—veered off to the southeast toward the capital city construction site. Though the final thoroughfare was evident, much of the construction was still in progress.

"Galerius goes out daily at eleven hundred hours to inspect progress on the capitol city," Volk began, pointing to the top of the map and tracing the main road. "He always uses this roadway. It lies halfway between the current palace and the construction site. His next stop is an inspection of the fleet and military training centers, but that's not important now."

"You sure about this?" Kern asked skeptically.

"Yes, he even uses the same land craft," Tasker chimed in. "Only two guards and a driver go with him."

"The terrain is *very* isolated," Volk added. "And we didn't see any of those *creatures* there either."

"What creatures?" Curran Zeidler asked. The rest of the *Endurance* team looked on curiously too.

"Big, ugly beasts," Volk warned, cracking a half-smile. "Almost four meters tall, four or five times bigger and uglier than Tasker."

"Thanks," Tasker sarcastically wagged his head at him.

"I don't know if that's possible," Gunn quipped. "Tasker's already pretty ugly."

Kern silenced the erupting laughter among the Coverts with a curt wave of his hand. "What are you talking about?"

"It's those life forms from the reconnaissance data that the computers couldn't interpret," Volk explained. "They look human—but their *not*. They're all over the construction sites and the habitat located outside the main settlement. The Europans use them for heavy labor."

"They can't be indigenous," Kara offered. "This planet doesn't have the ecosystem to evolve such creatures."

"So that means Europan genetic engineers did," Michael mused. "I don't think Aurelian Galerius cares about the ban on genetic engineering—*Weightless* re-alteration aside. I'll bet their ultimate purpose is military."

"One thing's for sure," Tasker looked around soberly. "They're *big* and *mean-looking*. I don't want to find out anything else."

"Let's just stay away from them," Kern said, drawing everyone's attention back to the map. "Since they're not in the area we intend to use, their existence is not an issue. So what else is important about the proposed ambush point?"

"Blasting crews and excavators were in the area," Volk replied, pointing to the unfinished roadway veering off to the southeast. "But they moved off to a project in the capitol city just yesterday. We don't expect them to return for a couple of days. All other work crews were redeployed to the capitol city construction site as well."

Kern smiled broadly. "This is what we're looking for. We'll go in tomorrow. If we can nab Galerius at just the right time, we'll have an hour or more to get back here before they notice he's even gone."

"But we should have a backup plan, in case we're found out," Zeidler added, fixing an intentional gaze on Kern.

"You're right," Kern nodded and turned toward Michael. "Can you have your team ready to come in with the *Aurora*?"

Michael shook his head in the negative, leery that somehow the Coverts were setting him up. "That won't work. The *Aurora* is too slow for a quick escape off-planet."

"But we'll need the *Aurora* to bring in heavy munitions—if things get ugly."

"You can always call the ship remotely," Tom countered. "The AutoNavs can fly it in when needed. Otherwise, the ship stays hidden here in the cavern, where it won't give away our position to the Europans."

"And after capturing Galerius," Michael pressed, looking around the table at the Coverts, "We'll have to hide here until it's safe to carry out the rest of our mission. We need to figure out how to destroy that Europan fleet, stealing one of those ships in the process to get home.

So we should keep the *Aurora* on the ground if possible."

The whole *Endurance* crew went silent at the comment. The Coverts traded inconspicuous but odd looks among themselves.

"So what do you suggest?" Kern finally asked, looking around at his team as if warning them off.

"Keep a low profile for the ambush," Michael exclaimed. "—everything done on the ground and in minimalist fashion. My team will go with you and provide additional cover."

"That doesn't work for us," Kern shook his head defiantly. "You'll get in the way."

"You'll need every gun you can get if things go wrong," Michael said, playing his hand for all it was worth—and ignoring Kara's wary gaze at him. "We'll take orders from you and keep out of your way—but we'll be there if you need us. Given the danger, I'm not sure why you *wouldn't* want reinforcements."

"I don't like it," Kern exclaimed. "None of you are trained for this."

Michael looked him in the eyes. "Now that the *Endurance* is gone, we're in this together. You need all the help you can get, and we need you to keep us safe."—pausing deliberately—"We're *going* with you."

Silence fell over the group. The two leaders traded posturing gazes. The rest of the Centauries and Coverts nervously watched the unspoken exchange.

Finally, Emir Kern let his face turn unconvincingly affable. "If your team stays back and out of the way like you promise ... I'll find some way for you to help out."

The tension in the room subsided, save an occasional contending glance between Michael and Kern. The rest of the crew's demeanors returned to normal—except Kara. No, she remained unsettled the entire time the team worked out the details of the imminent ambush.

The heavyset Europan, bearing a significant number of stripes and decorations on his uniform, walked over to the soldiers gathered on the operations floor of the Europan Strategic Command. The small group studied the holographic images hovering above the table: an aerial view of the northern hemisphere of the planet, superimposed with orbit paths and a computer-enhanced magnetic field.

As the man sidled up to the table, all discussion stopped.

"General Taun," an officer greeted him.

"What do you want to show me, Commander?"

The officer gestured to the two visitors: an older man and a younger man. "This is Lieutenant Kalb and Ensign Tighe of the terra-tanker controllers group. Five days ago, they made us aware of some suspicious activities involving tanker operations. We have reason to believe that unauthorized off-planet flights are occurring."

"What kind of flights?"

"We're not sure," the officer replied. "We haven't detected any unauthorized flights *leaving* the planet—just approaching. At first, we thought it was smuggling activities, but we haven't detected any unauthorized outposts anywhere on the planet. If they were smugglers, they couldn't conduct business so close to New Tyre."

"You just haven't found them yet," the aging general countered.

One of the other Europan officers spoke up, "We're still doing reconnaissance across the planet. We should have better information soon."

"We can't wait much longer," another interjected.

"I agree," Taun nodded. "I need to report this finding to Lord Galerius, but I don't want to go to him until we know more. He has ears everywhere … every hour I wait is another hour he might find out through other channels."

"We *have* found something very interesting," the commander offered. He pointed to the holographic display. "A small transport entered the atmosphere at the northern pole six days ago. Though we lost the ship's trajectory shortly after it entered the troposphere"—pointing to the red pulsing circles scattered across the planet's surface—"none of our passive security scanners detected the ship. That means it was traveling close to the surface to keep from being detected."

"That's obvious," Taun exclaimed. "But where did it go?"

"We don't exactly know."

"So you're wasting my time?"

The commander rather winced. "Sorry for the long explanation, Sir." He fiddled with the projection controls. Several red lines appeared, weaving erratically from the pole and down across the planet's surface.

"Since the unidentified ship was avoiding our low-level scanners, we plotted all possible trajectory points." He gestured to the red lines stopping near the settlement's perimeter. "We think they are *very close* to us."

Taun gazed at the display for quite the long time. "So then, they *are* smugglers. Where do you think they're running their operations from?"

"We're not sure," the officer shrugged. "We sent out reconbots across the region. We'll know more soon."

Kara Ricci stepped out of her warm tent into the cold, darkened cavern. With an abrupt, solitary shiver against the chill (for she was still in her nightclothes), she pulled the draping cutaway jacket fast around her slender frame.

Lingering at the tent's entrance for quite a while, Kara nervously deliberated her decision. With her mind aflutter and her fears unresolved, sleep remained elusive. So taking a deep breath, the young woman reluctantly turned and followed the path of marker lights deeper into the cavern.

The markers led her past a number of other darkened sleeping tents. Kara watched her every step on the shadowy path, being careful not to trip or otherwise draw the attention of the rest of the crew, who were fast asleep.

Eventually, Ricci came to a solitary tent sitting off to itself at the rear of the cavern. Pausing for a long moment just outside the makeshift quarters, Kara surveyed the whole area, making sure no one had taken notice of her. Satisfied, she pulled aside the door flap and disappeared into the warm tent.

The glow from the marker light just outside cast a dim light across the quarters. Looking into the shadows, Kara found Emir Kern tucked into his sleeping bag, fast asleep. After stealing a brief moment to admire his countenance, she knelt beside him.

"Emir?" she softly and cautiously beckoned, waiting for him to come to.

However, Kern remained lifeless.

"Emir?" she called again, this time a little louder and with a hand nudging his shoulder.

Once again, the man didn't move.

Frustrated, she waited in the darkness for a moment. When he remained asleep, she doubled her efforts.

"Kara, I know you're there," Emir rather laughed, his eyes still closed. "You can't sneak up on a covert operative."

"Then why didn't you respond?"

He smiled, opened his eyes, and shot a playful grin at her. "I was enjoying the intrusion."

"I *need* to talk to you," she begged.

The groggy man propped himself up on one forearm and gazed at her, noticing the nightclothes and the loose cutaway draping her form. "Are you sure that's all?"

Catching his playful, rather suggestive half-smirk, Kara pulled the cutaway tightly around herself. "*Be serious.*" Her eyes pleaded with him. "I want to talk with you about tomorrow—about your plans for Galerius."

"What about it?"

"Promise me you'll take Galerius back for trial."

His face immediately sobered. "Kara, don't ask me to do that."

"But you're putting the whole crew in danger."

Emir searched her worried expression. "Not if Gillen keeps you Centauries back like he promised. That's why I agreed to let your team come along. It'll be over before he even knows what's happening"—looking at her probingly—"… unless he *already* knows?"

The young woman shrunk under his penetrating gaze. "I didn't tell anyone."

A lie, she thought. *An unfortunate but necessary lie.*

"Good," he replied, his face returning to normal. "My men have waited a long time for this moment."

"But what about doing what's right?"

"Why?" he grimaced. "Just because that's what your good friend, *Michael Gillen*, wants?"

Kara recoiled. "No, we *promised* to bring Aurelian Galerius back. *That's why.*"

However, Kern just shook his head. "I made no such promise. Such a promise would be foolish too." When she looked at him quizzically, he added, "Kara, we won't get out of here alive if we kidnap Galerius. They'll turn the planet upside down to find him—the man probably has locator implants too. They'll know where he is, and then we'll have nowhere to hide."

After letting her ponder the thought, he looked at her with much determination. "No, give them a dead body instead. The security forces will scour the settlement for Europan conspirators. It works to our advantage both ways: We get away, and my men and I get our revenge.... I'm really *saving* the mission—and the crew."

The two went silent as Kara pondered his words.

"Not if Michael doesn't agree with your intentions," she countered, welling up a little. "He'll try to stop you. That means we could all end up dead."

Kara watched his eyes churn uneasily. His face waxed over with that same tormented expression she had seen days earlier.

"I'm okay with that."

The terrible truth hit her! She saw the cold reality lingering in his eyes; the young woman trembled at his awful gaze. "You *want* to die!"

Emir fell under the power of her angst. He paused self-consciously, though attempting a reassuring gaze. "Kara. I can't predict what will happen tomorrow, but there's no turning back. We've suffered too long over our families' deaths." His face twisted with an unrelenting resolve. "We *want* this.... I couldn't persuade my men otherwise—I couldn't persuade myself otherwise."

The two sat silently in the darkness for a long time. Kara slouched back and let her head hang low. While she stared down at the floor, her eyes welled up painfully.

"Kara, I need your support tomorrow."

The young woman said nothing.

"I know you want more from me," Emir offered tenderly. "I'm sorry. I can't give you more. I *want* to—but I *can't*." He gently lifted up her chin with his fingers so that she looked him in the eyes. "Regardless of what I do or don't do tomorrow, we're probably going to die."

Seeing the trepidation building within her, Emir leaned in closer. "You're very special to me." When she reflected back the same longing

267

amidst bitter tears, he placed his hand under her cheek and held her face for the longest time. He watched her tears trail down her cheek and over his fingers. "We still have *tonight* ... before everything changes."

Kara gazed desperately at him, searching him out—pitying him. Nervously, her fingers played with the heart-shaped locket hanging from her neck. Finally, she shook her head sadly. "That's not enough. That's *never* enough."

With one last pleading look, the young woman stole away.

Sitting alone in the darkness and hearing her footsteps move farther away, Emir Kern listened to each fading step. Silence returned. Yet he kept his vigil in the darkness, waiting—wishing—for the sound of her footsteps to return. However, silence remained. Her words haunted him too. So letting out a heavy sigh, he sank back into the makeshift bed. Unsettled by the confrontation, the man put his hands behind his head and stared up pensively at the tent ceiling.

Far on the other side of the cavern, Kara arrived back in her tent in a rush and threw off her cutaway. She desperately wanted to scream—not an option in the subdued cavern. So she fell headlong into her pillow and cried silently, wiping the tears from her eyes as fast as they came. Her mind spun madly over the thoughts of what would happen the next day. Desperately, the young woman searched for the ever-elusive solution to the looming crisis.

However, as she sat in the darkness weeping, only one thought came to mind: Morning was fast approaching.

CHAPTER TWENTY ONE

The High Wall

Michael Gillen plodded along among the Coverts and Centauries up the remote hillside, following well behind Emir Kern and Curran Zeidler. Everyone wore full combat gear in anticipation of the upcoming ambush. Kate walked close to him on one side, while Tom kept pace on the other side. Kara, who wore the telltale signs of a bad night's sleep, followed a short distance behind the trio. Every now and then, he looked back and traded uneasy glances with her.

The thick, lush undergrowth and trees—a stark contrast to the base camp's desolate topography so many kilometers away—made his progress enjoyably difficult. The pleasant aroma of untouched wilderness filled his lungs. Though laboring to carry his share of the equipment for the ambush, he took in the beautiful, Earth-like wilderness surroundings with much satisfaction. And it wasn't just him: Both Coverts and Centauries alike marveled at how the Europans had transformed the settlement from barren rock.

Although the fascinating surroundings provided a temporary respite, Michael's thoughts ran wild with more pressing matters;

his stomach had twisted into knots too. On the fortieth day since *Endurance*'s arrival at 18 Scorpii, the capture of Aurelian Galerius was upon him.

Certainly, he looked forward to capturing the brutal dictator. Fate had given him the opportunity to return Galerius to the *Weightless* for trial, to the very people who held Jonathan Gillen and his inventions in contempt. Today was his chance to redeem the senseless murders of his father, mother, and brother; to prove wrong anyone holding a negative attitude toward the Gillen name. This was *his* chance to bring peace to the Gillen family, not only among the *Weightless*, but also throughout all of Terrae Solaris—if only fate would smile on him.

However, he and the rest of the Centauries had waded into dangerous waters. They were at the mercy of Emir Kern and his men, a team driven by rage and lusting for revenge against Aurelian Galerius. Knowing Kern's intentions, Michael shuddered at what might happen when he and the other Centauries tried to stop him.

Oddly, the young man also couldn't shake the feeling that someone was watching them. Of course, he attributed the sensation to his nervousness about the upcoming ambush and an overactive imagination.

Michael watched Kern and Zeidler, who had hurried well ahead of the rest of the group, reach the top of the bluff. They knelt and surveyed the terrain on the other side of the bluff.

"Tasker, Volk," Kern turned and quietly called down the hillside, taking just the briefest moment to glance away from the construction site below. "I thought you said this area was *clear?*"

The rest of the Coverts sidled up beside Kern and Zeidler at the top of the bluff. Cautiously peering over the rise, Tasker and Volk's mouths dropped in unison.

"I *know* we overheard them say they were being redeployed," Tasker pleaded.

"Well, they're here," Kern grimaced.

Michael, walking the last few steps with the Centauries to the top of the bluff, knelt by Kern and peered over the rise.

Spread out below lay the southeast channel construction area, less than half a kilometer east of where they would ambush Aurelian Galerius. The dusty, rock-laden, rough-hewn passage cut through the pristine bluffs, creating a channel for the unfinished road running through it. A formidable high wall stood in the distance, carved out of the bluff lying on the other side of the channel. The chiseled wall prominently encroached out onto where the unfinished road would eventually run. From that point on to the south, the construction tapered off until surrounded by untouched wilderness bluffs.

Immediately, Michael spotted Kern's concern: the six-man construction crew working in the passage below. They mulled about in front of a massive excavator machine, which towered almost as high as the hill on which they stood. Two dirt-covered, heavy-duty utilibots hovered halfway up the high wall. One machine cut deep, narrow holes into the rock face with a laser drill, while the other stuffed the holes with cylinder-shaped rods.

"What are they doing?" Michael asked.

"They're removing that high wall," Kern replied. "Looks like they plan on taking down half the hill, given the amount of explosives packed into those holes."

Just then, Kara came to kneel closely behind Kern. Putting one hand on his shoulder, she peered over his other shoulder down at the construction crew below. Michael shot an inconspicuous grimace back at Tom and Kate, who returned the sentiment. Kara had tagged along closely to Kern the whole morning—at least when Michael was near him—putting herself between him and Michael.

"They're gonna ruin everything," Eric Gunn interjected, looking at the work crew below.

Kern watched the construction crew for a long moment in thought. Finally, he turned back to his team. "We've got no choice but to dispose of them." He took hold of the pistol at his side and motioned for his team to follow.

"Emir, they're just civilians," Kara begged, grabbing his forearm just as he began to stand up. "They shouldn't have to die."

"Better them than us," Brent Tasker countered while gesturing for the rest of the Coverts to follow him.

"Emir, please don't do this," Kara pleaded, holding him back once more.

"Kara, we have no choice."

Michael watched the interaction, relishing the disagreement transpiring between them. Since Kara was the key to countering Kern's plans for revenge against Aurelian Galerius, he knew the discord boded well for him.

"I have sedatives," Kara offered, holding up her pack containing medical supplies. "I'll make sure they're out the rest of the day."

Kern held his watch up to her impatiently. "Kara, we don't have time."

The two looked at each other for the longest time, trading pleading gazes. Kern's face slowly waxed over in sour resignation—much to Michael's chagrin.

"Fine," Kern shook his head in disbelief before turning to his team. "Okay, guys, let's go capture them so the doc here can do her thing."

The Europan construction worker, lying bound and gagged in the grassy ditch, stared up nervously at Kara Ricci kneeling over him. His eyes trained on the hypodermic she skillfully wielded in her hand. When she plunged the sharp needle into his arm, the man winced. He shot her a disdainful glare as she emptied the syringe's contents into his flesh. His contempt didn't last long. No, the man's eyes waxed closed, and his whole body went limp. Lying unconscious next to his companions, who were also bound, gagged, and unconscious, the construction worker would never know that Kara had actually saved his life.

"Good job, Kara," Emir Kern commented, standing behind her and watching.

The *Endurance* crew stood around her on a shallow hillside at the tapered end of the southeast channel. The high wall, the massive excavator, and the freshly charred remains of two utilibots sat a hundred meters to the west. Having captured the construction crew, the Coverts had marched the workers to the isolated area to let Kara sedate them.

Kern turned to his team. "Cover them up so no one finds them."

While Brent Tasker, Glen Volk, and Eric Gunn began covering the sedated workers with loose branches, leaves, and the like,

Curran Zeidler pointed to the excavator to the west. "I'll move the excavator to the ambush point. It'll make excellent cover."

"Good thinking," the leader said. "Pile rocks and dirt at various intervals throughout the area too. It'll look more realistic, and we can use the piles for cover if things go wrong."

"Got it," Zeidler nodded and set off for the machine.

"Gillen," Kern called to him, pointing to the high wall, "Move your team's land craft over there. It'll still be out of the way but closer to the ambush site."

"Sure," Michael replied, gesturing for Phil Marcotte and David Tashjian to comply. Immediately, the two men set off up and over the hillside toward the vehicle.

Kern motioned, leading Michael, Tom, Kate, and Kara toward the high wall and ambush point to the west. Gunn, Tasker, and Volk stayed behind to finish concealing the unconscious construction workers. Quickly finishing, the Coverts soon came up from behind and rejoined the group. That was when the excavator far ahead of them roared to life. Everyone watched Zeidler navigate the massive machine down the road and away from them, eventually disappearing around the curve of the hill. The small band continued walking.

A minute later, an abrupt noise came from behind them, causing everyone to turn and look. Marcotte and Tashjian barreled over the hill in the Centauri land craft, the vehicle hanging in the air a split second before landing with a heavy thud. Speeding haphazardly down into the channel and past the small band—kicking up quite the dust storm— the nimble vehicle came to a stop at the base of the high wall.

"Is this good?" Tashjian asked Kern when the team reached the place where he had stopped the vehicle by the high wall.

"Yeah," the Covert leader replied, still walking toward the ambush point a half-kilometer away and deep in thought. "But we could have done without all the noise and dust."

"Sorry," both of them replied almost in unison.

While passing the vehicle, everyone took turns gazing up at the impressive high wall towering over them. Kara, who was trailing the small band, stopped at the vehicle. She knelt, took off her pack, and opened one of the vehicle's side compartments. Then she started rearranging her pack and stocking more supplies into it from the open compartment. No one noticed, for the rest of them all stared up at the towering rock wall while continuing to walk westward.

"Do you want us to disarm the explosives?" Tasker asked Kern, gesturing to the charge wires hanging from the drill holes high up on the chiseled rock.

"We don't have time," Kern replied—

He abruptly stopped. His face lit up too. So turning toward Tasker and Volk, he said, "Before we go too far, move our other land craft to the north—just over the bluff at the ambush point—and hide it there. That way, we have two ways of getting out of here if anything goes wrong."

The two men dropped their shoulders and sighed, indicating their obvious disapproval for Kern not thinking of the idea earlier. However, they nodded and set off toward the nearest accessible bluff.

Kern led the rest of the team—absent Kara—toward the ambush point to the west.

Walking with the rest of the crew, Michael finally noticed that Kara wasn't among the group. He looked around, finally spotting her back at the land craft parked by the high wall. She still knelt in front of the open storage compartment while loading supplies into her open pack.

Eager to talk with her alone one last time—nodding tellingly at Tom and Kate to keep going—Michael fell back from the group. When everyone else disappeared around the corner toward the ambush site, he jogged the short distance back to meet her.

"What are you doing?" he asked, coming up to her just as she stood up and closed her pack.

"I'm packing more medical supplies," she almost snipped at him. "I think we're going to need them, since you won't listen to me."

However, Michael remained unfazed and preoccupied.

"So you know what to do, *right?*" he eagerly looked down at her, referencing the Centauri planning session earlier that morning.

However, the question only unsettled the young woman that much more. "Michael, please don't ask me to do this."

He took her by the thick of her arms, his gaze intentional. "Kara, everyone's safety depends on *you* doing what we talked about ... you know that, right?"

"Don't put me in the middle," she begged, pleading by expression for the longest time. "I don't like this, Michael. Someone's going to get hurt. Just let Emir—"

"*Emir?*" Michael recoiled, grimacing sourly. Still holding her by the thick of her arms, the young man shook her ever so slightly. "You're still part of the team, right?" However, her gaze betrayed her thoughts. "*You're a Centauri!*"

"And you're the mission commander!" she said, breaking his grip. "Our safety—yours too—should be your top priority."

"Don't you remember what they sent us here to do? We knew it would be dangerous."

"But Command didn't know about the warships," she pleaded, "or the invasion the Europans are planning against Earth States. They expect *you* to reprioritize the mission—give up capturing Galerius, if necessary."

"Don't try playing on my sense of duty. I'll make sure we accomplish what we need to." He gave her the once over and shook his head cynically. "No, this is all about your feelings for Emir Kern—nothing else. He's manipulating you and you can't even see it."

"I can see that trying to stop him is madness … you're going to get us all killed."

"I'm okay dying if it means doing what we came here to do."

"But that's the point, Michael," Kara continued to plead. "We didn't come here to stop Emir. We came here to ensure Earth States' future." However, when he simply rebuffed her comments, her gaze steeled. "Is stopping Emir Kern worth letting your friends die? Will you be so certain it was worth it when *Kate*'s dead?" she paused for effect, softening her voice intentionally. "What about you, Michael? Is *your* life worth *so little*?"

Michael gazed at her curtly. He could tell she was playing the opportunity for all it was worth. Of course, he fumed over the attempt. "Don't make your concerns out to be some attempt to protect me from myself. You've sided with Kern … you've turned on me, Kara."

"Don't say that," she shot back, her face waxing over in shock. When he remained skeptical, Kara looked at him sadly. "Do you really think I'd be here if I didn't care for you?" Yet he remained silent. "After all we've been through? After what we *shared* so long ago?"

"That's ancient history."

Kara folded her arms protectively in front of herself, her expression falling. "I'm sorry you believe that. I care for you more than anyone, Michael."

"Then why are you fighting me at every step in stopping Kern?"

She watched him rather sulk for a moment. "Maybe it has nothing to do with Emir Kern."

"So you *don't* have feelings for him?" he scoffed, holding a dubious gaze through a long silence.

"I didn't say that," Kara replied uneasily. "But maybe this isn't about what *you want* either, Michael." Then her eyes sharpened. "I've got a lot invested in this mission too—more than you know."

"I thought you were here because of *me*," he sneered.

Kara huffed and looked at him through a long silence. Visibly frustrated that all her appeals had failed, she waxed over deep in thought while keeping his gaze—looking as if she were mustering her courage too. "There's something you should know."

Her gaze waxed oddly, felling Michael silent.

Taking a deep breath, Kara pulled the heart-shaped locket from the neckline of her shirt. The medal Kern had given her dangled from the chain right next to it, and she could see that he took note of the gift. Brushing off his suspicious gaze at the medal, she opened the locket and held it up to him.

Michael looked at the picture of the eight-year-old girl inside, seeing Kara's odd gaze at him from behind the locket. He shrugged. "What does your niece have to do with anything?"

Kara hesitated. "... Her full name is *Caramia Micaela* ... it's the name I gave her when she was born. *Caramia* means *my beloved....* Mia's not my niece, Michael ... she's my daughter."

Michael fell speechless, his face betraying his astonishment and the guilt washing over him. He looked around warily—self-consciously too. "*Your daughter?*"

"I had her my first year at NSEA," Kara confessed, her eyes welling up a little. "Cyril granted me an extended leave of absence from NSEA—he wanted to protect me. So I went away to my sister's, had Mia, and came back to NSEA."

"Cyril knew?" he asked, though that wasn't his *real* question.

"Yes," she lamented, not wanting to continue. "He knows everything about her." A sentimental smile came over her as she gazed at the picture. "My sister called her *Caramia* for such a long time, just as I requested. But as she got older, Mia had her own ideas. Eventually, she decided she liked *Mia* better ... and once she fixates on something, she won't let it go"—looking up at him again—"a stubbornness she inherited from her father. *Caramia Micaela ... my beloved from Michael.*"

Michael stood there speechless, his eyes wide.

"She's why I'm here," Kara said before looking down awkwardly. "I know what happened between you and I was a long time ago ... and I know it was only one night...." Remaining pensive for a long moment, she looked back up at him—her blue eyes shimmering. "*But we have a child, Michael* ... Mia bonds us together forever. I know it sounds silly ... but it's true." Then she averted her eyes again self-consciously.

"Why didn't you tell me about her?" Michael barely eked out, still reeling from the startling revelation.

However, Kara didn't even hear him. "But when we found out about the Europan warships and Galerius' intentions to invade Earth States, I realized they'll attack the military bases on the Moon." She looked him straight in the eyes, her own eyes betraying a dreadful fear. "Michael, you know that civilians were the heaviest casualties of the war, right?"

"*Yeah?*"

Kara fought against welling up. "Mia lives with my sister and brother-in-law in the Mons Hadley Fleet Base settlement." Her eyes pleaded desperately. "Michael, Mia's right on the front lines of the invasion. She's in danger and no one even realizes it." Her eyes filled with tears—so quickly that they trailed down her face from the start—and her chin quivered. "Michael"—her voice trembling—"I need you to stop those ships ... and you *need* Emir to do it." When he remained silent, she begged, "If you won't change your mind for me ... then do it for your daughter."

The two went silent once again. Kara's expression and tears pleaded for help, while Michael remained overwhelmed by the startling revelation. He remained deep in agitated thought while Kara continued holding up their daughter's picture.

Finally, his face twisted scornfully. "Why are you telling me this *now*?" Before Kara could respond, he abruptly turned and set off away from her—at a rather telling pace.

"Michael!" she pleaded.

The young man continued walking away, his footsteps becoming more urgent. Unexpectedly, he stopped and turned around. The most indignant look covered his face.

"This changes nothing!" he huffed, shaking a finger at her. "If you want to protect *your* daughter, then do what I told you! You have your orders!"

Huffing once more, Michael turned around and set off toward the ambush site.

CHAPTER TWENTY TWO

A Dusty Highway

"**M**ike, what's wrong?" David Tashjian whispered to a rather preoccupied Michael Gillen, who lay on his stomach on the dusty ground beside him. Both men kept hidden behind a cluster of large rocks, holding their rifles at the ready. At David's prompting before speaking, both had muted their communicators.

Michael glanced toward the ambush point in the center of the road before him, ensuring no one was close enough to eavesdrop. "What do you mean?"

"You haven't been yourself since we arrived at the ambush point. You're not having second thoughts about stopping Kern, are you?"

"No," Michael assured him, shaking his head. "I just can't wait to get off this rock and go home."

David pondered the thought for a moment. "I don't know. How often do you get to go on a forty-six-light-year vacation? All the sneaking around and Europans aside … I rather like this place."

Michael nodded somewhat uneasily. The two men then unmuted their communicators and returned their gazes to the ambush site lying before them.

The predetermined capture point lay on the main road about a half-kilometer west of the high wall in the southeast corridor. Kern had chosen the place because of the natural cover: Unlike most of the roadway surrounded by vertically carved, barren rock walls, these bluffs descended naturally to the sidings and lay overgrown with thick vegetation. Several makeshift paths also led away from the site in different directions, allowing for an easy escape.

Neither Centauri could see anyone. Brent Tasker and Tom Andrews lay hidden just to the east on the same side of the road, and a prominent bulge in the rocky hillside sat between the two positions. The rest of the *Endurance* crew hid with Emir Kern, who lay in wait behind the massive excavator on the opposite side of the road. Curran Zeidler and Kara Ricci were hidden high above in the machine's control cabin.

Michael struggled to calm his rattled nerves. Thoughts over what would soon happen churned uneasily in his head. Never were the Centauries more vulnerable to Emir Kern and his men. The young commander began second-guessing himself, considering that perhaps he shouldn't have waited out Kern's treachery. Perhaps he and the Centauries should have overtaken the Coverts back at the base camp. Perhaps arresting him sooner for sabotaging the *Endurance* would have been the right thing to do.

Of course, Michael needed the Coverts to capture Aurelian Galerius.

But more than anything, Michael couldn't expel Kara's startling revelation from his thoughts. *He had fathered a child with her.* All the dreaded implications and guilt distracted him, making him doubt himself at such a critical time. And he fumed over Kara's impertinence. She had spitefully opened an old wound—probably to garner sympathy so that he would let Kern carry out his diabolical plan.

"Transport coming from the southwest," Zeidler's voice came over the communicator. "Same make as we're expecting."

"Look alive," Kern whispered into his communicator from his position behind the excavator. "Make sure your detection dampeners are active. Tasker, don't shoot until I give the signal—but don't let the transport go one inch over the capture point either."

"Got it."

All transmissions ceased when the sound of a motor broke the air.

The small, open-air transport rounded the corner in the distance, moving at a moderate pace. Aurelian Galerius sat peacefully in the vehicle's back seat, having not a care in the world. A driver and two guards accompanied the dictator, just as expected.

From her vantage point high above in the excavator's control cabin, Kara watched Emir Kern far below as he crouched at the foot of the machine. Though he remained calm and emotionless while lying in wait, Kara sensed a dark, foreboding rage boiling within him, overwhelming him. Though the expression barely registered on his face, she could see it there nonetheless.

"*No*," she whispered desperately under her breath, shaking her head too.

Zeidler, sitting next to her, failed to notice her concern. Instead, the man remained singularly focused on the approaching transport, his eyes betraying the anger boiling within him too. The other Coverts she could see all waxed over with the same bitter expression.

Everything was happening just as she had foreseen.

When the craft came within one hundred meters of the capture point, Kern whispered into his communicator, "*Now, Tasker.*"

From his concealed position on the opposite side of the road, Brent Tasker methodically trained his rifle on the vehicle as it sped toward the ambush point. The rifle wasn't his normal gun; that gun lay to his side. Instead, the gun in his hand shot focused electromagnetic pulses. He pulled the trigger. With a quick but imperceptible blast, the transport—all its electronics fried—glided to a full stop right over the intended ambush point.

From where he lay hidden, Michael nervously watched while keeping his rifle ready. The scene before him turned comical. Bewildered at the craft's unexpected stall, the driver tried restarting the engine several times—nothing. With each failed attempt, Galerius grew increasingly annoyed.

Shrinking under his leader's mounting impatience, the driver stepped out and went to the engine compartment in the front. One of the guards followed. Together, they opened the compartment and examined the lifeless motor.

Yet whatever may have been comical quickly disappeared. The Coverts rushed the transport like lightning, causing Michael to wince at their precision. Eric Gunn took out both the driver and guard with single shots, while Zeidler did the same to the second guard from the excavator cabin. Before the dead bodies even fell into heaps on the ground, the Covert team surrounded the vehicle. Even Zeidler arrived in split seconds, having slid down the rails of the excavator's ladder with his gear in tow over his shoulder. All Covert guns trained on a stunned Aurelian Galerius, who threw his hands into the air in surrender.

Galerius didn't say a word. Instead, the small, frail man sat trembling. Though dressed in attire clearly conveying his high position, the balding, grey-haired man radiated a demeanor devoid of any nobility or power, as if he were a shadow of his own repute. No, his weak, blue eyes filled with fear as he stared up at his captors.

"Aurelian Galerius!" Kern declared just loud enough so that the Centauries could hear from their support positions. "By the authority given us by the Allied supreme commanders, you are under arrest for crimes against humanity. You will be taken back to Solaris for trial. Once found guilty, you *will* be executed." Then he turned to his team. "Tie him up. Make sure he has no locators or weapons and get him to the land craft."

As the Coverts executed the capture, the Centauries—except for Kara—emerged from their positions and coalesced curiously in front of the excavator.

"You need any help?" Michael asked Kern as he and David Tashjian crossed the road well clear of the transport. Just as he had instructed the rest of the Centauries to do after the initial capture, he and David carried their rifles rather casually. Kern's men briefly glanced up, noticing their relaxed—rather naïve—demeanor. Surely enough, the small band went right back to work restraining Galerius and paying them no mind.

"No, Commander, we've got it," Kern replied, surveying the rather undisturbed surroundings. "This went better than expected. Take your group and redeploy to the high wall. We'll take Galerius out in our land craft to the north. Keep monitoring us for instructions. You never know when we'll need the *Aurora*."

Michael nodded as he and David met the other Centauries—absent Kara—in front of the excavator. "Okay, guys, let's get our equipment and head east."

Kern, morbidly content watching the Centauries disappear around the excavator, muted his communicator. He nodded tellingly at his men. They in turn muted their communicators, while Zeidler inconspicuously pulled the satchel of incendiaries from his gear. Ensuring the Centauries were still out of sight on the other side of the massive machine, the Covert leader leaned in toward the dictator.

"You haven't said a word yet," he chided the old man in hushed tones. "You're a disappointment—nothing but a coward without your security." His voice hushed even more. "Allow me to introduce us: We're survivors of the Ceres Fleet Base attack—you remember that?"

Galerius said nothing. He simply stared back in fear, mesmerized by the hatred emanating toward him.

"Our families burned to death in that massacre," Kern seethed. "Now, it's your turn to burn!"

"*Please don't!*" Galerius begged desperately, causing Kern to look around warily once more—no sign of the Centauries.

The man's pleas for mercy went unanswered. Tasker restrained the old man to the vehicle with handcuffs, while the other Coverts grasped eagerly at the firebombs inside the satchel. With much delight, the soldiers affixed the active charges to the dictator's clothing. They indulged themselves in the morbid ritual, relishing the terrible moment and losing themselves in their lust for revenge.

"Too bad it's the middle of the day," Kern mused, placing one of the incendiaries squarely on Galerius' chest. "I love the sight of a bonfire at night."

Weapons clicking to the ready brought the Coverts' morbid celebration to a sudden end. The Centauries had circled around the excavator and quickly surrounded them, though Brent Tasker and Eric Gunn reacted fast enough to draw their weapons: Tasker at Michael and Gunn at Phil Marcotte. Otherwise, each Centauri covered one of the Coverts. Kara, as Michael had ordered, remained in the excavator cabin high above, strategically kept out of the way.

"Put down your weapons!" Michael commanded, standing behind Emir Kern with his rifle pointed at his back. He wedged the barrel's

283

end uncomfortably under the Covert's shoulder blade.

None of the Coverts budged. Instead, they only steeled with resolve—particularly Kern.

"Gillen, don't do this," Kern yelled back. Upon seeing the Centauries unshaken by the warning, he added, "I don't want to hurt anyone except Galerius."

"We're taking him back to Solaris for trial—just as we were ordered to do."

"You don't know what you're getting yourself into, Gillen. Take your people and leave!"

"No, Kern! I won't let you stoop to this level."

"*Stoop to this level?*" Kern gritted his teeth and narrowed his eyes contemptuously. He half-turned his face so that Michael could see his grimace from behind. "At least I'd never point a loaded gun at a fellow serviceman—not until I had to defend myself, that is."

"But you're okay disobeying a direct order?"

"I don't care about my orders," Kern shot back. He nodded at the dictator. "*What good's a trial?* We know he's guilty ... guilty of things deserving a far worse punishment than being burned to death! We can end his reign here and now!" Looking at the faces of his wayward team, the man choked up. "*It's our right!*"

Michael surveyed his own team, noting how the Centauries' eyes betrayed their disdain for the brutal dictator. Even Kate, who was closest to the Covert leader (and had the best view of his tormented expression), reflected back something of sympathy for him. So Michael replied, "You're not the only one who suffered under this Cretin."

However, Kern only spiraled deeper into the madness plaguing him. "You don't know what we've been through. You can't see the faces of your wife and children ... *burned beyond recognition*"—gritting his teeth in such agony—"*You don't know the pain of losing someone you love like that!*" He went silent for an unbearable moment, and his eyes betrayed the insanity overwhelming him. "Maybe it's time you do—"

Kern brought his pistol up into Kate's face! Her eyes shot open wide! The barrel's end hovered just a hand's length away from her nose, and she could see Kern's finger squarely on the trigger as he stared her down. The startled, young woman froze in terror, though the pistol she kept trained on Zeidler trembled tellingly in her hand.

Michael winced at the sight of Kate staring down the pistol. Yet his anger boiled, and his resolve against the Covert steeled all the more.

"Kern, don't do this," Zeidler pleaded. "This isn't going to help."

"Yes, stop this!" Kara desperately cried out, appearing from around the excavator. She hurried around the perimeter of the standoff, aghast at the sight. "Emir, *please* … put down your gun! Michael, *you too!*" However, when neither man relented, she pleaded once more, "We're all on the same side!"

Michael studied Kara's exasperated expression, surprised at her appearance—and unsure of her intentions. However, though he had ordered her to stay in the excavator until summoned, Kara's presence seemed to have a calming affect on Emir Kern—though the Covert was far from cooperative.

"I can't do that, Kara," Kern exclaimed, keeping his gun trained on Kate. He half-turned his head toward Michael. "Gillen, this is up to you. We can all leave peaceably if you just let us finish what we came here to do."

"*Don't let him do it, Michael,*" Kate eked out with a trembling voice, her eyes mustering a nervous but defiant stare at the Covert leader.

Kern moved the pistol around ever so slightly, as if choosing a target among her fear-stricken features. "Don't be foolish, Kate. I don't want to kill you … but I *will* if you leave me no choice."

"*I'm not afraid of you.*"

"Kara," Michael called out as if challenging Kern, "Do what we talked about: Take the prisoner out of here. Take our transport—leave in the *Aurora* if you have to."

"Michael, don't make me do this."

"Kara, that's an order."

Kara paused anxiously for a moment, shooting pleading looks at Kern. Finally, the young woman moved toward Galerius and the continuing stalemate.

"Are you going to shoot *her?*" Michael wagged his head from behind at Kern.

The Covert, stymied by the surprising move, kept silent as Kara moved amid drawn weapons toward Galerius.

After ripping the incendiaries off the dictator and throwing them to the ground, Kara drew her pistol and shot off the cuff chains restraining him to the vehicle. The whole time, she moved slowly and deliberately, attempting to put out of mind the unnervingly cold stares from the Coverts—and the guns they kept ready in their hands. Finally waving for the old man to comply, Kara anxiously surveyed the ghastly scene. She realized just how dangerous things had turned.

Kern remained frozen in place the whole time, keeping his pistol to Kate's face and staring her down—quite an effective tactic. At the same time, the man appeared as if searching for his next move to counter the surprise.

"Let's go," Kara ordered, grabbing Galerius by the scruff of the neck. She wrenched him out of his seat and through the vehicle's open door; the old man struggled to comply. With her gun drawn, Kara pushed him outside the perimeter of the standoff. That was when she spotted Kern inconspicuously signaling his team.

She suddenly seized the old man in a chokehold, putting the dictator between her and the others and bringing her pistol to the man's head.

"Stop this!" she ordered everyone. "Put down your weapons, or I'll kill him myself. He's not worth it!"

Everyone looked on, stunned and silenced—Michael especially. Yet all guns remained trained on their intended targets.

Tightening her chokehold on the dictator, Kara labored to maintain her poker face. After all, she didn't intend to carry out the threat; she was bluffing. Nevertheless, her threat needed to appear genuine, for she had just put herself in the middle of the tenuous conflict.

"Kara, don't do this," Michael warned, his face betraying his outrage over her unexpected move. "Just take him back to the *Aurora*."

"No, Kara," Kern retorted, finding his resolve once more. He rather shook the pistol in Kate's face for emphasis. "Leave Galerius here. He's not worth the lives of your friends—that's what your glorious commander should worry about."

"You're the one pointing your pistol at my friend's head," she scoffed.

"Then remember what I told you about locator implants? We'll never make it off the planet if we take him alive."

Kara watched the two men posturing against each other—their teams following suit as the tension grew. Neither Michael nor Emir was relenting. No, they only steeled against her threat. And the other Coverts all looked as if ready to strike against the Centauries.

They were defying her threat.

Her resolve withered before them; her bluff had failed. Both men noticed her hesitation too. No doubt, they would avail themselves of her weakness to gain the advantage.

"Michael," she looked at him nervously, "What if Galerius *does* have hidden locators?"

"We'll worry about that when we have to. Just get him out of here."

Kara's eye's betrayed her desperate ambivalence toward both Michael and Emir. Still holding the dictator in a painful chokehold with her pistol barrel firmly against his temple, the young woman looked to Michael briefly, and then to Kern for the same, and then back to Michael again. She kept doing this repeatedly; each time her gaze waxed that much more anxious.

She didn't know what to do.

Kara's face soon fell in surrender. She looked to Michael as if to plead for his forgiveness—but his gaze only turned reproachful. With much reluctance, the conflicted, young woman pushed Galerius back toward the vehicle, just as Kern had asked her to do—

Until Michael aimed his pistol squarely at her head!

Kara immediately stopped, her face filling with dread.

The pistol wasn't the same weapon Michael was using for the standoff. No, his rifle remained cradled in his right hand and trained on Kern from behind. He had instead pulled the pistol out from behind his protective vest. He brandished two deadly weapons now—three, if the bitter look shooting back at her counted.

"*Michael!*" Kara cried out, wrenching Galerius around to shield herself from him.

"Kara, I won't let you disobey a direct order."

The old man gasped for air, and he pulled at her arm wrapped around his throat. However, the prisoner's welfare faded from importance. All her attention focused on Michael. Despite her desperate gaze pleading for sympathy, he kept the pistol pointed at her head. His determined expression didn't change either. No, Kara regretfully realized he would kill her unless she complied.

Something inside her died that very moment—died painfully.

She backed away in a panic, pulling the old man with her.

"Don't move, Kara," Emir Kern warned in a disturbingly calm voice, his eyes reflecting the darkness churning within him. He raised his left hand, flaunting the incendiaries' remote detonator in his grip. His thumb hovered tenuously over the trigger. "This ends here, Gillen.... Since you won't see things my way, we'll all go up in flames—unless you let Kara do the right thing. Kara, put Galerius back in the transport."

The two teams remained in the dreadful impasse.

Gazing down at the incendiaries scattered on the ground among their feet, Kara realized just what dire circumstances had befallen her. She saw the maddening resolve in Emir's eyes to push the trigger. He would not budge—even for her. Michael had become no different from Kern, as if Kern's madness had infected him too.

If she didn't quickly make the right decision, everyone would die.

With a thousand thoughts and emotions overwhelming her, Kara dropped her head in bitter defeat. She lowered the pistol in her hand and released her chokehold on the dictator. Galerius immediately snapped forward, gasping to catch his breath. This drew the attention of some in the stalemate. Michael and Emir saw the distraction the dictator drew and looked at their teams tellingly—

The shriek of an energy blast ripped the tense silence!

The *Endurance* crew shuddered at the noise echoing throughout the construction site. They looked around at each other, anxiously searching for the perpetrator and victim. However, the stalemate remained in force.

Instead—outside the stalemate—Aurelian Galerius gasped, and his eyes glazed over in shock. His whole body contorted at the pain shuddering through him. For one brief moment, he searched his captors' faces for a reprieve; none came. Finding no deliverance, the old man slumped over onto the ground and died.

Kara Ricci had executed him.

Dreadful silence fell. The irresolvable conflict that had enslaved the two teams perished, replaced by a morbid and awkward sense of unresolved justice. They looked down at the dead man, as if staring into an abyss. One by one, they lowered their weapons in defeat.

An unsettled peace imposed itself upon the crew.

"There," Kara said matter-of-factly, holstering her pistol and brushing her hands together. "Now there's nothing to fight about."

Though her voice remained calm and her expression resolute, the young woman's eyes reflected the oddest, most unnerving gaze.

Leaving the dumbfounded group, she went over to the side of the hill where her backpack lay. Rifling through its compartments, Kara began organizing herself to leave. She remained indifferent over the passing conflict, preoccupying herself instead with the task at hand.

The rest of the *Endurance* crew randomly formed a small circle around the corpse. They gazed down at what had been Aurelian Galerius. They stood around as if mourning for him, though that clearly was not the case. No, the man was a murderer. Having been weighed and found wanting many years before, the brutal dictator deserved to die; Galerius had merely gone the way of all his victims.

Nevertheless, the crew remained unsettled.

From his place standing over the dead man, Michael looked down at Galerius' remains. His mission was over. A dead man could not be tried. He could not be brought back to answer his accusers, to look into the faces of his victims' families. He was no longer a prize to be brought back to the *Weightless*, nor the token that would restore the Gillen name. Kara knew all this, and yet she had pulled the trigger. How could she have done that to him?

Across from Michael, Emir Kern also stared down at the dead man. The dictator had died too quickly and suffered too little. Kern filled with remorse—that his chance for revenge had been stolen from him. He could never assuage the torment he had carried for so long—*never!* The tragedy that happened at Ceres would always haunt him; he would never find peace. His one chance to avenge his wife and children had vanished. Kara knew all this, and yet she had pulled the trigger. How could she have done that to him?

However, neither man could alter what had transpired. They were still deep within the Europan settlement too.

Finally, Kern looked at the team—the entire team. "We'd better get out of here."

Hesitantly, the teams began dispersing in random fashion, though each person lingered over the dead man for as long as they felt the strange need. Eventually, they did leave, forming two long trains.

Kern climbed the bluff, leading his men north toward their hidden land craft. Michael turned down the road to the east, waving the Centauries toward the other vehicle parked at the high wall in the southeast channel.

Still preoccupied at the side of the road, Kara knelt beside her backpack and fiddled with her gear. She remained indifferent and to herself the whole time the crew dispersed. Instead, she spent that time ripping open packets of antiseptic cloths and meticulously wiping her hands. She became more desperate with each new packet.

Nevertheless, whatever covered her hands would not come off.

Finally recognizing the need to leave the area—*giving up really*—Kara packed her things away and flipped closed the medical kit. The white cross on its cover caught her eye.

Kara abruptly stopped. She stared oddly at the drawing, falling mesmerized by its simplicity. As her eyes lingered, she didn't even realize that one of her fingers was tracing its outline. After gazing at the picture for some time, she shook off the odd feeling and loaded the kit into her pack.

Noticing the long train of Centauries following Michael to the high wall, Kara quickly stood up, slung her backpack over her shoulder, and started in their direction. Just as she took her first step, Kara once again caught sight of the dead man out of the corner of her eye.

She only took a few steps before stumbling to an abrupt halt. Something was wrong. She looked up anxiously at her friends ahead of her, though no one was turned to see.

Something was definitely wrong! Her heart felt like wax and her bones as if they were withering within her. She paused and braced herself against the chiseled rock, hoping the sensation would pass; but it only worsened. Then, an incredible wave of nausea washed over her.

But nothing was physical. No, the world pressed in on her. The terrible reality of killing the man hit her right in the pit of her stomach. Unable to bear up under the condemnation swelling within her, Kara fell helplessly to her knees and trembled uncontrollably.

She knelt there for a long moment, desperately trying to calm herself. However, the young woman's efforts were to no avail. She could still see herself pointing her pistol at the old man's back; she could feel her finger pulling the trigger—*why did she do that?* She could still feel the deadly charge leaving the gun and striking him—the smell of charred flesh. She could see him writhing in agony before her as the life ebbed out of him—all because of what she had done. So Kara abruptly doubled over and threw up.

Completely undone and beginning to weep, Kara frantically tried composing herself. She even labored through her tears a few meters toward the Centauries. Nothing worked. No, she couldn't vomit out the painful emotions accosting her any more than gouging out her eyes could remove the ghastly images from her thoughts. The dread building within her overwhelmed her that much more. With her strength evaporating, the young woman fell onto the ground and wept harder.

Kate, who had looked back and saw Kara fall to the ground, came to kneel over her.

"Come on Kara," she beckoned, wrapping her in a half-embrace and kissing her forehead. "We need to leave."

However, Kara remained distraught. "*What have I done?*"

"I know … but it's not safe here."

Kara barely acknowledged the statement. Instead, the young woman just stared vacantly at nothing.

"Kara?" Tom greeted her when he arrived. Letting his awkward reaction to her condition pass, he looked at her intentionally. "We've got to go, Sis. It's too dangerous here."

By then, her condition had drawn attention. Michael and Phil both stopped in the distance and looked back at the spectacle. David, who was midway between the two groups, heard the commotion and started toward her.

Through tears, Kara looked up in the direction of the bluff. Emir Kern stood on top of the hill, waving his men past him and down the other side. She looked to him, almost calling—beckoning; she was desperate. She needed him more than ever. She needed his strength, his assurance that everything would be okay.

She needed *him*.

Emir stood away on the bluff for a long moment, returning her gaze. However, his gaze did not console her. No, he looked at her bitterly. His distant expression cut her to pieces, and the short gap between them became as if a chasm. Finally, Emir dropped his head in defeat and disappeared over the bluff.

Kara, sitting among her Centauri friends, was nevertheless alone.

She sat there for some time, almost comatose. Although Kate and Tom tried coaxing her to move, Kara didn't respond. She barely even noticed David coming to her side.

Amid the chaos surrounding the moment—weapons fire suddenly broke the air!

At first, the four distracted—and combat inexperienced— Centauries looked around in a stupor. But the split second of bewilderment evaporated when they looked in the direction of the artillery fire. Their faces waxed over in dread. Europan troops appeared from the west, coming from far over the rise. Though starting as only a trickle, the invaders began spilling into the area—moving in fast.

The Centauries looked at each other desperately: They were in grave danger!

CHAPTER TWENTY THREE

An Interruption

Aghast, Michael Gillen watched Europan troops spill into the construction sight from the west, approaching his team in a rage. At the same time, other troops rushed over the bluff in the direction of the Coverts to the north. Weapons fire echoing from just over the bluff soon followed.

"Kern!" Michael called into his communicator, "What should we do?"

"Do you need our help?" Kern called back.

Young Gillen paused in anxious thought, fighting his preoccupation with the unnerving sight before him. Finally, he replied, "I think I can get my team out of here."

"Good," Kern said. "Troops are moving in on us too. We're getting pressure from two different directions, so I doubt we can get to you anyway. We may as well forget a rescue by the *Aurora*: Zeidler tried summoning the ship, but it's not responding for some reason. Get your team out in the land craft parked by the high wall. I'll meet you back at the base camp. We can figure out our next step from there."

"Got it," Michael acknowledged.

Meanwhile, Tom Andrews, who was still at the ambush site with Kara, David, and Kate, wrestled his startled friends behind a pile of dirt as deadly gunfire shot past them. Soberly pondering the close call for a brief moment, Tom surveyed their vulnerable position: They needed to escape before falling victim to the swell of oncoming soldiers.

"David," Tom called out over the din of artillery, "We need to split up: Get Kara out of here and go toward Mike down the roadway. Kate and I will cover you until you're safe." Then he pointed to a makeshift pathway leading up through the bluffs. "I'll take Kate this way and meet you back at the high wall."

Tashjian complied, taking Kara—who appeared shaken but mostly herself once again—into his grasp. He escorted her protectively from behind, leading her closely along the rock face toward the east. At the same time, Tom and Kate laid down cover fire, halting the Europans' progress and forcing the lead soldiers to duck for cover.

Seeing Ricci and Tashjian eventually disappear around the curve of the hill, Tom took Kate by the hand.

"Come on, Sunshine," he said, whisking her away. The two disappeared into the thick undergrowth at the bottom of the bluff, hurrying up the narrow pathway toward the southeast.

The firestorm intensified as more troops spilled into the construction site. Michael realized he needed to act before the soldiers overwhelmed his team.

Risking his own safety, he dashed back to the ambush point amid a firestorm of hostile artillery. Passing David and Kara going in the opposite direction, he waved them on to the high wall and raced toward the ambush point.

When he arrived back at the ambush point—the Europan troops quickly closing in on him—the young man climbed the towering excavator into the operator's cabin high above. After several intense moments of him fiddling with the confusing controls, the leviathan roared to life. Continuing to learn the controls, Michael soon had the massive machine rolling forward. Just as the first wave of Europan soldiers appeared in the vehicle's aft mirrors, the anxious commander punched the accelerator. The vehicle suddenly lurched forward, accelerating to a steady pace toward the southeast channel.

Laboring with the steering mechanism to keep the machine traveling straight, Michael navigated the excavator to shield the Centauries from Europan artillery. Laser blasts harmlessly pockmarked the vehicle's thick metal aft hull.

The excavator eventually caught up to Kara and David. Slowing down, Michael waved them into the protective cover of the machine. He did the same for Marcotte a short distance down the channel. The three walked close to the massive vehicle to avoid Europan gunfire, keeping one hand on its steel frame to avoid falling under its sizeable wheels.

Michael steered the leviathan down the unfinished road, protecting the vulnerable Centauries while keeping pace ahead of the advancing troops. However, with no real defense keeping the assault at bay, the Europan soldiers began closing the gap.

Michael turned the excavator down the southeast channel toward the hidden land craft. From his vantage point high in the cabin, he spied Tom hurrying Kate along up on the steep hillside that overlooked the construction site. Surrounded by untouched vegetation, the two were following a path that ran to the top of the bluff overlooking the high wall.

Returning his attention to piloting the excavator, Michael realized that the channel was quickly narrowing. If he attempted to continue down the passage, the excavator would cut off the land craft's escape route, thus trapping everyone.

Instead, he maneuvered the excavator as far down the passage as possible, eventually bringing the machine to a stop against the canyon-like wall. Its position against the bluff provided Ricci, Tashjian, and Marcotte protection from oncoming fire. They could return fire to cover him while he attempted to dash to the land craft too. If all went right, Tom and Kate would arrive just in time to flee the oncoming horde.

Satisfied, the young commander began descending from the cabin, keeping well clear of the side facing the oncoming soldiers.

Hurrying to the end of the winding path they had followed for some time, Tom led Kate by the hand to the top of a bluff. They took up position where a small notch cut into the side of the hilltop.

The small, fort-like impression overlooked the southeast channel. Directly below them sat the massive excavator, shielding Kara Ricci, David Tashjian, and Phil Marcotte from the coming Europan onslaught. Michael was descending the machine's ladder while hostile fire streamed narrowly around him—much to Kate's dismay. Fifty meters to the east in front of the high wall sat the waiting land craft: the Centauries' only means of escape.

A searing round of energy shot past Tom, barely missing his head. He dove for cover, yanking Kate down with him.

"We'll have to stay here until Mike powers up the land craft," Tom declared, still crouching lower than the top of the notch. "It's too dangerous to try descending the hill with the soldiers approaching." Then he activated his communicator. "Mike, were up on the hill. We can't make it down to you from here."

"I saw another path opening up into the channel a little farther east," Michael's voice came from the communicator. "—the same one we saw when we arrived earlier today. See if you can connect to it. I'll pick you up there, just as soon as I pick up Kara, David, and Phil."

"I copy," Tom replied. "We'll meet you there."

The two stood back up, though sidling up protectively behind a large rock. They surveyed the landscape to the east, looking for the path that Michael had mentioned. However, the elusive trail remained hidden from sight.

As she looked down onto the channel below, Kate's heart leapt into her throat! Michael charged out from behind the excavator, making a quick but erratic path to the land craft parked beside the high wall. The Europan soldiers sent a firestorm of artillery his way while advancing. Michael dove between the craft and the high wall, barely escaping the barrage.

Kate and Tom watched him return fire far below to slow the troopers' progress. Ricci, Tashjian, and Marcotte did the same from behind the excavator. Kate watched the deadly exchange, desperately wishing Michael would retreat into the protection of the land craft.

However, his strategy worked. The lead Europan troopers took cover behind some rocks in the distance. Unfortunately, Michael had made himself a target. The entire squad of Europans concentrated all their firepower on him, trapping the young man behind the vehicle.

That was when everything changed.

A massive concussion rocked the entire area, enveloping everything in its fury and thundering something terrible! With the powerful tremor still surging through her, Kate looked on in horror!

Perhaps the soldiers had fired large mortars. Perhaps artillery fire had compromised the explosives planted in the high wall earlier by the blasting crew. No matter, the scene turned surreal. The high wall towering over Michael exploded violently! Massive rocks fell headlong, crushing the transport and burying the entire area! A cloud of thick dust billowed into the air, temporarily obscuring the dreadful sight. When the thick haze began dispersing, only a single, mangled corner of the land craft jutted out of the rubble. The rest of the vehicle—Michael too—lay buried under five to seven meters of boulders and debris.

Mortified—throwing aside concerns for her own safety—Kate jumped up to rush to her husband's rescue.

"Kate!" Tom yelled, grabbing hold of her arm as energy rounds streamed narrowly over her head. "Don't! You'll be killed too!"

Yet the terrified, young woman was inconsolable. Her eyes betraying her own madness, Kate wrestled out of his grip. She ran desperately and with abandon. However, not too many steps out, Kate slumped to the ground unconscious.

She had been hit from behind.

Kara Ricci, David Tashjian, and Phil Marcotte—still reeling from the explosion—looked on in horror through the dissipating dust cloud, taking in the dreadful sight of the high wall collapse. Their close proximity gave them an unenviable view to the gruesome spectacle: One moment, Michael knelt beside the land craft; the next, he was gone—*their friend was gone!*

They only had seconds to ponder their loss. Europan forces rushed upon them violently. The three Centauries found themselves suddenly swallowed up into a maelstrom of aggrieved Europan soldiers. A thousand powerful hands—or so it seemed—seized them all at once and beat them cruelly. The weapons Kara, David, and Phil held ready in their hands simply vanished in the chaos. The Europans flailed them about, forcibly driving them face down into the dirt.

The siege was over.

The guards showed no mercy, wrenching the battered Centauries off the ground and butting them around with their rifles. They herded the hapless prisoners out into the open and into a close huddle, all the while hurling insults at them.

"Take off all your military equipment!" one of the lead soldiers barked.

Kara, David, and Phil timidly complied, taking off the items and heaping them on the ground. While surrendering the equipment to the thugs, effectively stripping down to their mission uniforms, the three remained disoriented by the chaos. Fear of a summary execution quickly rose in their minds.

Eventually, Tom appeared at the top of the bluff, followed by a single trooper holding him at gunpoint. After the two men descended the path to the bottom of the bluff, the trooper marched him over to where Kara, Phil, and David stood captive.

"Did you see what happened to Michael?" Kara cried out to him, just as the guard rifle-butted Tom into the group.

"Yeah," Tom winced from the blow. "It was terrible. Kate saw it too."

"Don't talk!" the Europan soldier guarding them barked. He looked squarely at Tom. "Take off your military equipment like the others!"

Though everyone went silent, Kara whispered to Tom, "*Where's Kate?*"

"*Up on the hill, unconscious,*" Tom whispered back inconspicuously while removing his gear. "*A guard is up there watching her until she wakes up.*"

Kara looked up at the steep hillside before turning back to him. "*Is she okay?*"

"No talking!" the same Europan soldier barked.

Tom just nodded his head.

The soldiers marched the Centauries the very short distance back to the main road. The place provided visibility to both the ambush point to the west and the high wall collapse near where the Europans had captured them.

Kara nervously surveyed all the Europan rifles pointed at her and her friends, wondering what terrible fate awaited them.

Emir Kern fired his pistol from behind the large tree on the hillside. A stretch of trees and thick brush lay in the middle of the conflict, essentially blinding each faction to the other. He couldn't see them, nor could they see him. So he fired in random directions toward the hillside, hoping the rounds kept the advancing soldiers at bay.

The Coverts had made considerable progress north since the surprise Europan attack. The barren construction area lay well behind them, and the new terrain was thick with overgrown trees and vegetation: perfect protection for anyone on the run. For the first time, the Coverts had a fighting chance to escape.

Yet that fact came as little consolation to the seasoned lieutenant. He smarted over his stupidity. His obsession with revenge against Aurelian Galerius had blinded him, making him myopic to the trap forming around the *Endurance* crew. Having made a terrible judgment call, the entire team—Coverts and Centauries alike—were in grave danger.

Worse, the Centauries' combat inexperience made them helpless against the Europans, and Kara was with them!

He ducked behind the tree when energy rounds streamed dangerously close to his head. He hoped that the round had been a lucky shot, taken by an Europan shooting randomly from over the crest of the hill to draw out a target.

When an unexpected break in the artillery fire occurred, Kern waved his men on. Without hesitation, they sprang from their cover—incoming rounds resumed right behind them. Running past him and down into the valley below, the men darted back and forth to avoid the firestorm. Kern laid down heavy cover fire as they moved. Once certain his charge was clear, the Covert leader followed them closely down the hill.

With a single chance to escape, the small band ran with abandon through the undergrowth. The sounds of gunfire faded farther away, indicating their pursuers didn't realize the Coverts were on the run. The window of opportunity would not stay open long. Fortunately, the welcome sight of the land craft sitting hidden among the bushes came into view.

They arrived in sequence at the vehicle very much out of breath. Tasker dove into the driver's seat and brought the vehicle to power, while the others hastily threw off the pile of loose brush concealing it. Within seconds, the entire team jumped aboard. Tasker peeled out, masterfully piloting the craft through the rough thicket. Kern wasted no time barking out orders, while Zeidler characteristically kept one step ahead of him. Already, the subordinate worked the gear inside his pack.

"Tasker," he commanded, taking off his helmet, "Keep in the brush until Zeidler gets a fix on the surrounding area. Zeidler, find a route through the Europan forces—*and what's the status of the Centauries?*" Abruptly—furiously—Kern slung out a round of obscenities and hit the side of the craft with his fist. "I can't believe we let ourselves get caught like that!"

"We were too focused on Galerius," Zeidler exclaimed, bracing himself against the craft's jostling while working his equipment.

"No, Gillen got the best of us! If he hadn't intervened, you would have kept your eyes on the scanners—we would have seen the Europans coming."

The Coverts remained silent, letting Kern's fuming pass.

Zeidler studied the scanners while listening to his communicator. Keeping focused on the unit's display, he gave Tasker the coordinates to weave through the combat zone. His expression suddenly turned grim—as did the other Coverts—and he glanced at Kern. "Turn on your communicator."

"Yeah, I just heard something about a rockslide," Eric Gunn, listening to his own communicator, announced from the back.

Kern picked up the communicator attached to his helmet and put it to his ear. He immediately heard several Centauries speaking. Kara was one of them.

"I think Gillen's dead," Zeidler announced. "—something about him getting buried in some sort of explosion."

Though calling to them while transmitting, Kern realized the Centauries weren't actually using the communicators—unfortunate. He reckoned the Centauries must have left them on accidentally, and he and his men were listening to the bleed-over from their conversations. Kara's frightened voice came in and out of the chaotic and broken conversation, each time tying the knots in the Covert leader's stomach that much tighter. Eventually—abruptly—he heard the garbled ruckus of a violent siege—Kara screaming amid the chaos—followed by indiscernible dialogue before the transmission finally went silent.

Kern looked over Zeidler's shoulder at his scanner. Hundreds of red dots swarmed toward the Centauri team. The combat-lacking Centauries were doomed.

The man regretted leaving the Centauries—and leaving Kara stung terribly. No doubt, she would come to a tragic end. He filled with remorse upon realizing he would never see her again. Yet he was powerless to do anything about her dire circumstances: He and the Coverts were in imminent danger too.

"Let's return to the base camp," Kern sighed. "Maybe we can find a way to help."

The small group of captured Centauries—Kara Ricci, Tom Andrews, Phil Marcotte, and David Tashjian—huddled in the center of the construction site, staggered by the gruesome turn of events and filled with an incredible despair.

Caught in an assassination plot, they were prisoners of the Europan Royal Guard. As the soldiers mulled around them like rabid dogs—and many more were arriving every minute—the Centauries pondered their imminent and horrible fate. Surreal images of torture and execution filled their minds.

Death beckoned them.

From her unfortunate vantage point, Kara saw Aurelian Galerius' body lying on the road in the distance—the man she had executed. More than all the others, Kara lay heavy with the dread of what had happened. She had done something unimaginable: She had taken a life—a miserable cretin but a life nonetheless. Unable to bear the sight or the thoughts tormenting her, the distraught, young woman turned away.

However, in that direction just a short distance away, Kara could see the huge pile of rubble covering the place where Michael lay buried. A soldier stood in front of the heap, holding a scanner that searched for life signs. Kara so wanted the soldier to call attention to the others, abruptly alerting them to an unexpected finding. That didn't happen. No, more than satisfied that the massive rocks had done their job, the man walked away to report.

Michael was dead.

And of course, Kate still lay unconscious somewhere up on the hillside above.

Kara stood helplessly within the small circle of captured Centauries, her arms folded tightly in front of her and shoulders drawn in close. She whispered a prayer for deliverance under her breath, though not to anyone or any god in particular. No, Kara was not a religious person. Her pleadings were no more than a fleeting wish, for she knew they would all be dead soon.

The soldiers detained them several minutes, until two military transports arrived. While the crafts powered down, a high-ranking commander stepped out of the main transport.

302

The officer, an older man with a rugged frame and square jaw, approached the four. Studying each of them carefully, his face emitted an obvious disdain and a no-nonsense intention. His eyes lingered on Tom, whose mission uniform bore the highest rank. The officer studied him curiously.

After circling them once, the commander looked over to where Aurelian Galerius' body lay. He lingered on that sight for some time. Finally glancing back at them scornfully, he addressed the ranking soldier standing next to the Centauries. "Are these the only prisoners?"

"No, Sir," the soldier replied. "We're guarding an unconscious woman up on the hill. Another small group fled to the north. We're still in pursuit and should capture them shortly." Then he pointed to the rubble at the base of the collapsed high wall. "Another assailant was crushed under the rock slide over there. Our scanners show no life signs."

"Let me know when you catch the group heading north," the commander acknowledged. "Don't let them escape."

The soldier nodded.

The commander surveyed the entire area once again, starting with the rock pile and ending with the ambush point. He caught sight of Aurelian Galerius' body once again, his eyes lingering on the corpse. "Which one of them did this?"

"The Covert team," Tom replied quickly, so quickly that his response took the other Centauries by surprise. "—the ones who escaped to the north. They wanted him dead."

One of the soldiers, who boasted a large set of binoculars slung around his neck, pushed forward. Pointing accusingly at Kara, the man exclaimed, "She did it, Sir."

"That's not true," Tom retorted boldly. He fixed a confident gaze on the Europan commander, unnerving his lesser inclined companions. "I was right there when they did it."

"I know what I saw," the Europan soldier declared.

However, Tom didn't shrink back. "I'll prove it." He nodded in the direction of the bluff. "The unconscious woman up over the hillside ... take me up there, wake her up, and ask her what she saw. If she doesn't give the same answer ... *shoot me*."

Had Kara had not been under duress, her jaw would have dropped. *What's he doing?* she thought, completely stunned. Though Marcotte and Tashjian kept visibly indifferent, Kara could tell they were thinking the exact same thing.

The Europan officer looked at him for a long moment, his gaze appearing somewhat curious to the other Centauries. Finally, he waved for Tom to move. "Okay, let's go." Then, he turned to the Europan soldier with the binoculars. "Come with us—bring a medical kit so we can revive the woman."

The soldier quickly complied.

Kara stood in place with Phil Marcotte and David Tashjian, nervously watching the four men ascend the hillside. Even when the small band disappeared over the bluff, the trio kept their eyes trained on the place. Many long moments passed, and the hillside stayed the same.

Kara gnawed at her fingernails; the vain prayer she offered under her breath grew more desperate. Unless having concocted a rather cleaver scheme, Tom was surely a goner. *And for what?* They were all going to die anyway.

The hillside remained quiet. The longer Tom and the Europans remained over the bluff and out of sight, the more desperate Kara grew—

A solitary gun blast pierced the tense silence!

Kara threw her hand to her mouth as the dreadful sound echoed from where Tom had disappeared! Her eyes welled up and her face twisted painfully. She looked desperately at her equally shaken companions.

Less than a minute later, another shot broke the air from the same direction! Once again, the same haunting echo.

Kate!

Kara desperately wanted to scream, and her face twisted even more painfully. She looked at her companions with such despair. Unable to bear the thought of what had happened, the inconsolable woman looked away from the hillside, preferring instead to shelter herself within the protective shadow of Phil and David.

With unbearably long moments passing before them, the three remained silent and gazed in horror at each other. A terrible dread washed over them once more: Their turn to die awaited them.

As the appalling images of what must have happened up on the hillside tormented her, Kara began entertaining thoughts of denial. Perhaps Tom *did* have some sort of cleaver plan. Perhaps he had disarmed the guards and officer—maybe the shots were Tom killing the Europans *instead*. Perhaps Tom and Kate were still alive. Perhaps Tom was already in the process of effecting their escape.

But then, the Europan commander appeared at the top of the hillside and made his way down the path. A guard followed him—but not the one with the binoculars: another one. She reckoned the new guard was the soldier who had guarded Kate. No matter, both men proceeded along, unfazed by whatever had happened above. Kara conceded that Tom and Kate were dead. The other guard still up on the hillside was probably burying their bodies in a shallow grave.

Upon reaching the end of the path at the bottom of the hill, the Europan commander made a beeline over to two soldiers standing right next to the remaining Centauries.

"What did you do?" Kara pleaded as he passed.

The officer looked at her coldly. "He made a deal, and I held him to it."

Callously disregarding her horrified reaction, the man held up a small reader to one of the guards. "Here are your orders. Everything will be ready by the time you arrive." Then he pointed to Marcotte and Tashjian. "Take these two."

The subordinate held up his own reader to the officer's device and scanned in the orders. After looking at the small screen for a moment, he took a step and waved for Marcotte and Tashjian to follow him to one of the transport vehicles.

David and Phil hesitated and looked back at a petrified Kara Ricci.

The other Europan guard gave them no quarter, pushing the two forward with the pointed end of his rifle. When David resisted, the guard struck him hard in the back with the butt of his rifle. Tashjian immediately buckled over in pain.

"Don't!" the lead guard warned the other guard sternly—much to the shock of the three Centauries. He regarded Tashjian affably. "Sorry … please come with us."

David, struggling to compose himself, traded looks with Phil and Kara. Reluctantly, the two men complied, though looking back apprehensively at Kara the whole time. Helplessly, Kara soon watched the transport pull away with her two friends. Her shoulders slumped when the transport disappeared out of sight.

Kara was alone, surrounded by Europan thugs.

Several unbearable minutes later, Kara heard the sound of a small convoy in the distance. The steady noise grew louder, and the convoy eventually appeared from the southwest. Four elaborate transports approached, surrounded by hundreds of heavily armed soldiers marching in lock-step formation. Flags adorning the middle vehicle denoted a person of high position within the Europan government.

The sight of the motorcade fell ominously on the terrified Centauri.

After maneuvering around the stalled transport and dead bodies at the ambush point, the convoy stopped just twenty meters in front of where Kara stood guarded. A driver stepped out of the decorated vehicle and opened the passenger door. At this, every soldier not guarding her snapped to attention.

Aurelian Galerius—very much alive and well—emerged from the transport.

Kara looked over at the dead body lying at the ambush point in the distance. Any strength she had gathered evaporated, and her heart sank when the cold reality of what she had done set into her. She had not killed Aurelian Galerius; she had killed his double—she had murdered an innocent man!

The man stepping out of the transport was unquestionably Galerius. Though physically identical to the double she had killed, he approached with all the regal honor and terror that preceded him by reputation. This man was not spindly or cowardly, as the dead man had acted. No, he was both powerful and unflinching.

Kara felt herself withering before the man. The ruthless dictator's presence and the cold reality of her crime pressed in on her. She tried to steady herself—only somewhat successful at the attempt.

She was all alone, at the mercy of a man who was devoid of mercy.

As the brutal dictator made his way toward the gathering of soldiers, the Europan commander rushed to meet him halfway. Immediately, the officer handed the small reader to Galerius and began a rather lengthy explanation.

Kara couldn't hear, for the two men were too far away. Oddly, the brutal dictator appeared preoccupied while listening; he surveyed the area intently while the man spoke. When the officer came to a certain point in the explanation, Galerius' face waxed incredulous. The officer pointed toward the hillside. Then, he nervously gestured to the reader, causing the old man to examine the device's display for quite a while.

Resigning to whatever concerned him, Galerius continued listening. That was when the officer pointed to the dead body double lying in the distance—and then to Kara.

Kara's heart leapt into her throat.

Galerius approached her, studying her carefully. After circling around her once, he looked over at his double lying dead on the ground before fixing his gaze upon her.

"As you can see," Galerius said, his eyes narrowing in contempt, "You were not successful. I am very much alive."

The dictator waved two guards standing by toward her. The soldiers moved in and cuffed the young woman's wrists. Kara's face immediately drained of all color.

"If you were hoping to die today, that won't happen," Galerius exclaimed with resolve. "I'm giving you a temporary reprieve—not that I would execute an assassin such as yourself so quickly anyway. But know that you *will* be executed … when the time is right. Until then, you will be treated like the murderer you are."

Kara's heart waxed cold in her chest at the brutal dictator's piercing gaze. Terror filled her every thought. She had become the object of his scorn, the focus of all his rage. Perhaps even her most morbid thoughts could not portend what torments awaited her.

Kara, still restrained and her head hanging low, was taken away, while the commander escorted Aurelian Galerius up the hillside.

CHAPTER TWENTY FOUR

Up on the Hillside

Kate Gillen opened her eyes, only to find herself lying face down on the dusty ground. She felt not herself: Fatigue covered her as if deep waters, while most of her muscles ached terribly. She wasn't even sure where she was or what had happened.

She pushed off the ground just enough to wipe away the dust covering her lips. A sour grimace suddenly washed across her face, and she hastily spit out an unpleasant mouthful of dirt and saliva.

"Yuk!" she whimpered. With her face still twisted, she spit several more times to expel the rest of the stubborn, gritty substance from her mouth.

Turning on her side and surveying her surroundings through blurred vision, the young woman finally recognized her position: the notch carved into the top of the bluff. Though her head remained foggy, memories of weapons fire flooded her mind—and the terrible jolt of a round striking her. Kate immediately perked up. She swiveled around on her hips and sat straight up, patting her entire torso in a desperate attempt to find her wounds.

Surprisingly, she had none.

Still foggy, Kate looked around again. In front of her, a dead Europan soldier lay face down near the mouth of the notch. Tom Andrews lay unconscious well behind her—a gaping wound in his upper right chest and a blood-covered shirt caught her eye. Interestingly, most of his combat gear lay heaped beside him.

Suddenly, everything came back to her, jolting her into complete consciousness.

Kate stumbled over to where Tom lay and shook him vigorously. "Tom, wake up! I need your help ... Tom, wake up!"

However, the man remained unconscious.

Frustrated, Kate strained to a standing position and surveyed the area for help. However, the terrain lay deserted all the way to the horizon. All traces of the Europan forces were gone. The Excavator in the passage below sat alone near the rockslide covering Michael, and the other Centauries were nowhere in sight.

She was alone and in desperate trouble.

Hurrying over to where her field pack lay, Kate searched the pack for her medical kit. Once successful, she returned to Tom's side and began tending his wound, which didn't seem as bad to her at second glance.

When Andrews stirred, she gently slapped his face to get his attention. "Tom, wake up!"

"What happened to me?" he asked in a fog, wincing as she tended to his injuries.

"I don't know. I just regained consciousness myself."

Tom stared up at her blankly for a long moment before his normal expression returned. "They got me from behind." He feebly pointed to the dead Europan soldier lying at the mouth of the notch.

Kate looked across the way. The dead man lay slumped over on his stomach, concealing much of his mortal wound. Broken and charred pieces of a pair of binoculars were scattered near the corpse's head.

"I guess I was the better shot," he added.

"Where is everyone?"

"*Gone*," Tom replied soberly—recoiling when Kate applied a disinfectant to his wound. "It was mayhem, Kate … I couldn't do anything but watch. After the high wall collapsed, two squads of goons showed up and flanked Kara, Phil, and David. Kern and his team came back to help, but it was no use. They had no choice but to surrender. That's when the Europans executed everyone—right on the spot."

Kate's shoulders fell, and her face waxed over in dread. Tom lifted his arm—straining under terrible pain—and placed a sympathetic hand on her shoulder. "They loaded the bodies onto a transport and got out quick, as if they thought we had reinforcements coming. I thought they were all gone, but"—nodding his head in the direction of the dead Europan soldier—"this guy came out of nowhere…. We need to get out of here before they come back."

Kate shook her head defiantly as she finished dressing his wound. "We've got to help Michael! Let's go!"

"Kate, we need to leave. Don't—"

His pleadings came too late, for the distraught, young woman was already getting up to rush down the hill. Instinctively, Tom grasped at her—quickly thwarted by the pain shooting through his chest.

Kate left like a shot.

Fighting his injury, Tom struggled to his feet and chased her down the embankment. He followed as quickly as his weakened condition allowed. Catching up to her at the rock pile, he watched her strain to move a rock twice the size of her head.

"Help me!" Kate pleaded. But when he just stood to the side watching in disbelief, she drew her pistol and shot the rock into pieces. The shots echoed throughout the bluffs several times.

"You're going to draw attention to our position," Tom warned.

"Go! Bring the excavator over here—"

Tom grabbed her by the thick of one arm, forcing her to look at him. "Don't, Kate! Michael's gone. He would want you to leave."

"No!"

"Kate, listen to me!" Tom pleaded, still grasping her arm and looking her squarely in the eyes. "The Europans already checked for his life signs … they didn't *find* any." He nodded sadly toward the massive rocks lying in the pile. "You don't want to see him like that."

"I can't leave him!" she shot back, her gaze waxing graver. "He *needs* me." But Tom's sympathetic gaze pleaded for reason—the massive pile of debris too. Kate could no longer hold fast to her denial. Her face twisted painfully. The young woman fell to her knees, all the while grasping desperately at Tom's good arm for consolation. Breaking into tears, she cried, "*I need him.*"

Straining, he knelt and wrapped her in his good arm. "I know, Sunshine ... he was my best friend." He held her for a long moment— too long for such a dangerous time. "... But we have to leave ... *now.*"

Tom stood up and took her hand in his, all the while gazing reassuringly at her. "We'll be okay. Trust me."

She looked at him for the longest time.

"Okay," she finally surrendered. Taking the briefest moment to compose herself, she started to rise, letting Tom help her to a standing position—

Rifles clicking to the ready stopped both of them in their tracks. Four Europan soldiers suddenly appeared directly behind the two Centauries, pointing their weapons at the Centauries' heads. One of the guards looked warily at them from behind his rifle. "Drop your weapons, or you're dead!"

Phil Marcotte and David Tashjian walked the luxurious corridor, their thoughts heavy with whatever dire fate awaited them. The Europan escorts leading them kept a very comfortable, casual pace. Though the Europans didn't say much, their tone was amiable and their words devoid of abuse—a stark contrast to the welcome the two Centauries had received back at the failed ambush.

They were somewhere in one of the palace wings, snaking through the large passageways. Finally, the lead guard approached a particular door. With a quick swipe of his hand over the security sensor, the thick door swung open. The escorts stepped aside, directing Marcotte and Tashjian through the entryway. The Centauries reluctantly entered the room, trading anxious glances with each other as they did so.

The lavish suite in which the two men found themselves bordered on the extravagant. The immediate room set before them was a nicely furnished living area, while a kitchen and dining area sat in the back. To the side lay a small hallway, leading to several bedrooms and baths.

Marcotte and Tashjian nervously paced, waiting for the dignitary that owned the residence to appear.

"Here are your quarters," the lead guard stated, much to the astonishment of the two men. "—compliments of Aurelian Galerius. We've stocked it with anything you should need or want. If you find something missing, please let us know."

The two men looked at each other quizzically.

Marcotte, brimming with morbid curiosity, gathered his courage. "I don't understand."

"I'm not at liberty to explain," one guard replied. "Our orders are to provide for you as any guest of the King. There's just one limitation: You can't leave. Attempting to escape this suite will nullify the King's hospitality, and you'll instead be treated like common prisoners."

The two Centauries traded quizzical looks once again.

The guard, ignoring Marcotte and Tashjian's bewildered expressions, resumed reciting his instructions to them. Upon completing the rather exhaustive list of *do's* and *don'ts*, the guards left and locked the doors behind them.

Once again, the two Centauries warily paced the lavish room. Memories of staring down Europan rifle barrels earlier that day lingered prominently in their minds.

Finally, Marcotte turned to his companion, his eyes wide with astonishment. "Shouldn't we be dead?"

"And if Galerius is dead, who's this *King* they were talking about—who's putting us up here?"

"Nothing makes sense," Marcotte mused. His face turned sober. "But this is *still* a prison cell—and where's Kara?"

The empty prison cell deep beneath the Europan military complex was typical of any Europan military cell: dimly lit, cold, damp, and with filthy stone walls. In a word, the cell was spartan—worse, it was repulsive. Despair hung heavily in the air, a foreboding omen of terrible things to come.

The cell had remained empty for most of its existence. Yet with the clang of the lock and the heavy groan of iron hinges turning, the thick metal door swung open. Light from the outside corridor streamed in.

The dance of shadows on the cell floor interrupted the steady light. Kara Ricci fell headlong through the entryway, landing hard on her side onto the filthy stone floor. The door slammed shut behind her.

She was all alone in the shadowy chamber.

With her hands still bound in front of her, she lay on the cold floor a shadow of her former self. Her face was pale and her expression gaunt. Dirt covered her clothes—the result of soldiers knocking her to the ground repeatedly—and the fabric was torn here and there. She was sore; her legs ached from the long march from the construction site, while bruises from being rifle-butted covered her arms and torso. The pain was unbearable.

So Kara went limp, letting the cold dampness from the rock soak into her.

Numbness quickly overwhelmed the young woman. However, the sensation did not come from her injuries or the cold radiating from the floor. No, she was numb within and in a dire state of shock. Her world had crumbled before her eyes. All that was dear to her had vanished, vanished in the blink of an eye—vanished in the blinding flash of a single pistol round.

She had killed an innocent man, and something inside her had died too.

Painfully, the life that could have been hers cried out accusingly. There were many facets of such regret—too many to reconcile. The face of her daughter, whom she had given up so long ago, came to mind. Kara could still see the eight-year-old playing games with her, completely unaware of who she was. Kara's sister gazed at her from the ether, begging her to find herself—a dream that would never come true.

But above them all, she could still see Emir's face as he stood on top of the bluff. All the wonderful possibilities he might have offered simply faded away. Instead, his estranged expression—that look of having been betrayed by her—had frozen itself agonizingly into her conscience.

Her thoughts haunted her relentlessly. She couldn't put them out of her mind. She was being devoured from within, becoming as if food for a tormenting justice.

She would find no reprieve. No, her crime had sealed her fate.

The images of her destiny filled her mind. She shuddered as she saw herself rotting away in the dreadful cell. Each new day would become more unbearable than the former. She would be all alone, and the appalling conditions would impose themselves on her, stripping her of her humanity. She could see herself under the cruel treatment of her jailers, suffering unspeakable and unendurable pain and humiliation. The desperate prayer she had offered under her breath earlier that day had gone unanswered. Her life would now be one of ever-increasing sorrows, until that fateful day when Aurelian Galerius finally put her to death.

She knew she had earned her terrible fate by pulling the trigger.

However, her own sense of justice brought no consolation. She was terrified; she couldn't bear the images of her imminent suffering; the dread of her own mortality caught her in the pit of her stomach. She needed to get out of there; she needed to leave; she needed someone who could advocate for her release. But the footsteps were already fading down the corridor outside. Once she was alone, there would be no chance for relief.

She would be left to die.

The madness imposed on her by knowing her fate overwhelmed her. Desperately, she turned and struggled to sit up, finally falling hard against the door. She raised her hands, which were still bound, above her head and pounded on the formidable door.

"*Please, someone!*" she cried out. "*Please don't leave me here! Come back!*"

She continued to pound, to call, *to plead!* But the footsteps faded into the silence.

All hope, even the mirage of hope that existed merely in the shadows of her tormented mind, vanished. She would receive no reprieve; no one would advocate for her; her life would become one of cruel, painful suffering—until she was finally put to death.

Resigning to her fate, Kara fell into a deep despair. She collapsed onto the rocky floor and wept bitterly.

The land craft rushed through the jagged canyon in haste, demonstrating little regard for its own safety or that of its passengers. Emir Kern watched the landscape whiz by from his seat inside the vehicle, all the while barking at Brent Tasker to push the craft even faster. No amount of delay was allowable. No, they needed to get back to the base camp immediately!

The journey had gone tediously. The Europans had cut off the direct route between the ambush point and the base camp. Europan security forces, fully alerted to the Coverts' presence, had frustrated them at every turn since their narrow escape. Therefore, they had spent their time zigzagging their way back to the *Aurora*, their only real hope of escape.

As the land craft sped on, the canyon opened up into the familiar prominence outside the base camp.

"Zeidler," Kern barked, "Any sign of hostiles?"

Zeidler studied his surveillance equipment. "None that I can see."

Kern turned to the whole team, "We need to move fast. Tasker, start the *Aurora*'s power-up sequence. Zeidler, plot a course around the planet's security grid: Find a place where we can disappear for a while. Gunn and Volk, throw as much of our gear into the ship as you can before we launch."

Kern's orders finished just as the land craft arrived at the mouth of the cave. Having no time to hide the vehicle or stow it away in the transport, Tasker brought the craft to a screeching halt. The Coverts jumped out and rushed into the cavern. Just at the point where their eyes adjusted to the light differential, they came to a sudden halt!

The *Aurora*, loaded with most of their munitions and supplies, was gone.

The crew stood there for a moment, stunned.

"*What in the...,*" Zeidler gasped.

Attempting a recovery from the startling revelation, Kern and his men ran to where the command center had sat behind the *Aurora*. All the gear there remained untouched, save a fresh layer of dust covering everything. The provisions stacked to the side of the cave remained in place, as did the sleeping quarters in the rear of the cavern. The only thing gone was the *Aurora*.

"At least we know the Europans weren't here," Tasker exclaimed.

Zeidler shook his head. "But where's the ship?"

"What do we do now?" Volk interjected. The question fell over the small team ominously. Without having the *Aurora* to escape, the Coverts would quickly find themselves at the mercy of the Europans. And Europans were not merciful.

"We'll take the land craft and go into the mountains," Kern declared. "Everyone, start putting supplies into the vehicle—only what's necessary. We'll need more fuel too."

Volk, Tasker, and Gunn complied, diligently searching the supplies and remaining ammo for the needed articles.

Zeidler, noticing a single, blinking indicator light on the command center's presentation unit, called to Kern, "Look at this."

Everyone gathered curiously around the unit.

"What do you think it is?" Zeidler asked Kern.

The man shrugged impatiently. "Turn it on so we can find out."

The Covert complied. The unit lit up and began playing a stored message. Immediately, every mouth dropped at the familiar image standing before them and the words the electronic specter delivered. As they watched the transmission with morbid fascination, they traded uneasy glances among themselves.

Finally, the projection dissipated, and the projector went dark.

Vacant stares washed over the stunned Coverts.

"I can't believe it!" Volk exclaimed.

However, Kern had not the luxury of wallowing in the unexpected and dire turn of events. "Let's get out of here before the whole planet descends on the cavern—*move!*"

The Coverts rushed out of the cave and jumped into the land craft for a quick escape. Kern, who was the last one to reach the vehicle, abruptly stopped and put his ear squarely to the air. His men saw the disturbing hesitation and stepped out to listen too.

All of them heard the familiar sounds of approaching troops and vehicles in the distance.

Deep in the bowels of the palace, the prison cell door swung open. Kate Gillen fell headlong through the entryway, quickly followed by Tom Andrews. The two beleaguered Centauries landed hard onto the filthy stone floor, with Tom barreling into Kate forcibly.

Satisfied with how they had manhandled their charges, the guards slammed the iron door shut, locking them in. Footsteps echoed from outside, moving away from the cell.

Tom and Kate were alone.

"You okay?" Tom asked as he sat up, abruptly grabbing his chest in pain.

"Yeah," Kate replied, though preoccupied with the stinging brush burns her hands had sustained from the fall. Wincing, she gingerly rubbed them together to shake off the dust. "Just a little bruised and dirty." However, upon noticing Tom writhing in pain and holding his chest, she took him in her arms. "How's your injury?"

"Don't worry about it," he dismissed, gesturing in the direction of the guards' footsteps. "I'll be fine as long as the welcome wagon stays away from me. They sure aren't gentle."

The two prisoners helped each other off the floor and stood up, looking around the chamber. The cell was rather large, boasting of stone walls hewn from the rock foundation. A single, undersized light left the place poorly lit and shadowy. The air hung cold and damp and smelled of must. In the corner sat two small, unimpressive cots, placed perpendicular to one another against the walls. Dreadfully unattractive bath facilities lay in the corner opposite the cots.

"I guess it's *home sweet home*," Tom said dryly, his humor scarcely cutting through the heaviness of the situation.

Kate barely acknowledged his comment. The formidable cell had seized her attention. As she surveyed her surroundings, the frightened, young woman's expression worsened with each passing moment.

She folded her arms around herself, backing toward the corner as if the walls were closing in on her.

"I don't like this," she exclaimed, shaking her head warily. Her lips quivered ever so slightly too.

Tom immediately put a reassuring hand on her shoulder. He looked her in the eyes with all the courage he could muster. "Don't worry. I'll take care of you."

"I don't think you can," Kate lamented, the fear still swelling within her. "We've got as much time as it takes them to put together an execution squad."

"If they wanted us dead, we would already *be dead.* No, they want to find out who we are and how much of a threat we pose."

"I've heard how they treat their prisoners—especially women," Kate gasped, desperately fighting to keep her imagination at bay. The effort was futile. Despite Tom's reassuring gaze, Kate grew inconsolable. The anxious, young woman fell back against the wall, slithering down onto the floor while welling up.

Tom sat down beside her in the shadows against the wall. Ignoring the pain in his chest, he wrapped his good arm around her and watched the first few tears trail down her cheek.

"I miss Michael," she sobbed. "I miss our friends. … I can't believe they're gone."

"Me too, Sunshine … me too."

Helplessly, Kate leaned in toward Tom and hid her face in the crook of his neck. Nestled safely within his reassuring embrace, the young woman fell to pieces.

While he prepared himself to keep a long vigil with Kate, Tom's thoughts returned to the hillside overlook, just after the Europans had captured Kara, Phil, David, and him. He stung from his deception; he smarted at how quickly the idea had come to him—but delighted in all the wonderful possibilities the deception would bring him too.

However, right then was a time for remorse. Not that he regretted what had become of the Europan soldier with the binoculars. No, that man received everything he so rightly deserved. Moreover, his death was necessary to make the deception plausible; the Europan commander agreed with him on that point. Yet now that he had accomplished the initial deception, the young man found himself at a loss as to how to undo its impact.

However, after pondering the question before him for some time, Tom eventually realized that he found no allure in undoing the deception—at least not right then. No, the deception was necessary. And as he looked down at Kate nestled against him and crying on his shoulder, he knew it was for her own good.

Evening began falling over the desolate construction site. Shadows grew thick and full across the ground, draping coldly over the entire landscape. There were no heroes to be found, no clandestine duty to fulfill. There were no sounds of gunfire, no cries of desperation. No, the place once again sat barren and silent.

In the darkness lay a large pile of rocks against the high wall, burying all but one mangled corner of what had been a land craft. The rubble sat arrayed as if a memorial to the ill-fated mission of the *Endurance* crew.

Their mission was over. Aurelian Galerius still sat in power over Sco-II, more emboldened than ever. Emir Kern and his men had scattered to the wind, soon to be hunted down like common animals. The Centauries were no more, whether kept in an extravagant suite or in misery awaiting a death sentence. The darkness that fell over the land had fallen over the *Endurance* crew as well.

Two of the most hideous creatures—rags draping the leathery skin covering their thick, muscular frames—appeared at the top of the bluff. Casting long shadows upon the rocky ground, the massive creatures plodded along down the pathway to the bottom of the channel; their undersized heads turned back and forth warily, and their brooding eyes anxiously searched the terrain.

Coming to stand before the rocky debris piled in front of the high wall, one of the creatures spotted the corner of the crushed land craft jutting out. He pointed a gigantic hand at the mangled metal, and the two conversed in indiscernible, hushed tones. All the while, they looked around nervously.

Drawn by the arrival of the small band of humans earlier that day, the creatures had witnessed such an odd thing: *humans fighting humans*. That was why they had waited so patiently before coming out into the open; they needed to see it for themselves—find out who these humans were.

However, the remnants of the conflict left little clues.

Just as the beasts turned to leave, a subtle noise caught their attention. Near the base of the rockslide, close to where the mangled corner of the land craft jutted out of the pile, a single stone toppled from its place. The small stone fell away, tumbling erratically and harmlessly over its companions to the bottom of the pile. The cause for the unnoticeable disturbance remained aloof, for the massive pile sat firm and still.

The two creatures looked at one another curiously.

Then, another stone on the pile moved. This stone didn't topple to the bottom like the first. Rather, it merely shifted aside. Soon, all of the smaller stones filling in around a larger rock there began churning; some shifted, while others toppled off the pile.

Finally—unexpectedly—the small stones shot into the air! A fist erupted out of the pile, until the greater part of an arm protruded into the air. The filthy limb was bruised and bloody—and it belonged to Michael Gillen.